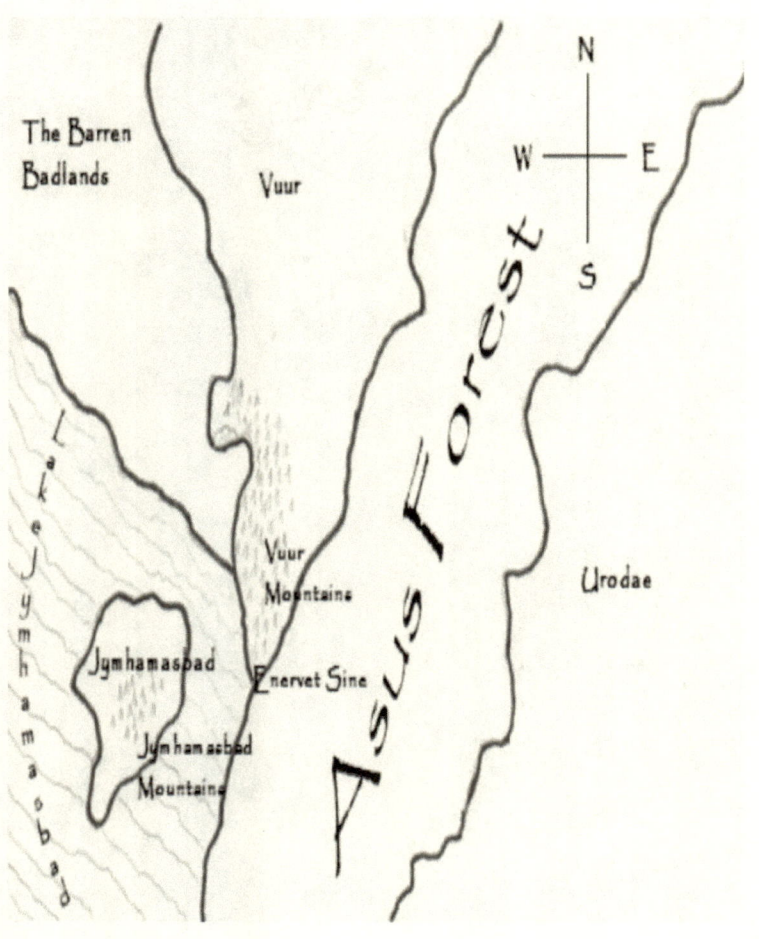

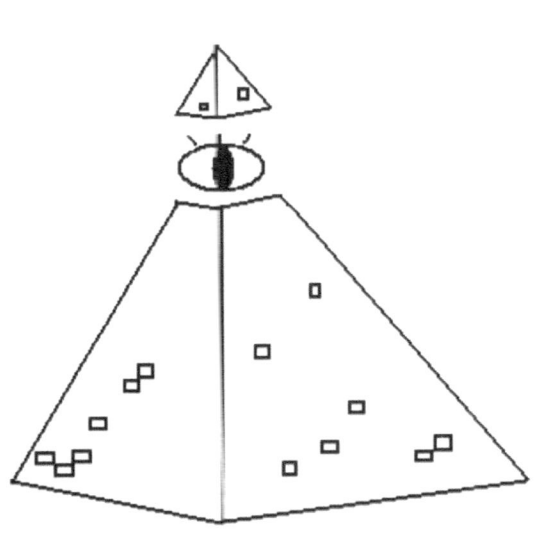

The Secret of Christopher Topher

Copyright ©2015 by Gee Williams

All rights reserved.

First edition published August 2015

This is a work of fiction. Names, characters, places and incidents
either are the product of the author's imagination or are used
fictitiously. Any resemblance to actual persons, living or dead, events
or locales is entirely coincidental.

Cover art ©2015 by Gee Williams and Liza at Impeccable Prose

Edited by Liza at Impeccable Prose

The Omen Experience™
Copyright ©2015

Hardcover: ISBN 978-0-9965083-0-8
Paperback: ISBN 978-0-9965083-1-5
eBook: ISBN 978-0-9965083-2-2

A portion of the proceeds are donated to the National Association of
the Deaf to battle against discrimination of the deaf and hard of
hearing

ACKNOWLEDGEMENTS

Thank you to: Dawn, Jas, and Amare for their support, my editor and critique partner Liza Dolensky, friends and beta readers Carl Dean, Kimberly Gorman, and Cathy Torrisi. A special thanks goes out to my daughter Alena for staying on me to complete the book and its title.

The Secret of Christopher Topher

by Gee Williams

The Omen Experience ™

Contents

Chapter 1
Off to School

In a small, Midwestern town lived a twelve-year-old kid named Alexander Smiley. Alex was neither big nor small but of average height and stature. He wore black-framed glasses and his standard combination of a black t-shirt, blue jeans, and black high-top sneakers every day. Alex enjoyed riding his bicycle, studying, and reading historical books on ancient civilizations. His passion was studying ancient Egyptian culture and he was able to read and translate some ancient Egyptian text. He was neither athletic nor popular but was very smart. He was an only child who lived with his parents in a small, bungalow-style house on a street teeming with kids his age. Unfortunately, Alex didn't have many friends. He had only one, to be exact. He met her each morning at the school bus stop. Her name was Karen Stubblefield.

Karen lived right next door to Alex, and they had known each other for as long as they both could remember. Karen was a very sweet person who was petite in stature but had a fiery personality. After Alex finished his breakfast of Froot Loops and toast one warm and sunny May morning, he walked outside to meet her at the bus stop, like every other school morning.

"What's up, Alex?" asked Karen. "Did you finish reading your history assignment?"

"I finished it this morning," Alex said. "Last night, I got caught up reading an article about ancient Egyptian languages I got from the town library. I just found myself struggling to read an article about the American Constitution again. It seems like that's the only thing we study in that class."

"Well you know Ms. Gateway," chirped Karen. "She's very patriotic. The only things we are going to learn in her class are Bill of Rights this or Constitution that. You know she served in the military a while back. She's a hero here in Brownsville."

"I have no problems with her being a proud military person. I just wish she would be more respectful," said Alex. "She can be so stubborn and degrading. One time I suggested, and very

1

nicely I might add, that we learn about the ancient pyramids of Egypt or the Great Wall of China. She looked me up and down and asked, 'Did your father ever get that seven-fifty-an-hour part-time job he was looking for? You know you can lose your house if your father doesn't keep up with the mortgage.' How she found out I don't know. And even worse, she said it in front of the entire class," said Alex, feeling ashamed, even though he was talking to his best friend.

"You should have either gone to the principal or told her off. You need to start standing up for yourself, Alex!" said Karen.

"I know," said Alex. "I'm just one who doesn't like to stir up commotion."

Karen was about ready to offer up more advice but the school bus arrived. The two of them boarded the bus to Brownsville Middle School.

The school day was as uneventful as any other day for Alex. Homeroom, math, biology, and art class before lunch, and English, gym, and history class in the afternoon. It was the last two classes that Alex feared the most -- not because he hated the subjects that Ms. Gateway taught or for his lack of athleticism in gym class. It was in these two classes that Alex had to face the school and town bully, Lenopolous Gary. Lenopolous was six foot two and weighed two hundred pounds. He was rather large for a middle-schooler, and it was rumored that he'd been held back a few times. He walked around the school with a fierce, mean face and never smiled unless he was administering harm to a fellow student. Throughout the day, except for the occasional run-ins with him in the hallways, Alex was able to avoid Lenopolous. But when the two o'clock bell rang, which signaled the end of English class and the beginning of gym class, Alex knew he would be in a world of trouble. It was well known that the gym teacher never demanded respect or had control of his class. Lenopolous made sure to use this to his full advantage.

"Hey, twerp," Lenopolous yelled at Alex, while at the same time bouncing a volleyball off Alex's head. "Make sure ya don't screw up this time. I don't like losing. I hate when we're on the same team. So get ready."

2

"Okay, Lenopolous. I'll try my best," said Alex, at which he was greeted with Lenopolous giving him a major wedgie.

"Leo. You call me Leo. I hate the name Lenopolous. How many times do I have to tell ya?" His classmates screamed with laughter.

"Sorry Lenop ... I mean Leo," Alex forced out as he regained his composure despite hair-raising fear and heavy pain. As the opposing team started the volley, Alex clumsily moved under the ball for a return strike. Unfortunately, his feet got tangled and he hit the ground as the ball fell on top of his head.

"Whatcha doin'?!" screamed Lenopolous while the gym class roared in laughter.

"My fault," Alex said.

After losing yet again due to Alex's lack of athletic skills, Lenopolous said, "I see it's time for another butt whoopin'. I'll see you after school." Alex was hoping that Lenopolous would start beating him up right in gym class. That way the gym teacher could stop the pummeling, even though that didn't always work.

After gym class was over and Alex had blow-dried his shirt (he kept a battery-powered blow dryer in his locker for this purpose, as Lenopolous regularly used Alex's shirt to wipe off his sweat), Alex slowly walked to Ms. Gateway's history class. There he got to face not only a condescending teacher, but more of Lenopolous, who sat in the back of the class and often threw balls of paper (or whatever else he could get his hands on) at those he could easily intimidate. The only saving grace was that Karen was also in the class.

"I hope all of you read your assignments last night. I want you to put your books away and prepare for a surprise quiz. My job is to weed out those of you who do not wish to learn in my class." This was a regular practice for Ms. Gateway. She showed preferential treatment to certain individuals, including Lenopolous, and she seemed to always turn a blind eye to his shenanigans.

"You have thirty minutes to complete the quiz," said Ms. Gateway. "In the meantime, I'll be in the principal's office discussing next year's history curriculum. Don't let me come back here and catch anyone cheating."

As Ms. Gateway closed the door behind her, she had a smirk on her face. She stared directly at Alex as if she knew exactly what was going to happen next.

Taking tests and pop quizzes was no problem for Alex, as he was normally (save for Karen now and then) the smartest kid in class. But being the smartest kid always had a price.

"Alex! Alexaaannndeeerrr ..." Lenopolous loudly whispered Alex's name for some quiz answers. Alex tried to ignore that annoying voice but the back of his head kept meeting the cover of a book.

"Alex!" Lenopolous screamed out. "You know the routine. I may be easy on whoopin' your butt if you give me those answers. Now hurry it up."

Karen, who didn't tolerate unfairness or bullies, had had enough.

"Lenopolous, you know if you maybe tried studying once in a while you wouldn't have to ask other people for answers."

"Whooooooo ..." cried the classroom as they waited cautiously for what would happen next.

"Oh, if it isn't Ms. Big Mouth, Alex's girlfriend," Lenopolous teased. "I think I'll take your paper for the answers. Plus your boyfriend has only fifteen more minutes before he receives his 'Royale Grande' butt kicking. Duayne, go get her paper."

"No problem, Leo," said Duayne as he got up from his desk and headed in Karen's direction. Duayne was one of Lenopolous' many minions.

"Give me that paper," shouted Duayne, snatching it from Karen's desk. "This will teach you to keep your mouth shut."

"Give me back my paper, you creep," shouted Karen. She was met with a notebook upside her head. Of course the notebook came from Lenopolous' direction.

"Shut it up! Or you're gonna get hit with this dictionary next," shouted Lenopolous, who looked as if he dared her or anyone else to make a peep. As Lenopolous started transferring the answers from Karen's paper to his, and the classroom sat in

4

stunned silence, Karen's eyes welled with tears. Alex, who had always wished he and Karen could be more than friends, had never seen Karen look so defeated. It angered Alex enough for him to stand up and speak for his friend.

"There was no need to hit her," shouted Alex, with his knees literally shaking.

"Wait a minute. You're talking to me?" laughed Lenopolous, with his cronies joining in.

"Yeah, you, you d-d-didn't hav-v-ve to hit her-r-r," stuttered Alex, feeling he'd faint from fear or crap his pants. Lenopolous thrived on people fearing him, and it was easy to see that Alex was scared out of his wits. But Alex's small showing of bravery surprised him.

"You know what? In ten minutes I'm going to give you the butt-kicking of your life," said Lenopolous. "You are going to wish you were never born. And as for your little girlfriend ..."

"All right class, settle down," interjected Ms. Gateway as she returned to the class. "Pass in your papers."

"Ms. Gateway," Karen cried. "Lenopolous took my paper and copied all my answers."

Ms. Gateway appeared unconcerned as she sighed and called out, "Leo, can you come here please? Karen is accusing you of taking her paper. Is this true?"

"Why no, ma'am," said Lenopolous. "I would never do such a thing."

Alex watched the exchange, knowing Lenopolous would get away with causing trouble again. He took his quiz paper, erased his name and put Karen's name on top so that she could maintain her honor-roll status. Alex felt he could afford an F. He had gotten A pluses on all his other tests in that class. One F wouldn't hurt.

"Ms. Gateway?" Alex interrupted, "I found her paper." Karen was baffled but did not say a word. Even Lenopolous couldn't believe it. But he wouldn't dare say anything lest he give his lie away. As Ms. Gateway snatched the paper from Alex's hands she gave him a cold stare.

"Where's your paper?" she asked.

5

"I decided not to take the quiz because I wasn't prepared. I'm sorry, but I didn't study," lied Alex.

"Well," said Ms. Gateway, feeling satisfied that she finally had Alex cornered. "It looks like someone earned himself a detention. Any more screw-ups and I'll have to call your parents. Then again what use would that be if they don't answer the phone because they think I'm a bill collector?"

"Okay, everybody out," Ms. Gateway shouted to the class as the bell rang. "And Alex, you can take a seat. I think a two-hour detention will be a just punishment. You can make up that quiz you failed to take. And don't expect the same test that I gave to the rest of the students." Then she added, "And definitely don't expect a good grade, no matter how well you do."

As the students filed out and Alex sat to serve his detention, he felt fortunate that he was actually able to retake the quiz. Even though it wasn't going to be the same quiz and he wouldn't get a fair grade, it was a quiz that he would no doubt pass. And he felt even more satisfied that Karen would maintain her honors status because of him. But as always, self-doubt and fear crept up inside him because he knew what would be waiting outside two hours from now -- a meeting with Lenopolous Gary.

When the clock was ten minutes from striking five, a cold sweat began to form on Alex's forehead as he peered out the window. The sun was still somewhat high in the sky and kids conversed on the school grounds. When people hung around school this late it usually meant there was either some sort of event going on or there was going to be a rumble. Unfortunately, Alex knew it was the latter, and that it involved him.

Five minutes till five o'clock. Is he lurking in the bushes? Is he behind one of the store buildings that I pass on the way home? Alex thought of ways he could duck and dodge Lenopolous. *Maybe if I called Karen she could warn me as to where that bully and his cronies are hiding.*

Alex pulled out his cell phone in anticipation of being dismissed from school. Once dismissed, he would call Karen. There was no time to waste. As soon as the clock struck five, Alex ran to the safety of the janitor's room. He wanted to avoid the halls and bathrooms lest he run into Lenopolous.

When Alex attempted to dial Karen's number, the stress made his fingers cramp. He was so nervous that he dialed the wrong number twice. Luckily, he remembered that he had her on speed dial.

"What's up, Alex?" asked Karen, picking up on the first ring when her caller ID displayed Alex's number.

"I need you to tell me where Lenopolous is hiding. I know he's out there," said Alex, looking from the janitor's room window.

"I normally see him hanging out at Dixel Park. And of course you pass the park on the way home. Maybe if you went through the junkyard to get home you would be able to avoid him that way."

"That junkyard gives me the creeps," said Alex, thinking about the piles and piles of junk, the garbage, and the dogs that guarded the area. He thought that this particular junkyard had a very negative aura about it and he made it a point to avoid it at all costs.

"Well, that's the best route I know," said Karen. "The only other thing I can think of is to ask your parents to pick you up."

"That's not going to happen," said Alex. "The one car we have broke down last week. So I guess I'll have to take the junkyard route."

"You'll be fine, Alex," said Karen. "I don't think that behemoth is smart enough to figure out what you are going to do."

"Let's hope not," said Alex. "He seems to sense fear from anywhere."

"Alex, you need to stop letting people push you around," demanded Karen. "If you never stand up for yourself, things like this will happen day after day for the rest of your life." She paused. "But I never did thank you for standing up for me. Thanks, Alex."

Alex calmed down. Karen's words of thanks gave him a warm feeling. "Karen, you're welcome. Anything for a friend." Karen hung up and Alex put away his cell phone. He wiped his

7

palms free from his sweat. Leaning his body against the storage shelves he let out a huge sigh. The time to dodge the school bully had come.

Chapter 2
The Junkyard

As Alex left the school building he peered left, right, and then left again. He tried to hide behind any tree he could find. There were students in the schoolyard but Alex wasn't noticed. When necessary, Alex could be very skilled at remaining unseen. The walk seemed long. It had been years since he had walked to or from school. He peered at the sky to see the sun beginning to set. A sense of urgency rushed through Alex's body. Not only did he fear Lenopolous, but he feared the darkness of night even more. Alex's walk turned into a light jog, and then into a full-out sprint. Before he knew it, an out-of-breath Alex arrived at the junkyard.

The junkyard gave off a putrid smell. Trash and junk were piled so high it blocked out the sunlight. Scrap metal, wood, and heaps of garbage were home to colonies of rats that moved nonchalantly from pile to pile. Hundreds of seagulls flew around the junkyard searching for food, like vultures waiting for someone or something to die. Then there were the guard dogs -- one pit bull and two beefy Rottweilers that waited to sink their teeth into anyone who trespassed.

Alex looked for a path through the endless piles of garbage and junk. *All I need to do is get through this junkyard, go three blocks east, and then I'm home.*

He checked the time on his cell phone. Seven forty-five. By Alex's estimate, the sun was going to set in approximately fifteen minutes. He knew he had to hurry, but he had to be super quiet or he would alert the guard dogs to his presence. As he quietly hopped the fence and treaded through the junk, he noticed a manhole cover that was jarred loose, partially covering an open sewer. He had heard stories of neighborhood kids who had fallen into this particular sewer never to be seen again. Alex was never one to believe in folk tales or fables, but he made sure to avoid the manhole, lest he become another folk-tale statistic.

Alex looked at the setting sun to gauge which direction he should head. He then thought of a plan on how he would find his way home.

I need to go north, northeast. That should take me into the Wallace's backyard. I'll cut through to Campo Street, through the Hampton's and then I'll be right down the street from my house. That should save me a good twenty-five to thirty minutes.

As Alex walked through the debris he received multiple scrapes and scratches, as the pathway through the junk was very narrow. Then an old metal car bumper caught hold of Alex's left leg and gave him a deep cut across the left thigh. "Ooouuuch!" Alex shouted out, forgetting that he needed to be quiet. Alerted by the shout, the dogs started barking wildly in the distance. The bumper had easily pierced Alex's skin even though he wore a durable pair of jeans. Blood freely streamed down his leg as the pain throbbed relentlessly. He removed his shoe and used one of his long tube socks as a bandage.

Hopefully that will slow down the bleeding, Alex thought. *Luckily I don't wear shorts or I would really be in trouble.*

He put his shoe back on and continued to walk through the heaps of junk and trash. His leg began to swell. He sat down on top of a rusted, old refrigerator to allow the blood to coagulate and the pain and swelling to subside. But he knew he shouldn't sit for long. *I gotta keep going,* thought Alex as he grimaced and limped to his feet. He knew every minute that passed gave him less room for error. The darkness of night was approaching fast.

Just when Alex seemed to be making some headway through the junk piles, he was unfortunate enough to step in a big pile of dog poop. As Alex cursed under his breath and scraped off his shoe, he noticed a convoy of rats having a feast on some garbage directly in his path. Anxiety began to take hold of him. The dog poop meant the dogs were nearby.

I have to hurry up and get out of here, Alex thought as he watched the disgusting display of feasting rats. *If I get bitten by one of these things I'll probably catch rabies. Then I'll have to get those painful shots.*

These thoughts made Alex quite queasy. He already figured he would have to get some sort of shot for his leg. Getting frustrated, he thought to take another route.

Let's see. If I go in the opposite direction, I can always hook back around and go north by heading west. Even though it'll take me farther out of the way, I should be somewhere near Lake Arnold. From there, that'll be about a forty-minute walk. Alex had to factor in that he was virtually walking on one leg. *Plus, I won't have to cut through anyone's yard. Hopefully, by taking this other route, I'll be able to avoid running into any more rats the rest of the way.*

Nightfall seemed to settle quickly and the piles of junk and garbage took on the appearance of giant, black mountains. Even though there was a full moon high in the night sky, the mountains of debris blocked out any moonlight, making it very difficult to see. Alex began to lose his sense of direction as he lost sight of his landmarks.

I could have sworn I passed this pile of garbage before. It was definitely this pile of trash that had a broken Xbox stuck halfway in it, Alex thought, as doubt and dismay crept in. *It's like I've been walking around in circles for hours. Maybe if I retrace my steps I'll find my way back to the path that leads to my block. Once I find that, I'll be on my street corner in no time. Those rats should be gone by now.*

As Alex retraced his steps, he passed heaps of trash and arrived at a path that looked familiar. The cry of the seagulls grew louder with every step as Alex limped through the maze of junk. As Alex lost his ability to see, he felt his way through the debris. He slipped on a bottle and fell to the ground in a heap. The loud noise resulted in wild barking that sounded too close for his comfort. As Alex picked himself up from the ground to dust himself off and wipe heaven-knows-what off the side of his pants, he was met with the sound of a low, fierce growl.

At first the growl came from in front of him. Then Alex heard two other, different, growls -- one from his left and the other from behind him. As the growls slowly grew closer, Alex knew he was in trouble. They were coming from the guard dogs and they were closing in for an attack. Alex's mind raced a mile a minute as he tried to think of ways to avoid being mauled to death. As the dogs approached, Alex was able to make out their silhouettes in the darkness. The pit bull was coming in from the front, one of the Rottweilers was coming in from the side, and the second and larger Rottweiler was coming in from behind. Alex had to think fast. He knew that if he were attacked, that moment would likely be his last. He also thought that had he stood up to Lenopolous, he wouldn't be in this predicament. The thought of getting punched out was looking really good in comparison with the situation he was in now. Scared, exhausted, and hobbling on a bad leg, he had seconds to act. He knew he wouldn't be able to outrun them, but maybe he could use the mounds of junk to his advantage. The mountain of junk towered on Alex's right. The pit bull stood in front of him while the two Rottweilers stood to his left and his rear.

In two nanoseconds, Alex was scaling the mountain of junk like Spider Man, with the dogs in hot pursuit. But just as Alex was beginning to advance, the large Rottweiler grabbed the pants on his bad, left leg. Searing pain such as he had never felt before shot into Alex. With a rush of adrenaline, he managed to pull his leg away, leaving the Rottweiler with a mouthful of torn jeans.

Luckily for Alex, Rottweilers are not climbing dogs, and they couldn't scale the mountain of junk. So Alex quickly climbed, while being repeatedly cut and scratched by the debris. He knew that the cuts, scratches, and bruises he was receiving were nothing in comparison with what those dogs would administer if they caught him.

The pit bull remained relentless in his chase, being more nimble and better able to tread the mountain. Between quickly climbing and occasionally slipping backward on a piece of garbage, Alex was feeling the hot breath of the pit bull on his backside. "Down! Get out of here!" cried Alex as he reached the top of the junk pile. "Get away!" He slung a broken bottle and kicked at the dog, upsetting the pit bull even more. He managed to get hold of a two-by-four. To keep the dog at arm's length, Alex swung the piece of wood wildly. As the dog moved in closer, showing its sharp fangs, Alex considered his dire fate. He glanced down below to see the light of the moon shine upon the open manhole he had passed a while back. This gave Alex an idea. Make a mad sprint to the manhole.

Down the mountain Alex ran, slipping and sliding along the way with the pit bull in hot pursuit. The pit bull was gaining ground, snapping at Alex's back. As Alex descended on the manhole, he heard the growls of the two Rottweilers closing in on him from the side. Alex knew he had to make like a baseball player and slide into the manhole. Even though Alex was not athletic, he had to make the perfect slide or he would literally be dog meat.

"Aaaaaah!" screamed Alex as he deftly maneuvered between the Rottweilers and, outrunning the pit bull, slid into the manhole opening, just large enough for him to fit. Alex had made the perfect slide and was alert enough to grab the stepladder in the manhole lest he fall to the bottom of the sewer. He looked up at the manhole opening as the three dogs growled and barked wildly while they peered down at him. Alex felt a sense of relief as he confidently and smugly looked up at the dogs, proud that he had outwitted them. He then carefully descended the manhole. He heard rushing water but could see nothing below but endless blackness. Alex took a deep breath and began to calm down from his adrenaline rush. The pain in his leg grew worse. As he gingerly continued his downward climb, one of the metal steps gave way, and Alex was airborne, arms and legs sprawling with nothing to grab onto. As Alex fell he let out a loud scream and disappeared into the dark abyss.

Chapter 3
Mr. and Mrs. Smiley

The clock read nine-thirty as Karen waited by her phone for a return call or text from Alex. She had left at least six or seven messages on Alex's voicemail since school let out. Normally, Alex promptly returned her messages. When she didn't hear from him she knew something was wrong. Her mind was filled with bad thoughts. *Did he run into Lenopolous? Did he get kidnapped? Or even worse, did he run into the junkyard guard dogs?* She looked out her bedroom window over to Alex's house. She noticed that Alex's bedroom light was out but the other lights in the house were on. Karen quietly checked her parents' bedroom to discover that they had already settled down for the night. So instead of asking for permission, she decided to take matters into her own hands and sneak over to the Smileys' to inform them about Alex.

As Karen approached the house she wondered how the Smileys would react to the news that Alex was missing. Alex had told her that his parents, while not particularly affectionate, were very protective. Because of his father's work schedule, the interaction between them had dwindled as Alex grew older. Karen found Alex to be very guarded about his family life. It seemed odd to her that in all the years she had known him, he had never invited her inside his house. Marion Smiley was a stay-at-home mom who recorded soap operas that she watched over and over again. No one dared to disturb Mrs. Smiley while she was watching her soaps, lest they receive a stern tongue-lashing.

She, like Alex's father, was a political junkie. While she was recording her soaps, she watched the TAPC (The American Political and Congressional) news channel spit out its daily propaganda. Never mention the President; she hated him with a passion. Alex never understood this deep hatred for the President, but to Mrs. Smiley he was an arrogant, controlling, and evil man. Alex didn't see him that way. To him the President seemed compassionate, smart, and strong-willed. He seemed to

14

care not only for the people of the United States, but of the world.

Alex's father, Phillip Smiley, believed that anyone involved with the government was evil. Mr. Smiley was rarely at home and worked relentlessly to make ends meet. He worked part-time at the local car dealer's parts warehouse during the day and worked odd jobs during the evening. He struggled to pay the mortgage and other bills that the family accumulated on a monthly basis. Their phone rang constantly with creditors looking for their past-due payments.

Karen hesitated before pushing the doorbell. *Should I call the police instead?* she thought as her mind raced with pessimism. *No. I'll contact Alex's parents first. Maybe they know where he is.*

Karen rang the doorbell three times before the door opened. It was Mr. Smiley. He still had on his warehouse uniform from his day job. He was a tall man with an upright stature and, like Alex, wore glasses. Karen noticed the stairs on Mr. Smiley's grey uniform and the tired expression on his face. Still, he greeted her with a friendly hello. "Well, well. Look who's here," said Mr. Smiley with a smile. "What brings you here this time of the evening? I don't believe Alex is home."

"Well, that's precisely why I'm here Mr. Smiley. Alex hasn't been home since school let out and I think he's in trouble."

"Okay, come on in," Mr. Smiley said in a rush. "Sit down on the couch and tell me what you know."

"Who's at the door?" asked Mrs. Smiley as she came in from the kitchen wearing a white robe and slippers, with a scarf on her head. She held a cup of tea, ready to watch another episode of her daily soaps.

"It's Karen from next door. She believes something has happened to Alex," Mr. Smiley answered.

"Okay. Wait a second while I put the DVR on pause," said Mrs. Smiley. "Karen, can I get you something to drink?" she asked.

"No, thank you," Karen answered, taking quick notice of why Alex had never invited her over.

The living room walls were covered with posters and paraphernalia from every soap opera and political event that had ever been. There was a bookcase loaded with *Soap Opera Digest* magazines, and the living room coffee table was stacked with political magazines that reported negatively on the President. Karen glanced at the couch and saw where Mrs. Smiley's favorite seat was. Years of sitting in the same spot had left a huge indentation. Through the kitchen door, Karen noticed piles of unwashed dishes in the sink, and an overflowing trashcan that gave off a noticeable stench. The telephone rang in the distance, ignored by Mr. and Mrs. Smiley. Mr. Smiley's absence during the evenings had taken its toll. But today, he'd taken the evening off to rest his weary body.

"What's going on Karen?" asked Mr. Smiley. His voice shook Karen out of her daydream. "Where do you think Alex is?"

"Well, I really don't know," Karen answered, struggling to keep her eyes off the soap opera paraphernalia. "Alex was threatened by Lenopolous Gary, so instead of taking the school bus home he tried to go home another way."

"What other way? He didn't take a ride from a stranger did he?" Mr. Smiley asked.

"No, he walked."

"Walked? Which way did he go?"

"I believe through the junkyard." Karen could see the expression on both Mr. and Mrs. Smiley's face turn to shock.

"I told him never to go through that junkyard," said Mr. Smiley. "How long ago did he go through that junkyard and why in the world would he do that?"

"It's my fault. I told him it was the only way to avoid running into Lenopolous. He left school around five o'clock."

"Five o'clock? Why so late?" Mrs. Smiley asked.

"Because Alex was serving a class detention."

"A detention? For what and in whose class?" Mr. Smiley said.

"In Ms. Gateway's class."

"Ms. Gateway, huh? That explains a lot," said Mr. Smiley as

16

he seemed to recall something very painful from his past. "But that's not important right now. We need to find Alex."

"Shouldn't we call the police?" asked Mrs. Smiley.

"No, we need to take care of this ourselves. The car isn't working so we're gonna have to make it happen on foot. Dear, why don't you stay here at home just in case Alex shows up?" Mr. Smiley suggested to Mrs. Smiley. "Karen, you have your cell phone, don't you?"

"Yes, I do," Karen answered.

"Good. Give my wife the number so she can call us if he shows up." Karen wrote the number on a piece of newspaper and handed it to Mrs. Smiley. Mr. Smiley then went down to the basement and returned with a flashlight and a can of mace. "Ready, Karen?"

"Yes, I'm ready, Mr. Smiley." They went out the front door into the moonlit night.

"I'm sorry that I suggested that Alex go through the junkyard," Karen said to Mr. Smiley as they scurried down the street.

"No need to apologize. If Alex had stood up for himself, this wouldn't have happened. But then again, a lot of his passiveness he got from me." Karen gave Mr. Smiley a surprised look. She had no doubt that Alex got his smarts from Mr. Smiley, but she always had the impression that Alex's dad was strong-willed.

"Karen, you should know that your history teacher, Ms. Gateway, isn't who you think she is," said Mr. Smiley.

"What do you mean?" asked Karen.

As they raced toward the junkyard, Mr. Smiley thought about his work for the U.S. government as a scientist studying extraterrestrials, physical phenomenon, time, and space travel. He recalled working closely with Ms. Gateway, who'd been an undercover FBI agent.

"Let's just say that I worked very closely with her and we disagreed on a lot of issues."

Mr. Smiley's statement left Karen very puzzled. She noticed a pained expression on his face.

He reminisced about discovering something that would have

been considered world-changing. In his opinion, the discovery was greater than all seven Wonders of the Ancient World combined. He also thought that the discovery could cause great calamity, disrupting world peace and harmony among all the people on Earth. The U.S. government and the Roman Catholic Church agreed.

The Church claimed it wasn't in the public's best interest for the discovery to be known. The U.S. government had its own reasons for not wanting the discovery to be made public. In reality, both institutions wanted him to keep quiet. When he made another discovery, both Church and government officials got angry. He was forced to leave the military.

They did everything they could to break him down, painting him as a thief and a liar, taking control of his bank accounts. They always had an eye on him. The government made Phillip Smiley Public Enemy Number One. This ensured he would never have a meaningful career, and would have to work odd jobs to make ends meet. To this day, Ms. Gateway had threatened him because of his discovery, and continually took out her frustrations on Alex. Because Mr. Smiley feared what the government could do to him and his family, he had always been afraid to stand up to Ms. Gateway.

"Mr. Smiley, are you okay?" Karen asked as they continued across the neighborhood.

"I'm fine. Let's just hurry up and get to that junkyard to see if Alex is okay."

Karen attempted to reach Alex on his phone, but once again she only reached his voicemail message:

"Hi. You've reached Alex. I'm not able to answer the phone right now, but if you leave a message, I'll get back to you."

Chapter 4
Muddy Waters

The sound of running water echoed in the cavernous tunnel where Alex lay dazed and sore from his fall. The layers of mud and filth had saved him from being severely hurt or killed. The dripping waters from the tunnel's ceiling, combined with the unbearable stench, slowly wakened him from unconsciousness. As he awoke, the pain from his leg, bruised body, and aching head made him feel as if he'd been hit dead on by a Mack truck.

The sounds of flapping bat wings and chirping rats made Alex try to expedite his recovery. He struggled to his feet, surrounded by darkness, with only a faint light coming from the manhole far above. He strained to listen for the guard dogs but heard no barking. There was no telling how long he had been unconscious.

As he slowly regained his wits he noticed that he had managed to lose his glasses. Twenty one-hundred vision in the dark wasn't going to help matters at all. *Think Alex, think. They have to be somewhere close by. If I just had a little light I could find those things.*

Unsure of which direction to turn, Alex got on his hands and knees and began to feel for his glasses. The only things he felt were empty cans, broken bottles, and other small objects that he couldn't make out. He made sure to feel around carefully or risk subjecting himself to more cuts and bodily injury. *I should've listened to Karen and gotten contacts.*

At that moment, Alex remembered excitedly that he had his cell phone and that it had a flashlight. *I'll use this,* he thought, pulling the phone from his pocket. In the phone's light, Alex searched the ground, looking like some sort of Sherlock Holmes.

After crawling on his hands and knees for what felt like an eternity, Alex was able to find his glasses buried deep in the sewer dirt. "Thank goodness" Alex yelped, which prompted barking from the dogs up above.

Great, they're not broken, he thought. *I'll just wipe these suckers clean and then try and get the heck out of here.* As he put on his glasses he felt for the first time in a long time that something was finally going his way.

Alex assessed his surroundings to figure out how far he had fallen down the hole. He guessed around fifty feet. He noticed that no less than eight metal bars had broken off from the sewer's wall. *Oh, man. How am I going to climb out of here? No wonder I fell. This wall is crumbling away. Plus, many of the bars are missing.* Alex didn't take into account that he would have to face the dogs again. They were the reason he was down in the sewer in the first place.

Wait ... I know what I can do. I'll call Karen. She'll think of a way I can get out of here.

But Karen didn't answer. He texted her but got no response. He had no other friends to call. He tried reaching his parents, to no avail. He dialed 9-1-1 but got no response. It was probably because he was so far underground.

This is what I get for dealing with these cheap phone services. Alex said to himself, dismayed as he had been all day. *Maybe if I scream someone will hear.* Alex directed his voice toward the manhole. "Hellp! Heeeelllp! Anyone there? Help!" The only response was the barking of dogs above and the screeching of bats below. A dejected Alex slumped to the ground in a pile of filth with his back against a sewer wall. *There has gotta be a way out of here.*

After taking a long moment to regroup, Alex looked at his cell phone and saw it was past midnight. His mood changed from dismay and boredom to frustration and anger. He started pacing back and forth, myriad thoughts running through his mind.

It's nine minutes past twelve. I hope someone is looking for me. But why should they? I never amounted to much anyway. Can't run. Can't jump. Scared to defend myself. Oh, and let me not forget to mention not ever having a girlfriend. Noooooo..... not Alexander Smiley. The girl I care about the most in this world talks to me every day and I'm too afraid to let her know how I feel. And why is that? She'd probably laugh in my face. But I wouldn't blame her one bit. Who would go out with a nerd who dresses the same every day?

20

And my parents -- what a joke they are. My father is never home, always working some odd job, but he never has any money. My mother would rather sit at home and watch TV, filling her head up with nonsense instead of finding a job. We have a broken-down car without a spare, and can barely pay the mortgage. Maybe it was meant for me to fall down in this hole. Maybe this is it. Maybe I can live the rest of my days down here, living off rats.

Alex felt he must punch or throw something. His phone was already in his hand so it was the most logical choice. "Arrggghhh!" he screamed as he threw his cell phone into the darkness of the vast sewer.

He didn't hear the thud as his cell phone hit the ground, but he knew it made an impact. Bats flew out of the darkness toward Alex like a swarm of locusts. He hit the ground face first. He didn't care if he got a mouth full of gunk, nor did he care about the rats. He was not going to die by way of bats. After the bats flew past him in a wild frenzy, Alex, still lying down, looked back into the darkness and saw the dim glow of his cell phone. Because of his lack of arm strength, the phone hadn't gone very far. *Eh, I might as well go get it,* he thought as he got to his feet and gingerly limped toward the speck of dim light in the darkness. He had finally calmed down. Things could be worse. He was not sure how much worse, but he needed to think of a strategy to get out of the stinky sewer.

As Alex reached over to pick up his phone, the light shone on a small metal object buried in one of the crumbling sewer walls. *What's this?* Alex thought as he took a closer look. *Hm. Looks like some sort of chest.* Alex searched for a stone strong enough to dislodge the object. *This one should work.* He used the stone as an icepick to chip away at the wall.

To Alex's surprise, the sewer wall crumbled easily and what he found was not a chest but an old briefcase. Alex's heart pounded with excitement as he pulled the briefcase free, thinking of what it might contain. *Wow! Maybe there's some money in here. Stolen bank money. Why would someone hide a briefcase in a sewer? Maybe there's a reason I fell down here. I'll be rich!*

21

Alex carried the briefcase beneath the manhole for more light. It was surprisingly light for something that had a stash of loot in it. He laid it on the ground for further inspection. The briefcase was black and had combination locks. Alex tried to open it but was unsuccessful on his first try. He fiddled with different combinations.

Eventually, Alex got desperate. *I'm going to get this thing open even if I have to break it!* He managed to find a piece of rock just thin enough to wedge into the briefcase opening. *Come on and open up,* Alex grunted, and pulled with all his might, using his hands and the rock to rip open the briefcase. Finally, it gave way.

What popped out was not money but paper scrolls -- seven of them, to be exact. He was disappointed that it wasn't money, but he picked up each scroll one by one. Under the faint light of the manhole opening and with assistance from his cell-phone light, he noticed that the scrolls looked and felt ancient. They were yellowish-brown, slightly wrinkled, with a few rips, but were otherwise in good condition. He rolled open one of the scrolls: *Oh, my god! This looks like ancient Coptic Egyptian writing.*

The scroll had a symbol at the top, followed by what looked to be a number, above a line of text that appeared to be a sentence.

The symbol at the top was a triangle in a circle with two crossing arrows. Just above the crossing arrows was a small circle. Alex had no idea what the symbol meant but it gave him the shivers. His heart beat rapidly as he scanned the writing. He recognized it as Coptic Egyptian -- an ancient text his father had taught him.

Alex's passion for ancient Egyptian culture and language, and his confidence in his ability to translate the writing, gave him courage to read the text. He easily read the numeral above the text. It translated as the numeral 1. Then slowly, after taking a deep breath, he translated and then chanted the Coptic text:

ⲉϩⲟⲩⲛ ⲡ ⲓⲣⲟ ⲉ ⲡⲓ ⲁⲧⲁ6ⲛⲓ ⲙⲏⲧⲣⲣⲱⲟⲩ

Alex chanted until he got the syllables and accent just right:

ⲉⲃⲟⲩⲛ ⲡ ⲓⲣⲟ ⲉ ⲡⲓ ⲁⲧⲁⲟⲛⲓ ⲙⲛ̄ⲧⲣⲣⲱⲟⲩ

The Coptic translates as:

Enter the door into the new kingdom.

Everything around Alex got deathly quiet. No bat or rat noise, no running or dripping water. In fact, Alex felt as if he were in a vacuum. And in what looked like something out of a science-fiction movie, the space directly in front of Alex began to ripple, opening up to display a bright light, accompanied by a humming like sound.

At first, Alex thought he was going crazy, that he had been isolated in the darkness for too long. But he soon realized that he must have opened a portal to another dimension. He had remembered that his father studied, and had often discussed with him, this type of phenomenon. But Alex had always thought his father was off his rocker, and would run and hide with embarrassment whenever his father bought the subject up. He was a believer now. The brightness and humming sound put him in a hypnotic state, which attracted him to the light.

Alex took slow, short steps as he walked into the light. Though cautious, he felt no fear. As he entered the opening he noticed that the rippling effect defied the laws of physics. He wished his father were there to see it. The rippling effect, along with the light and humming sound, made Alex's journey through the portal a beautiful experience. He had a feeling of soaring confidence -- not cockiness or arrogance, but positive self-assurance. He felt he could face anything or anyone and stand his ground.

As he continued through the portal he saw two objects in the distance -- one around his height and the other vastly larger. As he got closer, he saw that the objects were hideous creatures, running toward him at full speed. As they got closer, he could see they would be inexplicable to anyone in his right mind.

One of the creatures was of medium height and build with the face of a skull. It was dressed in hooded military apparel and looked to have weapons around its waist. Its most distinct feature was its eyes: red, fiery, and menacing.

The second creature was huge in stature and covered with coarse hair. Its face was twisted, with three eye sockets almost on top of each other. Its nose was wide and it had a huge mouth with huge fangs. Two of the fangs were visible -- one protruding upward and the other downward. Its military clothing included a breast plate and it carried an assortment of weapons.

When Alex saw the creatures he knew right away they meant to cause trouble. The creature with the hooded skull was pulling out a weapon. The larger and more grotesque creature simply growled, but the growl was the most horrifying sound that Alex had ever heard. All the confidence Alex had acquired left him in one fell swoop. It was time for him to turn and run for his life.

As he exited the portal, the light continued to shine brightly. Running, Alex tripped on the discarded broken briefcase, falling face first to the ground. The scrolls he'd been carrying sprawled across the sewer floor. But the creatures were coming. So Alex quickly grabbed the scroll closest to him and continued running down the passageway.

Alex had never felt as much fear or run so fast. He was so frightened, he forgot about the rats, the bats, and the pain in his injured leg. As he ran, the light from the portal illuminated the tunnel. After a short distance, he saw an opening, and Alex knew he was close to getting out. He could smell the night air.

He dropped to his belly to crawl through the opening. It was just wide enough. And it was the way out of the sewer and out of the junkyard. Alex was only a couple of blocks from home.

Once through the opening, he gripped the scroll like a baton and made like an Olympic relay racer, sprinting as fast as he could into the mid-spring night. He dared not look back. His only concern was to get out of that dreadful place and get home.

The creatures emerged through the portal. The opening quickly closed behind them, immersing the creatures in the darkness of the sewer. Nevertheless, they had easily found six scrolls and realized that one was missing. But that wouldn't be a problem. The unrightful bearer of the one missing scroll had left a muddy trail of footprints.

Chapter 5
In a Pickle

Jordan Lane was swarming with police cars. It looked as if every cop in Brownsville was either on Jordan Lane or somewhere near. All neighborhood streets leading to Jordan Lane were blocked off, starting with Mariah Avenue in the east all the way to noisy Heather Avenue in the south. Even Nicole Circle, the quietest street in the neighborhood, was closed to traffic. The chilly spring night was lit up with flashing red lights and sirens. Residents looked out their windows or stood in front of their houses to witness the commotion.

Mr. Smiley was face down on the pavement in handcuffs. Karen was being detained in a police cruiser awaiting transfer to the police station, where she'd be questioned before her parents could pick her up.

Several neighbors had seen Mr. Smiley and Karen cutting through backyards, and promptly called the police. With little going on in Brownsville, the police were looking for any type of action. They were on the scene in less than five minutes.

Within fifteen minutes the block was teeming with cruisers, and Mr. Smiley had been handcuffed and arrested. Even though Karen was a minor and had no criminal record, the police decided that she needed to be questioned. They felt that Karen must have some useful information because she was hanging around such a peculiar individual as Mr. Smiley, and they wanted to know about it. As the police dogs growled at Mr. Smiley, Karen pleaded her case to the officer.

"We didn't do anything. We were just walking down the street. You can't arrest us for that."

"Listen, you had a flashlight and a can of mace in your possession, and you were trespassing. And you were just 'walking down the street?'" the officer said while he sipped on a latte. "We're supposed to buy that? And as for you," the officer said to Karen, pointing at Mr. Smiley, "What are you doing hanging around someone like that? That guy is bad news."

"Bad news? How?" asked Karen. She had no idea why Mr.

Smiley was receiving such poor treatment. "What has he done to deserve this? I think you're the ones who are 'bad news.'"

"Okay, that'll be enough, young lady. Any more back talk and I'm gonna put you in the detention center for the night," retorted the officer, who grew more annoyed with Karen by the second.

Karen leaned her head against the back seat of the police cruiser. She closed her eyes and thought about the trouble she was going to be in with her parents. There was no doubt that she would be grounded for months. Sneaking out of the house was a no-no, let alone landing yourself at the police station. She also thought about Alex. The anxiety to reach him was at an all-time high. It had to be seven or eight hours since she last spoke to him, and he had never answered any of her calls or voice messages. *He isn't even answering my text messages. He must be in trouble.*

Her cell phone rang, buzzing and displaying Alex's number, which added to her frustration. If only she could answer. The policeman had confiscated her phone, and it sat in the front passenger's seat of the cruiser. It was well past midnight, almost one o'clock in the morning, and she was in the back of a police car while Mr. Smiley was on the ground in handcuffs. If only she hadn't told Alex to go home through the junkyard. *If Alex had stood up to Lenopolous in the first place, no one would be in this situation.*

The police loaded Mr. Smiley into the cruiser and the long, slow ride to the police station began with sirens blaring. There was so much commotion, an onlooker might have thought the police had captured someone on the FBI's Most Wanted list.

Karen and Mr. Smiley were mostly silent, looking straight ahead. Karen managed to quickly glance at Mr. Smiley and notice that he had an expression of shame on his face, as if he blamed himself for getting Karen into this mess.

When they arrived at the police station, Karen and Mr. Smiley received very different treatment. Karen was politely told that several people wished to interview her, then escorted to an interrogation room. Mr. Smiley was fingerprinted and posed for mug shots, then placed alone in a jail cell.

"Ms. Stubblefield, I'm Victor Riley and I work for the FBI. Do you mind if I ask you a few questions?" Karen dared not say 'no.' Riley was intimidating. He had a strong jaw line, a thick black mustache, and a bald head. He was six feet four inches tall and had a very menacing stare. His voice had a grainy timbre.

"No, I don't mind," Karen said timidly.

Riley looked straight into Karen's eyes. "Okay, then," he said. "Let's get started. Karen, I understand that you are a smart girl. I understand that you are one of the smartest kids in school and you're pretty popular. What I don't understand and would like you to explain to me is your fascination with the Smileys. You know -- your best friend Alex and his father."

"My 'fascination with the Smileys?' What do you mean? And how do you know Alex is my best friend?" Karen said.

"Okay, let's cut to the chase. What are you doing hanging around a court-martialed felon after midnight, and why is your best friend his son? Whadya know that you'd like to share with me? Huh?" Riley's pointed questions and intimidating manner had Karen frightened and confused.

"I don't know anything! I've known Alex and his parents for years. We're neighbors. Mr. Smiley and I were out late because we were looking for Alex."

"Why were you looking for Alex? What was he doing out in the middle of the night?" said Riley.

"We think he's lost. We believe he cut through the junkyard and lost his way home."

"Why do you believe he got lost coming home? And why would he cut through a junkyard at night? And if you were looking for your friend, I could understand carrying a flashlight, but why did you have a can of mace in your possession?" asked Riley.

"Because of the dogs. We were going inside the junkyard because that's where Alex was. Please, you have to believe me," Karen's eyes welled with tears. Riley, knowing that he had broken Karen to the point that she would tell him what he wanted to know, stared directly in her eyes while he asked his

28

next question.

"Karen, I'm going to ask you one more question, and how you answer will determine whether you go home or spend the night in a jail cell. Did Smiley or his son ever tell you anything about a dimensional portal or something to that effect?"

"Look, I don't know anything about any dimensional portal and that sounds totally crazy. You have to believe me. I don't know anything!"

Satisfied with her answer, Riley took a deep breath, stood up and left the room.

About an hour later, another officer came into the room.

"Ms. Stubblefield? Your parents are here. You can go home."

Karen had never felt so happy to see her parents. The expression on their faces was one of disappointment, but she was willing to face the consequences. Besides, she didn't have to spend the night in a smelly jail cell. At that thought, she glanced back over her shoulder to look at Mr. Smiley. He didn't notice her leaving. He had his face buried in his hands as he sat alone on one of the jail-cell benches. She felt very sorry for him and wanted to offer some words of encouragement, but the look on the Stubblefields' faces told Karen to not even think about it. She was going home to think about what she did. At least three months' worth of thinking.

The ride home was long and quiet. Longer than the ride to the police station. The silence in the car echoed Mr. and Mrs. Stubblefield's disappointment in their daughter. Karen wanted to explain what had happened, but she thought better of it and remained quiet. She just wanted to get home and get to bed, to end what had easily been the worst night of her life. When the family finally arrived home, Karen went straight to her bedroom, put on her pajamas and got into the bed. She buried herself under the covers hoping she would fall asleep quickly. But before she got comfortable, her cell phone rang. It was Alex.

"Alex, where have you been?" Karen whispered, knowing her parents would confiscate her phone if they heard.

"You wouldn't believe what happened to me," said an exhausted Alex. "Do you have time to talk? I have a lot that I need to tell you."

"I have a lot that I need to tell you, too, Alex, but I don't think we should discuss it over the phone. Are you home?"

"Yes. I got home about an hour ago," said Alex.

"Okay. I have an idea. Let's meet at the bus stop tomorrow morning and take off from there. And forget about school. There's a lot we need to discuss," said Karen.

"No problem," said Alex. "Sounds like you've had an adventurous night."

"Adventurous isn't the word," said Karen. "But I'm glad you're all right."

"Well, I'm beat-up and totally drained. I'm just lying in bed trying to comprehend what happened to me tonight."

Chapter 6
The Next Day

The buzzing sound of the alarm clock pounded through Alex's skull like a sledgehammer. It had been just four hours since the horror Alex witnessed in the junkyard sewer. The images of the two creatures chasing after him in the dimensional portal were still fresh in his mind. He had not slept a wink. He was too traumatized. Despite this, he had to rise, as he had made plans to meet Karen. Alex feared that he had done something really wrong, with dire consequences.

When he'd found an escape route and squeezed his way out into the fresh, crisp air, the sound of traffic and the light of the moon had been heaven compared with the claustrophobic, dark stench of the sewer. Though he climbed over fences and sprinted through yards, not once did Alex think about his leg wound or any of his other bruises. Nothing was going to keep him from reaching home.

When he did, Alex plopped on his bed in a heap, too tired and riddled with fear to notice that his parents were gone. Lying down, he stared at the ceiling, replaying his adventure over and over again before calling Karen. After they decided where to meet, he set his alarm clock and returned to his trance-like state until morning.

When the alarm went off, he quickly showered, wrapped his wounded leg with a bandage, ate some cereal, and headed out the door. While scurrying out of the house he called for his parents, but there was no reply. He knew then that there was trouble, and hoped Karen could fill in the missing pieces to the puzzle.

Karen waited for Alex at the bus stop. Having convinced her parents that she needed to go to school despite arriving home in the wee hours of the morning, she couldn't wait to tell Alex about her adventure. Ditching school, they headed straight to the town library. Isolated at a corner table in the quietest part of the library, Karen explained in a whisper what had happened to her and his father. Alex was surprised but not shocked, given the peculiar ways of the Brownsville police.

Alex started telling Karen about his adventure. He told her about the chase from the dogs, and how he'd escaped them by sliding into the sewer manhole.

"No wonder your father was worried when you went into that junkyard. He was worried about those vicious dogs. But what gets me is that the manhole cover was already ajar when you slid down the hole. That seems odd. Do you think that someone was looking for something in that sewer? Oh well, other than a few cut and bruises at least you're okay. Let's not tell anyone what happened."

Alex thought about her question. *Was someone looking for something in the sewer?* The only thing he could think of was the scrolls he'd found. He decided to show her.

"When I was down there, I found this." Alex pulled out the scroll from his backpack and opened it up, spreading it across the table.

"What's this?" asked Karen, looking puzzled.

"It's a scroll that looks like it contains an ancient Egyptian language. But I haven't had the chance to decode it yet," whispered Alex.

"What do you *think* it says and what's with this crazy symbol?" whispered an excited Karen.

"I'm not sure, but I believe it's just one piece of a major puzzle. I was able to read and decode one of the other scrolls. I found seven of these things," Alex stated.

"Seven? Well, what do these things do?" Karen asked.

Alex sighed before answering.

"The scroll that I was able to read opened up a dimensional portal to another world."

Karen's jaw nearly dropped to the floor.

"Well that's what your father must have been hiding. This is what that angry FBI agent kept asking me about at the police station," whispered Karen, trying to control the level of her voice. I didn't know what he was talking about.

"So you opened up a dimensional portal?" she asked. "I've only heard of those in sci-fi movies. I didn't know they actually existed. And did you go into the portal? What did you see? And why didn't you bring all of the scrolls?"

"After I chanted the text, the portal opened up and then I went in. It was beautiful," said Alex, reminiscing as he told his story. "But then I saw two creatures running directly toward me and they didn't look friendly. So I turned and ran. When I exited the portal, I dropped the scrolls on the sewer floor and didn't have time to pick all of them up. I just picked up the one that was closest to me and kept on going."

Alex went on to describe the creatures to Karen. The graphic images horrified her, but she remained strong.

"We need to get the rest of those scrolls, Alex. We don't want them to fall into the wrong hands. I bet you they are super important. And since we know that one of the scrolls opens a portal to another dimension, there's no telling what the others do."

Alex paused, deep in thought.

"I don't want to, but I'm willing to go back to the junkyard and get those scrolls for my father's sake," said Alex.

"That's the spirit, Alex," said Karen. "And you know I've got your back."

Alex and Karen decided to wait until the afternoon to go to the junkyard, to coincide with school letting out. They made sure they were prepared for the journey, taking a flashlight and a can of mace to protect them from the junkyard dogs. When they arrived, Alex took Karen by the hand and entered the junkyard sewer through the path by which he'd escaped the night before. Upon entering, he noticed that his cell phone had a very low signal. "No wonder we couldn't reach each other," Alex said to Karen. When they walked farther into the sewer, Alex noticed three things: First, there was no trace of light, which meant that the portal was closed. Second, the scrolls were missing. And third, there were two sets of footprints in addition to Alex's and they weren't human. Alex had a panic attack.

"Oh, my god! Those things came out of the portal. They're after me."

"Calm down," said Karen. "Maybe they went back into the portal. We don't have to say a thing We can act like nothing ever happened," said Karen.

"I'm afraid that's not possible," said Alex, looking like his days were numbered. He followed the trail of footprints. "Look, these footprints lead to this opening where I escaped. They're on to me. My god, I'm so screwed!" Alex began to cry. It had been years since Alex had cried and he couldn't remember ever sobbing so hard. "Why don't you just get out of here and save yourself?" cried Alex. "I think I want to end it right here."

That statement got Karen fired up.

"Now, you listen here. Quit feeling sorry for yourself and get it together," Karen demanded. "And quit thinking about killing yourself. Let's look at the facts. You kill yourself, the creatures get the last scroll -- and we don't know what the scroll does. Your father probably ends up in jail, and I lose my best friend."

This calmed Alex down. Then they looked at each other and embraced. "Don't worry, Alex, we'll get to the bottom of this," said Karen, whispering into Alex's ear. "But we need to talk to your father. I'm sure he has some answers."

With that, Alex and Karen exited the sewer and left the junkyard. Despite being on punishment, nothing was going to stop Karen from helping her friend. As they hustled to the police station, they comforted each other by holding hands.

Chapter 7
The Sétbætañ

The full moon and bright stars made the night sky look like a planetarium; the galaxy's beauty was on full display. There were no sounds of people or traffic, only those of crickets and owls in the distance. The creatures, the Sétbætañ, took care to stay under cover in the evening darkness. They were masters at cloaking themselves and keeping silent; they were skilled at sneak attacks. They had a keen sense of smell and were highly skilled fighters. Their weapons were not highly sophisticated but were more than enough to do the job. After traveling for the better part of the night, they were closing in. The creatures had only one goal: to capture the portal opener and possessor of the final scroll.

Exiting the portal, the creatures had been slowed down when they saw the scattered scrolls on the sewer floor. It was a great discovery. The creatures would have been satisfied chasing the being out of the portal and back into its own dimension. But seeing the scrolls, they'd known more was at stake. And when they'd discovered that the most powerful scroll was missing, they knew that they had to find it, and to capture the being or beings that possessed it.

"The being's trail leads this way," growled Cúbaneg, the skull-faced creature.

"Good. Let's move quickly," growled Ugnjengon, the large, grotesque creature.

Ugnjengon was an impatient soul with a very bad temper. He stood seven feet tall and was strong as an ox. Cúbaneg was more calculating, possessed the skills of a natural leader, and wouldn't hesitate to use force. The trail led right up to Alex's front door. The creatures knew that the possessor of the scroll was human.

"Let's break the door down," shouted Ugnjengon.

"No," countered Cúbaneg. "We do not want to alert and encounter any of the other humans, at least not yet. We will stay cloaked until we find easy access into the human dwelling."

It was ten thirty at night when Mrs. Smiley arrived home. She'd spent the entire day at the police station, looking for

35

answers on the whereabouts of Alex, and pleading for Mr. Smiley's release. Because she couldn't afford bail, Mr. Smiley would spend three weeks in the jail cell. In the short time that Mrs. Smiley was allowed to visit with her husband, they expressed their love for each other. Despite their shortcomings, Mr. and Mrs. Smiley expressed deep sympathy toward each other when trouble arose. Now mentally and physically tired, Mrs. Smiley felt a good night sleep was in order before she went back to the police station.

Entering the house, Mrs. Smiley paused at the slow squeak of the door. A cold shiver of fear penetrated her body as she shut the door behind her and reached for the light switch. She grabbed the family bible from the coffee table and recited a prayer. Calmer but still visibly shaken, she decided to catch up on the news instead of going to bed. Maybe some news on Alex's whereabouts would be broadcast. She would also watch some political talking points to clear her mind. Sitting in her favorite spot on the couch, holding the remote, she wondered where the deathly cold feeling of fear had come from. Never in her life had she experienced such a feeling of near death. *Maybe I'm just overtired,* she thought. After reciting another prayer, Mrs. Smiley attempted to settle in. While she continued to worry about Alex's whereabouts, she turned the television to the TAPC news channel.

The creatures had entered the house, following Alex's trail of footprints to his room.

"The human's not here," growled Ugnjengon.

"Then let's search for the scroll," said Cúbaneg.

The creatures searched every corner of Alex's room. Ugnjengon became frustrated.

"Noooo!" the creature roared before ramming Alex's drawer into the bedroom window. "It's not here."

"You must control yourself, you fool. Now you've alerted the human," whispered Cúbaneg.

"I'll destroy the animal," Ugnjengon said, drawing his weapon.

"No. Now's not the time. Now, cloak. Now!" said Cúbaneg.

Hearing the loud crash, Mrs. Smiley called out to Alex. "Alex, are you home?" When he didn't answer, she raced to his room carrying her bible and a sawed off shotgun she'd retrieved from under her couch. She opened Alex's bedroom door to discover a room in disarray along with a smashed bedroom window.

"Someone's kidnapped Alex!" she screamed figuring that someone had just taken Alex after he had returned to the house while she was away. Mrs. Smiley promptly dialed 9-1-1.

The creatures, invisible and silent to Mrs. Smiley, followed Alex's scent out of the house.

"It leads away from this dwelling," said Ugnjengon, who had calmed down.

"Good," said Cúbaneg. "Let's proceed. But let's not have any more of your foolishness. Ecaep will nct be pleased if we fail."

At the police station, oblivious to what was happening at the Smiley's home, Mr. Smiley, Alex, and Karen quietly and carefully went over the events of the previous thirty-six hours. They didn't want the cops or anyone else in the police station to hear.

The usually quiet police station was buzzing with activity. There was chatter about an apparent break-in and kidnapping across town. What's more, another person, who lived next door, was now identified as missing. In all the commotion, Karen had forgotten to let her parents know of her whereabouts. They were hysterical that their daughter hadn't come home after school and suspected that her absence was connected to last night's events. Both the Stubblefields and the police suspected foul play. The Stubblefields had learned that Alex was missing and suspected that Karen was with him. They'd always hated that Karen associated with Alex. Anything that involved the Smileys led to trouble. But because the Brownville police were unaccustomed to drama, and with Detective Riley out of town on business, they failed to realize that Alex and Karen were right at the police station.

The Smileys, on the other hand, were accustomed to drama. With their past involvement in the federal government, the constant job hopping, and Alex being bullied at school, this was just another episode of their own, long-running soap opera. Alex had always felt that a reality show of his family would be a big hit.

Amid the commotion, Mr. Smiley explained to the kids why he'd planted the scrolls in the junkyard sewer. Until Alex discovered them, they'd been hidden there for more than twenty years.

"The scrolls all possess unique powers," said Mr. Smiley. "Alex, like you, I discovered that one of the scrolls could open dimensional portals. If chanted correctly, its translation is: *Open the pathway to the new world*. Alex quickly reached in his back pocket and showed his father the scroll in his possession.

"Yes. I can't remember exactly, but this looks like the seventh of the sacred scrolls," Mr. Smiley said, drawing attention from the station staff. He lowered his voice. "I discovered these scrolls while working on an excavation project for the government. The U.S. government believed that certain fossilized plants contained DNA for life regeneration. And not the life regeneration about spiritual awakening or physical healing, but the actual resurrection of the dead. They thought it could be used on soldiers who fell in battle. Anyway, when I took a look at the writings on the scrolls, I noticed they were similar to the ancient Egyptian Coptic writings that I'd studied in church. This is what I eventually taught you, Alex," said Mr. Smiley. "So, in secret, I spent months trying to decode the writings. And after spending seventeen-hour days in the lab, trying to figure the ancient text, I was able to decode the scrolls, including the one that opens the dimensional portal."

"What did you see? What did it look like? And did it make any noise?" asked Karen.

"The portal opened with a big flash of light," said Mr. Smiley. "The flash of light was very similar to a flash of lightning on a stormy night, without the thunder. Then the portal appeared. It had a low humming sound."

"Yes. That's what I saw," said Alex.

"I discovered that anyone could enter the portal and it could be opened any time. The only thing is that the portal didn't stay open for long," said Mr. Smiley.

"How long did it stay open for?" asked Alex.

"For approximately a minute and then it would disappear."

"What would happen if you were in the portal and it started to close?" asked Karen.

"Nothing. You would return to the dimension you started in," said Mr. Smiley.

"How do the scrolls work? I know it's not by magic," said Karen.

"I believe they work by satellite. I've been researching my theory for years," said Mr. Smiley.

"Have you ever been to the other side?" Alex asked.

"Yes," Mr. Smiley said, hurrying to the next point of the story to avoid any further questions on the topic. "But things went wrong when Elizabeth went into my lab and found out about the portal."

"Elizabeth? Who's Elizabeth?" asked Karen.

"Elizabeth Gateway. Your teacher, and one of the government's many secret intelligence officers," said Mr. Smiley.

"What did she find?" asked Alex.

"She found my drawings and theories on how the dimensional portal and the scroll text worked. I had had my suspicions, but I learned that the government had been spying on me for quite a while. I was lucky enough to spot her in my lab while I was returning from home. But before Ms. Gateway could gather the authorities for my arrest, I took the scrolls that I'd kept in a briefcase and buried them in the wall of that junkyard sewer. The government has been looking for them ever since. And my secret has been safe, until your discovery," Mr. Smiley said, looking at Alex.

"Wow. And I thought I had an adventure," said Alex.

"Now we know why the manhole cover was open," said Karen. "Government agents must have been in that sewer looking for the scrolls."

"Exactly," said Mr. Smiley.

"What does this scroll say?" asked Alex.

Mr. Smiley paused but quickly dodged the question.

"You say that the creatures entered our dimension? Then you must leave, son. They're coming after you," said a concerned Mr. Smiley.

"And go where? I can't go home," said Alex.

"You and Karen will have to keep on the move. Don't let them capture you and more important, don't let them get that scroll," said Mr. Smiley.

"Well what should we look for, and –"

Mr. Smiley cut them off.

"You need to leave now. They're coming."

Alex and Karen left the police station and went out into the chilly spring night. They wondered out loud where they should go. After wandering aimlessly for about eight blocks, Karen suggested they sit down on the curb and rest. The street was dark and quiet. No one was out. Putting her face in her hands, Karen started to cry. "I have to reach my parents. They don't know where I am. I'm sorry, Alex."

"That's okay," said Alex. "This isn't your battle."

"But I said I wouldn't leave you and now look at me, ready to jump ship."

Alex consoled her as she cried. "Look, I'll be fine. Just call your parents."

Karen pulled out her phone and started to press the speed dial. But a cold chill engulfed them and all bodily movements seemed stuck in time. Two monstrous figures appeared. Seeing the creatures, Karen fainted. Alex stood, numb.

"You, Possessor of the Last Scroll," growled Cúbaneg in a horrific alien language unrecognizable to Alex. "Give me the scroll. You are coming with us. Ugnjengon, grab the other human," ordered Cúbaneg.

Ugnjengon grabbed Karen and slung her over his shoulder. Cúbaneg took the scroll from Alex and bound him in chains, pointing a semi-automatic weapon at his back. With that, the creatures opened the portal. Gripped with fright, Alex felt the end was near.

Chapter 8
The Land of Vuur

In possession of all seven scrolls, and with Alex and Karen in tow, the creatures felt great glory. With only a minute to cross the dimensional portal to reach their world, they ran at a brisk pace. As Alex ran, chained like an animal, the jaunt through the portal was nothing like his first, beautiful, experience. This time seemed like a trip to hell. Alex's mind raced as he wondered what fate he and Karen faced on the other side. Meanwhile, Karen was being carried like a sack of potatoes across the back of Ugnjengon. Repeatedly bumping her head against the creature's breastplate, she fell in and out of consciousness. They weren't headed to hell. Alex and Karen were headed to Caynonã, the home planet of the Sétbætañ.

The creatures were certain that reclaiming the scrolls and capturing human enemies would make them heroes among their people. They believed that they finally had the ammunition to defeat their longtime rivals the Luçimarks and that Ecaep, the leader of the Sétbætañ, would lead them to victory. As it was told by the ancients, war between the Sétbætañ and the Luçimarks had been waged on and off for more than two thousand miliyous. A miliyou is a Caynonãn year, equivalent to three Earth years. After centuries of living together peacefully in the land of Urodae, the Luçimarks declared war on the Sétbætañ and ended up ruling over all of Caynonã. Through war, the Luçimarks acquired their technology to travel to other worlds using dimensional portals.

One of the worlds they frequented often was Earth. The Luçimarks found that Earth could easily support life and decided to colonize the planet, giving birth to a new civilization. They'd taken the technology from the Sétbætañ by force. The Luçimarks, resourceful but arrogant creatures, considered the Sétbætañ an inferior race of beings. At the time, the Sétbætañ were smaller in number, and were enslaved by the Luçimarks. The Sétbætañ were intelligent and peaceful beings, but the Luçimarks oppressed the Sétbætañ by using their economic and

41

military advantage.

Tired of being oppressed, the Sétbætañ rebelled against the Luçimarks in a war that lasted for hundreds of miliyous. They made great strides in closing the Luçimarks' military advantage. After the Great Rebellion, the Sétbætañ were able to reclaim and utilize the advanced weaponry and dimensional portal transportation devices they'd created.

But the might of the Luçimarks was too much, and the Sétbætañ eventually succumbed. The Luçimarks then cast the Sétbætañ into Vuur, the dark and desolate lands of Caynonã. Thus, the Sétbætañ vowed to get their revenge by torturing the Luçimarks' new civilization on Earth.

Reaching the other side of the portal, Alex and Karen were thrown to the ground in a heap. When Alex looked up, he saw a barren world of darkness. The chill air held the stench of death. Wind blew dirt and sand in every direction. The thundering and lightning sky was dark, with a red tint that resembled blood. There were four moons that gave off a faint light. The most horrifying site was the thousands of demonic creatures that were chanting what seemed to be a name, facing a large stage made of rock. They were awaiting the arrival of their leader. Alex and Karen were in the desolate lands of Vuur.

Karen slowly regained consciousness. She was bound in chains. Her head throbbed. She tried to make out the creature on the stage. It addressed its audience in a hideous, alien language:

"Today is the day we get our vengeance on the enemy," it said.

The crowd cheered.

"Thanks to the work of our great warriors, Cúbaneg and Ugnjengon. They have captured what was stolen from us."

More wild cheering from the crowd.

"After two thousand miliyous, we now have in our possession the Ancient Scrolls. We also have a bonus. Look to the feet of Cúbaneg and Ugnjengon and look upon the maggot offspring of the Luçimarks."

The crowd went into a frenzy. As the creatures huddled around the kids, poking at them and shouting insults, Alex and

Karen huddled against each another in the fetal position. The being addressing the creatures was their leader. His face, like Cúbaneg's, resembled a skull. He wore a hood, was larger than Cúbaneg in stature, and was riding a red, bear-like animal. His eyes glowed red and he sported an evil grin. The other creatures looked like the monsters, devils, trolls, and gremlins you would find in your most frightening nightmares.

"But we'll have time to address them later. Cúbaneg. Ugnjengon. Give me the scrolls." The creatures handed the scrolls to their leader, and the leader held the scrolls up in the air. "Now, with these scrolls, you shall witness the triumph of your people. You will witness the triumph of the Sétbætañ. I command that all the greatest scientists that breathe among our people decode these scrolls created by our forefathers. I also command that the earthly vermin that cower before us be tortured for two days, before we feast on their flesh. Two days to represent the two thousand miliyous we have been oppressed by our enemy."

The crowd broke into more wild cheering.

"All hail the Sétbætañ! All hail Caynonã!"

The crowd went into a wicked frenzy, chanting their leader's name: "Ecaep ... Ecaep ... Ecaep ... Ecaep ..."

Alex and Karen were dragged across the ground by a giant, troll-like creature while the mob of hideous beings shouted and screamed. Several smaller creatures kicked and spat at them. The rough terrain scratched, scraped, and bruised their bodies as Alex and Karen were dragged to their fate. The swirling winds filled their mouths and lungs with dust and dirt. The chill air penetrated their bones, while the sounds of the creatures pierced their ears. Their screams were drowned out by the noise of the crowd. For Alex, it seemed as if time had stopped. Never in a million years did Alex imagine he would die like this.

Alex and Karen were dragged into a dark dungeon, where other creatures were being kept. The jailed creatures went wild upon seeing the humans. Some spat on Alex and Karen as they were dragged by.

Alex heard the sound of keys and the opening of a cage door.

He and Karen were thrown into the cage. The floor was covered with mud and ghastly muck. When the troll removed Karen's chains, it breathed heavily in her face. The stench caused Karen to vomit. The troll left them, slamming the cage door behind him. As he walked away, he looked at the humans with an evil grin. Though Alex and Karen were isolated from the others, they could clearly hear the sounds of the other captive creatures, who seemed to be hurling insults at them. Alex thought there was no way that he and Karen would survive the night.

As time passed, Karen slowly regained her composure. She had begun to get used to the inmates' noises and the filth beneath her feet. Alex also felt better, although he was resigned to his life being over.

"Alex, don't you give me that look. I know what you're thinking. You're thinking about giving up," Karen shouted. "We have to think of a way out of here. No one, and I mean nothing, is feasting on my flesh."

"Well, look at this place," said Alex. "It's not like we have a lot of room to maneuver. These walls are solid brick and there are no windows. Plus, there's not enough light in here, I can barely see you, and you're only two feet in front of me."

"Oooh, I have an idea," said Karen. "Take out your phone."

They both took out their cell phones. Alex noticed that there was no time displayed but the flashlights provided decent light. Enough to gaze at each other, which felt like the only thing they had left. Alex wanted to see something beautiful before he died. And to him, Karen was the most beautiful thing ever.

Just then something entered the dungeon. The sound of footsteps headed toward Alex and Karen, and they quickly put away their phones. Soon, standing in front of their cell were the guard troll, Cúbaneg, Ugnjengon, and Ecaep. Ecaep looked at them long and hard, then began to speak. To their surprise, he addressed Alex and Karen in English.

"You filth. You had our forefather's sacred scrolls in your possession. Now you will pay," Ecaep said, staring and pointing at Alex. "For six thousand of your Earth years we have been struck down by the hands of our enemy. But now we shall have our revenge. And we're going to start with you." Shaking like a leaf, Alex managed to tumble some words out of his mouth:

"But I didn't mean to --"

"Shut up!" said Ecaep, cutting Alex off. "You're a pitiful human. Weaker than most. Your female friend has more warrior blood than you." Humiliated, Alex's eyes fell to the dungeon floor. *Now how did it know that?* Alex wondered if the creature had ESP. Then Karen spoke up:

"I think *you're* pitiful."

"Ah, a human with some fight," laughed Ecaep. He then reached into his pocket. "You must be hungry, here."

When his bony hands emerged from his pockets, he threw into the cell two worm-like creatures that began to multiply when they hit the ground. Karen screamed. Laughing, Ecaep and the other creatures left. In a matter of seconds, the slimy creatures had multiplied into a heap. Alex knew he needed to act fast. Retrieving a large stone from the corner of the cell, he picked it up and with all his might smashed the stone on top of the worms. Green ooze spattered onto Alex and the cell floor. He did it repeatedly until all the worms were dead. Karen rushed into his arms. "Thank you, Alex." She was truly grateful for his bravery.

Alex and Karen grew tired. Despite his fear that he would never awaken, Alex just couldn't take the strain. The constant noise from the inmates, the numerous bumps and bruises, the battle against the worms, and dealing with the hideous creatures were too much. Without speaking, Alex and Karen slumped to the ground against the cell's back wall and held each other as they fell asleep. Whether they would see another waking moment was anyone's guess.

When Alex awoke, he was not sure how much time had passed. The sky was still dark red, with thunder and lightning. The dungeon walls were still filled with noise, and the air still reeked. Alex took out his phone, adjusted his glasses, and used the phone's flashlight to glance at Karen. She slept peacefully on his shoulder. He noticed a bruise on her forehead from banging it against Ugnjengon's breastplate. Still, her face maintained its youthful innocence. As Alex looked at Karen, he began to think about home, his family, and school. He wondered if his father was still in jail, and if his mother was worried about him. He wondered if anyone at school missed him. He even wondered about Lenopolous Gary. What he wouldn't do to have Lenopolous pounding his fists into him right now.

Without warning, a bright flash of light with a low humming sound appeared, jolting Alex from his daydream. The dungeon inmates went berserk. It was a portal. And coming through it was not a monster, or some grotesque creature, but a human, dressed in an army uniform.

"Hey, quick! Jump into the portal," said the human. Alex didn't hesitate. He quickly woke Karen and dragged her half-asleep body through the portal. The commotion alerted the dungeon guards and they scrambled to the cell. The troll guard nervously fumbled the keys while trying to unlock the cell door.

"Hurry, you fool," hollered Cúbaneg, knowing the portal would soon close.

"Enough of this," screamed Ugnjengon, as he snatched the keys from the troll guard and managed to open the cell door. It was too late. As the creatures stepped foot into the cell and then into the portal, the portal disappeared. Not clearing the portal in time, they remained where they were. Frustrated, Ugnjengon let out a thunderous growl and banged his fists repeatedly against the cell walls. Cúbaneg took out his anger on the troll guard.

"You pitiful fool. Why weren't you on patrol, guarding the cell? You knew those humans were supposed to be guarded with your life." Cúbaneg looked the troll in the eyes and said, "You have failed. Ecaep will not be pleased. You know what must be done." The troll dropped to his knees. At the instruction of Cúbaneg, Ugnjengon took out his long sword and beheaded the troll. As the troll's head rolled down the dungeon aisle, the prison inmates shouted at the top of their lungs.

The humans had safely reached the other side of the portal. When they stepped out, Alex and Karen noticed quite a difference.

Chapter 9
Urodae and the Luçimarks

Alex, Karen, and the soldier exited the portal into a world quite different from Vuur. While grasping their new surroundings, they took in its beauty and pleasantness. Blue skies, shining warm sun, and lots of vegetation. The air had a clean, sweet smell, with the perfect breeze. Their journey had taken them to Urodae, land of the Luçimarks.

"Don't get too comfortable daydreamin'. Those Setties can pop up anywhere, anytime," said the soldier, referring to the Sétbætañ. The soldier was a tall, well-built man who spoke with a Southern accent. "We have a bunker not too far from here. We'll be safe there."

"How do you know they won't appear at your bunker?" said Alex.

"Don't worry. They won't show up there. That bunker is built like a fortress. Plus, I've scrambled the portal navigation signal. It'll take a while for them to decode it," the soldier reassured them.

"How long is a while?" asked Karen.

"A week, minimum."

Alex, Karen, and the soldier walked about a mile to reach the bunker. It was isolated in a forest and looked like a huge warehouse accented with plants and an assortment of trees. To enter the bunker, the soldier input a code and laser scanned his palm. He led Alex and Karen down a narrow hallway into a big, open room filled with tables of food and decorated with strange plants. Alex and Karen looked around in awe.

"Well, dig in. I know you're hungry. Don't just stand there gawkin'," said the soldier. Alex and Karen pounced on the food.

"I don't think I've introduced myself," began the soldier. "I'm Captain Franklin Powers. But you can just call me Captain or Flip."

"Why Flip?" asked Karen, barely looking up as she inhaled her pasta.

"I got that name working in a burger joint at home. I was so good at flipping burgers, the locals started calling me Flip and the name stuck."

"I'm Karen."

"And I'm Alex. Thanks for saving us."

"Well, you're quite welcome. I just wanna let you know that I know about you two all too well. Especially you, Alex," said Flip.

Alex started to get nervous and his hands shook while he gripped his sandwich.

"What do you know?" asked Alex.

"I'd say quite a bit. Where would you like me to start? From you opening the portal in that sewer or getting captured by those Setties? Or should I talk about how your father is a traitor to our country, and may have enabled the annihilation of mankind by allowing those scrolls to end up with the enemy? So which is it?" said Flip, his voice rising.

"Now, wait a minute," Karen retorted. "First of all, how dare you spy on us. And second, Alex's dad is not a traitor."

"Karen, calm down. I can fight my own battles," said Alex, resigned to the fact that the captain knew a lot, if not all, about the Smileys. He figured that if he or Karen caused any trouble, they would end up back in some type of jail cell. "Flip," Alex said, "I know my family has a lot of issues and my father may be strange. But he proudly served his country and loved being a scientist. How does that make him a traitor?"

"Look, let's not play dumb. Your father had an agenda to conceal a highly dangerous weapon, the scrolls, from the U.S. Government. Second, without permission, he used the scrolls to open a dimensional portal and travel to this world. Last but not least, he made contact with the natives of this world, including making contact with the enemies of our allies." Flip then lowered his voice and looked Alex straight in the eyes before continuing. "So maybe he loved being a scientist, and maybe he served his country with pride some of the time. But given the facts, you still think your father isn't a traitor?"

Just before Alex was about to offer his rebuttal, a tall, thin, creature carrying a tray entered the room. The creature was physically similar to humans, but eight feet tall. Its hands were webbed, it had a very small nose, and its eyes were spread farther apart than a human's eyes. The creature was wearing a long, dark garment, and walked with an elegant stride. Seeing Flip, the creature placed the tray in front of him. It held three green, aspirin-like tablets.

Flip consumed one of the tablets.

"Thank you, Eloysina," he said. "They're not ready for these yet. I'll contact you when its time."

The creature nodded its head and left the room. Alex and Karen gasped in amazement.

"What was that?!" asked Alex.

"Not 'What was that?' but 'Who is that?' That was Eloysina, a native of this fine land," Flip said.

Alex and Karen rushed to the door where the creature was exiting. In the hallway they saw several creatures; some dressed like Eloysina, others dressed in military garb and carrying weapons that could have been Earthly.

Alex and Karen ran down the hall. Coming to a courtyard, they saw hundreds of the Luçimark creatures mingling with human military personnel. Some were drinking, some were eating, and some were laughing and talking – in human tongues. Others seemed to be showing off their weapons. Alex and Karen gawked in amazement but the creatures didn't pay them any attention. The creatures seemed to have a sense of entitlement. Feeling like her head was about to explode, Karen rushed back to the break room to confront Flip, with Alex in tow. Flip had a wry smile on his face. He was sitting on a table, smoking a cigar.

"Listen, Flip, or whatever your name is," said Karen. "Since you know so much about us and about what's going on, can you clue us in? Alex and I have been jailed, interrogated, and surrounded by freaks for the past several days. We understand they want the scrolls but why are you here and how do you factor into all of this?"

"You want answers? Then I'm gonna give you answers," said Flip. He gave an order on his radio. "Major Kremley, can you and Lieutenant Jackson please report to the break room? Our

49

guests want some answers." Flip looked at Alex and Karen and said, "Now the lieutenant, major, and I are gonna tell you some truths. And I hope you can handle it. 'Cause after we're through, you may wish you'd stayed in the fantasy world you've been living in all your lives."

Chapter 10
A Tale of Origin

Major Kremley and Lieutenant Jackson, dressed in military garb, entered the break room. They looked at Alex and Karen suspiciously. Kremley had an intensity that differed from Flip's laid-back manner. Jackson was focus and poised. They introduced themselves to the kids.

"Hello, I'm Major John Kremley."

"And I'm Lieutenant and scientist Granger Jackson."

"We understand that you got caught up in a situation instigated by your father, Phillip Smiley," said Kremley, staring at Alex.

"Now, before I allow Lieutenant Jackson to explain what's going on, I want you to realize that the United States is now at war," said Kremley. "And not only are we in danger, but the entire world is in danger. Everyone, and I mean everyone in the U.S. military all the way up to the President, is ready to protect our interests at all costs. Now, everything that you're about to be told is highly confidential information. You are ordered not to tell anyone. Not acquaintances, friends, or family." Kremley looked directly at Alex. "Thank goodness your father at least followed *those* orders." He then told Jackson, "You can begin when you're ready, Lieutenant."

"Let me start by giving you some historical background," Jackson began, pointing to an astronomy chart. "This here is the planet Caynonã. The planet we are on now. It is located in the Maczell Galaxy, which is about seven hundred and fifty thousand light years from Earth. About six thousand years ago the Luçimarks, the creatures that you see roaming around here, fought a war against the Sétbætañ, the creatures that we rescued you from. The Luçimarks defeated the Sétbætañ, and the Sétbætañ decided to seek revenge on the Luçimarks by waging war against their distant cousins, the humans." Karen cut Jackson off.

"Wait a minute. Are you saying that we are related to these … these … freaks?"

"Exactly. These 'freaks,' as you call them, are your great, great, great, great, great, great, great, great, great, great, grandparents," said a smiling Jackson. "They are beings who came to our planet and established human civilization. That includes the things that scientists can't seem to explain -- from Stonehenge, to the Great Pyramids of Giza, to the ancient writings in Egypt."

"Wow! That's why I was able to read the writing on the scroll. It was simply the ancient Coptic Egyptian writings that I studied with my father when I was small," said Alex.

"Actually, they're alien writings, to be precise," said Jackson.

"Why don't they look exactly like us?" asked Karen.

"Scientific research indicates that over time, the Earth's atmosphere dictated how we evolved physically. If you notice, the air is very fresh and easy to breathe here in Urodae. That would explain the Luçimarks' small noses. There's less need to filter the air. And because there's a lot of oxygen, organisms here grow larger, which explains their height," explained Jackson.

"What about the eyes?" asked Alex.

"Our guess is that binocular vision like we have is more important for hunting and avoiding predators. That type of vision is not as necessary on this planet, as Luçimarks consume only vegetation and have no natural enemies," said Jackson.

"Are there any other beings on Caynonã?" asked Karen.

"No. These are the only two races of beings on the planet and individuals can live up to seven hundred earth years," said Jackson. "You should know that the majority of the surface of Caynonã is barren rock and desert, much like Vuur. Urodae is the only hospitable land on the planet. The Luçimarks and the Sétbætañ used to dwell together in Urodae, but the Luçimarks wanted Urodae to themselves. That the Sétbætañ adapted and survived outside of Urodae is quite an accomplishment."

"How, exactly, did the Sétbætañ get their revenge on us?" asked Alex.

"I'll get to that in a minute," said Jackson.

"Anyway, the scrolls that you recently discovered were

hidden on Earth for centuries before being discovered by the Germans in 1906. The Germans were savvy enough to decode the scroll that allowed dimensional travel to and from this planet. They met and befriended the Luçimarks and they exchanged technological knowledge on weapons, and on space and dimensional travel. With this new technology, the Germans attempted to use the scroll technology in fighting both world wars. And as far as the weapons technology was concerned, the Germans were very successful. As you may or may not know, Germany perpetrated some of the greatest crimes known to mankind during this period. But perhaps the greatest crime against mankind happened after Nazi Germany was defeated in 1945.

"You see, the scrolls were confiscated by the Italian Co-belligerent Army, which fought on the side of the Allied forces not too long after the collapse of Italy's fascist government and Nazi Germany's surrender. All the Allied forces, in particular the United States, as well as the Roman Catholic Church, studied the confiscated documentation on what the Nazis had discovered about the scrolls and both races of alien beings. After proving the validity of its contents, the Church cut a deal with the Allied forces not to let the discoveries become public."

"Was it that the Church didn't want people to know that we are actually descended from the Luçimarks and were not created by God?" asked Karen.

"Yes. That was the first and perhaps one of the greatest crimes ever committed by the Church. They knew that if these discoveries were made public, it would fly in the face of the Church's teachings. But an even greater crime was that the Church used fear to keep the public in line."

"How so?" asked Alex.

"Well," Jackson continued. "You know how the Church would perform exorcisms on people possessed by evil spirits? What the Nazis and eventually the Allied forces discovered was that when the Sétbætañ set out to attack the humans, they attacked using subconscious methods."

"How did they do that?" asked Alex.

"They did it by using our fears against us and subconsciously persuading us to do bad things, such as lying, hurting, stealing, or killing. This was similar to what the Church and its religious zealots taught when describing how humans were possessed by evil spirits," said Jackson. "And how did they do that? Come over here." Jackson led Alex and Karen to the plants that were decorating the break-room.

Then Flip explained. "See, if you ingest these plants you will gain the ability to cloak, or disappear," said Flip.

"Was that tablet you took earlier made from these plants?" asked Karen.

"Exactly," said Flip. "People in the military have the ability to cloak and use dimensional portals to travel to other worlds just like the aliens. And we can do it without you knowing it."

"What does that mean?" injected Alex.

"It means that I can come into your bedroom and stand right behind you and you won't even know I'm there."

"So you've been spying on us, and that's how you know so much about Alex," shouted Karen.

"This girl catches on quick," said Flip. "So I can influence your thoughts by simply talking to you, or I could pretend to act like some sort of ghost, goblin, spirit, or spook to scare the devil out of ya. And if I wanted, I could attack you physically. Oh, yeah, and any time you see lightning without hearing the sound of thunder, that's a dimensional portal opening. The portal can open up pretty much anywhere, any time. However, don't expect that you'll be able to cloak after just taking one or two tablets. It takes a while for your body to integrate the plant into your system," said Flip.

"How long does it take?" asked Alex.

"About a week or two of regular ingestion."

"So you see why this technology is so important to us?" asked Flip.

Jackson resumed the story. "So in order to keep the new discovery in line with Church teachings, the Pope and his ministry relegated the Sétbætañ to the role of demons and the Luçimarks to the role of angels. This ploy was easy for the

Church to accomplish. The Sétbætañ resemble the demons of folklore in their physical characteristics and evil intentions. Their land of Vuur could easily be interpreted to be hell."

"I don't disagree with that," said Alex.

"The Luçimarks, on the other hand, may not exactly look like humans, but they come close enough," said Jackson. "And since they are easier on the eyes and Urodae is more heaven-like, it would be easy for the Church to continue the lies if the truth ever surfaced. The United States and the other Allied governments didn't care what the Church did. Their sole interest was in the Luçimarks' advanced technologies."

"So every religious thing we've been taught is a lie?" asked Alex.

"I'm afraid so," said Jackson.

"The concepts of God, angels, demons, et cetera, existed long before 1945," said Karen.

"True," said Jackson. "But these were simply beliefs held by Church followers, bred by the writers of the Bible and the ancient Dead Sea Scrolls. The images were passed down through the centuries by those who interpreted these writings in their own way. And because fear has always been used as a weapon by the Church, these interpretations were held up as truth. What the Church did not know at the time was that the Luçimarks left clues to their existence on Earth through the writings of the Bible and the Dead Sea Scrolls."

"Wow! My mother would die from a heart attack if she ever found out," said Alex.

"That's why she should never find out," piped in Kremley.

Jackson continued, "Why the Luçimarks used these writings to tell fables is anyone's guess. But the easy answer is that they were created to instill fear in the humans. Just like the Church is doing today, the Luçimarks probably used these writings to control the humans by painting themselves as God," said Jackson.

"Who would have ever thought that the Bible was written by a bunch of aliens?" said Karen.

"In short," said Jackson, "the Luçimarks and the Sétbætañ are just beings from another planet who have been intentionally mislabeled as divine beings by the Church to serve its own purposes and protect the military interests of the United States and its allies. To keep the scrolls' secrets hidden and to gain possession of their powers, the Church and the U.S. government cut a deal in which it was agreed that they would study the secrets of the scrolls, hiding their findings from the public. But someone in the U.S. army came up with the bright idea to bury the scrolls out West, somewhere in Utah. Why this was allowed to happen, I'm not sure. But this is where your father comes in," said Jackson, looking at Alex. "While on an excavation assignment, he lucked out and found the scrolls buried in a metal chest in the Utah badlands. Instead of turning them over to the proper authorities, he used them to experiment, keeping them out of the government's possession. We don't know your father's motives, but this is the reason we're in the mess we're in today."

While Alex and Karen stood dumbstruck, amazed at what they've learned, Flip thanked the major and the lieutenant and led them out of the room. When he returned, he tried to reason with the preteens.

"I know that we gave you a lot to digest, but I suggest you stop getting down on yourselves and get some rest. Now that you know what we're up against, you understand that we must go to war. The Setties will figure out how to use those scrolls to destroy not only the Luçimarks, but all of mankind."

"What do we do next?" asked Karen.

"We're going to take a trip on the ol' dimension portal back to Earth," said Flip. Alex and Karen shouted for joy, but Flip gave them a stern warning. "Listen, when we get back to Earth, don't expect things to be quite the same as when you left. Because the Setties have the scrolls, I'm sure they've already begun to exhibit their influence on Earth. Also, we've got to go to Washington."

"Washington? What for?" asked Karen.

"We have to report our findings to the President. He's waiting for us," said Flip.

Wow! Alex thought. *I've always wanted to meet the President, just not under these circumstances.*

Nevertheless, Alex and Karen were about to visit the most powerful man in the world, and it was going to be all about business.

Chapter 11
A Trip to Washington

To Alex, the journey through the dimensional portal back to Earth felt unbearably long. It had been days since he'd seen or heard from his family and he couldn't wait to be back in familiar surroundings. When Alex, Karen, and Flip exited the portal they were greeted by a not-so-pleasant surprise.

"Where are we?" asked Karen.

"We're back home on Earth, in Washington, D.C.," said Flip. "We need to catch a helicopter to the White House. I recommend that you contact your family now, before we get on board. It's doubtful that you'll be able to talk to them once we get to the White House. Try not to take too long."

"Wow. It sure doesn't look like Washington. Or Earth, for that matter," Alex said to Karen as he looked around.

Alex and Karen saw a world in complete panic mode. People were running amok in the streets, looting stores, and trying to leave the city via jam-packed highways. Television stations, radio broadcasts, and people on the streets blared that the end of the world was upon mankind.

An unearthly voice had caused the earth's skies to become dark red by chanting the text of the second scroll:

ⲤⲘⲞⲨ ⲈⲢⲞϤ ⲔⲀⲦⲀ ⲠⲀϢⲀⲒ ⲚⲦⲈ ⲦⲈϤⲘⲈⲦⲚⲒϢⲦ ⲐⲰⲖⲈⲂ ⲦⲪⲈ

The translation is:

Bless Him according to the abundance of His greatness as he spoils the heavens.

There were many reports of people experiencing paranormal activity. And there was a deathly chill to the air. To Alex and Karen, it looked and felt just like Vuur.

Despite the dire atmosphere, Alex longed to talk with his parents. He found some nearby shelter and pulled out his cell to call his mother. Before dialing the number, he noticed that the date shown on his cell didn't jibe with what he thought it should be. When Alex and Karen were abducted by the creatures and brought to Caynonã, it was late May. According to Alex's cell, it was now October. It was apparent that time on Caynonã moved at a much slower rate than time on Earth. Therefore Alex and Karen had not been gone for just days, but for months.

When Alex heard his mother answer, he screamed into the phone. "Mom! It's me."

"Alex! Where have you been? Do you realize we've been looking for you? Are you okay? Where are you? You realize we're in our last days?" Mrs. Smiley said.

Alex conjured up the greatest pack of lies he'd ever told.

"Well, Karen and I joined this religious sect that worshipped the 'end of days' and they wouldn't let us contact anyone in the outside world. But we managed to escape," said Alex. Given all that was happening, it was an easy lie to sell. He did tell her the truth about them being in Washington.

"Why in the world are you there? You need to come home," said Mrs. Smiley.

"Oh, um, the religious sect is stationed here in Washington," Alex said, trying not to laugh.

"Well you better get out of there before they find you. Plus you know the fools that put your father in jail are stationed there, led by that evil President."

Not about to stir the hornet's nest by saying that he was about to meet that evil President, he quickly changed the subject and asked his mother about his dad's whereabouts.

"He's still being detained. They moved him to a maximum security prison. They didn't give me a reason why they did it, they just did it," said Mrs. Smiley, knowing only that it probably had to do with Mr. Smiley's past involvement with the government. "Phillip is a good man," Mrs. Smiley said. "They've treated him horribly ever since he made his discovery. It's not his fault that the government is so corrupt. And that's the only reason he hid them. I wish this country would stand up for what's right. I know Phillip does. Now the Savior is coming to put this evil world to an end. It's written in the Bible. In the book of Revelations, to be exact," said Mrs. Smiley.

"Alex, it's time to go," shouted Flip. The helicopter had arrived.

"Alex, who was that?" asked Mrs. Smiley.

"Um, that was Flip. He escaped with me and Karen," lied Alex.

"You hurry home. I want our entire family together during the Rapture."

"I will. I love you."

"Love you, too," Alex heard his mother say before he put away his cell. Meeting Karen to board the helicopter, he asked what she had told her parents.

"I told them I was abducted by Lenopolous and that I'd escaped. I told them I was on my way home."

Alex laughed.

"That's not too far-fetched."

"I hope this meeting with the President doesn't take too long. I really need to get home to my family. They're worried to death," said Karen.

Flip interjected, "It depends on what information the President needs from you."

After Alex, Karen, and Flip boarded and sat down in their seats, the pilot made the helicopter take flight. What they saw below them wasn't pretty.

The sky was dark, with patches of fire and smoke covering the land. Traffic jammed the highways and drivers crashed into one another as they tried to escape the city. Buildings were left in ruins. Those who were not running amok packed churches, mosques, synagogues, and every other place of worship. Others held up signs that told of the world's impending doom, preached of the last days, or cowered in any shelter they could find. Police, fire, and ambulance sirens blared as public service workers tried to contain the chaos that was upon them. But as Alex looked outside he noticed one building that wasn't damaged -- the White House. Amid all the chaos and flames, the federal government buildings looked to be untouched.

The helicopter landed. Alex, Karen, and Flip were met by Secret Service agents who checked them for weapons, verified their identities, and led them into the White House. Once inside, the agents led the trio into a room with plush furniture, a super wide-screen television, and a table heaped with fancy foods. The walls were painted an inviting color of beige with crisp white trim. The windows had old-fashioned dressings. A crystal chandelier hung from the ceiling.

"Wow! Now this is living," exclaimed Karen as she looked around in awe.

Alex was most amazed by the wide-screen television.

"This has got to be the biggest wide-screen I've ever seen," he muttered.

"Just be careful not to touch anything," said Flip. "Remember, we are on official business."

Urgent-sounding chatter could be heard from outside the room. Something barely audible, about a State of the Union address. Alex held his ear near the door to listen. He heard talk of calming the citizens of the world, and readying the troops for battle. He heard a plethora of footsteps walking down the hall toward the room. When the door opened, two Secret Service agents entered and checked them for weapons.

"Didn't we do this already?" asked Karen. The agents didn't answer.

Two more agents entered the room along with the secretary of defense, some military generals, Major Kremley and Lieutenant Jackson. Finally, a tall, handsome man dressed in a dark suit and tie, and flanked by three Secret Service agents, walked through the door. It was the President of the United States.

Alex and Karen stood in awe until the President said, "Hello. You must be Alex Smiley and Karen Stubblefield."

"Ye ... Ye ... Ye ... Yes," stumbled Alex.

"Hi, sir," said Karen in a voice so meek it was barely audible.

"You two are international heroes and we're going to need your help to defeat this enemy. Major Kremley and Lieutenant Jackson have already briefed us on what happened. We'll just

61

need you to fill in the finer details. Captain Powers, I thank you for getting them here safely. Well, why don't we get started?" said the President as he sat down on the couch. Nervous wrecks, Alex and Karen followed suit. They were about to be questioned by the most powerful man in the world, President Christopher Marcellus Topher.

Chapter 12
Ascension to Power

President Topher became leader of the United States from humble beginnings. He was raised as an orphan in Philadelphia until he was adopted at age fifteen by a wealthy couple who owned vast amounts of real estate in New York City. The family lived in Greenwich, Connecticut. Christopher spent a lot of time with his adoptive father, who taught him the ins and outs of the real-estate business at an early age. He was a shy but extremely gifted child who possessed an uncanny ability to influence others. As he got older, he outgrew his shyness and was able to use his talents to the fullest.

As a baby no more than a few weeks old, Chris had been discovered outside the front door of a Philadelphia foster home by a caretaker who'd heard his cries from inside. Who his biological parents were, and whether he'd ever attempted to find them, were not publicly known. Chris listed his birthplace as Philadelphia, Pennsylvania. But neither he nor anyone else knew where he was actually born. Even though it was assumed that he'd been born and abandoned by his birth mother in Philadelphia, there were also rumors that he was not a U.S citizen. Because of this, his right to be U.S. president had always been in question. One conspiracy theory holds that he was likely born in the Middle East or Asia to non-Americans.

As a young boy growing up in the mean streets of Philadelphia, Chris used his special skills to avoid confrontation. Tall but slight, he needed to avoid physical conflicts. He also used his skills to get others to do his bidding. By the time he was in the seventh grade, he was class president. Sometimes he used shady methods, such as charming others to strong-arm potential voters into voting for him. But it wasn't as if he didn't use his smarts. Throughout grade school, Chris finished at the top of his class and was always voted Most Likely to Succeed. He had an almost hypnotic effect on his female classmates. Even at an early age, he was able to use his charm and wit to get what he wanted. He had an infectious smile, to boot.

When Chris reached high school, he got serious about pursuing a career in politics. Using his powers of influence and his business and social smarts, he joined the high-school debate team, leading his team to Nationals every year to challenge the top debaters in the country. He was elected high-school class president each year he attended. Several people who already had political careers took notice and tried to persuade Chris to get an early start in politics. But Chris decided to wait until after college, respecting his parents' wishes.

Chris attended Yale University where he earned a bachelor's degree and then a master's degree in business. He graduated summa cum laude and was the class valedictorian. He also earned a doctorate, finishing at the top of his class. In total it took him only six years to earn his PhD. There were rumors that he pledged Skull and Bones society, but he avoided questions on the matter.

Upon leaving Yale, Chris moved to Saddle River, New Jersey, to run his adoptive father's real-estate business and begin down the road to political success.

Chris won his first election as a local councilman. Later, as mayor of Newark, he was instrumental in improving schools, roads, housing, and in job creation. Considered an up and coming political force, he ran for governor of New Jersey and won in a landslide.

After six years as governor, Chris ran for the Senate, winning in a close race against the incumbent. During Chris's time in the Senate, he was regularly able to get opposing political parties to come to an agreement. His mantra was, "We are employees for the citizens of the United States, not the other way around." He even got involved in foreign affairs and was well-liked around the world.

After a short time as senator of New Jersey, he decided to run for the presidency. Though his challenger routinely ran ads to paint a negative picture of Chris, he won the election by the widest margin in history. As President he was able to succeed where his predecessors failed, reforming healthcare and Social Security, signing bills for job stimulus plans, transportation, and new clean energy sources. He was also able to assist in peace efforts overseas, changing the world's perception of the United States from bullying and arrogant to peaceful. This transformation was possible with the signing of the NONWES (NO Nuclear WEaponS) treaty, in which all countries agreed to the complete removal and destruction of nuclear and biological weapons.

President Topher was very popular -- perhaps the most popular president in history -- not only in the United States but around the world. He was given rock-star status wherever he traveled. He had never married, and women wanted him. Men wanted to be him. He was very charismatic and an excellent public speaker. And to no one's surprise, he easily won re-election. Both America and the world had never been better.

But despite all this, Chris had his detractors. The politically partisan TAPC news channel, was among them. They frequently aired conspiracy theories about the President's birthplace and his true intentions for America. And because he promoted new and controversial ideas, he was slammed by his political enemies.

Perhaps the most controversial of the ideas put into law by President Topher was the United Peoples Act which was the impetus for the creation of the BioCharge system. The system consolidated each individual's personal information on a microchip embedded in the hand. Now there was no need to carry cash or credit cards to make a purchase. All it took was a hand swipe.

The world economy was moving toward a BioCharge-only system. More than eighty percent of the nation's business transactions already used it, including those at banks, supermarkets, auto dealerships, and retail outlets. Even securities traders had adopted the system.

BioCharge was not limited to adults. Children were also imbedded with the chip. The government required that all citizens with the chip get quarterly software updates to ensure that the individual received the latest software bug fixes, and the government had the individual's most recent information.

The only people slow to adopt the system were the poor and

lower-middle classes who could not afford the portion of the embedment procedure not covered by the reformed healthcare policies, and those who believed that the BioCharge system represented the biblical "mark of the beast." Both Alex's and Karen's family were in this last category.

The system was created to reduce the need for cash and credit cards, and eliminate identity theft. Although there had been cases of thieves using a corpse's hand to steal merchandise, on the whole, the BioCharge initiative had been a success. Robberies and identity theft were at an all-time low. As countries around the world learned of its success in America, they'd adopted the system.

The downside to having these embedded hand chips was the loss of privacy. The government knew everything about you, from medical visits to retail purchases. The chips also contained your bank information, social security number, birth date, driver's license number, and credit score.

Although he'd led the implementation of the BioCharge System, the world now looked to President Topher to deliver them from one of its darkest hours.

After Alex and Karen had briefed the President, he called in all the military generals and contacted world leaders to devise a plan to prevent the looming attack. Then, to the surprise of Alex and Karen, a Luçimark, dressed in the military uniform of a high-ranking official, entered the room.

"General Akaie, we understand that you have some information about the scrolls. Can you please inform the President of your findings?" Major Kremley said to the Luçimark.

"Yes, Major Kremley," said the Luçimark, pointing to an image on a projection screen.

"As you are fully aware, the first scroll allows for travel in space and time to other worlds. This scroll was used by both the Luçimarks and the Sétbætañ to travel back and forth from Caynonã to Earth. The command is activated by correctly chanting the text on the scroll. Once the pronunciation has been mastered, physical possession of the scroll is no longer needed.

The second scroll is utilized to set the mood for war.

"If you look at the skies and notice the weather patterns," Akaie continued, "they're now very similar to those of the Sétbætañ homeland of Vuur. My spies have confirmed that the Sétbætañ create this war-like atmosphere to instill a mood of hopelessness among the humans."

"The third scroll is similar to the first, except that it allows large objects such as tanks and missiles to travel from world to world. This scroll can open dimensions for a longer period than the first scroll allows. It is normally used for full-scale invasions. My spies have confirmed that the Sétbætañ have mastered the technology from this scroll. I would strongly advise that all military personnel prepare for an attack, as it will only be a matter of time."

"What about the rest of the scrolls?" asked Flip.

"According to my sources, the Sétbætañ have yet to understand how scrolls four through seven function. Remember that it has been generations since all the scrolls were utilized," said General Akaie. "Each scroll has a number at the top. So they should be easy to identify."

"Make sure your people keep an eye on them. We have got to figure out what those other scrolls do. You'd better believe that those Setties will figure it out. And that third scroll alone is enough to put us in a bad position," said Major Kremley.

"I guess war is certain at this point," Alex said, putting his two cents in. Despite being with the most powerful people in the world, he was not the least bit intimidated.

"Yes, it is," said General Akaie.

"Okay," sighed President Topher as he straightened his tie. "It's time for me to deliver the address."

Major Kremley gave the President a serious look. "Have you made up your mind on what you're going to tell them, Mr. President?"

"Yes. I've decided to tell them the truth as they know it," said the President.

It was eight o'clock in the evening when the President got in front of the TV cameras and microphones to deliver one of the most important speeches in the history of mankind. President Topher was slightly nervous but confident as he spoke from the Oval Office. It was estimated that at least two billion people worldwide would watch or listen to the address.

"Citizens of the United States, of North America, and around the world, I will attempt to bring you a message of hope during a time of despair. As you now know, there have been rumors and speculation that the end of the world is upon us. As the President of the United States, the most powerful nation and protector of the world, I'm here to inform you that the end of the world is not upon us. What's upon us is an enemy that the Bible has warned believers about for centuries. The enemy upon us has been described in the book of Revelations as "the beast" and his armies.

"Yes, people of our great nation and the world, Armageddon has come. But I'm offering you a message of hope that the United States, along with her allies and the Church, will defeat the beast and his demons and send them back to hell, from which they came. I ask that each and every one of you great citizens of the world understand that it has been prophesied that good has, and will always, conquer evil. All you need to do is bear arms, fight the enemy, pray, and have faith. May God bless you, the United States of America, and all the nations of the world."

Chapter 13
Trip to the Vatican

The President's decision to hide the truth from the world was not a spur-of-the-moment decision; it was highly calculated. Anguishing for days about what to do after the Sétbætañ reddened the skies, President Topher, along with Major Kremley, Lieutenant Jackson, and the Secretary of Defense took Air Force One to Rome to seek the Pope's council at the Apostolic Palace in Vatican City.

Days before the President gave his State of the World address from the Oval Office, he and his team discussed in detail what message he should deliver. Major Kremley had a bold suggestion. "I don't see anything wrong with telling them the truth now. We can tell them the truth that we are at war against aliens. Let's not mention anything about religion. They don't need to know."

"But understand that we are not the only ones who know the truth about the religious aspect of the situation," said the President. "There's been too much chatter around the world that various governments have known about intelligent, extraterrestrial life. There have also been ongoing questions from the media and people all over the world regarding the sincerity of the Church and whether God exists. People are starting to put two and two together. The Church is feeling a lot of pressure and those who believe want answers. I can either tell them the truth, or let them continue believing what they believe. I'm just not sure if it's time to tell the masses the truth yet. If I told them, the Church and all religious institutions around the world would crumble. Sooner or later, though, we're going to need to come clean. It will be just another part of mankind's evolutionary process. People in positions of authority have been lying to the masses for far too long. The time has come to represent those who elect us with genuine honesty. It's my hope that the governments and religious institutions of the world can work together and come up with a proper solution. I would feel awful about going in front of the camera and lying to the world. Then again, telling them the truth could have grave implications. I can't wait to get to Vatican City so the Pope can help steer us in the right direction."

Europe was in an even greater state of flux than America. Arriving in Rome, the President and his team saw firsthand what was happening. As they toured the streets with representatives from the European Union Intelligence Analysis Centre, or EU INTCEN, they saw citizens looting and destroying property at an even higher rate than in the U.S. In and around Vatican City, mobs protested relentlessly against the Pope and the apparent detachment of the Church. Many atheists held protests at churches, chanting slogans such as "religion is a lie" and demanded the Church to tell the world the truth. Since the reddening of the skies, there hadn't been any communication with or signs of the Pope.

Catholics in Vatican City and throughout the world were looking for comfort and reassurance during the tribulation. It didn't help that Pope Gregory was one of the most unpopular popes in the history of the Roman Catholic Church. He had only held the papacy for three years, replacing one of the most popular popes in Church history, Paul James III, who had died of a heart attack. Although Pope Gregory was elderly, he possessed a fiery demeanor and wasn't shy when it came to giving his opinion. It was well known that the flock was unhappy with his leadership.

Unlike previous popes, Pope Gregory was seen as detached from the faithful. In his three years as the Bishop of Rome, he had yet to meet and greet pilgrims at the General Audiences that attract thousands. He didn't get along with the world's leaders, and even dictators complained about his coldness and lack of compassion.

Church tradition frowned upon removal of a pope, however, as it could lead to a perception of instability in the Church. Nonetheless, the Holy See routinely heard criticism and protest, and during this time of tribulation, these had grown loud and clear.

"As leader of the Catholic Church and Vicar of Jesus Christ, please give us some reassurance that God is still with us," the faithful implored. But the Church knew the truth of the current events. And this truth had the potential to end all religious institutions, most specifically the Catholic Church.

Arriving at Vatican City, the President, the secretary of defense, Major Kremley, and Lieutenant Jackson were greeted by several Cardinals and a seemingly nervous and agitated Pope. President Topher, not wanting to mislead America's Catholics, was looking for guidance on how to handle the apocalyptic situation. *Should I tell the people the truth? Or should I let the idea of the 'whole religious thing' continue?*

His rationale was that if he told the truth, it would show his sincerity as a leader and potentially galvanize the people to rally behind him to destroy the enemy. On the other hand, he could use the mantra of God to inspire the people to defeat the enemy. Without religion, many people would feel that their lives were meaningless. And religious people outnumbered nonbelievers. Still, the President was leaning toward coming clean.

Pope Gregory had a different train of thought. As the Cardinals, the Pope, the Secretary of Defense, Major Kremley, Lieutenant Jackson, and President Topher set down at the office table, the Pope had no problem letting the President know what was on his mind. He sat right across from the President. His speaking voice had a gravelly, almost-creepy timbre.

"Your thoughts of telling the world that aliens exist and are the forefathers of humans are foolish at best. Do you realize what the ramifications would be? People would stop believing in God. Humans need order and authority. Plus, you'll probably be wasting your time. The majority of worshippers have and will always believe in God."

"Yes, I realize the ramifications. But my belief is that it would affect just a small number," said the President. "People are smarter and more educated than in the past, and I think you have to give people credit for accepting truths. Look, how many years ago did people believe the world was flat? Or that the Earth was the center of the universe? Do I expect people to adapt overnight? No. Is it a life-altering piece of information? Yes. But

71

I fail to see the reason for not letting the people know the truth."

"You fail to see the reason? You think these people are more educated?" asked the Pope. "Educated people do not set buildings on fire or destroy ancient relics. Educated people do not cause mass riots threatening people of authority. Educated people do not hold pointless protests twenty-four-hours-a-day in front of religious institutions. Educated people do not run around killing others because they have no answers and succumb to fear. Look out the window, Christopher! Do you actually think those people are without need of God?"

The President did not appreciate being called by his first name, and he found the Pope's tone demeaning -- like a father scolding his son.

"Don't you mean the *fear* of God?" the President countered. "And how many wars throughout the centuries have been started and fought in the name of religion? And I'm not just picking on Christianity, but other religions as well. I think that it's time for the people of the world to become educated."

"You pompous fool," said the Pope. "Imagine this world without the Church. People would be on the brink on self-destruction. For centuries the Church has wisely guided believers, keeping them from rebellious destruction and giving them hope for life beyond this world. Is that something you wish to take away from them, Christopher? Hope?"

"Well, what about the nonbelievers? And those whose belief system differs from mainstream Christianity?" said the President. "Does the Church take pride in the many atrocities they've perpetrated on mankind in the past? What about the Inquisition and its murders, and the torture used by the Church against so-called pagans and Jews? What about the sex crimes committed by priests and even popes of the past? What about the Taiping Rebellion in China, where Christian rebels murdered more than twenty million people? What about Pope Pius XII and his lack of action during World War II, while the Nazis murdered more than six million Jews?"

The Cardinals, Secretary of State, Jackson, and Kremley sat in stunned silence. The Pope was beet red with anger.

"The Church accepts its past mistakes," said the Pope.

"Mistakes? These are outright crimes that the Church has committed," said the President. "And how many great leaders have we lost because of religion? Let's name a few. There's Malcolm X, killed by the Nation of Islam. Gandhi, murdered by a Hindu nationalist. And if he existed, Jesus, crucified by the Romans with assistance from the Jews. And what about all those religious cults responsible for mass murders? The Jonestown Massacre. Waco and the Branch Davidians. Heaven's Gate. The Order of the Solar Temple. You say that the masses have hope and will avoid rebellious destruction with religion? I beg to differ. The facts are indisputable. Religion has caused more pain and destruction on Earth than anything else in human history. All in the name of God. Oh, and did I mention how Christianity was used to justify slavery?"

"Silence!" screamed the Pope, pushing on the table to rise abruptly from his chair. "How dare you question the integrity of the Church."

"Look, I know you're a very popular political figure," said the Pope, returning to his seat and sipping his tea, trying his best to calm down. "You have done much to help bring peace to a world that not long ago was infested with warmongers with access to weapons of mass destruction. But I think that you are out of your league when it comes to matters such as these."

This back-and-forth between the President and the Pope made Lieutenant Jackson understand why this Pope was very unpopular. This last statement had Jackson puzzled. He wondered. *If the President was able to achieve world peace, something that no one has done before, why wouldn't he be able to handle this crisis and be successful?* The Pope's reasoning didn't make sense. But before Jackson could jump in, the President stated his point of view.

"Father, this is a matter of not only national, but world, security. As you just stated, I do have a track record. So I think that I'm fully capable of handling a situation like this," said the President.

"So what you're telling me is that you are willing to say to the world, 'Hey, you know the tenets you've believed in and have placed your faith in for more than two thousand years? Sorry, but we've made a mistake," said the Pope.

Then, before the President could offer his rebuttal, the Pope, aided by his golden staff, walked to stand directly before the seated President. He bent his frail body over to look the President directly in the eye.

"Christopher, let's be honest. What's your real motivation for this? Is it that you want all the people of the world to follow you? Is it that you want to be worshipped as the savior of the world? The messiah? God? No need to respond. Everyone in this room knows the answer."

The President shot back in a calm but pointed manner.

"Father, since we're being honest, at least that would be better than letting the world believe in a fairy tale that's perpetuated by a bunch of people whose only wish is to serve their own self interest. Imagine doing meaningful work for the people instead of living off their tithing? Is that why you don't want the truth to come out? No need to respond. Everyone in this room knows the answer."

Major Kremley, the Secretary of Defense, Jackson, and the Cardinals were shocked. Never had they witnessed two leaders, one from the political world, and the other from the religious, disagree so venomously. Pope Gregory's blood was boiling. Standing over the President, he shot back.

"It would be wise to temper your tone, Mr. President. You may be favored by many, but not by everyone. You've come here seeking council on matters of religion, and I have given it. I'll leave it up to you to do what you feel is best. Just remember this: what you say will affect millions, and their faith runs centuries deep. I'd further advise you not to act the hero. You have no idea what secrets lurk in the shadows of history."

With that, the Pope and his Cardinals abruptly left the room, leaving the President and his team alone. They were escorted out of the Vatican by a young priest, who led them to a taxi reserved for high-ranking officials. On the ride to the Roman airport, Major Kremley offered his assessment.

74

"I guess the Pope is in favor of keeping his standard of living."

"Maybe so," said the President. "But right is right, wrong is wrong, and the truth is the truth. But when do you know the right time to tell the truth?"

Chapter 14
Defending Against the Surge

As the days passed after the President's speech, the mood of the citizens was more upbeat. People were shopping, traveling, and conversing as they'd done before the skies turned red. The President's address had helped put everyone at ease. Sporting events were held. Even the stock markets were open. Even Alex and Karen felt more at ease. Lodging at Washington's Watergate Hotel, they ordered room service at a rapid clip. Karen was in a relaxed mood as she convinced her parents that staying in Washington was the smartest and safest thing to do. Meanwhile, Alex daydreamed, staring out the hotel window, his thoughts on his father in jail. Because of the recent events, Alex's mother decided to dedicate herself full-time to the local church, believing that Jesus would soon return to Earth.

"Hey Alex, you hungry? I'm about to call room service," Karen asked as she picked up the phone.

"No, I'm good," said Alex. "I'm just wondering what our military has planned to do? It's like we're just sitting here waiting to be attacked like wounded prey," said Alex.

"Alex what do you expect them to do?" said Karen as she lay on the bed munching on the potato chips she'd just ordered. "We have no plan of attack because we don't know how to locate them," said Karen.

"But we do have a way," exclaimed Alex. "We could use the dimensional portal. Heck, Flip and his people know the way."

"Well, I don't think it's that easy. I'm sure that Flip and the Major have already thought of that. So I guess we're out of luck," said Karen. "Maybe those Setties decided not to attack after all. It makes no sense worrying about something you can't control."

Later in the evening, Alex looked out on the dark skies as lightening flashed, sensing that a storm was on the way. There was no accompanying boom of thunder. Alex knew that the time had come. He scrambled down the hall to warn Flip. Time seemed to move in slow motion as he heard the screams of horror from the streets below.

"Oh, God! Jesus help us!" screamed a lady as she witnessed the unspeakable horror of the Sétbætañ appearing out of thin air.

"What is that? Oh, God!" people screamed, as the creatures emerged from the portals with weapons and tanks in tow.

The Sétbætañ had unleashed the power of the third scroll, waiting for the humans to relax before executing their attack. An unearthly voice had chanted its command:

ⲈϨⲞⲨⲚ ⲠⲒⲢⲞ Ⲉ̀ ⲠⲒ ⲀⲦⲀ6ⲚⲒ ⲙⲚ̄Ⲧⲣⲣⲱⲟⲩ † 2ⲁⲡ †ⲂⲱⲔⲒ

The Coptic translates as:

Enter the door into the new kingdom to condemn the slave.

Boom! Boom! Boom! Boom! The creatures shot their tank's cannons into nearby buildings, which disintegrated into piles of debris. The creatures attacked people at random, killing or severely maiming them. When Alex and Karen reached Flip's hotel room, the door blasted open. Flip was wrestling a Settie that looked like a giant wolf.

"Get out of here," Flip shouted to Alex and Karen as he struggled with the creature. "Go and get some help."

The Settie was seven feet tall with long claws, protruding fangs, and the strength of four men. The wolf-like creature overpowered Flip as they wrestled to the ground. It raised a hairy hand with protruding claws, ready to deliver a death blow. Alex picked up a broken piece of door frame and clobbered the creature across the head. As the frame made impact, the creature looked at Alex with glaring, bloodshot eyes and jumped off of Flip in pursuit.

"Ruuunnnnn!" screamed Alex as he and Karen fled with the wolf-creature on their tails.

As Alex ran, he thought of that fateful night in the junkyard when he was chased by dogs. This felt like déjà vu. Being on the sixth floor of the hotel there was no easy escape route. It was either find a stairwell, find an open elevator, or jump out a window.

The creature was hot on their heels. Alex felt the creature's claws swipe at his feet. His heart pumped with fear and his glasses fogged with sweat. He and Karen were now in a full-out sprint. They spotted an open elevator, but knew they needed more distance between them and the creature.

Thinking quickly, Karen ran off in a different direction. She figured it was best if at least one of them survived. The beast stayed on Alex, but Karen's slick move caused the beast to hesitate, buying Alex a little time. Alex entered the elevator, frantically pressing the Close Door and First Floor buttons. As the doors slowly closed, Alex's life flashed in front of him as he saw the beast rushing up to the elevator. The doors took an eternity to close. With the doors nearly shut, the beast managed to hold them ajar with his hairy and powerful hands. As the creature slowly forced open the doors, it stood tall in front of Alex and let out a deafening growl. With his back to the elevator wall, Alex awaited his fate.

Just as the beast was about to deliver a fatal blow, three blasts of gunshot pierced its chest. The beast wobbled and fell forward, pinning Alex to the floor at the back of the elevator. Karen stood in the doorway flanked by Flip, who was pointing a sawed-off shotgun.

"Are you okay?" said Karen, running to assist Alex.

"Yeah, I'm okay," Alex said, as he and Karen pushed the heavy creature aside.

"Now y'all listen here. Don't you ever pull a stunt like that again," said Flip, looking directly at Alex.

"You could have put these people's lives in jeopardy. Do you understand me, soldier?" said an angry Flip, referring to the hotel's other guests.

"Yes, sir," said Alex.

"Now, I want you two to go back to your rooms and take shelter. I'm gonna go and get some supplies. And I want you guys to start taking these," said Flip, giving them a vial of green pills.

"And Alex, thanks," said Flip. He searched the beast for weapons then took the elevator down.

Alex walked Karen back to the hotel room, feeling a sense of pride in having helped save a life. Being thanked by a captain of the U.S. military made him feel ten feet tall.

Worldwide, media reported that Satan's army had invaded but were being met with resistance in every land. In America, the armed forces attacked from land and air. The Sétbætañ, however, had the element of surprise on their side. Mastering the use of the third scroll allowed them to dial in on any location and send troops at will. The third scroll also extended the portal's time constraints, allowing hundreds through at a time, with large machinery. This made winning the fight against the creatures nearly impossible. The military saw enemy tanks appear, firing, from out of nowhere. The third scroll also allowed the Sétbætañ to use the dimensional portal to fire missiles from their home world onto Earth.

This put the Earth's armed forces at a huge strategic disadvantage and they began to doubt they could win the war. They were also outmanned. Some Luçimarks were fighting alongside them, but it was not enough to stem the tide as the Luçimarks were being killed at a faster rate than the humans. Many other Luçimarks saw the situation as 'your problem not mine.' Luçimarks were selfish and arrogant beings. The truth was that even though they were the forefathers of the humans, the Luçimarks didn't care about their well-being or survival.

Alex and Karen split their time between looking out the hotel window and getting updates from the TV news.

"Oh, my god! Look what they did to Paris," said Karen, viewing the wreckage on the news app on her phone. Parts of Paris had been completely destroyed. And that was the case for all the major cities around the world. According to the news reporters, not one significant human-made structure was left standing, including the Eiffel Tower in Paris and the Statue of Liberty in New York.

Back at the White House, President Topher was informed by an Army general and Major Kremley of the dire circumstances facing the American citizens.

"Mr. President, you need to be aware that we're losing the battle on all fronts -- by land, air, and sea. And we have no idea where they are getting all these weapons," said the General. "Our initial intelligence reported that the Sétbætañ didn't possess half the weapons or manpower they've shown over the past few days. Mr. President, we've never encountered anything like this."

"What can we do to counter the power of that scroll?" asked the President.

"There's not much we can do. We'll just have to continue to learn their technology so we can counter their attacks," said Kremley.

"We need immediate answers. I'm responsible for billions of lives," said the President, referring to the world's population.

Kremley added, "Mr. President, I would suggest more manpower, but the Luçimarks don't seem interested."

This last statement set off the normally even-tempered President. "They don't seem interested? Well they'd better get interested in a hurry," he shouted, storming out of the Oval Office. The General and Major were befuddled.

Back in Vuur, in a structure that resembled a fortress, Ecaep, Cúbaneg, and Ugnjengon mapped out battle plans against the Earthlings. They felt confident they were winning the war, but the humans showed resolve despite great strategic disadvantages. Ecaep was not one to welcome long, drawn-out wars. He wanted victory as soon as possible. The key to a quick victory was the translation of the seventh scroll.

So far, the Sétbætañ were able to decode scrolls one through six, even though only three of the scrolls had been utilized. In order to gain the knowledge to decode the seventh scroll, Ecaep decided it was time to utilize scroll number four. He explained his reasoning to Cúbaneg and Ugnjengon:

"I've discovered that a human holds the secret to the seventh scroll and I've locked in on the location of the human."

"How did you find out this information?" said an excited Cúbaneg.

"There are traitors among the humans," said a boastful and

grinning Ecaep. "Now hand me the scroll." Cúbaneg went into a large, cast-iron vault containing all the scrolls and selected the fourth. He handed it to Ecaep, who began to recite in a chant-like fashion:

ⲉϩⲟⲩⲛ ⲡⲓⲛⲓⲱϯ ⲛ̀ⲟⲩⲣⲟ ⲉⲧ ⲱⲛϩ ⲛⲉⲙ ⲡⲓⲥⲉⲗⲁⲛⲟⲛ
ϩⲁⲡ ⲡⲓⲗⲁⲟⲥ ⲉⲧ ⲡⲉ ϩⲁⲡ ⲙ̀ⲙⲟⲛ

The Coptic translates as:

Enter the great king who lives with the Selanon.
Condemn those who condemn us.

The ground shook, followed by a loud, monstrous roar. A giant portal opened and the normally red Vuur sky turned black with grotesque, winged creatures. These creatures, a sub-species of the Sétbætañ called the Selanon, were spies. They made a horrifying, bird-like sound that could pierce human eardrums. But the worst was yet to come. Out of the shadows of the deep Vuur night emerged a creature so horrifying that it was beyond human comprehension. With a blink of an eye, both the Selanon and the creature entered the portal with clear instructions: They were to capture the human who possessed the knowledge of the seventh scroll, and to destroy all in their path.

Chapter 15
Enter the Krieatine

Back in the hotel room, Alex and Karen remained low to the floor while occasionally sneaking a peek out the window. What they saw was not pretty. The Sétbætañ had destroyed roughly seventy percent of Washington, not including the federal buildings and a few nearby. Debris was piled everywhere along with human remains. President Topher and the other high-ranking officials were safely moved to a secret bunker. The U.S. military combed through the debris to locate survivors. Karen said a short prayer in thanks that the Watergate Hotel had little damage amid the bombing and gunfire and that she and Alex were safe. They guessed that the encounter between Flip and the wolf-creature was just a random incident and that the Sétbætañ deemed destruction of the hotel unimportant.

While safely nestled, the preteens wondered out loud how their families were doing. At this point no one could tell what was going on. There was no television, radio, telephone, or internet. All avenues of communication had been disrupted by the Sétbætañ. Only the military had the technological means to communicate abroad. And even though they were safe, Alex felt that he and Karen needed to make a move to help in the battle against the Sétbætañ.

Back in Brownsville, the town was mostly intact. Even though there were no media to deliver the daily news, the town's citizens felt confident that good would prevail over evil. Citizens gathered in churches in record numbers not only to pray but to strategize about how to destroy the creatures if confronted. Unfortunately, others felt that the time had come to join their loved ones in heaven and had committed suicide by a variety of methods, from drinking cyanide to self-inflicted gas poisoning. These acts were done individually and in groups, the latter usually headed up by leaders of religious cults.

At the town jail, Mr. Smiley occasionally asked Detective Riley if he had heard what was going on around the world. With no method of gathering news, Riley would simply tell him, "I have no idea, Smiley. And you only have yourself to thank for that."

Yes, Mr. Smiley felt the burden of blame for what was happening. The blaring sirens and constant chaos were taking a toll on his mental well-being. He was being transferred from one maximum security prison to another that was seventy miles upstate. Because of the distance, Mrs. Smiley wouldn't be able to visit him as often. Late one night while still at the town jail, he was awoken out of a rare, deep sleep.

"Get dressed," said Detective Riley. "You're being moved upstate."

"Why?" said a half-asleep Mr. Smiley, trying to make out two silhouettes in the dark. "I thought that we were leaving in the morning?"

"Because we believe you are a primary target of the enemy and we need to move you now," said another voice, which belonged to Gateway.

"Target?"

"Look, quit playing games, get your stuff on and let's get out of here," said Detective Riley. Mr. Smiley quickly put on his clothes and gathered his things. Detective Riley opened the jail cell, grabbed Mr. Smiley by the shirt and held up the broken suitcase that was recovered from the sewer. He looked Mr. Smiley coldly in the eyes.

"Remember this, Smiley? This piece of evidence is gonna put you away for good. And I'll be glad to be rid of ya. Think about it. All you had to do was give us the scrolls. But, noooooo. You had to send the entire U.S. government on a wild-goose chase. At least those monsters won't destroy our town if you're not here. They'll have to kill you somewhere else. And that's something I should've done myself a long time ago." The cold look on Riley's face sent shivers down Mr. Smiley's spine.

Mr. Smiley left the town jail into the cold November night. It was his first taste of freedom in six months. Even though he was in handcuffs, flanked by Riley, Gateway, and several police officers, breathing in the crisp, cool air was liberation enough. In the back of the police cruiser, he felt a sense of relief as he leaned back comfortably in the seat. Part of this relief came with the absence of Riley and Gateway. The other part was that despite the belief that he was being targeted by the Sétbætañ, he held hope that things would turn for the better.

Mr. Smiley sat in the back of the cruiser while the police discussed protocol. A loud roar invaded the night air. The police looked to the night sky but saw nothing. Then the roar repeated, louder. This time the police saw the source of the sound. It was a creature that stood three hundred fifty feet tall. It walked upright on two legs. Its body was covered in horns and it had elongated, gnashing teeth protruding from its grotesque mouth. It had four sets of eyes. Two arms protruded from its sides, another from its chest. When it walked, it shook the earth. Weaponry had no effect. The creature was able to take heavy fire. It had great physical strength. A hideous beast, it had a humanoid look similar to an ogre but with amphibian traits. This beast was an ancient warrior for the Sétbætañ. It had last fought when the Sétbætañ battled the Luçimarks during the Great Rebellion centuries ago. It was the Krieatine.

"Let's get out of here," screamed the police.

Mr. Smiley looked out the cruiser's window as he saw the police scrambling for safety. The creature crushed any vehicles and buildings in its path. Many townspeople were snatched up and swallowed whole by the Krieatine. And they should consider themselves lucky. Others were ground to death by the creature's teeth or crushed beneath its feet. It was truly hell on Earth.

"I've gotta get out of here," screamed Mr. Smiley as he saw the Krieatine approach the cruiser.

Hands bound with handcuffs, Mr. Smiley attempted to open the lock of the cruiser door with his mouth. "Almost got it," he said aloud as the door lock slowly shifted open. He needed to move fast. The creature was getting near. "Come on... Got it!" Mr. Smiley said as the cruiser door popped open. He tumbled out of the car with the creature in full pursuit. As the Krieatine reached its middle hand to grab him, Mr. Smiley ducked into an alley where he spotted Gateway and Riley hiding in the cellar hatchway of a coffee house.

"Get out of here," screamed Riley as Mr. Smiley used his foot to jar open the hatch. The creature's long arm reached down the alley for Mr. Smiley.

"Sorry, Smiley," said Gateway, taking a crowbar and whacking him in the leg. Mr. Smiley removed his leg from the hatchway with a scream as Riley slammed the doors shut. As the foul beast grabbed at him, Mr. Smiley dove headfirst into a dumpster. The darkness of the alley combined with the Krieatine's poor eyesight provided camouflage. The creature roared with frustration.

In the dark, smelly dumpster, Mr Smiley thought of his past failures and how his discovery had placed all of mankind in peril. He thought about his family. He'd have given anything to be out of the predicament he was now in. He heard the shuffling of the creature's hand as it searched the alley, accompanied by a low, monstrous growl. He knew the Sétbætañ wanted him alive because the creature could have easily destroyed the alley and killed him by now. Despite this, Mr. Smiley dared not peek out of the dumpster. He knew that he held the fate of the world in his hands.

Just then a loud, piercing, bird-like sound polluted the air. It was the Selanon. The sound was so sharp that it forced Mr. Smiley out of the dumpster. He struggled to gain his footing, running hand-cuffed down the alley, looking for an opening to a main street. The night sky was filled with flying, gargoyle-like creatures that attacked people at will. The military couldn't shoot fast enough. There seemed to be no defense against the flying creatures or the Krieatine. As Mr. Smiley ran, he felt the piercing sensation of claws sinking into the skin of his shoulders. The pain became excruciating as one of the Selanon creatures took flight with him in its grasp. Before long, Mr. Smiley was hundreds of feet above the ground, flying among the Selanon with their bird-like, piercing cries. Looking down at the people running and screaming in horror, he fell unconscious.

Chapter 16
Visiting Familiar Places

After waiting several days in the hotel, Alex and Karen were getting restless. Phone communication was unavailable. They were wondering what had happened to Flip, who'd promised to return. A welcomed voice echoed on the other side of the hotel door.

"Hey Alex, Karen, open up. It's Flip."

"It's about time," Karen said, jubilant and stern at the same time.

"What's going on out there? I haven't seen the Sétbætañ in days," said Alex.

"Well, there's been a lot going on," said a somber Flip. "The Sétbætañ have nearly wiped out all of the major cities around the world, and the military is really struggling to keep them at bay. There have been countless lives lost."

"Thousands?" asked Alex.

"Try millions," said Flip.

"What do we do now? We just can't sit here. We somehow need to get to those scrolls," said Alex.

"I agree," said Flip. "But we'll need to be cautious. I received a report that the Sétbætañ attacked your hometown of Brownsville. Karen, your family is safe. Alex, your mom is fine but they have your father. I feel I owe it to you to let you know."

Alex sat in stunned disbelief as tears began to well up. Karen did her best to console him. Flip continued.

"We found out that your father holds the secret to the seventh and final scroll. That's why they got him. But don't worry. We're going to do all in our power to get him back." Flip patted Alex's shoulder, but there was a trace of uncertainty on his face.

"Why didn't the government protect him?" shouted Karen. "They must have known he was a potential target, right?"

"Listen, I don't make the rules," said Flip, annoyed. Not at Karen's question, but at the understanding that she was correct. Why hadn't the government protected Mr. Smiley, with so much at stake?

"Look, I gotta go," said Flip. "I want you guys to remain here. Do you understand me?"

"We understand." said Karen. Alex didn't answer. His face was blank. He was angry.

When Flip left the room, Karen turned to Alex.

"How do you feel?"

"How do you think I feel?" said Alex, staring at the hotel-room door. "I feel like I failed everyone."

Alex had always been deemed different. His peers saw him as too smart, too kind, too nerdy, and just plain weird. Nothing he ever did pleased anyone. Even his racial make-up caused disdain. Alex was of mixed ancestry, just like his parents. His father was African-American/Irish, and his mother Hispanic/Polish. To his peers he was too black, too Hispanic, or too white. It didn't help that his parents were perceived as weird. He wasn't good at sports, wasn't considered good-looking, wasn't good at making friends. Alex had never fit in.

The only true friend he had ever had was Karen. While his classmates made fun and chastised him, Karen always had his back. Even though her parents didn't approve of Alex, this never deterred Karen from building a friendship with him. Because of this, Alex felt indebted to her. If there were one person he was afraid to lose, it was Karen.

As Alex continued to daydream, Karen noticed what sounded like the drumming of heavy rain on the rooftop. When she looked out the window, she saw not rain but fiery hail falling from the sky. The hail wasn't burning down buildings, but it burnt anyone it touched and did great damage to vegetation. This was the power of the fifth scroll, unleashed by the Sétbætañ: to destroy all food crops.

ΠΙΡΗ ↓ ЄΠЄϹΗΤ 2ι ϯФЄ

It translates as:

The sun will come down from the heavens.

87

It was clear that the Sétbætañ were close to their goal of completely annihilating all of humanity. All that was needed was the unlocking of the sixth and seventh scrolls. Alex gathered his composure and joined Karen at the window.

"Look at this. I can't believe this is happening," said Karen.

"I'm not surprised by anything anymore," said Alex, moving away from the window. "You know I can't just sit here with my father in the hands of those monsters."

"Alex, I can only imagine how you feel. But I don't think Flip would want us to do anything irrational," countered Karen.

"You know, you're right. Flip wouldn't want *us* to do anything irrational. So that's why I'm gonna do this myself," said Alex.

"What are you talking about?"

"I'm going to get my father."

"How do you expect to do that?"

"I know the chant of the first scroll. I did it once and I can do it again."

"What if they're waiting for you on the other side?"

"That's a chance I'm willing to take."

"You know that I'm coming with you."

"No, you're not. Not this time."

With that, Alex closed his eyes and started the chant. He knew it had to be perfect for the portal to open:

ⲈϨⲞⲨⲚ ⲠⲒⲢⲞ Ⲉ̀ ⲠⲒ ⲀⲦⲀ6ⲚⲒ ⲘⲚⲦⲢⲢⲰⲞⲨ

ⲈϨⲞⲨⲚ ⲠⲒⲢⲞ Ⲉ̀ ⲠⲒ ⲀⲦⲀ6ⲚⲒ ⲘⲚⲦⲢⲢⲰⲞⲨ

ⲈϨⲞⲨⲚ ⲠⲒⲢⲞ Ⲉ̀ ⲠⲒ ⲀⲦⲀ6ⲚⲒ ⲘⲚⲦⲢⲢⲰⲞⲨ

On the third try, it opened.

As Alex walked into the portal, he looked back and saw Karen in tears. He wanted her with him but he knew the stakes were too high. He turned and ran through the portal. As the portal closed and Alex disappeared into thin air, Karen cried. She didn't cry because she was afraid, but because she wasn't sure if she would ever see Alex again.

When Alex reached the other side, he was near the Vuur prison where he and Karen had been held. Alex figured that if his father had been taken captive, he would be in that same prison. Despite a steady downpour creating poor visibility, his portal location couldn't have been better. He knew he had to be careful not to attract attention approaching the camp. The slippery footing and lack of camouflage would make it difficult. The only things in the barren plain between him and the prison were a few boulders.

Hiding behind boulders for cover, Alex got within two hundred yards of the camp. Through wet and fogged glasses he spotted two objects walking toward him. Alex ceased moving and wiped the fog from his glasses. The objects began to run. They were troll guards of the Sétbætañ prison. Alex realized that he had been spotted. Unbridled fear ran up his spine. The trolls were huge, standing eight feet tall and weighing no less than a ton. The troll guards were now within ninety feet of him. Mumbling to himself, Alex wished he could just disappear. He promised himself that he would not scream when the trolls attacked him. He stood still, closed his eyes, and braced for impact.

But nothing happened.

The trolls had run right past him and looked around, confused. They weren't the only ones. When Alex happened to look down at his feet, he saw nothing. As a matter of fact, his whole body was invisible. The green pills that Flip had ordered him to ingest had taken effect. He had learned to cloak by simply telling himself to disappear. As the confused trolls cursed and searched for the intruder, Alex quietly and quickly moved toward the prison camp.

Alex entered the camp, moving past several troll guards as he approached one of the dungeons. He tried to listen in on the troll guard's conversations to pick up any useful information. But the trolls were speaking an alien language. Moving down a dark, dingy hallway, Alex saw the dungeon where he and Karen had been captives. The unpleasant memory sent shivers down his spine. As he passed, the alien inmates made noises and shouted, as if they had sensed his presence. He picked up his pace.

Then Alex spotted a dark, narrow, tunnel-like path on the left, just past the dungeon. Not knowing why, Alex felt a strong urge to go down the path, as if someone or something were guiding him. The path was long, quiet, and pitch-black. Its floor was a hard ground and its walls were solid rock. Unable to see properly, Alex used the walls to guide his way. He began to think that the journey down the path was a mistake, and was about to turn around, when he heard a faint voice rise out of the darkness. He followed the voice to see where it would lead him.

As Alex continued down the pathway, the voice grew louder and he saw a faint light. Listening closely, he realized it was not just one voice but several. He decided to investigate.

Approaching the voices, Alex made sure to be extra quiet. The long, dark path opened into a large, dark room with what looked like a giant, dim, interrogation light. The walls were covered with what looked to be strange torture devices. Chains hung from the ceiling. In the middle of the room, on a table, was an unidentifiable figure. Surrounding it were two creatures. One had the legs of a horse, the torso of a man, and the head of a devil. The other looked like a man-bull, similar to a Minotaur. The creatures were torturing and cursing the figure on the table.

"What's the secret?" said the creature with the devil head.

"Looks like we're gonna have to rip him in two," said the man-bull.

Alex got closer, hiding behind one of the large tables near the end of the path.

"Let's see how he'll like this. This will break him down. Though we must admit, he's a tough one," said the man-bull as he picked up a device that looked like a long, thick strap with nails.

"Aaaaaaah!" screamed a human voice as the man-bull administered the strap. "Aaaaaaahhhh!" the voice screamed even louder when the man-bull struck again.

"Tell us the secret of the scroll," screamed the creature with the devil head. The human did not answer.

Alex knew then that the figure on the table was his father and that his father's life and the existence of mankind were in jeopardy. He thought feverishly about how to free his dad.

While the creatures continued to interrogate Mr. Smiley, Alex grabbed a sword from the wall and slowly approached. He made sure to stay low. A floating sword would be a dead giveaway. As he slowly and quietly crawled toward the feet of the creatures, the man-bull urinated on the ground, missing Alex by inches. The smell almost made Alex vomit.

"Looks like he needs another one, eh?" said the man-bull. Mr. Smiley looked like he was about to lose consciousness.

"Give it to him good," said the devil-headed creature as the man-bull raised his arm to deliver another blow.

Just then Alex took the sword and stabbed it into the foot of the man-bull with all his might.

"Aaaaahhhhh!" the man-bull screamed as the devil-headed creature looked at him, puzzled. "I've been stabbed in the bloomin' foot!"

Before the devil-headed creature could react, Alex took the sword and delivered a fatal blow, slicing across its neck. He then quickly sliced the torso of the man-bull, sending both creatures to their deaths.

Alex looked at the creatures lying in pools of greenish-black blood. It occurred to him that it was the first time he had ever killed anything. He had no regrets. He actually felt a sense of power surge in his body for possibly the first time in his life. He would do anything to save his father.

Alex used the sword to quickly unbind Mr. Smiley. He was naked, with welts, cuts, and bruises all over his body. He wasn't breathing properly and he appeared to have a broken leg. Mr. Smiley had been tortured for two days with an assortment of whips, stretching devices, and baseball bats.

"Alex, God bless you, son," said a weary Mr. Smiley as he looked into Alex's eyes. Alex's cloaking potion had begun to wear off just as Mr. Smiley regained consciousness. "But you shouldn't have come."

"Dad, I couldn't just leave you here," countered Alex,

covering his father in bandages and old alien rags that he'd found in the room.

"Alex, we need to keep those monsters from using the last two scrolls. I know where they are," said Mr. Smiley.

"Well we'll need something to help support that leg."

Alex looked around the room. He found some lengths of wood to use as a splint. He tied the wood to his father's leg with bandages, and then helped his father off the table. Mr. Smiley used all the strength he could muster to rise up from the table. He was exhausted and took short breaths between every word.

"Dad, are you okay?" asked Alex.

"I'll be okay. We've got to get to those scrolls. But we must stay low."

Mr. Smiley's adventure to Vuur had not been pleasant. He'd been carried like an eagle's prey by the Selanon. Dropped to the ground from fifty feet in the air, he had broken his leg on impact. He'd been taken by troll guards to a room with the vault containing the scrolls. There he was greeted by Cúbaneg, Ugnjengon, and Ecaep who'd tried to force him to translate the scrolls. But he'd remained strong-willed and refused, so they had imprisoned and tortured him. The techniques were similar to those practiced by the ancient Scots, including the echelle, or ladder or rack, in which a person, lying on a long table, is stretched violently. Mr. Smiley had had several joints pulled from their sockets. He was repeatedly whipped with chains, and cut with various knives.

Now, thanks to his son's heroics, he was free to retrieve the scrolls and save mankind. Even though he knew what he was in for if he was recaptured, the opportunity to save mankind gave him the courage to persevere.

It quickly became apparent that Mr. Smiley's injuries were too severe. He grimaced and groaned when Alex tried to support him. Alex helped Mr. Smiley back onto the table. A feeling of hopelessness clouded his mind as Alex wondered what to do. Sensing this, Mr. Smiley began instructing Alex on how to get back the scrolls.

"Alex, go and grab those binoculars on that desk." Alex got

the binoculars, which looked like the kind used by Army commandos in World War I.

"Now look over in that direction and tell me what you see." Mr. Smiley pointed to a small window in the far right corner of the room. As Alex focused the binoculars and looked through the window into another room, he saw a large, cast-iron vault being guarded by several creatures, one of which looked familiar. Seeing the creatures, Alex quickly lowered the binoculars. He told his father what he'd seen.

"Alex, I need you to get those scrolls out of the vault. Those creatures will be back in here very soon and that's when you'll grab the scrolls."

"I'm not leaving you, Dad."

"Just do as I say," said Mr. Smiley.

"How am I gonna get that vault open?" asked Alex.

"Don't worry. I have a plan".

The plan was for Mr. Smiley to draw the creatures away from the vault room to inform them that he would translate the scrolls. Once the creatures had opened the vault, a cloaked Alex would grab the scrolls and return to Earth. This meant that he would have to leave his father behind. Though Alex pleaded with him, Mr. Smiley insisted that Alex must do what was in the best interest of mankind, even if it meant sacrificing his father. Alex removed Mr. Smiley's alien rags and bandages, and the splint he'd made for his broken leg. He piled wood and rags over the bodies of the dead creatures to conceal them.

But the cloaking potion had permanently worn off. No matter how hard Alex tried to cloak, he couldn't. He would have to get the scrolls the old-fashioned way, using stealth and brains.

As Alex slowly and quietly moved toward the vault room, Mr. Smiley used all his might to let out a loud scream. It was enough to get the attention of the creatures. Out of the vault room they came, four in number. Two were wolf-like creatures. Alex recognized the other two. They were Cúbaneg and Ugnjengon. Thrilled that they were about to get the final scroll translation, these creatures never questioned the whereabouts of Mr. Smiley's torturers.

"Ready to talk now, eh?" said Cúbaneg. He ordered one of the wolf-creatures, "Go and get the scrolls." The creatures jubilantly huddled around Mr. Smiley.

Ugnjengon began to get suspicious when his keen sense of smell picked up the scent of the slain creatures.

"You must open the vault," the wolf-creature said to Cúbaneg.

"It's not in the vault. It's on the shelf next to the vault. You know that," screamed Ugnjengon.

Frustrated by the incompetence of Cúbaneg's minions, the quick-tempered Ugnjengon started kicking things around the room. He kicked away the debris that had been covering the slain creatures.

Realizing they had been tricked, the creatures scrambled back to the vault room. They searched high and low for the scrolls, tossing tables, shelves, and chairs, and ripping apart anything in their path. "Arggghhhh!" screamed Ugnjengon.

Alex was well on his way back down the dark, narrow tunnel. In the vault room, he'd been shocked to discover that the scrolls were not on the shelf next to the vault but had been left unattended on a table. He quickly grabbed them and escaped unnoticed.

He saw that one of the scrolls, the sixth, had more text on it than any of the other scrolls did. He didn't know what it meant, but he had a feeling it would be of significance.

Going down the dark path the second time seemed to take forever. Alex figured that once he got into the open he would open the portal back to Earth. Because he couldn't cloak he would have to be even more cunning than before. At last, Alex saw faint light. He figured it would be smarter if he opened the portal before stepping off the path so he began his chant:

ⲈⲂⲞⲨⲚ ⲠⲒⲢⲞ Ⲉ ⲠⲒ ⲀⲦⲀⲞ́ⲚⲒ ⳘⲘⲦⲢⲢⲱⲞⲨ

He didn't quite get it right.

ⲉϧⲟⲩⲛ ⲡ ⲓⲣⲟ ⲉ̀ ⲡ ⲓ ⲁⲧⲁϭ ⲛⲓ ⲙ ⲛ ⲧ ⲣ ⲣ ⲱ ⲟⲩ

He chanted again. Still not right. Alex knew it usually took him three tries to be successful. A creepy voice echoed from the darkness. It said:

"If you value your friend's life, you'll hand over the scrolls."

The voice came from the light at the end of the pathway. When Alex looked out to see the source of the voice, he had to fight to keep his bowels from emptying. In Cúbaneg's hand was a gun. At the end of the barrel was Karen's head.

Chapter 17
Making Tough Choices

Karen's decision to follow Alex was pure impulse. Her feelings for Alex had grown throughout their ordeal and she'd decided that nothing was going to keep them apart. When Alex disappeared into the portal, Karen knew right away that she would follow him. She'd been secretly practicing the chant of the first scroll and mastering the ability to cloak. She was well-prepared and ahead of the game.

When Karen arrived on Caynonã, she wasn't in the badlands of Vuur, but three miles from the prison camp in the dark forest of Asus. Approximately four hundred square miles, the Asus forest separated Urodae, land of the Luçimarks, from Vuur. Estimated to be twenty-five hundred Earth years old, Asus had trees so tall they blocked the light of the planet's sun. The forest contained plants and creatures ranging from docile to dangerous. It was rumored to be the home of both the Selanon and the Krieatine, though no one knew for sure.

Lost and scared, Karen had to find her way out of the forest to Vuur. She was determined to find Alex. She figured if things got too dicey, she could always chant herself back to Earth and then attempt a later return to Caynonã.

Because of the vegetation, the forest air was easier to breathe than in the badlands of Vuur. The forest floor was thickly covered in an assortment of small and large exotic plants. She did her best not to step directly on any of them for fear of being poisoned. Or worse yet, eaten.

Visibility was very poor. Thick fog rose from the ground. Karen had a flashlight but could only see directly in front of her. Because of the fog, the light only reflected back into Karen's eyes. She turned it off and felt her way by carefully touching tree trunks and large rocks. In the distance, the dark and fog could be cut with a knife.

After traveling for more than two hours, Karen felt weak with hunger. She had made sure to come prepared, stuffing her backpack full of sandwiches, drinks, and a first-aid kit. She'd also brought a compass -- an item of critical necessity in unknown lands. She soon found that it didn't work. Its needle just spun around in circles. This was probably due to the planet having a different magnetic field than the Earth's. She carefully shined the flashlight toward the ground to help guide her way. She dared not shine it directly ahead, for fear of being spotted by something awful and terrifying.

Noises echoed in the deep darkness of the forest. Some sounded like strange bird calls, and some sounded like weird whispering. But it was another noise that bothered Karen most and sent shivers down her spine -- the low growl of a wolf or other carnivore.

My God, what did I get myself into? But I have to keep going. I have to find Alex. If only I knew which way to go.

Though the air was still, Karen felt a slight chill as she walked away from the growling. The bird calls and whispering noises grew louder. Then, everything went quiet except for a rustling in some nearby bushes. Karen stopped in her tracks and stood as still as death.

"Who's there?" Karen whispered, hoping that nothing would answer. "Alex?"

Karen heard more rustling and growling. Her curiosity got the best of her and she shined the flashlight into the bushes. Through the thick fog and the dark night she saw two pairs of eyes and protruding fangs that made her heart pound so hard it felt as if it would come out of her chest. Karen knew any sudden movement would be fatal. *Don't run. Stay still. It'll go away.*

The creature emerged from the bushes. It was a xyheilamander -- a huge, carnivorous, bearlike creature that roamed the Asus forest. It was the same sort of creature that Karen saw Ecaep riding when she and Alex were first captured and brought to Vuur. The xyheilamander weighs about two tons and can measure eleven feet when standing on its hind legs. It has two pairs of eyes -- one pair for binocular vision and the other on the side of its head. Its fangs are two and a half inches long, and its claws four inches. It has wooly brown fur all over its body, which can change to black, white, dark green, or blood red. It uses this ability to camouflage to blend into its surroundings when hunting. A change to red usually means it's on the attack. Despite its size, it's a particularly fast animal. It's also very powerful and can kill with one strike of the paw. It has no natural enemies.

Karen's first impulse was to run like crazy, but she quickly noticed that the creature didn't have an aggressive demeanor. It seemed more curious about her than anything else. And it looked to be injured. One of its hind legs was bleeding. It slowly circled Karen on all fours, sniffing and making funny gargling noises.

Karen kept as still as possible. The creature was huge, larger than an adult rhino or hippo. Through the darkness and fog, this xyheilamander appeared to be brown. The animal clumsily nudged Karen's backpack. She figured that feeding the animal some food might keep it from feeding on her. She slowly reached into her backpack and pulled out a sandwich.

"Here boy, here boy," said Karen as she held out the sandwich. The creature didn't seem hostile at all. As a matter of fact, it seemed quite gentle.

"Come on, boy. Want some sandwich?"

The creature slowly sniffed the sandwich with its large nose. Karen let it drop onto the ground. The creature then gobbled up the small delicacy in one bite. It still seemed very hungry.

"Want some more, boy?" Karen went back into her backpack and pulled out another sandwich. Once again the creature quickly gobbled it up. Then, with its nose, it knocked the backpack out of Karen's hand. The xyheilamander then proceeded to rummage through the backpack, eating every edible thing it found. The animal once again started to circle Karen, wanting more.

"There's no more, boy. I'm all out. You ate it all," said Karen in her most gentle voice possible.

The creature started to growl, and it got louder by the second. Karen was surprised that she didn't feel all that alarmed. She tried to soothe the creature by stroking its thick, woolly fur.

"Easy there boy, it's okay," said Karen. She had begun to admire the great beast while she was stroking its fur.

Without warning, the creature's growl turned to a loud roar, like a pride of angry lions. Its woolly brown fur turned red and the beast stood face to face with Karen. It was now obvious to her that the creature was in attack mode. Karen was frightened beyond belief. But if she were going to die, she was going to die trying her best to escape. Without thinking twice, Karen bolted into the foggy, dark forest.

As Karen ran, the creature lumbered behind. The creature's injury prevented it from making a quick snack of Karen, but it wouldn't give up easily. In fact, xyheilamanders were known to pursue their prey up to fifty miles. Besides being powerful and great at camouflaging, the creature had an excellent sense of smell.

Karen ducked and dodged tree limbs and trunks. She squashed plants and other small things in her path. After running for her life for what felt like miles, she was exhausted and needed a break. She had outrun the creature.

Daybreak was finally arriving and Karen could see faint glimmers of light emerging through the tops of the trees. She decided to take a rest at the foot of a large, white, tree trunk.

Karen dreamed she was walking into her parent's house. Her parents were sitting at the kitchen table with smiles on their faces. Detective Riley was also at the table. He wasn't smiling and got up and approached Karen. Something seemed wrong. Karen screamed for her parents but they were no longer there. She tried to escape but the doorknob wouldn't turn. Detective Riley was upon her, reaching out to grab her. Karen woke suddenly from her slumber. As she opened her eyes, she saw four xyheilamanders surrounding her, ready to attack. The largest of the creatures was the xyheilamander that Karen had outrun miles ago.

Karen quickly surveyed her path for escape as the creatures started in toward her. There was no place to go but up. Without hesitation, she began to climb the huge tree, pleased that her tomboy skills were paying off. The creatures swiped at her feet. If any of those swipes had connected, Karen would have lost a limb. She dared not look down. It wasn't the height she was afraid of, but the creatures. Luckily, they were unable to climb trees.

"I should be out of their reach by now," said Karen as she ascended. She was so high up that she could feel rays of sunlight on her skin. She looked down and saw the creatures standing at the foot of the tree trunk.

While Karen sat on a branch, she began to feel uncomfortable. The creatures were camped at the bottom of the tree and she wasn't going anywhere anytime soon. It made sense to find a comfortable resting place. As she maneuvered upward, from branch to branch, she was shocked to find she was not alone in the tree. Resting on a branch was a gargoyle-like creature grinning directly at her. It was one of the Selanon.

"Nooooo!"

The shock and horror at seeing the creature scared Karen to her wits' end, causing her to fall out of the tree. She saw the ground rushing towards her with the certainty of death. The Selanon caught her in its talons just before she hit the ground occupied with angry xyheilamanders. As the creature flew off with her in its grasp, Karen breathed a sigh of relief that her life had been spared. Then she fainted. Death may have been a better alternative to where she and the creature were headed.

Chapter 18
In the Face of Death

The trip to Jymhamasbad was a long and painful journey. Flanked by Cúbaneg, Ugnjengon, and roughly thirty other Sétbætañ, Alex, Karen, and Mr. Smiley were bound in chains on a large, gray boat moving steadily across the deep, dark waters. The red sky was warlike and the air was chilly and stifling. Alex, who still had images of Cúbaneg pointing a gun at Karen's head in his own, was scared, tired, and dazed. Karen, who not long before was being chased by xyheilamanders, and then carried off by Selanon, was feeling light-headed and weak. This may have been due in part to her contact with the poisonous plants of the Asus forest.

Mr. Smiley was in the worst shape of the three. He was naked save for a rag around his waist that served as a loincloth, and the cold wind pierced his bones. Despite suffering a broken leg, cracked vertebrae, and shortness of breath, the Sétbætañ made him carry out the journey bound in chains and standing on his feet. Every second for Mr. Smiley was a second drenched in pain. Only his strong will prevented his demise. Had he known where they were going, however, he may have felt that dying in that boat was the better alternative.

Jymhamasbad is an island thirty miles southwest of Vuur where prisoners of the Sétbætañ are sent for execution. The island is surrounded by the deep and deadly cold Lake Jymhamasbad, which can only be crossed by boat. Falling in meant quickly freezing to death, even before drowning. Many Sétbætañ have died a quick but horrible death in the watery graveyard.

Alex, Karen, and Mr. Smiley thought for sure that the creatures would toss them in the lake to be rid of them once and for all. But the creatures had another plan. The Sétbætañ's preferred method of execution featured slow, painful torture until the prisoners' death. The methods of execution included poisonings, hangings, and bloodletting. Their goal was for the humans to die painfully and slowly, and the Sétbætañ were

101

unmerciful when dealing with those they hated.

Ecaep had instructed Cúbaneg and Ugnjengon to concoct the perfect method for killing the humans. Now that the creatures had the seventh scroll's translation, Alex, Karen, and Mr. Smiley were expendable. On the journey, Cúbaneg whispered to Mr. Smiley. "This will be the last of your trips to our planet, you filthy human. Once we reach Jymhamasbad, you and the other human vermin will wish they had never been born."

Cúbaneg and his thugs had captured Alex on his way back to Earth via dimensional portal. He had the sixth and seventh scrolls in his possession and getting back to Earth could have meant ending the war and saving mankind. Even though Mr. Smiley was the only one who knew the translations, Alex was thought to also have the ability to decode the text, enabling the humans to turn the tables on the Sétbætañ by using the scrolls against them. Mr. Smiley's plan to recapture the scrolls and Alex's execution of it had very nearly worked. Unfortunately, Cúbaneg would not let the humans escape with the scrolls without paying a heavy price. That price was Karen's life.

While Cúbaneg was getting the seventh scroll translation from Mr. Smiley, he was also tracking Karen in Asus, using the Selanon to report back her every move.

When the Selanon delivered Karen to Cúbaneg, he used her to capture Alex, and then ordered his soldiers to bring Mr. Smiley to him. Once Mr. Smiley saw Karen and Alex in the grasp of the Sétbætañ soldiers, he knew that Cúbaneg had him in an untenable situation.

"Now, you fool. Translate the seventh scroll or these human maggots die. It'll save my people the time and energy of figuring out the translation ourselves. We have no need for you to translate the sixth scroll. We've done that already," said Cúbaneg, holding a gun to Karen's head. Ugnjengon had one of his huge hands around Alex's neck, ready to squeeze and crush his trachea at Cúbaneg's order.

"Don't hurt them, please," said Mr. Smiley, using every muscle in his body to strain out the words.

"You must make the choice. It's either the translation or the death of these humans."

"I'll give you the translation."

"You've made a wise choice," said a grinning Cúbaneg.

Cúbaneg ordered one of his soldiers to hand a tablet-style computer to Mr. Smiley.

"Enter the translation," Cúbaneg ordered.

As Mr. Smiley's shaky hands touched the screen, random thoughts raced at a thousand miles per second: *Should I fool them and give them the wrong translation? My God, I'm about to jeopardize the entire human race. My wife. I pray she hasn't given up hope. Maybe we should all sacrifice our lives for the survival of mankind.*

Cúbaneg saw Mr. Smiley stalling. He nodded his head toward Ugnjengon, whose large hand tightened ever so slightly around Alex's neck. Within a second, Alex started gagging and his face turned blue. Mr. Smiley quickly typed the translation into the tablet.

"You have the translation. Now please, let him go," said a frantic and breathless Mr. Smiley.

When Ugnjengon loosened his grip, Alex collapsed to the floor. Cúbaneg then ordered his soldiers to bind the preteens and spoke nose to nose with Mr. Smiley.

"I remember the last time you were here. You were new to our world, alone and frightened. You didn't know what to make of your situation. But we were merciful and shared with you the plight of our people. Your traveling to our world let us know you were in possession of the sacred scrolls, of our technology. But we were merciful to you despite your being the offspring of our enemies. You promised to deliver the scrolls to lord Ecaep. But you betrayed us. You betrayed our people by planning to share the scroll technology with the Luçimarks."

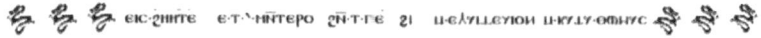

Mr. Smiley's discovery of the alien planet was by pure luck. When he found the scrolls in the Utah desert, he decided to keep them secret from the government -- not because he was a traitor, but because his years of research taught him that the scrolls had significant and potentially dangerous powers. Familiar with how the government worked, he knew that the scrolls could easily fall into the wrong hands.

Working in his lab, Mr. Smiley noticed that the language of the scrolls was similar to ancient Coptic Egyptian writings, widely used until the seventeenth century. The familiar text and numbers at the top of each scroll gave them a cryptic appearance. Mr. Smiley used his extensive scientific background and his access to highly classified government documents on alien beings to decipher the scrolls.

After many months working feverishly in his lab, Mr. Smiley's worst fears were realized. He discovered that the U.S. government and the Roman Catholic Church had known about the scrolls since the end of World War II. He also discovered that the government had been searching for the scrolls since they'd been buried in Utah in the 1950s. Both the government and the Church knew the power and the source of the scrolls.

This discovery angered Mr. Smiley. He felt betrayed by his country and by the Church. He became determined to find out the whole truth for himself -- to decode the scrolls and discover their ancient secrets.

Through hard work and determination, Mr. Smiley was able to decode all of the scrolls. He felt it necessary to prove his theories by utilizing the power of one of the least dangerous scrolls, the first. Spending time with Marion, the future Mrs. Smiley, would have to wait. It was time to find out what truths the Church and state had been hiding from the people.

When he'd first arrived through the dimensional portal, Mr. Smiley was two miles outside the prison camp of Vuur. To say he was frightened is an understatement. Mr. Smiley was certain that he had just walked through the gates of Hell. With its red skies, constant thunder, and blowing dust winds, Mr. Smiley knew he was on an alien planet.

At first, Mr. Smiley didn't know what to make of the situation. Taking the dire landscape into account, he was surprised that he was still alive. The atmosphere could have had gas or pressure levels different from Earth's, or contain poisonous gases. But the planet seemed able to sustain complex organisms such as humans or other sophisticated beings.

As Mr. Smiley ventured farther, peering through binoculars he noticed a prison-like building being guarded by grotesque creatures. Though frightened, he approached the camp very slowly, hoping to make friendly contact. Without warning, he was knocked unconscious. He woke up alone in a prison cell, surrounded by more cells containing other imprisoned creatures. Rubbing his splitting head, Mr. Smiley tried to guess how long he had been out. It didn't take long for a couple of visitors to arrive. Shocked by the grotesqueness of the creatures, Mr. Smiley nearly lost control of his bladder.

"Are you a spy?" asked the creature who turned out to be Cúbaneg. Ugnjengon was with him.

Mr. Smiley was flabbergasted when the creature spoke to him in English.

"No. I've come in peace from the planet Earth," said Mr. Smiley.

"The planet Earth, eh? Well, how did you get here? By what means?"

"I arrived by a dimensional portal. The portal was opened by chanting the text of an ancient scroll."

At this, Ugnjengon let out a fierce scream. Cúbaneg turned toward him to calm him down, then proceeded with his questioning of Mr. Smiley.

"Ancient scroll, eh? And you found this scroll on Earth?"

"Yes."

"Was this the only scroll you found?"

"No. There are six others."

Cúbaneg was pleased with the answers to his questions. He was surprised how easily Mr. Smiley was volunteering the answers. Being a creature that possessed great manipulative powers, he decided to dig a little deeper.

"So how do you think these scrolls ended up on Earth?"

"I believe that they were placed there."

"And who do you believe placed these scrolls on Earth?"

"I'm not sure."

"What would you say if I told you the scrolls belong to us?"

"I'd say you should have them."

Cúbaneg ordered the troll guard to open the prison cell and release Mr. Smiley.

"Come with us. You will meet our lord, Ecaep," said a jubilant Cúbaneg.

As Cúbaneg and Ugnjengon escorted Mr. Smiley out of the prison camp, word began to spread that the long lost scrolls had been discovered and that a human, of all creatures, was going to help the Sétbætañ reclaim them. A small crowd began to gather as Cúbaneg, Ugnjengon, and Mr. Smiley got closer to Ecaep's lair. Mr. Smiley, still in chains, was as nervous as he had ever been. The creatures worshiped their leader as a god.

After traveling approximately ten miles by foot, the group arrived at Ecaep's castle. It was huge and dark, resembling a castle in a Dracula movie. The exterior was decorated with gargoyles. There was a huge drawbridge at the entrance. Several trolls were stationed on the grounds around the castle, and other creatures were stationed around its upper deck. Ugnjengon ordered the troll guards to lower the drawbridge.

The group entered. The castle was huge and dimly lit with candles. They proceeded down a long, dark hallway. Sounds bounced off the castle walls creating a cavernous echo. The air smelled of damp basement. Mr. Smiley passed rooms along the hallway, and could see that some were decorated with ancient war weapons such as swords, while others held more modern machinery, such as automatic assault weapons. Still other rooms were decorated with gold, silver, and jewels. The group had reached the back of the castle. Before them, sitting on a jeweled throne, was Ecaep, the reigning lord of Vuur. On the wall above the throne was an inscription:

ⲠⲒⲚⲒⲰⲦ Ⲛ̀ⲞⲨⲢⲞ ⲪⲎⲈⲦⲤⲈⲘⲤⲒ ⲞⲒⲬⲈⲚ ⲠⲒⲐⲢⲞⲚⲞⲤ

It translates as:

The great king who sits on the throne.

Cúbaneg, Ugnjengon, and all the other creatures in the castle ceased movement and chatter. They bowed before Ecaep in worship.

"Step forward, human," boomed Ecaep. Mr. Smiley, frightened out of his wits, moved forward.

"I understand that you are in possession of the sacred scrolls."

"Yes, I am. I –

"Kneel before me while addressing me, human."

Mr. Smiley quickly went to his knees. He made sure to bow his head and never looked up.

"Yes, I am. I found the scrolls that you seek on my home planet, Earth."

"Are they with you now?"

"No, my lord, they are on Earth. It is my intention to deliver them to their rightful owners, which would be your people, my lord."

Ecaep ordered Mr. Smiley unchained. Mr. Smiley could be very useful to him. He shared some of the history of his people and the people of Earth with Mr. Smiley.

"I am well aware of your planet," Ecaep stated. "I'm aware that your planet is very violent and that humans fight among themselves often. Like you, we have our enemies. And our enemies have stolen from and enslaved our people. We were forced to live like maggots upon the dirt of our world, and to give up all things created by our people. As some humans may understand, we grew tired of the beatings, the theft, and the humiliation. We rose against our enemy. We call those miliyous The Great Rebellion.

"And here we are, exiled in this wasteland called Vuur. Though we hate this land, it is our only haven from those who seek to oppress us. But not all of our people are here. Many have been detained by our enemy, to serve them even to this day. These people need our help. Our eternal enemy no longer outnumbers us. With the scrolls in our possession, our people

107

will claim victory and we will live free again."

The small crowd in the castle went into a frenzy. Ecaep continued.

"Many Earth years ago the enemy stole our technology and took it to your planet. This technology is contained in the scrolls. We have searched for centuries to find them. Now through you we have reached our destiny. Now we shall go to Earth to recover the scrolls."

The crowd got even louder. Mr. Smiley, however, was not comfortable with the idea of aliens invading Earth.

"My lord, would it be possible for me to deliver the scrolls to you? I worry that your mighty presence may cause great stress and panic on my planet."

Cúbaneg went to discuss this with Ecaep.

"My lord, we shouldn't trust this human scum," reasoned Cúbaneg. "If we do not accompany him to Earth, he may never return."

"Oh, he will return, alone or with others," said a confident Ecaep. "Humans are war-mongering beings just like their creators. They always seek power. And if they cannot find ways to acquire power among their own, they are willing to travel to other worlds to feed their desires. Their lust for power will eventually cause them to betray their own forefathers. Let's just see if this maggot is like the Luçimark filth."

Finally, Ecaep rose from his throne and delivered his decision. He was willing to gamble that Mr. Smiley would return with the scrolls. He ensured this by issuing a threat.

"Human, I will allow you to travel alone to recover the scrolls. But know this: If you fail to return, you and your world will feel my wrath. Now, go."

Mr. Smiley was led out of the castle and into a sparsely wooded field. As a skeptical Cúbaneg looked on, Mr. Smiley recited the chant to return to Earth. When the portal opened, Mr. Smiley jumped in and ran as fast as he could.

When he arrived back home, Mr. Smiley noticed that time had sped forward. Though he'd been gone only a couple of days, the calendar on Earth had shown him gone for several weeks.

The first thing he wanted to do was contact Marion because he had missed her. He also knew she would have been wondering about his whereabouts. But time was of the essence. He had to get the scrolls. Exiting the portal, Mr. Smiley found himself fifteen miles from his destination. It was ten o'clock at night. Because the busses were no longer running and there was a cab strike on, he would have to travel back to his lab on foot.

"My God, I miss Marion," said Mr. Smiley, jogging at a brisk pace. "But I have to get those scrolls back to those creatures. Our world depends on it."

When he'd arrived at the lab, the first thing he noticed was that his answering machine was filled with messages. He wanted to listen. He longed to hear Marion's voice. But he dared not, knowing it could be some government agent whose shrill would make him sick to his stomach.

The second thing he'd noticed was that someone had gone through his documents. He had no time to investigate. He needed to deliver the scrolls back to the creatures in Caynonã. It would ensure they would be kept out of government hands. To keep them safe, he had hidden them in the drop ceiling of the lab.

" ... four, five, six, seven. Yes, these are all of them," said a relieved Mr. Smiley, happy that no one found them. He placed the scrolls in a suitcase and opened a portal. But this time, he would arrive somewhere vastly different.

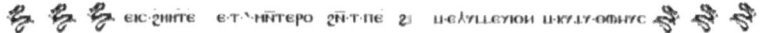

When Mr. Smiley exited the portal, he was one mile outside of Urodae, land of the Luçimarks. He was greeted by warmth, blue skies, and fresh air. He was also greeted by three creatures that looked quite different from those he'd encountered on his first visit. These creatures, though very tall, looked similar to humans. At gunpoint, Mr. Smiley was placed in a mobile cage along with creatures that looked like the ones he'd met last time he'd gone through the portal. They all were being taken to the government's council for questioning.

Though the weather and the atmosphere were great, the

situation seemed dire. Mr. Smiley was in a cage with seven others -- grotesque creatures that looked very sad and worn down, as if they didn't care if they lived another day. In contrast, the creatures in command were strikingly beautiful, confident, and proud. They rode beside the mobile cage on beasts similar to horses. Without question they considered themselves the superior race of beings.

The mobile cage soon came to a halt at what appeared to be a concentration camp. It was filled with creatures that looked to be on their last legs. Mr. Smiley also observed that the ruling race of creatures was hostile to the creatures they enslaved. Now he understood why Ecaep and his people were so bitter. He also noticed the creatures looking at him and his suitcase, conversing in their native tongue. Mr. Smiley clutched the suitcase tightly. Before long, he was placed back in the mobile cage and led away from the camp. Unbeknownst to him, he was to be questioned by the leader of the Luçimarks, the Supreme Leader Mataralin.

Mr. Smiley arrived at not a gloomy castle, but a palace. It was very grand, towering over all other buildings in Urodae. Though he was led out of the mobile cage at gunpoint, Mr. Smiley stood in awe of the beauty of the palace and its majesty. It took the poke of a gun barrel to awaken him from his daydream.

Walking through the palace, Mr. Smiley saw floors coated with solid gold, chandeliers of pure silver, and tables lined with rubies and diamonds. Rays of the planet's sun shined beautifully through the many stained-glass windows. After a few more steps, he saw sitting on a throne before him the leader of the Luçimarks.

Like all Luçimarks, Mataralin was tall and thinly built. He was a selfish leader, caring little about anyone but himself. He spent his days counting his jewels. His subjects responded to his every whim. The following was engraved on the wall behind his throne:

ⲍⲱⲥ ⲉ̀ⲣⲟϥ ⲕⲁⲧⲁ ⲡ̄ⲁϣⲁⲓ ⲛ̇ⲧⲉ ⲧⲉϥⲙⲉⲧⲛⲓϣϯ

It translates as:

Praise him according to the abundance of his greatness.

Mataralin was clothed in garments of pure silk, and wore a crown of solid gold. He spoke in a low but commanding voice as he addressed Mr. Smiley.

"Step forward, human."

Mr. Smiley stepped forward.

"What are you doing in our lands?" asked Mataralin.

"I come here in peace from the planet Earth," answered Mr. Smiley.

"And how did you get here?" asked Mataralin.

"Through space travel," said Mr. Smiley, hoping he would not be pressed to explain how.

After a brief pause, Mataralin continued.

"What do you have there?"

"Just some of my personals, my lord. Some clothes, food, and things of that sort," said Mr. Smiley.

"You're able to fit food and all of your garments in that small case?"

"Yes, my lord."

Mataralin's tone grew dark. He knew of only one way the human could have arrived on his planet.

"I hope that you're not lying to me. Because if I open that case and find out it's not as you say, then one of my guards will promptly remove your head."

"I'm sorry, my lord. Please, forgive me. I carry some scrolls that I found on Earth," said a nervous Mr. Smiley.

"What?" shouted Mataralin. This was the most animated he had been in years.

"Some scrolls, my lord. When I --"

Before Mr. Smiley could finish his sentence, Mataralin ordered his guards to seize the briefcase. They smashed it open and took out the scrolls. Mataralin ordered his guards to hand him one so he could take a closer look. Though he could not personally decipher it, he knew what it was.

"These are indeed the sacred scrolls," said Mataralin. There was a collective gasp. Once again Mataralin's tone turned dark.

"So after all these Earth years, you humans decide to sneak back to our planet and deny that you have the scrolls in your possession? Even though we created your civilization? Helped you with your technology? Helped you defeat your enemies? We originally hid the scrolls on your planet for safekeeping. This is the thanks we get?"

"My lord, please understand. I have nothing to do with the humans who came before me. I found these scrolls on my planet. I just came to return them to their rightful owners."

"And who would you say are the rightful owners of these scrolls?" asked Mataralin.

"I would say you are," lied Mr. Smiley.

"Excellent answer," said Mataralin. "Who other than your ancient ancestors could create such a technology?"

Knowing the creature was lying about creating the technology, Mr. Smiley had to think of a way of retrieving the scrolls and return to Earth. He saw that Mataralin was having problems translating the scroll.

"My lord, I humbly ask that I help decode the scrolls for you," said Mr. Smiley.

"Very good," said Mataralin. "I'll give you all the time you need." He ordered one of his guards to return the scrolls to the briefcase and escort Mr. Smiley out of the palace.

"Guards, take the human to the science lab to translate the scrolls. Our scientists will help with the translations."

As the Luçimark guards led him from the palace, Mr. Smiley snatched the briefcase and made a mad dash into the woods, chanting the text of the first scroll as he ran. The portal opened. Mr. Smiley was on his way back to Earth. The Luçimarks were too late and the portal closed on them.

Returning to his lab, Mr. Smiley spotted Mrs. Gateway and other government officials rummaging through his papers in search of the scrolls. Mr. Smiley knew the government intended to use the scrolls for their own purposes. It was then that he

112

decided to hide the scrolls, from the government and the aliens.

He knew of a sewer in the junkyard he used to cut through on his way to and from school. With the scrolls locked away in his briefcase, Mr. Smiley descended the sewer manhole. With the help of his flashlight he spotted a huge crack in one of the sewer walls. It was just large enough to fit the briefcase. He placed the briefcase in the crack, and then used mud and debris from the sewer floor to conceal it. Without lights, the briefcase was perfectly hidden. Unless someone carefully searched the walls of the vast sewer, the briefcase could remain hidden forever.

Back on Caynonã, Mataralin, a stubborn leader who never took responsibility, cursed the guards for their incompetence. Like the Sétbætañ, the Luçimarks knew how to reach Earth by using the power of the first scroll. But without all seven scrolls, neither race of beings possessed the technology to directly locate a specific person or thing.

In the woods just west of the palace were the peering eyes of the Selanon. They returned to Ecaep to report their findings. Like the Luçimarks, the Sétbætañ had been tirelessly searching the Earth for the sacred scrolls. Returning with the head of Mr. Smiley would be a bonus.

"Listen," said Mr. Smiley. "I wasn't trying to give the scrolls to the Luçimarks. I escaped when I knew that they were trying to regain possession of the scrolls. Listen to me. This technology has already been shared with the humans. Why can't we, your people, and the Luçimarks come to a sensible solution? Ecaep's hatred will destroy all of us!"

"You fool. I should sever your head right now for your insolence," said Cúbaneg. "You humans don't even get along among your own races. How dare you pass judgment on the Sétbætañ. We are a proud race that's been forced to serve at the feet of the Luçimarks for centuries. Now it's our time to be the masters and for the Luçimarks and all of their ancestors to be the slaves."

"I believe that the humans, your people, and the Luçimarks can work out a peaceful solution," said Mr. Smiley.

"No. There's no solution except the destruction of the Luçimarks and their maggot offspring! Our little chat is now over. It's time for you to die."

The creatures put Alex, Karen, and Mr. Smiley in chains. They then boarded the boat to begin their journey across Lake Jymhamasbad.

"Why don't we take the portal?" asked one of the creatures. "It would hasten their deaths."

"No, our lord Ecaep would prefer that we transport the humans at a leisurely pace," said Cúbaneg. "He says that the anticipation of death is worse than death itself."

To pass the time while traveling, the Sétbætañ sang songs of war and death. It was a joyous occasion, as they now had all seven scrolls and their primary target, Mr. Smiley, in their possession. Alex and Karen were considered bonus prizes and would be executed for their meddling. With the Sétbætañ in control, the Krieatine had been ordered to return to Vuur. They couldn't wait to carry out the execution of the humans.

They sang with great enthusiasm, like pirates after acquiring spoils. For the humans, time seemed to drag as they were bound in chains and, like animals, forced to stand despite the rolling waves.

Arriving at last in Jymhamasbad, death was upon them. Alex, Karen, and Mr. Smiley knew that only a miracle could save them now.

114

Chapter 19
Enter the Dragons

It could be said that Karen's meeting with a xyheilamander was an once-in-a-lifetime experience, because once you've met one, your life is over. Her quick thinking and running ability, however, enabled her to see another day.

Unfortunately, she, Alex, and Mr. Smiley were now locked in a twenty by fifteen foot cage, which had several smaller cages above it. These smaller cages were filled with hundreds of large, snakelike creatures called mallie dragons. Native to Caynonã and highly poisonous, they could paralyze an adult human with one bite.

A mallie dragon can be distinguished from a snake by the long fin running from its head to its tail. The dragon has poor eyesight and the fin helps it locate prey. Once a victim is paralyzed, the mallie dragon eats it alive.

Unlike Earthly snakes, mallie dragons do not swallow prey whole. Instead, they devour it by chewing the flesh with long fangs and sharp teeth strong enough to snap and grind bone. Because of this unique trait, the mallie dragon often fails to leave any trace of its victim. It is said that once paralyzed, the mallie dragon's victim feels just enough pain while being eaten.

This was the plan of Cúbaneg and Ugnjengon -- for the humans to be eaten alive. The minimal level of pain meant that the victim would remain conscious while dying a slow and horrible death. It should also be noted that some Sétbætañ creatures are cannibals and that they also have a taste for human flesh. Ugnjengon was one of them. So there was a chance that the humans' last moments would involve being eaten alive by the mallie dragons, and also by Ugnjengon.

In preparation for execution, Alex, Karen, and Mr. Smiley were stripped, covered with a jelly-like substance, and hog-tied with rope. The jelly-like substance gave off a sweet aroma that was attractive to the mallie dragons. The Sétbætañ creatures laughed and mocked the humans, who cowered in different corners of the cage.

"They're gonna make a good meal for those dragons," shouted one creature.

"Forget about the dragons; I want some," shouted another creature, laughing.

Alex had conceded that the end had come for him and his loved ones. Though he was hog-tied, he sat up in a corner of the cage with his head down, rocking back and forth. The ropes that secured his wrists and ankles pierced his skin and burned like fire. The creatures had crushed his glasses and his vision was a blur. As he closed his eyes, he prayed to God for help even though he knew He didn't exist. When he opened his eyes, he could not help but glance at the Sétbætañ creatures that mocked him. He heard the horrific sounds of snake-like hisses above him, but dared not look up.

In another corner of the cage, his father was gasping for air. Suffering with a broken leg and back, Mr. Smiley looked ready to be put out of his misery. In the opposite corner of the cage was Karen. Still weakened by the poisonous forest plants and suffering from seasickness, she looked as helpless as Alex had ever seen her. Her confidence and strong will were broken. But soon their misery would be over, compliments of the mallie dragons -- huge, slithery, hungry creatures ready to enjoy a scrumptious feast.

As the sun set in the evening sky, the Sétbætañ began the execution ritual with the blowing of a huge horn. The creatures surrounded their victims in a circle.

In unison, the creatures chanted and sang songs of victory. Then, under the direction of Cúbaneg, the creatures stopped chanting and bowed their heads. A tall, distinguished-looking creature began to speak.

"We meet here for the execution of these humans. May the dragons leave no trace of this Earthly filth created by our eternal enemies, the Luçimarks. We say this in the name of our father who dwells forever, Ecaep."

The creatures resumed their chanting and Cúbaneg motioned to Ugnjengon to release the dragons. To do so, Ugnjengon had to pull a huge lever located near the top on the side of the cage.

And because Ugnjengon had great stature and strength, reaching and pulling down the lever would be no problem. The process would take all of five seconds. As he prepared to grab the lever a loud cannon blast was heard. It came from the other side of the Jymhamasbad Mountains.

Another, even louder cannon blast boomed in the background and the Sétbætañ knew there was trouble. That trouble came in the form of the United Alliance Marines -- a collection of marines from the nations of Earth. This combining of military forces had been President Topher's idea. And Flip was leading the charge.

"Fire!" shouted a voice from the brigade as the Alliance released ammunition from a tank now in the creatures' view. The missiles landed squarely within the pack of creatures. Several died instantly. The Sétbætañ needed a new plan of attack -- fight back or retreat. The creatures decided to fight back.

As they scrambled in chaotic fashion to defend themselves, more missiles landed, destroying any shelter the creatures had had. One missile just missed the cage holding Alex, Karen, and Mr. Smiley. The impact was enough to blow the door open. Alex, the only human still conscious, had a new sense of hope as he strained to see that the attack was coming from a human brigade.

Maybe we can survive this after all.

The mallie dragon cages were violently rattled loose by the missile blast, leaving them dangling off the edge of the larger cage beneath. One more strong vibration would certainly send them crashing to the ground. Alex knew he had to untie himself and lead the others to safety. While the creatures were preoccupied firing back at the Alliance, Alex quickly rubbed his tied wrists against the jagged bars of the cage. He continued to look up nervously at the rattling cages of the mallie dragons.

"Come on!" Alex said to himself out loud as he struggled to free himself. The ropes finally gave way. Relief came to Alex's burning wrists. He quickly untied his ankles. He needed to get to Karen and his father posthaste.

Meanwhile, Cúbaneg and his crew were having problems.

117

"Fire the cannons!" yelled Ugnjengon. Boom! Boom! Boom! the cannons echoed, along with machine-gun fire. But the cannons had no effect. The Alliance was moving in quickly on the undermanned Sétbætañ. Cúbaneg felt it was time to retreat. The Earthlings wouldn't stand a chance with the Sétbætañ at full strength.

With the majority of Ecaep's army wreaking havoc on Earth, Cúbaneg and his crew just didn't have enough in them to withstand the forces of the Alliance. As he ordered his fighters to retreat, a Sétbætañ soldier noticed that Alex had freed himself. Panicking, the creature walked through the open cage door with enough force to dislodge one of the mallie dragon cages above. It crashed down on top of him, opening on impact. The dragons poured out of the cage like running water and quickly bit the creature. "Nooooooo!" he screamed, attempting to escape. But the poison from the multiple bites quickly took effect and the creature fell to the ground not far outside the cage. The mallie dragons were able to locate the paralyzed creature and begin their feast. The creature screamed as he watched the dragons dine on his flesh and bone. He felt slight pain before succumbing.

During the Sétbætañ retreat, Alex had managed to untie his father and Karen. Karen had come around and was able to help Alex drag Mr. Smiley to a corner of the cage away from the dragons. But it wouldn't be long until they smelled the jelly, and escaping the cage looked nearly impossible with the dragons blocking the exit.

"How are we gonna get out of here with all of those snake things blocking the exit?" asked Karen.

"I'm not sure," said Alex. "But we're gonna have to move soon. Those snakes are gonna run out of Sétbætañ to eat."

Missiles continued to explode and the Sétbætañ continued to scatter. Mr. Smiley regained consciousness. Even though his every breath was painful, he had his wits about him.

"Alex, I want you to listen to me and listen well," said Mr. Smiley through short breaths. "I need you to get Karen out of here. You two can get past those snakes. It's your only chance."

"Dad, I'm not going to leave you," said Alex, propping up his father's head in his arms.

"Listen to me, son," said Mr. Smiley. "I am counting on you to save yourself and Karen. I also need you to help get the scrolls from those monsters. Mr. Smiley had begun coughing up blood. "And promise me that you'll never let your mother see me like this. Even after I'm gone. I have no more to give."

"Yes, dad," said Alex.

The sound of Alliance gun and missile fire was deafening. The Sétbætañ had gone into full-scale retreat. Alex and Karen could only lip-read what Mr. Smiley was saying. He was too weak to project his voice. But Alex and Karen were clear on what he wanted -- for them to get to safety and leave him behind. He didn't want to be a burden. As the tanks moved in, Alex and Karen saw their opportunity to make a move. They figured their best course of action would be to get safely out of the cage, then find help for Mr. Smiley.

"Dad, try not to move. We're gonna get you some help," said Alex. Tears welled as he softly placed his father's head onto the ground. He took Karen by the hand and instructed her to walk toward the cage door with their backs against the cage. The middle of the cage was filled with mallie dragons trying their best to home in on their next victims.

"We must walk quickly," said Alex as he guided Karen against the perimeter of the cage. "Once we find some help we'll come back and get my dad." Karen was looking in horror at the mallie dragons that covered the ground. One false move could send the dragons in their direction. Several were packed in the cage doorway. There was no way to pass without getting bitten. But time was of the essence. Several dragons had started crawling toward Mr. Smiley.

"I have an idea," said Alex. "Give me a boost so I can reach the top of the cage."

Despite being naked and terrified, the kids' minds were focused solely on getting out of that cage. Karen's cupped hands gave Alex support as he was hoisted to the top.

Hanging from the top, Alex could use his strength to swing

out of the cage doorway. Despite being scrawny, Alex was very good at playing a game called Lava Pit on the monkey bars at school. The object of the game was to avoid falling off the monkey bars and onto the "lava pit" on the ground. The last person on the monkey bars was the winner. Only now, to fall to the ground meant certain death.

Alex swung out of the cage doorway and ran full speed toward the brigade. Besides dead bodies, there were no Sétbætañ in sight. Before long, the tanks were right upon him. As he approached, he screamed and waved his arms frantically so he wouldn't be mistaken for the enemy. On the ground next to the tanks were several soldiers. Alex could hardly make out their blurry figures. As he got closer, he began to see a figure that looked familiar. It was Flip! Alex was overjoyed. Flip approached with a smirk on his face.

"Hey, you don't believe in wearing any clothes?" joked Flip. "Where are the others?"

"They're in this cage just over here," said Alex as he quickly led Flip and his men in the direction of the cage. "Hurry! My father's dying."

Flip could see that the cage was infested with mallie dragons. They were surrounding Karen and Mr. Smiley, ready to strike.

"Get back against the cage and take cover," ordered Flip. Karen did her best to push Mr. Smiley back toward the cage wall.

"Fire!" ordered Flip. The deafening sounds of machine guns filled the night sky as the green and black blood of the dragons exploded into the air. The threatening mallie dragons were dead. Flip and his men quickly stormed the cage to assist Karen and Mr. Smiley.

"Be careful, he's really gasping for air," said Karen. Tears welled up in Alex's eyes.

"Where's the medic?" screamed Flip. The doctor, Flip, and Alex quickly came to assist Mr. Smiley. The doctor placed Mr. Smiley's head on a pillow. Between irregular breaths, Mr. Smiley weakly forced out some words. Though he had his eyes closed, he could feel Alex's presence.

120

"Don't … let … them … use … that … seventh … scroll. It … will … destroy … all … of … mankind."

Alex didn't get a chance to respond. Mr. Smiley breathed a couple of short breaths and died. Karen tried to comfort Alex. He sobbed, blaming himself for all that had happened.

"If I would've stood up to that bully this never would've happened," said Alex.

"Don't blame yourself, Alex," said Flip. "There are others who need to take the blame in this whole mess and that starts with the U.S. government. We had the opportunity to work with your father a long time ago but didn't do it. Now we're in the mess we're in. Looking back on things, as far as I'm concerned, your father is a hero."

Keeping his promise to his father, Alex decided to bury Mr. Smiley on Caynonã. Doing this would ensure that Mrs. Smiley would never see Mr. Smiley's body. Flip and his men helped bury him in the fertile soil beneath a large tree. As the Alliance's campfire warmed the chilly night air, the military chaplain gave a brief but powerful sermon. It was clear that he was still a believer. As for Alex, he knew that he had to follow his father's last wish. He had to retrieve the seventh scroll. If not, neither the Earthlings, God, nor any other power would be able to stop the Sétbætañ.

Chapter 20
On the Trail

Spearheaded by President Topher, the United Alliance Marines had been created by the world's leaders to hunt down and annihilate the Sétbætañ. By mimicking the third scroll's technology, the Alliance was able to send tanks and hundreds of troops through a dimensional portal to Jymhamasbad. Thanks to Flip, and to a lesser degree to Alex, the U.A.M. located the creatures and sent them running. They'd used a new homing device that could track people or objects across other worlds or in other dimensions.

Back at the Watergate Hotel, when they'd learned that Mr. Smiley had been captured, Flip had placed a small homing device on Alex's shirt collar. He'd gambled on Alex trying to rescue his father, and his gamble had paid off. Luckily for Flip, the U.A.M., and the human captives, Alex's shirt was not far from them after it had been ripped from his body. Now, by order of the President, it was time to go through the dimensional portal and destroy the aliens with the myriad of weapons and new technology at the Alliance's disposal.

Since Mr. Smiley's death, Alex had experienced a sort of spiritual rebirth. After mourning, Alex began to accept his father's passing as serving the purpose of a greater good. Alex's heart hardened and he no longer was haunted by images of mallie dragons or of creatures ripping off his clothes and smearing him with goo. If fact, his father's death had made him a stronger person, less afraid, and even more proud to be Mr. Smiley's son.

According to Flip, the U.S. government now recognized Mr. Smiley as a hero for his attempt to save mankind by averting interglobal war. To the general public, the late Mr. Smiley grew to be seen as the person who bravely went face-to-face with the devil and his army before succumbing. When told of the news by military officials, Mrs. Smiley was particularly proud of her slain husband for facing the devil and his demons head-on. Though she cried over the loss of her husband and worried about the safety of her son, she believed that God and the power of good would prevail. As for Alex, he had stopped feeling sorry for himself. His mission was to assist the U.A.M. in destroying the Sétbætañ.

The Alliance was made up of three hundred and sixty-seven thousand soldiers. Of these, just over four thousand were Luçimarks. The majority of Luçimarks were uninterested in helping the humans fight the war, despite the fact that the Sétbætañ had waged war against them and their offspring, the humans. The Luçimarks were arrogant enough to believe that they could squash the Sétbætañ at any time. But they were either unaware of, or ignored the fact that, with the scrolls in the Sétbætañ's possession, the Sétbætañ were now a force to be reckoned with.

Three thousand Alliance troops had been sent on the Sétbætañ invasion. Flip was in a battalion of three hundred fifty in which he led a company of one hundred fifty. Of these, twelve were Luçimarks. The battalion took extra care to kill any lingering mallie dragons. They also gave Alex and Karen a fresh set of army clothes and gave Alex a new pair of glasses. Though he could not see with the new glasses as clearly as with his own, they worked well enough. While Flip and his men set up camp, he suggested the best course of action for the preteens.

"Alex, Karen, it's time for you to go home," said Flip. "You've done a fabulous job. We've got to get you two to safety."

"I'm not going anywhere," said a stone-faced Alex. "You can take Karen home but I'm not leaving."

"Well if you're not leaving, I'm not leaving," said Karen, slipping on a warm sweater. "We're always gonna be a team, Alex. And I'm not gonna leave your side."

Flip groaned.

"Look. This is cute and all, but fightin' a war against extraterrestrials is no walk in the park. I can't afford to have two dead preteens on my conscious."

"This isn't about you," Alex said sternly. "Those things killed my father, and they've killed millions of others. I can't believe

123

you're talking about sending us to safety. To safety where?"

Flip responded calmly.

"Listen, I understand you've just had a big loss."

"I don't think you do," fired back Alex. "You know, I blame myself for all that's happened. Heck, my father blamed himself and took that guilt to his grave. But I realize now that if the government hadn't been so crooked and tried to steal the scrolls for their own agenda, my father would be alive today and we wouldn't be in this situation."

"Those scrolls were government property," said Flip. "You can't steal from yourself."

"Oh, come on, Flip. Stop with the crap," said an exasperated Alex.

"Will you two stop it?" said Karen. "Now listen. Nothing is going to bring your father back, Alex. And Flip, you can forget about us going back home. You know as well as I that it's worse back on Earth than it is here. Alex isn't going back home. Look in his eyes Flip. You know it and I know it. And I'm not leaving his side. So you tell us what we need to do to help because we're all in and ready to fight."

"All right, all right," said Flip. "You two just signed your death certificates. But it ain't gonna be on my head when my men are heaping six feet of dirt on ya. I guess I can teach y'all how to protect yourselves. Lord knows you're gonna need it."

Flip took out two semi-automatic weapons, a handgun, and an M-16 rifle. He gave the handgun to Karen and the M-16 to Alex.

"What am I supposed to do with this?" said Karen. "And why does he get the rifle? Is it because he's a guy?"

"Come on," said Flip. "It doesn't make any difference. Trust me. They kill the same way. Alex, why don't you trade with her?"

"No way," said Alex.

"I swear, if the Setties don't kill me, you two will. Brent, fetch me another rifle, for God's sake."

Brent was a young marine in Flip's company and part of Flip's squad. He snickered at the pettiness of the kids.

"Okay, here ya go," said Brent, handing the rifle to Karen in a disparaging fashion. "Now ya know where the bullets come out, don't ya?"

"I think you better worry about where I'm about to put this!" said Karen, pretending to ram the grip of the rifle into Brent's butt.

"Okay, kiddies. That's enough," said Flip. "Let's get to training so you two can use these things. And this is going to be a crash course. We're setting out at zero four hundred tomorrow morning to hunt those creatures down. And Alex, you've just earned yourself another weapon," said Flip, handing him the handgun.

Through many months of trial and error, the military had finally figured out how to track Earth time on the planet of Caynonã. With help from the Luçimarks, the CIA had discovered that the creatures dwelled in Vuur, just northwest of the Asus Forest. This was contradictory to the belief that the Sétbætañ dwelled near their concentration camps, southwest of the forest.

It was four the next morning, and the troops on the island had to cross Lake Jymhamasbad to get back to Vuur. All the troops, including an exhausted Alex and Karen, were trained and ready to go. But without any method of transportation, they were literally marooned.

"Can't we just use the dimensional portal to get across?" asked Karen.

"We could, but the portal would only hold a few people at a time. I believe one of the scrolls has the command. Didn't you use that command when you first rescued us, Flip?" asked Alex.

"Alex, you're right. I used one of the commands from the sixth scroll," said Flip. "The command is called intradimensionality. But there's no way we could fit a whole brigade into the portal. I have another idea. Since our technology has grown to the point where we can now make contact with other worlds through dimensional portals with a simple phone call, I'll contact one of my buddies to send us some transportation."

Flip made his call and within seconds a dimensional portal

opened. Through came a small black submarine. The submarine could hold thirty people, so had plenty of room for Flip, Alex, Karen, and a squad of fourteen soldiers. The submarine landed safely in the water, docked comfortably against the shore.

"Don't you love it? The power of the third scroll. All right, everyone aboard," ordered Flip. The soldiers, followed by Karen, Alex, and Flip, boarded the submarine.

"This is so cool," said Alex, climbing down the ladder into the submarine. Karen's eyes were as wide as saucers as she looked around in amazement. All the buttons, levers, and odd gadgets seemed to operate in harmony. In the submarine to meet them was the ship's commander, Master Sergeant Rane Mackie.

"Welcome aboard the Arowana," shouted Mackie as the troops loaded. "Get as comfortable as you can 'cause I believe we're in for a rocky ride."

As soon as the last soldier boarded, the Arowana undocked and dove into the icy Lake Jymhamasbad water.

Alex and Karen attempted to get comfortable. The request for a submarine had made them wonder why one was needed. It wasn't as if the island was miles from the mainland, and they'd arrived on Jymhamasbad in a medium-sized boat. Flip's crew and the rest of the U.A.M. thought a submarine could prove useful for underwater exploration.

As Flip, Mackie, and the other soldiers discussed strategy, Alex and Karen entertained themselves by playing a game of Go Fish. It was the only card game Alex knew, besides Solitaire. Playing cards or video games was not Alex's cup of tea. Reading books or surfing the web for historical facts piqued his interest. It seemed as though it were taking forever to cross the lake. Alex guessed they'd been underwater for at least two hours. And with a high-powered submarine, that just didn't make sense. It had taken roughly two hours for the Sétbætañ creatures to sail their makeshift boat across the lake. But Alex didn't realize that there were floating rocks, possibly formed by an erupting underwater volcano, and debris in the lake. Mackie had to navigate the submarine with precision, as an astronaut would guide his spaceship through a meteor storm.

Before long, a very odd-looking, large object was spotted on the submarine's sonar panel. It could easily have been a huge boulder or volcano. But the object was moving fast toward the Arowana. Alex and Karen were so absorbed in their game they were oblivious to what was happening.

"Soldiers, brace for possible impact," shouted Mackie as the sonar started beeping rapidly.

"That thing is too big and it's coming in too fast for us to take a hit," shouted Flip. "We need to slow it down. Let's see if it can handle a missile at point-blank range.

"Will do, captain," shouted Mackie. "Get ready to fire. Three… two… one…"

Mackie fired. Seconds later the crew felt the waves generated by the missile's impact rock the submarine back and forth.

Alex and Karen gripped their seats tight.

"Soldiers, brace for impact," shouted Mackie once again. "Three… two… one… fire!" This time the missile failed to hit its target, which had moved completely off the sonar screen.

"Where the heck did it go?" asked an exasperated Flip.

He didn't have to wait long to get his answer.

The Arowana started shaking violently. Alex and Karen were thrown from their chairs to the hard floor. Chaos ensued as the crew scrambled to take their positions. The playing cards showered the area like confetti.

"What's going on?" screamed Karen as the Arowana continued to shake violently.

"Just take cover!" screamed Flip, trying to remain upright.

What was rocking the submarine wasn't waves from the impact of any missile. It was the impact of the Krieatine. The creature that had attacked Brownsville in its attempt to capture Mr. Smiley dwelled beneath the lake and had been summoned by the Sétbætañ to attack. Now that it was close up, the sonar screen showed a clear image. That image horrified the crew.

"What is that thing?" screamed Flip. "It's tearing this ship apart.

The creature had immobilized the vessel with its three strong arms, and then violently rocked it back and forth. Leaks began to sprout inside the submarine.

"Ya better think of something quick, commander," yelled Flip. "My crew and I can't go out like this."

"I'm gonna try to loosen its grip by backing up," said Mackie.

Mackie tried reversing direction and for a second, the creature seemed to lose its grip. That gave Mackie an idea.

"I'm gonna rock this boat back and forth," shouted Mackie.

Mackie repeatedly switched between forward and reverse gears. The creature's ability to maintain its grip was weakened and it began to fatigue.

"Come on, Mackie, drive this boat!" screamed Flip.

Mackie continued the back and forth action. Something had to give soon because the pressure from the struggle had the Arowana taking in quite a bit of water. Once again, Alex and Karen found themselves in a dire situation that didn't seem to have a possible positive outcome.

"The water's almost up to my knees," shouted Alex.

"We could drown," shouted back Karen.

The vessel broke loose. This angered the Krieatine. Mackie figured he had better take a shot while he had the chance.

"Fire!" shouted Mackie. With this order, a missile fired from the Arowana and hit the creature on its leg at point-blank range. This only managed to slow it down. The creature was still in pursuit.

"Fire!" shouted Mackie. This time the submarine quickly emitted two missiles that hit the creature squarely on its torso. This rocked the Krieatine, causing it to trip over a boulder and fall flat on its back. The crew roared in jubilation. But the creature was not to be deterred. It managed to return to its feet and continue its attack.

"I can't believe how strong this thing is," shouted Flip. "The missiles aren't doing a thing."

"I've got another idea," said Mackie.

Mackie fired another missile at the creature, hitting it on the side of its torso. The Krieatine staggered backward, trying to maintain its balance. Then Mackie released a long, steel cable from the vessel and attempted to wrap it around the creature's

128

neck.

"Got it," said Mackie.

"Fire!" shouted Mackie once again.

This missile rocked the creature backward, tightening the wire around its neck. Mackie's plan had worked. The creature was strangling.

"Again, fire!"

Once again the creature was knocked backward while the submarine pulled in the opposite direction. The Krieatine's aggression was dwindling.

"Keep doing it, it's working," screamed Flip, his confidence growing.

Just then, the creature managed to grab the wire and started pulling the submarine toward itself. Mackie gunned the Arowana in the opposite direction. The engines started to smoke. The struggle was taking its toll on the vessel.

"Just cut the line. It's too much stress on the engines," shouted Flip.

As Mackie started to retreat, he came up with an idea. There was a reef of jagged rocks just above the creature's head. Mackie fired a missile into the reef, crashing it down on the creature. The weight of the rocks pinned the creature to the lake floor.

"Finish it off," Flip ordered as the Arowana shot two missiles at the creature's head.

Mackie's gamble had proved successful. The impact of the missiles destroyed the powerful but helpless creature by blowing off its head.

The crew cheered as relief settled in.

"Take us up to the surface. We're right where we need to dock," said Flip.

As the submarine rose to the surface, rocks and remains of the Krieatine softly bounced off the vessel. The Arowana and its crew were safely ashore.

"Now *that* was an adventure," quipped Alex.

"I'm so glad to see dry land," said Karen.

As the crew exited, a sand storm began to form under the dark-red sky. The surroundings made it clear that the crew had arrived at its destination in Vuur. Waiting for them were the other members of the U.A.M., led by General Darius Miller. They numbered over three thousand strong. Thus far the humans had done a good job of keeping casualties to a minimum. And every soldier would be needed in the U.A.M.'s next endeavor.

Chapter 21
Decoding the Scrolls

The humans and the Luçimarks first exchanged technologies in 1918, when some German explorers discovered the scrolls in a cave near the town of Stuttgart, Germany. The Luçimarks, always looking for an advantage against their adversaries, received weapons technology in exchange for some of their alien technology the Germans were seeking.

Though the Luçimarks weren't able to translate all of the scrolls they'd stolen from the Sétbætañ, they were able to translate one -- the first scroll, which allowed dimensional space travel. Sharing this technology with the humans would pacify them and make them feel obligated to provide the Luçimarks the weaponry they needed.

The Luçimarks also needed a place to hide the stolen scrolls from the Sétbætañ who were searching both Earth and Caynonã for their prized possessions. The Luçimarks had been coming to Earth for centuries prior to meeting with the Germans, and felt that hiding the scrolls on Earth would be best. When searching for the scrolls to return them to Caynonã, they found them missing from their hiding spot in the cave. They finally recovered them when they discovered a human searching for something in the spot where the scrolls had originally been hidden.

Recovering the scrolls took the Luçimarks twelve years. Thus from 1906 until 1918, the Luçimarks had roamed the Earth invisible to human eyes, searching for the scrolls. When the Luçimarks discovered that the scrolls were in the possession of the German government, they cut a deal with the Germans that would prove beneficial to both parties.

The Luçimarks' desire for guns and weapons of war stemmed from their continued desire to dominate the Sétbætañ. Through years of researching the ways of their human creations, they knew that the humans had a tendency to wage war against one another. The weapons that the aliens desired included automatic and semi-automatic guns, tanks, missile launchers, chemical weapons, and military aircraft. Though it had been years since the Sétbætañ had risen to challenge the Luçimarks, an occasional air raid on the land of Vuur would keep the Sétbætañ in check. The Luçimarks were impressed not only with the humans' ability to create guns and firearms, but with their ability to create weapons of mass destruction, which could be used as a last resort.

While the Luçimarks craved guns and war weapons to maintain their advantage over the Sétbætañ, the Germans sought possession of the scrolls to enable dimensional space travel. This technology was discovered through years of research by the German scientists after the scrolls were removed from the cave. They convinced the Luçimarks it would be best to continue hiding the scrolls here on Earth, away from their enemy. They promised the Luçimarks that they would take care in hiding the scrolls. The Sétbætañ considered this an act of war by the humans.

The Germans believed that access to dimensional space travel could give them an overwhelming advantage over their enemies during battles. The problem was how they could pull it off. Much of what they discovered about the scroll's powers seemed like black magic. But through continued research the Germans learned that the opening of dimensional portals was a scientific, not supernatural, phenomenon, involving voice recognition and satellite technology. Much of today's advanced communication technology was already in place in the early twentieth century. But the public was led to believe it could only be the result of supernatural phenomena.

During World War II, the CIA discovered that voice recognition technology was originally introduced to humanity in 1918. And while the Russians and the Americans led the masses to believe that Sputnik was the first artificial satellite, the Luçimarks had been launching satellites into orbit for decades.

The CIA learned that the technology worked like this: The writing on the scroll must be recited aloud, with precision, at a level above a whisper. The satellite recognizes and translates the command contained in the text, sending a signal back to the

Earth's surface to open a dimensional portal. The satellites were programmed to open a portal to the world of the programmer's choosing which would bring the traveler close to their desired location. The scroll text must be recited correctly or the technology would not work. The gravitational orbiting of the satellites around Caynonã and Earth could cause a traveler to land in an altogether different location on the chosen planet. Because of this natural phenomenon this could mean landing in Urodae instead of Vuur.

The satellites were programmed to follow any command recited from the text on any of the seven scrolls, including reddening the skies, causing firestorms, and awakening alien creatures. These satellites still orbited both Caynonã and Earth. They were invisible to humans and dispersed among the human-made satellites.

The text of the scrolls is in an ancient alien language created by the Sétbætañ and used for communication by both alien races. Called Coptic Egyptian on Earth, this language was used by the Luçimarks when they colonized the planet. It was the language first adopted by their creation, the humans.

The scrolls had been created by the Sétbætañ to fight the Luçimarks. Not only had the Sétbætañ created the language, they had also built all the necessary equipment to make them functional, including the satellites orbiting Caynonã. The language, the scrolls, and the satellites were created years before the birth of Ecaep. The satellites and scrolls were stolen by Luçimark Supreme Leader Mataralin and strategically placed around Caynonã, Earth, and other planets.

But the Sétbætañ had made the text difficult to understand. They'd created subtle nuances that made it difficult to decipher and nearly impossible to translate. The Luçimarks inability to decode and use the scrolls frustrated them. But simply having the scrolls in their possession gave the Luçimarks an advantage, and placed fear in the hearts of the Sétbætañ. Knowing the scrolls' capabilities, and lacking the resources to recapture them, the Sétbætañ felt their best strategy for survival was to lie low and exact their revenge by torturing the humans.

133

Their hope was that the humans would turn on their creators and join the Sétbætañ in their fight against the Luçimarks. But the Luçimarks used religious propaganda, influencing the humans to worship them as loving angels or gods, and fear the Sétbætañ as devils. This was done through texts such as the Bible and the Dead Sea Scrolls, and through the use of supernatural phenomena. This trickery proved successful, as evidenced by human belief in deities throughout history.

Despite possessing the scrolls for more than thirty-nine years, the Germans did not get a chance to use the technology as they'd intended. During World War I, they were more interested in intraworld than interworld travel via the dimensional portal. During World War II, the Nazis had envisioned using the scrolls to launch surprise attacks on their enemies. But neither they nor the Luçimarks knew that intraworld travel was possible. They had not translated the sixth scroll.

The Germans believed that the first scroll was the only one that contained the command for dimensional travel. They believed the only way to launch a dimensional surprise attack on France, for example, would be to launch that attack from Caynonã. The Luçimarks wanted no part of Earthly wars. They had their own problems. Through their numerous battles, the Sétbætañ were able to acquire and copy the Luçimarks' German weapons technology.

The Luçimarks did not allow the Nazis to launch attacks from Caynonã. So the Nazis attempted to expand on the technology on their own. Fortunately, Germany was defeated and the scrolls confiscated before they could succeed.

Chapter 22
The Calm Before the Storm

As the soldiers were settling down after pitching their tents, a giant sandstorm began to develop under the dark Vuur sky. The winds howled, blowing with great intensity. Many soldiers worried if their shelter would make it through the night. That was the least of Alex's worries. He was focused on his mother and how she was coping with the changes in the world. Now that he was settled, and the technology had been expanded to allow interplanetary communication, Alex had the opportunity to contact his mother to see how she was doing. Using Flip's device, he quickly dialed his mom's cell number.

"Hello?"

"Mom, it's Alex."

"How are you, my son?" said Mrs. Smiley, overjoyed at hearing Alex's voice.

"I'm fine mom, how about you?"

"I'm doing okay given the circumstances. I've been staying with your aunt and uncle for a while now and we've been rationing food and water for months. I'll be glad when this is all over. Everyone feels that we are winning the war. It won't be too long before those demons are sent back to hell. When will you and Karen be returning?"

"It should be soon, mom."

"Good. We still plan on holding a funeral for your father when you come home. I wish I could have seen him one last time."

Alex was not confident when or even if he and Karen would return. He was afraid to ask what time of year it was. He had originally calculated that they'd been gone for weeks. But with his mother's statement that they'd been rationing food for months, there was no telling how much Earth time he had lost.

"Well I look forward to seeing you," said Mrs. Smiley. "When you get back I know a new church that we can go to. It's called The Church of New Beginnings. Nearly everyone's a member. Over a thousand members already. They were going to call it The Church of the Apocalyptic Survivors, but the church leaders thought it sounded too scary. They hold three-hour services on Sundays, Tuesday, Fridays, and Saturdays. And they only ask for thirty-five percent of your earnings for tithing."

"Thirty-five percent?" said Alex, not even mentioning the number of hours and days church members were required to attend. "That's highway robbery. What if you're unable to work to earn any money? And isn't feeding yourself more important?"

"The church teaches that if you pay God first then treasures will follow," said Mrs. Smiley. "And that includes food. Think about it. Thirty-five percent isn't all that much. Plus, most of the church members get monetary help from the government anyway. But no thanks to that idiot Topher."

"Oh, come on, mom. Can you give the guy a break? I think he's doing a pretty good job given the circumstances," said Alex.

"There's something about that man, I tell you," said Mrs. Smiley. "TAPC News reported he was going to try and negotiate with the demons. Think about it. Negotiating with demons. Things that are killing us. I swear, he's the devil himself!"

Realizing he'd be fighting a losing battle, Alex decided not to argue. "Okay mom, we can go to church once I get back. It was great to hear your voice."

"Yours too, hon," said Mrs. Smiley. "I love you."

"Love you, too."

After the kids spoke with their parents, all the soldiers were ordered to bed.

"We have a big day tomorrow," said Flip. "We've got 'em on the run. Those Setties see that we're three thousand strong and it's apparent that they can't take the heat!"

"Do you think we'll run into them tomorrow?" asked Karen.

"I don't think; I know," said a confident Flip. "We've been tracking them ever since they left Jymhamasbad. "Come here," said Flip as he led Alex and Karen from out of the canopy into the cold Vuur wind.

"You see those mountains over there?" asked Flip. "That's where the Setties are. Just over those mountains, the Vuur Mountains. And when we get there, we're gonna splatter some

Settie blood. Now you two report to your quarters."

Flip left Alex and Karen to go to his quarters.

"Great. I can't wait to use that rifle they gave me," said Karen, mimicking shooting. "What's wrong Alex? You look nervous."

"I'm more concerned than nervous," said Alex.

"Come on, Alex. You heard what Flip said. It sounds like it should be a piece of cake. Plus, I hear that we're really kicking butt back on Earth."

"I just don't think it'll be as easy as he thinks," said Alex.

Flanked by tanks, jeeps, Humvees, and other military vehicles, the troops marched out in high, dusty winds toward the Vuur Mountains. Alex and Karen rode in a Humvee with Flip, Mackie, and Brent. They noticed the temperature begin to rise as they approached the mountains.

"Man, it's sure gotten hot," said Flip, wiping his brow. "And the wind is still blowin'."

"Feels like we're under a hairdryer," said Karen.

The troops approached the mountain range, marveling at how the highest peak towered toward the sky. Earth scientists had concluded that it rose ten thousand one hundred and fifty-nine meters, dwarfing Mount Everest in the Himalayas. Unlike on Earth's mountain ranges, the temperature on the Vuur mountain ranges increased with elevation.

"Okay troops, let's get to the other side of this mountain," ordered General Miller.

Alex looked at the challenge in front of them. *There's a chance that most of us will never see this side of the mountain again*, he thought. He tried not to be pessimistic, but he felt the need to be realistic. Karen, who seemed to sense Alex's quiet and concerned mood, broke the silence.

"So what do you think, Alex?"

"I don't know what to think Karen. I really don't."

As the Humvees and tanks climbed to the other side of the Vuur Mountains, the temperature climbed steadily. Despite the usual cloud cover, the temperature rose from fifty-four degrees Fahrenheit in the morning to eighty-one degrees by noon. By early afternoon, the temperature had risen to one hundred three. The blowing wind provided no relief. The searing heat combined with the wind to bake the troops like a convection oven. Sand blew off the mountain, smashing into the troops' faces like hard-driven snow. Many of the troops began to suffer from heat exhaustion. Brent was one of them.

"Ya gotta keep yourself hydrated, man," said Flip, helping the medics administer liquids to Brent.

"I am, but it's doing no good," Brent said.

"His vitals are not looking good, sir," said the medic. "Many of the other soldiers have the same symptoms."

"Check as many soldiers as you can to see if they have any symptoms," ordered General Miller. "We need to make sure that we're strong enough for battle."

The troops stopped their progress over the mountain and got medical assistance. Alex and Karen made sure to stay hydrated. In fact, Alex drank so much that he had to relieve himself several times. Needing to stop, Alex spotted a small cave in the mountain that was partially hidden by a sand dune. He figured the cave would provide temporary shelter from the searing winds, sand, and heat. While relieving himself in the cave, he noticed a flashing light in the darkness. Thinking that it was a fellow soldier, he decided to investigate.

"Anyone else in here? Hello?" said Alex into the darkness.

"I guess not," Alex said to himself, his voice echoing off the cave walls.

As Alex was getting ready to exit the cave, a small figure began to uncloak in front of him: the vy-imp, a species of Sétbætañ. Vy-imps are no more than two feet tall, and skilled at spying in small spaces and caves. The small, bright, beady eyes of the creature illuminated in the darkness of the cave, staring evilly at Alex. Alex screamed. His loud pleas for help were drowned out by the howling winds. Not wanting to waste another minute, Alex attempted a mad dash to the cave exit. The imp blocked his path at every turn. It was quick on its feet and stopped Alex from advancing. The imp made horrible, loud sounds in a pattern that suggested it was calling for help.

Frightened and desperate, Alex leaped over the imp and, tripping on its head, fell face-first to the ground. The imp had fallen to the ground but managed to grab hold of Alex's foot.

"Let go!" screamed Alex, kicking the creature in the head. The imp tightened its grip and continued to call for backup.

"Get off!" screamed Alex, as he kicked the imp's head with all his might. He tried dragging the creature but fell back to the ground. The imp was extremely strong for its size.

After a long struggle, Alex remembered the handgun he'd been given. Flip frequently reminded him to carry his weapons at all times. He tended to forget. But luckily, Alex decided to strap on the handgun before going into the cave. He was trained to carry the gun in his black holster. And Flip had trained him well. He took the gun, switched off the safety lock and pulled the trigger. The bang from the gun echoed loudly as the creature's grip went limp. Blood and brain matter sprayed all over the cave floor. Alex got up and ran out of the cave.

"There's a monster in there!"

"Calm down, son," said Flip. "What, exactly, did you see?"

Before Alex could answer, hundreds of Sétbætañ began to uncloak. They came out of mountain caves, and from behind sand dunes and boulders. They had led the troops into a trap.

"It's an ambush," screamed Flip.

Within seconds, the Sétbætañ attacked. They fired guns, fought with swords, launched grenades, even engaged in hand-to-hand combat. Cúbaneg and Ugnjengon were leading the charge.

"Destroy the evil humans. Kill those who have destroyed one of our mightiest warriors, the Krieatine!" shouted Cúbaneg.

The creatures attacked at full force. Gunfire and grenades rained down on a military force unprepared for the ambush. They had underestimated the Sétbætañ. And the heat exhaustion afflicting so many of the troops made fighting back even more difficult. The creatures were killing the weakened soldiers with ease. Flip and his gang had to act fast.

"Everybody cloak! Everybody cloak!" screamed Flip.

To the soldiers' surprise, nothing happened. Even Alex and

Karen were unsuccessful. Alex knew he had taken plenty of the cloaking tablets prior to setting out across the mountain. *Maybe it's from the extreme stress.*

Even Flip, who was the most experienced at cloaking, was unable to disappear. The inability was driving him nuts.

"What the heck is going on, did we get ahold of a bad batch of plants?" asked Flip, of no one in particular.

The fault rested with human anatomy. The extreme heat had prevented the soldiers from properly digesting the plant enzymes that allow cloaking. Sétbætañ anatomy, however, is constructed to handle extreme heat, and the creatures used their cloaking ability to its full advantage.

"Noooo! Aaaaaahhhh!" screamed soldiers, as they were picked off left and right by the creatures. The soldiers' advantage in numbers was dwindling because of the Sétbætañ's strategy. Alex, who'd been the first to spot the creatures, noticed that the majority of them were coming out of hiding spots in the mountain.

"Flip, they're coming from the other side of the mountain," said Alex.

"You heard 'im general," said Flip.

"I gotcha. Fire into the mountain on my command. Fire!" ordered General Miller.

A rocket hit the side of the mountain. Scores of dead Sétbætañ rained down the side of the mountain. The confidence of the soldiers was restored.

"Again ... fire!" A rocket was fired into another section of the mountain. This time, hundreds of Sétbætañ were killed.

"We've got 'em on the run," yelled Flip.

Thanks to Alex and the quick thinking of the U.A.M., the Sétbætañ had suffered a devastating setback that included a significant loss of lives. The creatures were forced to retreat and devise another plan of attack. It wouldn't be easy. They had just lost one of their greatest warriors in the battle.

While the creatures retreated with the humans in pursuit, Ugnjengon kneeled over Cúbaneg, who'd been on the mountainside.

140

"No! Get up. Rise, my leader. Ri_iiise!" shouted Ugnjengon. There was no response from Cúbaneg's limp body. Ugnjengon lifted his leader, slung him over his wide right shoulder, and trekked across the mountain, avoiding the onslaught of the humans.

The humans pressed on with their attack. Hundreds of Sétbætañ fell in their path. The humans had the creatures in disarray. With the loss of Cúbaneg, their army was a rudderless ship.

The aura of death permeated the castle as Ugnjengon walked toward Ecaep's throne. It was a long and lonely walk, quiet throughout. Each thudding step the creature took echoed in the hallways. The lighting was dim, reflecting the somber mood. The Sétbætañ soldiers, lined up on either side of Ecaep's throne, looked at Ugnjengon and the body he was carrying in disbelief. Ugnjengon looked at Ecaep solemnly, as he lay Cúbaneg before him.

"What has happened to my mightiest of warriors?" asked Ecaep.

"It was the humans! They have taken him, like the Krieatine, from us," said Ugnjengon.

"And what about the rest of our army?"

"The humans have killed many of our soldiers and they're marching toward our land."

"They are marching toward their deaths," said Ecaep. "We shall wait for them as an arachnid awaits its prey. Go, round up every beast, large and small, and prepare them for war.

"Yes, my lord," said Ugnjengon.

"Wait a minute, I have another idea," said Ecaep. "I wish for you to gather the troops. But before we deal with the humans we're going to pay someone a visit. And we're going to settle our differences with the scum once and for all."

Chapter 23
The Battle of Caynonã

Over fifteen thousand Sétbætañ, soldiers and civilians, mourned the death of Cúbaneg in a funeral fit for a king. The funeral was held in a stadium-like structure with chains of gold hanging from its rafters, and sheets of silver covering its walkways. Ribbons of red silk lined the main floor, matching the blood-red color of the sky. Five hundred soldiers stood on the floor of the stadium, facing Cúbaneg's body. Ecaep stood on a podium directly over the slain leader, preparing to give his speech. All of the creatures, civilians included, raised weapons pointing to the sky. Cúbaneg's popularity and admiration among his people was second only to Ecaep's. For years, Cúbaneg had led his armies into battle against the Luçimarks, led the search initiative for the scrolls, and helped lead the technological advancement of his people. This was one of the most tragic days in Sétbætañ history.

"Today we mourn the loss of a great warrior, brother, friend," said Ecaep to the masses. "But this day also represents the beginning of a new chapter of the Sétbætañ where we no longer forgive or show compassion to our enemies.

"We have come to the hour where we crush our eternal enemy, the Luçimarks. For centuries they have held their swords to our necks. Stripping us of our technology, land, and resources. For miliyous they have equated our culture with the underbelly of a maggot. Enslaved, tortured, and slain our people. But no more. No more shall we bear the pain that they inflict. With the power of the Ancient Scrolls, we shall turn the tables and inflict the pain, the torture, and the death upon them. We will start a new Great Rebellion in which all of our enemies are eradicated. This is what our slain warrior Cúbaneg would want. Let's not allow the greatest warrior in the history of the Sétbætañ to die in vain. This is the will of your lord Ecaep. I know this is what you desire. Let's once and for all destroy the Luçimarks and all of their offspring."

The crowd went wild. As Ugnjengon took the podium, the

crowd began to stomp.

"Hold up your weapons," screamed Ugnjengon.

The crowd obliged and he let out a loud roar.

"To the death!" he screamed.

"To the death!" screamed the crowd.

Ugnjengon led the crowd of soldiers from the stadium.

The humans tracked the enemy's movement. During the battle on the mountain, they'd placed homing devices on the surviving creatures. And though the humans now had the creatures on the run, many soldiers had lost their lives. Some fell in battle and others, including Brent, had died of heat exhaustion. The number of U.A.M. soldiers was decreased considerably, but this did not discourage Flip and the other military leaders.

"We really got 'em on the run," Flip said to General Miller. "But I'm a little concerned about where they're headed."

"Where's that, captain?" asked Miller.

"They look to be headed toward the Asus Forest."

"The Asus Forest?"

"Yes, and there's no way we should go chasing them in there."

"We need to head them off. You know that Urodae is on the other side of the forest?" said Miller.

"I know," responded Flip. General, we'll need more troops and we need to warn the Luçimarks.

"You handle redirecting of troops and I'll handle getting us more men," said Miller.

"No problem, general," said Flip. "I hope we can get to Urodae in time to give the Luçimarks some help. Besides going through that forest, going over the Vuur Mountains is the quickest way."

After three days of travelling, the Sétbætañ arrived in Urodae. With troops numbering over fifteen thousand, they were an imposing force. Not only did they have a seemingly endless number of foot soldiers, but they were assisted by countless flying dragons and Selanon, which littered the blue Urodae sky until it turned black. Giant trolls assisted by tanks, cannons, and rocket launchers led the front line, flanked by thousands of vy-imps. Wolves, devils, and other monstrous creatures made up the rest of the army. Many of them carried assault rifles and swords. Some were armed with mallie dragons. Though most of the soldiers traveled on foot, some rode xyheilamanders for both transportation and added defense. Other creatures traveled by air with assistance from the Selanon, who carried them by the shoulders.

Despite the planned raid, and thanks to the humans' warnings, the Luçimarks were prepared. Sort of. The Luçimarks were used to surprise raids by the Sétbætañ. In the past they were able to defeat their enemy with numbers alone. But this time their arrogance would betray them. Not only did the Sétbætañ arrive with more than fifteen thousand foot soldiers -- their largest army ever -- but they were assisted by the Selanon, providing the aerial attack. These creatures had acted only as spies in previous encounters. The Sétbætañ army totaled eighteen thousand troops.

As Ugnjengon and his troops approached Mataralin's castle, they were headed off by four thousand Luçimark soldiers. The Luçimarks knew they were ill-prepared when they saw the vast Sétbætañ army in front of them. Knowing he had the advantage, Ugnjengon readied his soldiers for battle.

"My soldiers, today is the day we get vengeance for Cúbaneg's death. Now is the time to crush those who have crushed our people. In the name of Ecaep, let us battle to the death!"

The soldiers began to stomp in unison. The Selanon, flying overhead, screeched with high, piercing voices. Never before had the Sétbætañ looked so intimidating.

Just hours before the Sétbætañ invasion, Mataralin and various Luçimark officials huddled in a remote castle room, circulating blame for their current predicament.

"What were our military leaders thinking? Those beasts are on the march and we don't have enough troops," asked Mataralin.

"It's clear that we've underestimated the resolve of the Sétbætañ," said Inspyron who acted as the Luçimarks' prime minister. "In our past encounters, four thousand troops were more than enough to handle them."

"Well it won't be enough this time. Have your heard of the vastness of their army? Our spies report that they have more than fifteen thousand troops and that doesn't include the Selanon and other flying creatures," retorted Mataralin. "Our minister of defense felt that those stupid humans needed our help in their fight against the Sétbætañ on Earth I have told parliament all along that we should've minded our own business. The humans mean nothing to us."

"My lord, you do realize that ignoring the battle on Earth was impossible?" said Inspyron. "The Sétbætañ's main goal was to use the recovered scrolls not just against the humans, but against our people. And even though you care nothing for the humans, you must admit that they have been valuable allies against our enemy in the past. Also, our informants tell us that there are roughly twenty-seven hundred human soldiers here on Caynonã. They're headed to Urodae to assist us in battle."

"I wouldn't care what those monsters did to them, here or on Earth," shouted Mataralin, growing more irrational by the second. "What have the humans helped us with? Some weapons? It's not as if we couldn't have created them ourselves or stolen them from the Sétbætañ. And how many troops have we wasted trying to help them?"

"Around ten thousand, my lord."

"Ten thousand? I thought we sent seventeen thousand."

"We did, my lord. Unfortunately, we lost ten thousand in

battle."

Mataralin, who had been standing, sighed and slumped down in a nearby chair. He, along with the other congressional leaders, felt powerless to stop their impending doom. The only way the Luçimarks had a fighting chance was not only to bring back the remaining troops, but to rely heavily on the humans. This would give the Luçimarks thirteen thousand seven hundred soldiers, which would come close to matching the Sétbætañ forces. But time was not on their side. The U.A.M. was close to joining the Luçimark army, but it would take time to gather the Luçimark troops still fighting the war on Earth. And the great Sétbætañ army was emerging from the Asus Forest. Mataralin, knowing that the survival of his race rested on his shoulders, did what he felt was best for his people.

"Inspyron, given the circumstances, we need to bring back our troops," said a deflated Mataralin.

"And what of the humans on Earth?" asked Inspyron.

"They're going to have to fend for themselves."

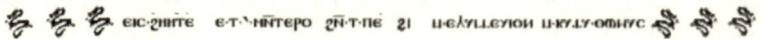

It was sundown when the U.A.M. joined the Luçimark troops. The Sétbætañ chanting and screeching grew louder as they readied themselves for war. Despite their disadvantage in numbers, the Luçimarks had the higher ground. The castle sat on a hill overlooking the land. Not only were they on the defensive to guard Mataralin's castle, but they also had to protect the rest of Urodae. Flip, Alex, and Karen could not believe their eyes as they looked down upon the Sétbætañ army. Flip saw the fright and doubt in the kids' eyes.

"Now you listen to me, and you listen well," said Flip. "You are U.A.M. soldiers now. So I want you to get that look off your face. The Luçimarks have got our backs."

In no way did Flip's words comfort Alex. Both he and Karen saw that it was all about the numbers. The Sétbætañ army outnumbered them by thousands and it looked as though each creature was holding a weapon. A plethora of guns, missiles,

146

knives, cannons, tanks, and swords were at the Sétbætañ army's disposal. The U.A.M./Luçimark army, despite some highly sophisticated weaponry, such as the Punisher super rifle, looked like small potatoes by comparison. Seeing that Karen was very frightened, Alex turned and looked into her eyes. He was also frightened but had learned how to control it. He grabbed her hands.

"Karen, I want you to know that I've got your back."

"I know you do, Alex. You've always had my back. And you should know that I have yours."

"I know you do," said Alex.

Just as Alex and Karen embraced, an emblazed arrow emerged from the night sky and landed among the Luçimark troops. This was followed by thousands more. They landed on the castle, setting fires, or pierced the protective gear of the soldiers. Flaming arrows lit up the night sky as they rained down upon the U.A.M./Luçimark forces. It was the beginning of an attack by the Sétbætañ, who began to storm up the hill toward Mataralin's castle.

"Fire your weapons," shouted General Miller.

"Get inside the castle," Flip shouted to Alex and Karen as Sétbætañ foot soldiers began scaling the castle walls. The Sétbætañ's flying creatures landed on the castle in the defensive areas occupied by the U.A.M./Luçimark army. Many Selanon dropped Sétbætañ foot soldiers onto the castle grounds for battle. The U.A.M. did their best to slaughter as many of the flying creatures as possible, but the numbers were too great. As she and Alex headed inside the castle, Karen was attacked by a Selanon creature.

"You get off her," shouted Alex. The creature had pinned Karen to the ground. Karen screamed in horror as the creature tried to bite her face.

Alex, who had only fired a gun once in his life to kill the vy-imp, took out his gun and fired repeatedly. He was so nervous, it took him three shots to level the creature with a bullet to its chest. Karen quickly leaped off the ground as the creature fell limp. Now angry, she wanted to shoot as many of the Sétbætañ

147

as possible.

"Why did you use that hand gun when you have an assault rifle?" shouted Karen. "Let's kill some Setties."

"You're welcome," responded Alex.

Flip was even more concerned about the kids.

"Get in that castle now, soldiers."

"No, we're going to stay out here to fight," said Alex.

Flip saw the fire in Alex's eyes and dared not challenge him. He welcomed the kids to fight by his side.

"Okay, then. What are you waiting for? Help me kill some Setties."

To counter the Sétbætañ aerial attack, the Luçimarks took to the skies with retired or abandoned fighting aircraft such as the Boeing P-12 and the German-built Heinkel. But these World War II planes didn't have the impact of other bombers from that era. The flying creatures and the missiles from the Sétbætañ ground soldiers were able to quickly counterattack, bringing the planes crashing down from the sky. Mataralin watched his army's destruction from the castle.

"Look at this. Do you see what I'm seeing?" Mataralin said to Inspyron. "Our army is getting destroyed. We gave the humans superior weaponry and this is how they repay us? Look at the inferior aircraft we have, thanks to them."

"The sniper rifle, grenade, land mine, rocket launcher, and the machine gun are weapons that helped them against their earthly enemies. Those are weapons that we gave them during their World Wars. This is what they give us in our time of need? Those fools betrayed us."

"I wouldn't blame the humans, sir," said Inspyron. "Back in Earth year 1938, the humans offered us several of their retired bombers, which would have been more than effective in defeating the Sétbætañ. It seems that it was never a priority to completely destroy their race, only to frighten them and keep them enslaved. Therefore the gift of the bomber planes was not accepted."

"What idiot agreed to that?" asked Mataralin.

"You did, my lord," said Inspyron.

148

Alex and Karen sprayed gunfire on any enemy creature within reach. Cannon fire and miniature rockets rained on the Sétbætañ army at a furious pace. Many of the creatures were blown up by hundreds of strategically placed land mines on the castle hill. General Akaie and his Luçimark army used rocket launchers and threw grenades at the Sétbætañ. The U.A.M. army did the same. But the Sétbætañ were like a swarm of locusts. What's more, the army's gunfire wasn't effective on the flying dragons. Their skin seemed to be made of armor. And just as in a fairy tale, they breathed fire.

"Look out!" screamed Flip, as fire from one of the many dragons burned his men.

Alex and Karen were holding their own. Karen had developed into a good shot. She picked off Selanon one by one.

"Take that, and that!" yelled Karen, shooting the creatures dead.

Alex was also on a roll as he bragged about his kills to Flip.

"How do ya like that, Flip?"

"Pay attention and don't get cocky," responded Flip.

Alex's confidence was soaring and he had the look of a man on a mission. Not only was he doing a great job shooting the creatures, but he'd also learned how to handle a sword. He put numerous creatures to death with his sword-fighting skills. It was apparent to Karen that this was no longer the Alex of Brownsville.

A dragon tackled Alex from behind. It didn't breathe fire on Alex as it swooped down out of the chaotic skies, but landed on top of him. Flip, Karen, and other army members fired on the creature.

"Don't worry, we're going to get it off of you," shouted Flip as he and the others unsuccessfully fired at the creature.

Alex, who only had his hand gun because his rifle and sword had been knocked away on impact, looked into the menacing eyes of the dragon. It seemed to be grinning as it opened its mouth, ready to burn Alex to a crisp. With no other options, Alex took his hand gun out of his pocket and fired a bullet directly into the creature's throat. The creature fell on Alex in a heap. Flip and Karen ran to get the creature off of him.

"My God, what did you do to kill that thing?" asked Flip.

"I shot it in the throat," said a relieved Alex.

"All right, troops. Shoot the dragons in the throat. I repeat, aim for the throat. It's their weak spot," ordered Flip.

Following Flip's order, the dragons crashed out of the night sky. The U.A.M. army was overjoyed. Even the Luçimarks were pleased. Alex was a hero.

Their jubilance didn't last long. The Sétbætañ countered by firing bundles of mallie dragons from cannons. The mallie dragons, in small cages, were released upon impact with the castle's deck, biting and poisoning any soldier within reach. One of the slithery creatures landed near Alex, and bit him just above the ankle. The venom quickly took effect. Alex crashed to the ground. He watched helplessly as the mallie dragon opened its mouth to feast. Luckily for Alex, Karen was nearby.

"Flip, that snake bit Alex," yelled Karen.

"Don't worry, I've got it," said Flip.

Within seconds of shooting a Sétbætañ in the head with a semi-automatic rifle, Flip turned and shot the mallie dragon dead-on with a semi-automatic pistol. Though Alex was safe from being eaten, Flip knew that he needed immediate medical attention.

"Cover me, soldier," Flip shouted while he tended to Alex.

"Alex, are you with me?"

"Yes, but I can't move."

"I'm gonna get you out of here, but we need to get you some shelter. Just lie here with your eyes closed until I come back. They'll think you're dead."

Alex, now nearly paralyzed, lay waiting while Flip splattered Sétbætañ blood all over the castle walls. The U.A.M. were slowly driving the Sétbætañ army back from the castle as the enemy's casualties mounted.

But the Sétbætañ, in possession of the sixth scroll, were able to perform intradimensional travel. They could use portals to travel on the same planet. As the U.A.M./Luçimark forces fought a group of Sétbætañ at their front, the creatures would transport and attack from behind.

Damaged by Sétbætañ missiles, the castle walls had begun to crumble. This made it easy for troll guards to break through the castle walls and attack the U.A.M. The trolls were followed by the rest of the Sétbætañ army as they stormed the castle. Those creatures that did not breach the castle walls fired cannons, ammunition from tanks, and flaming arrows. Once inside, the Sétbætañ murdered anyone in their path. While Flip called for his remaining troops to retreat, he wondered where the rest of the Luçimark troops were.

"Where are those troops?" screamed Flip.

"I'm not sure, but we've got to retreat behind the castle and protect the citizens of Urodae," yelled General Miller.

"General, take control of what's left of the troops, I'm headed back to Earth," said Flip.

"Why is that, Captain?" asked General Miller.

"Alex was bitten by a mallie dragon. The kid needs top medical assistance or he may end up a quadriplegic. Plus, I need to get our troops at home prepared for battle against these creatures. You know they're coming after us."

"Understood, Captain, and make sure you brief the President. We'll see you there."

"Karen, grab what you can. I'll carry Alex. We're headed home," said Flip.

Flip, Alex, Karen, and a few select soldiers took a portal back to Earth. Flip's first call of duty was getting Alex immediate help. The poison had seized his body. He was completely paralyzed. Without medical attention, within forty-eight hours the paralysis would become permanent. Karen wept while she watched her friend, who was now unresponsive. And though they were returning home, Karen didn't know whether she should be happy or sad. Not only was she upset about Alex's condition, but reports were that it was as hellish on Earth as it was on Caynoñã. Though it would be the first time in weeks she would get to see her parents, she knew that she must keep focused. The mission remained the same: destroy the Sétbætañ.

Beyond the castle and deep into Urodae, the Sétbætañ

stormed the country and destroyed everything in sight. All creatures, large or small, young or old, were at the mercy of the Sétbætañ. Villages and crops were set ablaze, buildings destroyed, dwellings looted, and Luçimark creatures murdered. The once beautiful and peaceful land of Urodae was now a chaotic mess of flames and death. The Sétbætañ were in control of the war. Mataralin was in full panic mode as he watched the enemy approach his lair at the base of the castle.

"Where are those blasted troops?" Mataralin asked Inspyron.

"Reports are that our troops are going to remain on Earth. The minister of defense says that our armies are overwhelmed and need to seek refuge."

"What? How dare that fool. I'm the one who gives the orders here," countered Mataralin. "I order you to tell the minister of defense to return our troops."

After several tries, Inspyron was able to contact the minister of defense. Zixselec had been in charge of the military for as long as Mataralin had been leader of the Luçimarks. Their relationship was a tenuous and stressful one. In many matters involving their people, the leaders differed in opinion. And because Mataralin was the official leader of the race, his ideas and decisions, good or bad, took precedence. Knowing the Luçimarks were on the brink of destruction, Zixselec demanded to hear the orders directly from Mataralin and not through a third party. Incensed, the Luçimark leader snatched the communication device from Inspyron to speak with Zixselec.

"Why is it that I receive your insolence?"

"Because of your incompetence, our race is on the verge of extinction. I will not give you any more soldiers. They're safer here on Earth," said Zixselec.

"This is mutiny. How dare you go against my orders," shouted Mataralin.

"I'm just doing what's right for my soldiers. You are fighting a losing battle, Mataralin. And it is well overdue. For thousands of miliyous your bloodline has waged war against a people who only wished to live in peace. Those who disagreed with you and your forefathers were persecuted and murdered. And now because of your greed, and your desire to enslave those who differ from you, the hour has come for your comeuppance. I want to make sure that my people are worlds away from your destruction. You have heard my last words."

Mataralin was in a rage.

"How dare you say that they are your people. Those are my people. I'll have your head propped on my sword. Do you hear me? Answer me! Do you hear me?"

Zixselec was no longer listening.

"What do we do now? I need answers," Mataralin said to Inspyron.

"We need to get you to safety, my lord," said Inspyron. Turning to one of Mataralin's guards he ordered, "Take the Supreme Leader to the Cambridge Tower."

"You'll be safe there," he said to Mataralin.

But it was too late. Led by Ugnjengon, the Sétbætañ army slammed through the doors of Mataralin's lair. The room went silent as Ugnjengon grabbed Inspyron and snapped his neck. A xyheilamander ridden by Ugnjengon mauled a Luçimark official to death. Members of the army killed all of Mataralin's guards with gun or sword. Mataralin cowered in front of his throne. Ugnjengon put his blade to the Luçimark leader's throat. Just then, a voice halted the execution. It belonged to Ecaep.

"Step aside, Ugnjengon. He's mine. I want everyone to leave us, at once. I need privacy to talk to my old enemy."

Confused by the request, all of Ecaep's soldiers, including Ugnjengon, left the room, shutting the massive doors behind them.

Walking slowly and confidently with sword in hand, Ecaep spoke.

"It's times like these that make living worthwhile. To see my eternal enemy cower before me. The scum who cast his people as gods and my people as demons in the eyes and minds of the humans. To see the enemy who has deprived and killed our people utterly defeated. Tell me Mataralin, how does it feel to look upon the steel of death?"

"Listen Ecaep, we can negotiate. I will give you what you

please if you spare my life."

"You will give me what I please? Then I want five thousand of your people to serve as slaves to the Sétbætañ."

"Well then, let it be done," said Mataralin.

Ecaep looked upon him with rage and let out a fierce scream.

"You would give the lives of your own people to save your own? Despite the fact that they no longer live? My soldiers have pillaged your lands and left death in their path. This is proof that you are nothing but a coward. A piece of filth. Scum. You are lower than anything in the universe. Bow your head, you cowardly maggot."

"No! No! Spare me. Please, spare me. Take our females instead. Take as many as you'd like," screamed Mataralin, weeping.

"Take your females instead? What a surprise that you would offer that," said Ecaep. "It was a little over two hundred miliyous ago that I was held by your people as a slave and treated like the rotted wood on which the termite feasts. And during that time, I fell for one of your females. Do you remember?"

Mataralin did not answer, but looked at Ecaep in horror.

"She had a child. You promised to keep the union a secret from your parliament, but you lied. You told anyone in shouting distance. You were weak then as you are now. You gave in to the evils of your ancestors. You and your leaders called my offspring an atrocity, an abomination. You cast my child and its mother into the fiery pits of Enervet Sine," said Ecaep, tears running down his face.

"The child could not live, Ecaep," said Mataralin. "You blame me, but you know that you would have done the same."

Ecaep did not counter.

"Why didn't you allow my union with the Luçimark female? Was it because it would have meant peace for our races?" asked Ecaep.

"No, it was not that. You understand that she was my daughter. My loving daughter. You ruined everything," shouted Mataralin, weeping.

"You slime," shouted Ecaep, enraged. "You killed your own

154

daughter and grandchild! No, it was you who ruined everything. By killing my child and the one I loved, you destroyed any hope of our races obtaining peace."

"Please, go after the humans instead. Spare my people. And after you destroy them we can live in peace together, on Earth."

"Too late. I care nothing about living in peace on Earth. That planet will burn. And like you and your people, the humans will be destroyed," said Ecaep.

A weeping Mataralin lowered his head. Ecaep then raised his sword and beheaded Mataralin. He took the leader's severed head to the castle balcony and lifted it high for his soldiers to see. When they saw the head of the fallen Luçimark leader, they roared in triumph. He addressed his army.

"Now, we shall finish the revenge of our people and of Cúbaneg, and crush the humans. Nothing shall stop us. We will make that planet burn."

Ecaep slung the severed head into the Sétbætañ army. Chanting and roaring in jubilation, Ecaep and his army entered the portal to Earth.

Chapter 24
Frozen

The sound of bombs, gunfire, and military machinery filled the snowy February-morning air in Brownsville. Ecaep and his massive army had invaded Earth in what they hoped would be their final conquest of the Luçimarks and the human race. The Sétbætañ troops who had not participated in the battle of Caynonã held their own despite being outnumbered. The Sétbætañ creatures were using the scrolls' advanced technology to their full advantage, from portal openings to fiery hail storms. They claimed conquest after conquest. Remote areas of the Earth lacking military power were easily overrun. Even the United States, Europe, and China were having a very tough time. With the addition of a massive number of troops, and confidence on their side, the Sétbætañ were poised for an easy victory.

Throughout Brownsville and the rest of the country, mobile hospital units had been set up. In a Brownsville unit lay Alex, surrounded by his mom, Karen, and her parents. He could hear his mom and Karen's parents chattering and weeping over his predicament, and how Jesus would make things right. He could hear the doctors tell his mom all they were doing to alleviate his paralysis. He felt Karen's presence at his bedside even though he couldn't feel the touch of her hand. Alex was immune to the cold wind and snow that blew through the unit's meager coverings as he lay immobilized.

President Topher was addressing the nation for what seemed like the hundredth time in the past nine months. Karen looked at Alex and blamed herself for his condition. If she had been more assertive in dissuading Alex from going to Vuur, he wouldn't be lying in a hospital bed, a quadriplegic. But then, Alex's mission had been to rescue his father -- something worth dying for.

Looking out from the hospital onto the snowy, deserted street, Karen felt as if she had gone through a time warp. The amount of time that she and Alex had spent on Caynonã didn't compute. A few weeks on that planet was months on Earth. She felt as if part of her life had been stolen from her. But what she and Alex had experienced was proof of Einstein's Theory of Relativity.

The genius of the ancient Sétbætañ race was that they had proved Einstein's theory. Before their secrets and discoveries were stolen, they'd confirmed the existence of the wormholes necessary for time and space travel. These wormholes were the dimensional portals through which travelers moved at or close to the speed of light to other worlds. When Karen and Alex traveled from Earth to Caynonã, they traveled at a speed approximately thirty-three percent of light speed. This made the time on Caynonã seem to move slower, explaining the planet's one-to-three time ratio compared with that of Earth. After spending time on Caynonã, Alex and Karen actually traveled slightly into the future when they returned home. This explained their experience of lost time. They actually had lost time. This phenomenon proved that Einstein was correct, though at the time he had been unaware that this proof existed.

After nearly two sleepless days in the hospital unit, Mrs. Smiley and the Stubblefields needed to rest. Mrs. Smiley was still staying with relatives. The Stubblefields remained at their home. Though the war activity in town was relatively light compared with what was happening in larger cities, the town residents took no chances after dark. The episode with the Selanon and Krieatine was still giving the locals nightmares. Karen asked to stay with Alex a little while longer. Mrs. Smiley and the Stubblefields left, to give Karen and Alex some privacy.

"Alex, I know you can hear me," whispered Karen. "I need you to get up. At least respond. You can't stay like this. I don't know what I would do without you," Karen said.

Getting no response, Karen wept. She was beginning to lose hope. It had been almost forty-eight hours since he'd been bitten. She massaged Alex's arms and legs, hoping for any reaction. There was nothing. Then she began to gently shake Alex. There was still no reaction. She remembered Flip saying that Alex had no more that forty-eight hours to recover or he would remain paralyzed. Becoming desperate and frantic, she tried doing chest compressions. When the nurses rushed in to stop her, they noticed that Alex was showing some movement in his extremities.

"Hey! I need someone in here. I think he's moving," a nurse called. "This girl started pumping his chest and he moved."

Karen smiled for the first time in days. Mrs. Smiley and Karen's parents came back inside the unit when they heard the commotion.

"What's going on?" asked Mrs. Smiley.

"We think we saw some movement when pressure was applied to Alex's chest. I'm not making any promises, but I think there may be light at the end of the tunnel," said the doctor.

"Oh, thank Jesus! And thank you, doctor," said a joyful Mrs. Smiley.

"Don't thank me, ma'am. Thank this brave young lady. She's the one who may have discovered the secret to getting Alex moving again," said the doctor. The Stubblefields smiled proudly at their daughter.

With no time to waste, the doctors cleared everyone out of the room and used a defibrillator on Alex. The idea was that shocking his heart would rush blood through at a higher-than-normal rate and counteract any poison lying dormant in his body. As the doctors repeatedly shocked Alex's heart, movement slowly returned.

"We got him moving," shouted one of the doctors.

"Oh, thank the Lord," said Mrs. Smiley.

After about an hour, Karen checked to see if Alex had regained consciousness.

"Alex? Alex, can you hear me?" she asked, holding his hand.

"He's still unconscious," said a doctor. "But he should come around soon. We'll make sure to keep an eye on him. It would be best if you got some rest and returned in the morning."

"You know that wouldn't be a bad idea, honey. You haven't slept in two days," Mrs. Stubblefield said. Mr. Stubblefield nodded in agreement.

"All right, mom, but I'm going to be back here first thing in the morning."

With that, Karen kissed Alex on the forehead and said her goodbyes. She left the hospital unit with a huge smile on her face, comforted by the knowledge that her best friend was going to be all right.

Not too long after Karen, her parents, and Mrs. Smiley departed the hospital unit, the doctors moved Alex to the local clinic, just down the block. Despite the loss of utilities and extensive damage wrought by the Sétbætañ, many nations had been able to reestablish power and satellite communication after months of disruption. National leaders could now keep the masses abreast of what was happening and advise them on what to do. For those injured and hospital-ridden, a clinic with power, food, and fresh water was a welcome relief.

Still fading in and out of consciousness, Alex was placed in intensive care with other patients who'd suffered life-threatening injuries. Once he'd fully regained consciousness, he would be placed in a recovery ward. The unit was dim, with the sounds of TAPC News in the background. Televisions in every hallway in the clinic showed news twenty-four seven, giving updates on current events. President Topher was frequently broadcast around the world.

Alex dreamt he was in Vuur, fighting against a Sétbætañ warrior. The warrior was very powerful and was in possession of one of the ancient scrolls. They were fighting a great battle on top of a mountain, a sword in each of their hands. As the battle went on, he was getting the better of the beast and drove it to the ground, ready to deliver the final blow. Just then he heard Karen's voice.

"No, don't do it Alex. No!"

When Alex paused to look, the warrior pushed him down the mountain. As he fell, Alex saw his father, pressed against the side of the mountain, holding one of the scrolls. Continuing his fall, he saw two vy-imps pointing and laughing at him. When he looked at the ground, he saw three mallie dragons with their mouths wide open. When Alex hit the ground, there were no mallie dragons, no vy-imps, nothing but a dim, dirt road. He walked down the road and found a small gold chain with a cross. The cross shone brightly in the light of the full moon. As he went to pick it up, a raven swooped in to grab it and took flight. The raven seemed to mock Alex, cawing loudly as it soared through the air. Alex chased the raven into a church full of people. At the pulpit was a man with his back to the congregation. The man turned around. Alex saw that it was President Topher. The President was solemn. Tears were running down his cheeks. As Alex approached, the President faded away, leaving only the raven, with the cross around its neck. Then he heard the voice of Ms. Gateway whisper.

"Now that Smiley's dead we should be in the clear."

"But we have another problem that must but eradicated," said someone else.

The voices were actually in the hallway just outside the intensive care unit. One did belong to Ms. Gateway, another to Detective Riley, and a third to Pope Gregory. The Pope was making visits around the world to pray with worshipers during this time of crisis. Thanks to the doctors and Karen, Alex had regained consciousness and full range of motion. From his hospital bed, he saw Ms. Gateway, Riley, and the Pope right outside the open door, and despite their attempts to keep their voices low, he could hear them fairly well. Keeping still as death, Alex listened in on their conversation. What puzzled him most was the Pope's presence. Why was the Pope having a conversation with Detective Riley and Ms. Gateway in a clinic in Brownsville, of all places, at three in the morning?

"Who else do we have issue with?" asked Riley.

"My issue is with that arrogant idiot on television," said the Pope, pointing to the President giving yet another address to the world.

"My fellow Americans and citizens of all the great nations of the world, I urge you not to worry, but to trust in our military to be victorious in the battle against this great enemy. In America and around the world, the United Alliance Marines are doing all they can to protect our lands from those who'd claim it for themselves, and take human lives. We will show the enemy that

160

we will not succumb to their evil. We will show them that all the nations of Earth will rise as one and defeat those who wage war against us. Good night and God bless."

"You see, he's beginning to crack," said the Pope, explaining the situation to Riley and Gateway. "Mr. Topher and I had a discussion months back about the Church's place in human society. He said that every government around the world and the Holy Catholic Church should come clean to all those who believe in God. That the Church should cease teaching that God exists. I, along with the other high-ranking church officials, vehemently disagreed."

"Do you think he'll tell the masses in one of his addresses?" asked Gateway.

"I don't think; I know he will," said the Pope. "Besides the aliens, only a select few know the truth -- the three of us in this hallway, and the high-ranking government and Church officials."

"How do you plan on stopping him?" asked Riley.

"I have a plan that will make Christopher step down from the presidency. I will not go into details as of yet, but you'll know when the time comes," said the Pope

The three of them walked down the hallway and out of the clinic. Alex got out of bed, crouched down, and looked out the ICU doorway as they were leaving. Still lacking energy and feeling wobbly legged, Alex was determined to find out what the Pope had up his sleeve and what he had planned for the President. But first, he had to contact Karen. Not only did he want her to accompany him on the upcoming adventure, but he wanted her by his side. He was beginning to feel giddy whenever she was around. He felt that she was slowly becoming more than a friend. Never in his life had he felt so grateful to be alive.

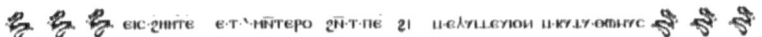

When Karen and Mrs. Smiley arrived at the clinic the next day, they found Alex walking around the room on crutches. The poison from the mallie dragon was still working its way out of his body, and he had trouble standing for more than a minute at a

time. He was determined to get back to full strength as quickly as possible. Karen and Mrs. Smiley were ecstatic to see Alex's progress and wondered how long he would have to stay in the clinic.

"How long did the doctors say you have to stay?" asked Karen.

"Until I fully recover," said Alex. "They want me to stay as a precaution."

"There's no rush, I want to see you at full strength. So take your time and get better."

"I can't take my time. I need to hurry and get well. I saw Ms. Gateway, Detective Riley, and the Pope here at the clinic."

"Are you sure you weren't hallucinating?" asked Karen.

"No, I wasn't," said Alex. "The three of them were here last night plotting to get rid of the President."

"Get rid of the President? What do you think they meant by that?"

"I'm not sure, but I plan to find out."

"Well you're in no shape to go anywhere. You can barely stand up. And don't you think you've been through enough already?" said Karen.

"Look, Karen, you and I know that Detective Riley and Ms. Gateway had it in for my father. If they knew that I possessed the ability to open dimensional portals, they would come after me. Now they're going after the President and I'm going to try and stop them."

"Why in the world would the Pope be involved?" asked Karen.

"I guess the answer adds another layer to the mystery," said Alex. But I need to know if you're coming with me or not. I'll understand if you don't want to. You've been away from your family for quite some time and I'm sure they miss you. My mother believes that I'm fighting for God, battling Satan's demons. So she understands that I'm on a mission."

Alex had his fingers crossed that Karen would join him.

"Alex, I've told you that I would never leave you. I'm with you through thick or thin," said Karen. "So I'll just tell my parents that I'm joining you on the same mission."

"Good," said Alex. "We'll need to get ahold of Flip. We're gonna need some supplies and some of those cloaking tablets. Do you think you can reach him?"

"I can reach him," said Karen. "Though it won't be easy."

"Nothing ever is," said Alex. "We'll just need to stay positive."

Chapter 25
The Sixth Scroll

For the first time since World War II, the entire world was in chaos. From the Americas to Europe, and from Africa to Asia, pillars of smoke rose to the stratosphere, choking out the sun and its cursed red skies. The battle between the U.A.M. and the Sétbætañ had taken its toll on the environment. Polluted water and burned crops disrupted the planet's ecosystem. Diseases from rotting corpses plagued the Earth. Civilizations lay in ruins.

Many who'd survived the onslaught from the Sétbætañ were without food or shelter. Posters of missing children circulated through cities and towns around the world. In New York City, millions looted stores and homes and searched trashcans for food. In Los Angeles, people were so desperate that they had resorted to eating their pets. In Shanghai, some gathered human corpses and took to cannibalism.

It was indeed a biblical prophecy fulfilled: The Final Battle, Last Days, Armageddon. The faithful were looking forward to the return of Christ. Several months before, the Alliance had seemed to be holding the creatures at bay. But the latest Sétbætañ onslaught had been too much for the humans. In many towns, the creatures broke into every home and slaughtered the inhabitants. The Earth's skies, already red, were now littered with the black silhouettes of the Selanon. The creatures took satisfaction in swooping down from the sky and mauling humans to death. They destroyed crops by burning them or infesting them with fast-multiplying alien worms. People jammed into churches for shelter and prayer. Those who roamed the streets wept loudly for God or whomever they worshipped to save them. Millions of people around the world committed suicide to escape their sorrows. But despite the dire circumstances, an overwhelming majority of people in America and abroad still believed in the leadership of President Topher.

In a secret location in Washington, D.C., the President and his military generals were devising a new plan of attack. Reports were that the Alliance's manpower was dwindling and that many rebellious factions around the world had taken up arms to fight the creatures. Though their cause was noble, these rebels were disorganized and untrained, and often unwittingly aided in their town's or city's destruction. The survival of mankind hung in the balance, and the confident but impatient President wanted the creatures gone by any means necessary.

"General Miller, what's our strategy for getting rid of these things?" asked Topher.

"Since we no longer have nuclear or biological weapons, our initial plan of attack was to counter the creatures by air. But because so many of the flying creatures are littering the skies, we're having a tough time getting off the ground. The creatures have also attacked and downed our fighter jets."

"What about ground troops?"

"We're in retreat, Mr. President," said Flip. He hadn't slept in days. "The Sétbætañ's ability to use the portal for intradimensional travel has really put us at a disadvantage."

"What is intradimensional travel?"

"It's a technological command from the sixth scroll," said Miller. "It allows a person or thing to transport from one point to another within the same dimension. We've used it before when we first rescued Alex and Karen. What happens when the enemy uses it is that we find ourselves fighting the creatures on one front, and without warning they're on another front attacking us from behind. I believe this is happening with the flying creatures also."

"That would be correct," said Flip.

Intradimensional travel was created by the ancient Sétbætañ for quick attacks on their enemies. The genius behind the technology involves quantum teleportation, in which particles from the same source can interact with one another no matter the distance. Thus, using the phenomenon of quantum entanglement, the Sétbætañ were able to teleport the particles of a being and put them back together at their destination. This technology was coveted by the Nazis during World War II. But because the Luçimarks had the scroll, and were unable to help the Nazis with the translation, the technology was never utilized.

This command is the first of two on the sixth scroll:

ϯⲭⲟⲙ ⲡⲓⲛⲓϣϯ ⲛ̀ⲟⲩⲣⲟ ⲫⲏⲉⲧϩⲉⲙⲥⲓ ϩⲓⲭⲉⲛ ⲡⲓⲑ̀ⲣⲟⲛⲟⲥ ⲟⲩⲱⲛ ϯ̀ⲫⲉ

The Coptic translates as:

The power of the king who sits on the throne opens the heavens.

"It's proven that we can use the technology," said Topher. "We just need to devise a plan to use it against them. And what about the command of the seventh scroll? Can we use that technology against the aliens?"

"Highly unlikely, Mr. President," said Lieutenant Jackson. Only the aliens know the translation. This is where the Sétbætañ have shown their technological superiority."

"So you're telling me that we don't have anyone who can translate the scroll?" asked the President.

"The only one I know of is dead," said Jackson. "Phillip Smiley."

"He's dead, but I can get hold of the next best thing," Flip said, reluctantly.

"And who would that be?" asked the President.

"Phil's son, Alex Smiley."

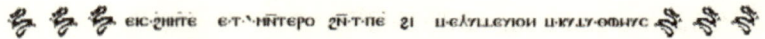

Back at the clinic in Brownsville, Alex was ready to be discharged. He was near full strength and ready to find out what the Pope and his minions were up to. Waiting for his mom and aunt to pick him up, he anxiously paced the room. He planned to connect with Karen soon as he got to his aunt's house to see if she had been able to contact Flip.

During his stay at the clinic, Alex had regularly conversed with the doctors and nurses, sharing his adventures. The clinic staff looked up to Alex and considered him a hero for surviving a condition that was foreign to modern medicine. They unanimously considered his recovery a medical miracle, as the cure had been discovered by accident. Now, those who'd been bitten by mallie dragons were quickly treated and released. Karen's bravery would save many lives.

When Alex arrived at his aunt's house, he immediately went to the guest room and called Karen. He was so happy to hear her voice. She felt the same way. Karen, who had been home for days, gave Alex the 4-1-1 on the neighborhood's current events.

"Though there's not a tremendous amount of damage, many of the local stores and schools have been shut down. Since the invasion by that monster and those flying creatures, everyone has been lying low."

"What about the neighborhood kids?" asked Alex.

"Many of them have been killed."

"What about the kids who went to our school?"

"Same thing, though some have formed gangs." Gangs were unheard of in Brownsville before the alien invasion.

"Who at our school was crazy enough to form a gang?"

Karen let out a long sigh before answering. "Lenopolous Gary."

Throughout his trials and tribulations, Alex had forgotten about Lenopolous. The mention of his name gave Alex shivers, imagining how any gang formed by Lenopolous would impose uncensored mayhem on the Brownsville residents.

The gang robbed people of their resources. Members often sold stolen goods back to their victims and to the needy at a premium.

"Were you able to get hold of Flip?"

"No, I wasn't. He won't answer his cell."

"Jeez, Karen! We have to get ahold of him. He has everything we need. Plus we have to warn him about the Pope."

"Don't get nervous, Alex," said Karen. "After Flip and I admitted you to the clinic, he told me he was going to Washington to brief the President. So, we need to go to Washington."

"And how are we going to get there?" asked Alex. "It's not

167

like we can take the bus or anything. There's no public transportation."

Karen sighed.

"Ye of so little faith. Meet me on the corner of Heather and Bella."

Still feeling the effects of the mallie dragon poison, Alex ran as fast as his weary legs would carry him. When he finally got near the location, he saw Karen standing next to an old Ford pick-up full of rust holes and dents. Inside was a middle-aged guy wearing a dusty brown hat and a ripped jean jacket. He reeked of alcohol.

"Alex, I'd like you to meet Walker."

"Howdy, Alex! Karen tells me yaw needs a ride to D.C. Well I got time on my hands and a full tank of gas. I'm ready to go when you are."

"Uh, yeah … can you hold on a minute?"

Alex grabbed Karen by the arm.

"Is this how we're supposed to get to Washington? By hitching a ride in a beat-up pick-up truck, driven by a drunk?"

"Keep your voice down," whispered Karen. "He was the best I could do. Unless you think our parents are going to give us a ride?"

"Okay, okay. Just let me ask him a few questions."

"Uh, Walker? Where are you from and why are you willing to take two teenagers to Washington?"

"Well, to answer your first question, I'm from right here in Brownsville. Lived here all my life. And to answer your second question, Karen told me all about your mission. My family was killed by those demons. Yep, a wife and two daughters. And all I want to do is my part in helping to put those demons back in hell."

Alex pulled Karen aside again.

"You told him everything?"

"Not everything. I told him we've been hired by the CIA to help the President," said Karen.

"And he believed that?"

"Just trust me Alex, we can use his help."

168

After spending a few minutes pondering, Alex and Karen jammed themselves in the cabin of the truck. Depending on the condition of the roads and the dependability of the truck, they were in for a sixteen-hour ride. Their hope was to reach Flip in time to warn him of the Pope's intention to get rid of the President.

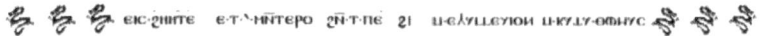

Back in Washington, the President and his top officials were meeting in an underground office at St. Patrick's Catholic Church. Its proximity to the White House afforded it military protection, so the church remained relatively unscathed. At a long, oval table with the President were General Miller, Lieutenant Jackson, Flip, Major Kremley, the Luçimark General Akaie, and several military officials. The President was responding to a summons from Pope Gregory to hold discussions on the delivery of food aid to churches throughout Europe, America, and the world. The Pope felt that the Church could play a vital role in helping distribute food to the needy in addition to providing spiritual guidance and shelter. The President looked uncharacteristically uncomfortable as he awaited the Pope's arrival.

"You're not looking forward to this are you, Mr. President?" asked Kremley.

"Based on our last discussion, I would say not. But the Pope does have a very good idea. Any way we can help people, I'm all for it. I'm not sure we can give him all he needs, but he's extending an olive branch while we settle our differences in a cordial manner."

While the President and his trusted officials waited, they heard in the hallway the sound of slowly approaching footsteps assisted by a walking stick. The Pope had arrived. He was flanked by several security officials along with undercover CIA officers Elizabeth Gateway and Victor Riley. The President and his officials stood to greet the Pope.

"Welcome, Your Holiness. I hope that you enjoyed a

comfortable flight on the Air Force jet," said the President.

"Given the circumstances I would say that the flight was reasonable," the Pope said. "As you know, I've been here in the United States for almost two weeks visiting churches, hospitals, and shelters, offering the suffering hope by spreading the word of God."

"I'm glad that you were able to lift spirits," said the President. "And I'm hopeful we can do even more despite the dire straits we are in."

The Pope gave the President a sarcastic look.

"Tell me, Mr. President. You have delivered a countless number of world addresses to millions, telling them to hang on to hope. How can you preach hope when you yourself do not believe in the source of all hope, which is God?"

The President sighed, knowing the Pope wanted to drag him into an argument. Out of respect, he calmly and honestly answered.

"It makes no difference what I think, Father. My job is to protect the people of this world. And if believing in fairy tales brings them comfort, then that's what I'll deliver."

That statement was enough to send the Pope into a rant.

"Your disrespect for God and the Church knows no bounds. Those so-called fairy tales are keeping many of the suffering alive. They realize that it is God who will give them salvation and not Christopher Topher."

"Father, I didn't mean any harm. You should know that I'm one to answer everything openly and honestly. I would like to move forward and discuss the government's plan for food aid in the churches. I think that you'll be pleased."

The Pope would not drop the subject.

"Tell me, Christopher, how are we doing in the war? Are we any closer than last month to ending it? How many civilians have died because of the incompetence of the U.S. Government and her allies?"

The Pope had got to the President.

"With all due respect, Father, I think that the government and our military have performed quite well under the circumstances.

170

For the first time in history we are fighting against beings from another world, with superior technology. My feelings now, as they have been from the beginning, are that lying to the public has been detrimental to our cause."

"And what, exactly, do you mean by lying to the public?"

"The whole Armageddon, God versus Satan, heaven versus hell lie we've been feeding mankind for more than two thousand years," said the President.

"Why don't we get back to the matter at hand and discuss those food-aid plans?" injected Kremley, trying to change the subject. It didn't matter. This was a debate that neither party was willing to let die.

"You do realize that the Church and the government that you presently lead made a deal years ago to keep sensitive information such as this from the public?" said the Pope.

"I do realize it. But that deal was made in the nineteen forties. As I told you during our last meeting, the world has changed. People are smarter and more informed. I believe that if we tell them the truth and the people know what they are really fighting against, we can rally and win this war."

"It sounds as if you are considering telling them that we are being invaded by aliens."

"I am," said the President. "But I don't plan to tell them only part of the story."

"You intend on telling them everything," said the Pope. "You do realize that would destroy the beliefs of millions of Christians?"

"It's time, Father. And it's time for the Church to realize its place in history. No more lies, no more threats, no more torture. After the war, we'll begin a new world order where people can live free, unrestricted by fear, false promises, and religion. I plan on giving the State of the World address tonight. Afterward, the people of the world will know the truth."

The Pope's face was beet red. With a menacing grin he took out a cell phone, dialed a number, and started chanting. He began quietly and then raised his voice as he repeated the chant over and over:

171

ⲙⲉⲃⲥⲉ ϩⲓⲧⲉⲛ ⲛⲓⲡ̄ⲣⲉⲥⲃⲓⲁ ⲛ̄ⲧⲉ ⲡⲓϣⲁϣϥ ⲛ̄ⲁⲣⲭⲏⲁⲅⲅⲉⲗⲟⲥ ⲛⲉⲙ ⲛⲓⲧⲁⲅⲙⲁ ⲛ̄ⲉⲡⲟⲩⲣⲁⲛⲓⲟⲛ
ⲭⲱⲣ ⲡⲓⲗⲁⲟⲥ ⲉⲧ ⲡⲉ ϩⲁⲡ ⲙ̄ⲙⲟⲛ

The Coptic translates as:

*Awaken through the pleadings of the seven archangels and
the heavenly hosts. Destroy those who condemn us.*

The Pope was reciting the second command of the sixth
scroll.

On the other end of the line, Sétbætañ officers and soldiers
recited the same text.

Within moments, many Alliance soldiers worldwide had
stopped attacking the creatures and turned on their own brethren.
They appeared to be in a trance. With the assistance of the
Sétbætañ, they placed unaffected soldiers under arrest. Those
who resisted were killed. Eighty-five percent of the Alliance
army was now under the influence of the Sétbætañ.

Civilians were also affected. Friend turned against friend,
child against parent, husband against wife. There was chaos in
the streets, in homes, even in churches. Many were placed into
custody. Many more were killed or maimed.

Affected members of the Alliance stormed into St. Patrick's
Church, killed several officers including General Akaie, and took
the President into custody. Flip, Lieutenant Jackson, and Major
Kremley were arrested. General Miller and several Secret
Service agents were shot to death while trying to protect the
President. It was a perfect coup, spearheaded by the Pope with
assistance from the Sétbætañ. Gateway and Riley pointed guns at
the President while the Pope gloated over his apparent victory.

"Christopher you have no answers as to what went wrong?"
asked the Pope. "Your days as President and world leader are
over."

"I know we've had our issues, but for you to conspire with
the enemy and kill soldiers and civilians to get back at me is
highest treason," yelled the President.

The Pope chuckled.

"You still think this is all about you. Wrong, Christopher. This is about protecting the Church and the word of God. You thought you were in control? Well, it looks now as if you never were."

"What did you and those monsters do to our soldiers, the civilians?" interjected Flip.

"You'll need to ask your leader that question," said the Pope, looking at Topher. "What's the matter? You don't know the answer? Let me refresh your memory."

The Pope walked up to the President, meeting him almost nose to nose. He was so close that the President could see the anger in the Pope's eyes.

"It's very surprising that you and your cronies forgot about the United People's Act. That Act, as I remember, allowed for the creation of the BioCharge system. Is it coming together now, Christopher?"

The President tried to remain stone-faced, though his eyes betrayed his fear.

"Your arrogance in having computer chips embedded in humans under the false pretense of making their lives easier has backfired," said the Pope. "I warned you and the U.S. Government that placing computer chips in humans was immoral and went against the teachings of the Catholic Church. Even though there's a separation of church and state, the BioCharge computer chip implanted into human hands gives credibility to the mark of the beast prophecy. If a person took part in the BioCharge program, that person would be at an advantage economically and socially, but the government would know all aspects of that person's life. This is what you, Christopher, championed for the people of this world, despite protests from the Church and its followers."

The President and his staff sat in stunned silence.

"But I digress," the Pope continued. "I simply invoked the mind-controlling technology of the chip. You remember this, don't you Christopher? Technology that was taken from the Nazis by the U.S. Government which was originally created by

173

the Sétbætañ?"

Flip thought he was having an out-of-body experience.

"Wait a minute," he shouted. "You've been in cahoots with the enemy all these years?"

"Like you and certain members of the U.S. Government, I have been in communication with the aliens. I just chose a different side."

"You slime. You piece of filth," shouted Flip.

"Watch your tone, captain. I can have one of your soldiers eliminate you with a snap of my fingers. And don't try and play like you and your government allies are innocent, you hypocritical twit. The U.S. Government has sought the power of the scrolls for decades. Their goal was to use the scroll's power for purposes of war. We only wanted to make sure that the scrolls were not discovered by the masses. Discovery of the scrolls would have been catastrophic to those who believe in God and the Church. The pope who presided over the Church after World War II was able to translate the Coptic text and record it in the Church archives. As a young cardinal, I kept abreast of the location of the text, fascinated by their meaning.

"As the years passed, I became curious about the origin of the text. Through research I learned that the Germans and the Americans were competing for the scroll technology and were in communication with the Luçimark beings. I later learned it was not the Luçimarks who'd created the scroll technology, but the brilliant Sétbætañ. I learned how the Sétbætañ race was persecuted and enslaved by the Luçimarks, and how their culture, ideas, and inventions were stolen from them. Naturally, being a man of the cloth, I was moved to meet members of this downtrodden alien race. I understood their anger toward their enemy. I managed to keep in touch with them through my promotion to the papacy.

"Mr. Topher, when you became President and started preaching the idea of having computer chips embedded in humans, I found out from the creatures the meaning of the text and found out that this technology was to be embedded in the chip. Thus, I realized that I could, at any time, use the command

174

to create a rebellion against those who did not abide by God's law. I knew you were against God from the beginning and had a plan to lead an army of unbelievers against the Church. I have the backing of the Sétbætañ, who have their own plans. But despite my beliefs, never in my wildest dreams did I imagine I would have to use the command to stop your madness."

Angry and confused, the President mustered a rebuttal.

"You're sick. I can't believe your level of paranoia. And you thought I was taking over the minds of people? Look at what you're doing. What you've done! You're killing people and you say it's to protect God's law? Come on, Father, think about what you're doing."

"What I do, I only do in the name of God," said the Pope.

"So you're telling us that the Church had copies of the scroll text all along? Was it just the text of the sixth scroll?" asked Lieutenant Jackson.

"No, Mr. Jackson, we have the text of all the scrolls except the seventh. But what makes this sixth scroll unique is that it contains two commands: one for intradimensional travel and the other for mind control. The mind-control command is only effective with the use of additional technology. Thanks to the U.S. Government, and the creation of the BioCharge implanted computer chip, the successful use of the mind-control command was possible."

"You're worse than the government that you hate," said Flip.

"No, you're confused, captain. We knew we couldn't afford to trust the government, and were afraid that the scrolls could be misplaced or fall into the wrong hands. So we decided that if we weren't going to keep the actual scrolls, then obtaining the text of the scrolls would be enough. We were proved correct when one of your government staff members inexplicably buried the scrolls in the desert. We were unable to record the text of the seventh scroll before its confiscation. The government was in such a rush to hide what they'd obtained from the Nazis. But having the text allowed me to learn the language of the scrolls, thanks to the teachings of the Coptic Egyptian churches."

"I still don't understand your purpose in sacrificing human

lives to save the Church," said the President. "What is it that you're trying to do? Create a world of aliens and Christians?"

"Far from it," said the Pope. "After you broadcast your resignation, the Church will step in and make things right with the world. Do you really think I care anything about those monsters? I only care about the sanctity of the Church. Mark my words, I will gain possession of the seventh scroll and lead in the destruction of the aliens. I will rewrite the Holy Writ and a new heaven on earth will be established to fulfill God's prophecy."

"I think you've underestimated me," said the President. "I'm not resigning. You'll have to kill me."

"Oh, I've never underestimated you, Christopher," said the Pope. "My plan includes wiping out the non-Christian population if you don't agree to my terms. If that happens, how would you ever be able to go in front of the television cameras and give your hollow speeches of hope and prosperity? And as for your being killed? I'll make arrangements for that in due time."

"The Christian people will figure out who the real monster is," said the President.

"Yes, you are correct. The Christian people are smart. And in due time, they will find out who the real monster is," the Pope said slyly. "Trust me. After you find out the truth, you will give your resignation with no questions asked. Now enough talk. Soldiers, take this vermin away."

The compromised soldiers led Flip, Jackson, and Kremley away at gunpoint. The President was led away by the Pope, Gateway, and Riley. The President's hands were tied and his mouth gagged. They pointed a gun at his head.

In the hallway, a pair of vy-imps had just finished uncloaking. They went back to report all they'd heard to Ecaep.

Chapter 26
On the Road

As the rusty, brown truck rumbled across the countryside, Alex and Karen felt every nook, cranny, and bump in the seemingly endless road. The nauseating smells of gasoline and alcohol, along with preprogrammed country music from the truck's AM radio, had the teenagers pining for better days. The scenery of frost-covered hills and barren farmland made them feel even colder in the unheated truck. Though they were seated close and body heat was helping to keep them warm, the cold winter air reminded them they would suffer an unpleasant fate if the jalopy broke down.

Walker seemed unconcerned about the possibility of anything going wrong. It was his civic duty to deliver the two undercover CIA agents to Washington. Every now and again he would strike up a conversation about the days he enjoyed with his family, before his wife and two daughters were killed by the Krieatine.

"I remember when we would wake up early on Sunday morning to go to church," he said. "My wife would cook up some eggs, bacon, and grits while the kids were washin' up, and we would rush to the breakfast table and go to town eatin' some good food.

"Once we got to church, we would talk with the other members in the congregation about how it felt being a Christian. We believed that you should have faith in God no matter how bad things were. Yeah we all have our problems, but I never thought things would take this bad of a turn.

"I'll never forget the day. It was a late summer afternoon. I had just returned home after droppin' the wife and kids off at the mall. I was watchin' the TAPC News channel and they were showing coverage of what was going on in New York City. Matter of fact, they were showing what was going on in just about every major city. The devil's army had begun their fight against God.

"I'm an avid reader of the Bible. I knew it was Armageddon. But where were the angels? Weren't they supposed to be fightin' in the battle? I said to myself, they'll come, just give 'em time. Well, they never showed up. It looks like we'll have to fend for ourselves. Where is Jesus when we need him most? Didn't you think that God's angels would save us? You two *are* Christians right?"

Alex and Karen looked at each other. Karen answered the best she could to avoid suspicion.

"Yes, we thought the same thing, that Jesus would return."

"'Cause we've been Christians all our lives," added Alex.

"Well, never did I think in all my years of livin' that those demons would come to little ol' Brownsville. I'll never forget the sight of the sky turning dark red, with hundreds of flyin' demons swooping down from high above and killin' folk. But that was child's play compared to what came next.

"It was that gruesome monster with three arms that attacked the town. It was the most ghastly thing I've ever seen. It must have been the devil himself. It was destroying everything in its path. The local news was tracking its every move. Though I was already worried, I became terrified when I heard that the monster was heading east. That's where the mall was located, in the eastern part of the city. I was unable to contact my wife, so I got in my truck and rushed eastward, only to run into a wall of traffic. While I was stuck, several of those flyin' demons started bashing my truck. I even saw some of the demons fly away with folk.

"With the traffic at a standstill, I took a chance and got out the truck and started running towards the mall. By God's grace I was never attacked by the demons. But by the time I arrived to the mall it was too late. The entire mall was leveled. I went through the debris to see what I could find, or at least listen for cries for help. But the only sounds I heard were the crackling of a raging fire, the cries of the flyin' demons, and the roar of the giant creature. They were deafening, horrific sounds. But as quickly as they appeared, they disappeared. It was as if they were lookin' for something or someone specific, found them, and left. Neither I nor anyone else cared. We just wanted to find our loved ones. I searched in the debris for days. The bodies

178

were finally found by a rescue team. Since then, my heart has been filled with the desire to destroy those demons by any means necessary."

While Walker told his story, Alex stared out the window onto the ravaged countryside. His eyes welled with tears as he imagined how his father had been taken by the Selanon. It would be the beginning of the end of Mr Smiley's life, as he was tortured and crippled by the Sétbætañ. Alex, much like Walker, felt the need to destroy the creatures by any means necessary.

"Are you okay, Alex?" asked Karen.

"I'm fine," said Alex. "I just can't wait to get to Washington."

Karen didn't press the issue, but she knew that Alex wasn't telling the truth. She knew that he was hurting. His father's death had taken an emotional toll.

It was close to sunset and everyone was cold and hungry. Not far down the road, they saw a convenience store with some gas pumps. As Walker drove closer he saw that the store was desolate. On the ground were two dead bodies. Alex guessed that they were former store employees. They decided to try their luck to see if any of the gas pumps were working.

"Voila!" said Walker as he began to pump gas into the gas tank.

"Hey Walker, you wants some chips?" asked Alex. He and Karen had looted the store for as much food as they could carry.

"Save me some for later," said Walker who preferred to drink an alcoholic beverage instead. "I'm just glad we were able to get some gas. We're not too far from Washington but I need to get some rest. I say we find a spot and continue in the morning. We should be there by mid-afternoon."

After pumping the gas, Walker stocked up on his favorite beverages. Though Alex and Karen didn't approve, they felt there was nothing they could do about it. Shortly after leaving the convenience store, Walker guided the truck off the road and into some woods.

"This is where we're gonna rest up for the night. I'm dead tired and got to get some rest. Do either of you know how to

179

drive?" asked Walker.

"No, we don't. But I don't feel we're doing the right thing by stopping. Plus, I'm freezing," said Karen. "How are we supposed to keep warm?"

"Oh, don't worry. We're not staying in the truck. We're gonna get out, pitch a tent, and make a fire," said Walker.

Alex looked down at the cold dusty road. There was no way he was going to fall asleep in the middle of nowhere. He didn't want to take the chance of not waking up.

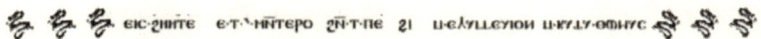

It was well past midnight. The hoot of an owl filled the cold night sky. Alex and Karen were huddled underneath an oversized blanket, trying to keep warm beside the campfire. They ignored the regular incoming calls from loved ones, letting their cells phones vibrate. Their calls to Flip remained unanswered. Walker had drunk his fill of alcohol and was fast asleep in the tent, snoring as loud as a bear. Alex wondered if the trip to Washington was for naught and if they would ever find the President.

The next morning, Alex and Karen were greeted by overcast skies and a cold, searing wind. They had managed to fall asleep despite trying their best to remain alert. Walker was still fast asleep and Alex was anxious to get back on the road.

"Walker. Walker," said Alex, reaching through the tent and poking him with a stick. "Walker, wake up!"

Startled, Walker woke quickly from his slumber. "Walker reporting for duty!"

"Walker, we have to hurry and get to Washington. Time is of the essence," said Alex.

"Well let's get into the truck and hit the road," said Walker.

Between catnaps, Alex caught glimpses of road signs. The trio was not too far from Washington. As he stared groggily at a sign stating they were fifty miles out, he thought about his entire adventure. How he'd avoided the bully by going into the junkyard. How he'd discovered the scrolls by ducking into a

180

sewer to escape the dogs. How he'd opened a portal to another world and been chased by alien creatures. How he and Karen had been abducted by the aliens and brought to their world. How they'd been rescued by Flip and told the truth about the history between the aliens, the government, and the Church. How he'd returned to the alien world to rescue his father and watched helplessly as he'd passed away. How he had fought gallantly against the aliens only to nearly lose his life to alien poison. And now, how he and Karen rode in a cold vehicle navigated by a drunk, en route to Washington, D.C., to rescue the President of the United States from the evil Catholic Pope.

The rescue of the President seemed an impossible task. The person Alex and Karen knew who was closest to the President was Flip and he couldn't be reached. And if the Pope was able to reach and abduct the President, where would he hide him? Would the Pope do the unthinkable and kill him? And if the Pope kidnapped him, how could they find him, especially without assistance from Flip? There had to be hundreds of personnel protecting the President. Could he be kidnapped? Maybe Alex and Karen were being overly paranoid. But there was something deep down in his gut that told Alex the President was in real danger.

As Walker, Karen, and Alex approached a town just outside of Washington, they noticed for the first time that there were other people about. As they got closer, they noticed that the people were in the middle of the road forming a barricade with their vehicles. As they rolled to a stop, they were approached by four men carrying rifles. Two wore bandanas, one red, the other white. The third man wore overalls and the fourth wore a tank top. The man wearing the white bandana tapped on the driver's side window with the butt of his rifle. Walker rolled down his window, hoping to get some direction.

"Uh, hello, we're trying to get to Washington. Is there a detour off this road somewhere?" asked Walker.

"Maybe, maybe not," said the man with the white bandana. "Smells like you've been drinkin' a lot of the hot sauce. Where are you guys coming from? Are those your kids?"

181

"No, they're not. They're just friends," said Walker, sensing trouble. "And we're traveling from Virginia." Alex and Karen kept their mouths shut.

"So you're traveling with two teenagers in which you're not their father, to Washington, D.C., nearly drunk, and you claim you're coming from Virginia but you don't have Virginian license plates. For what purpose, may I ask, are you coming to Washington? You know the city is under martial law?"

"Well, these kids got lost due to the war. I'm just bringing them back home," said Walker, lying as best as he could.

"So you two from D.C. somehow got lost way out in the sticks of Virginia due to the war. Is that true? Can either of you talk?"

"Yes, we can talk," said Karen. "And this nice man is taking us home."

The man with the white bandana went back to converse with the other men before coming back to the truck.

"You know? I think yer lying," said the man. "Now get out the truck."

The trio got out of the truck, and were met with rifle barrels. They were ordered to hold out their hands palms up. The man with the overalls examined their palms. He then looked at the others and without saying a word shook his head no. The other men, led by the man in the white bandana, went ballistic.

"So, you're part of the enemy, huh?"

"The enemy, what are you talking about?" asked Walker.

"The enemy is those who are fighting against the Church and for the Alliance."

"Whoa, whoa, whoa, slow down partner, you've got me confused," said Walker. "Fighting against the Church? We're fighting for the Church against the demons."

"No," said the man. "Those without the chip are the true enemies. We were fooled by the government, led by the evil Christopher Topher. He's the one who wants to destroy God and the Church."

"That's not true," blurted Alex. "You must be under some sort of spell to believe that."

"Ya see? He's a CIA government agent. He knows what he's talking about," said Walker.

"CIA? That proves he's against us. Now shut up and get into the vehicle," ordered the man.

With the steel of the rifles pressed against their backs, Alex, Karen, and Walker were stuffed into an army transport vehicle likely stolen from the Alliance. The men with the red bandana and tank top rode in the back of the caravan with guns pointed at the trio. The vehicle took off.

"Hey, where are we going?" asked Karen.

"A place where all of ya belong," said the man with the tank top. "Hell."

Chapter 27
Camp 349

With the majority of the world's population under the influence of the sixth scroll, those not under its influence were easily overrun. With assistance from the Sétbætañ, numerous prison camps were set up around the world for those without a chip. Each camp held as many as two hundred thousand prisoners. Alex, Karen, and Walker were now occupants of Camp 349, in Annapolis, Maryland, just outside Washington, D.C.

A former naval base in close proximity to Baltimore and Washington, Annapolis was a perfect location for a prison camp. The camp had fifty subdivisions equipped with food, storage, and torture chambers. Most of the camps in the United States were located on the east and west coasts with a few scattered in the middle of the country. There were no camps yet located near Brownsville.

Alex, Karen, and Walker were stripped of their belongings and issued orange prison jumpsuits.

The camp was packed, like the Nazi concentration camps of World War II. The sea of orange created by the thousands of prisoners was only broken up by the concrete walls of the watchtowers and the brown wooden walls of the buildings scattered throughout. The perimeter of the camp was enclosed with a forty foot steel gate topped with barbed wire. Outside the gate and among the prisoners were the armed rebels of the Sétbætañ -- hundreds of humans under enemy control due to the command of the sixth scroll. They occupied the watchtowers and descended upon the prisoners when chaos erupted. Fights between the prisoners would break out over food, blankets, or other coveted items. Their mental state had been reduced to the level of an animal's.

The most chilling sight and sound of the camp was the three-hundred-foot clock tower that rang a deafening bell on each hour. Each time the clock tower rang, rebels would randomly haul away several prisoners, ranging in number from three to as many as fifty. During their first few hours at the camp, Alex, Karen, and Walker noticed how everyone would look toward the clock tower in anticipation of the bell sounding. When the clock tower showed the time to be three o'clock, the bell let out three deafening peals. The prisoners screamed and shouted as the rebels took some of them away.

"Where are they taking them?" Alex asked an old man with a flimsy blanket, shivering from the cold.

"They're going to the chambers," said the old man, coughing between words.

"Chambers? Where are they?" asked Karen.

"The wooden buildings that you see scattered about," said the old man.

"What are they doing to them in there?" asked Alex.

"No one is certain. We only know that it ends in death."

"Why are they taking only some of the prisoners?" asked Karen.

"They choose people at random. And don't worry, they'll get to you soon enough," said the old man. "Now leave me alone and let me die in peace."

"Look at this," said Walker. "We're like trapped animals, awaiting our demise. You gotta get us out of this. Aren't you guys CIA agents?"

"Calm down, Walker," said Karen. "Alex and I have been in worse situations than this. Right, Alex?"

"I'll answer that as soon as we find Flip," said Alex. "What's the chance he's in here?"

"I don't have a clue," said Karen. "The only way we'll know is if we ask around."

The trio walked through the camp for days without any luck. They wished they could find any familiar face, let alone Flip's. Tears streamed down Karen's face as she witnessed the hopelessness of the crowd. Some were young, some were old. They were of all different shapes, sizes, and colors. Most were women and children. Karen shuddered at the thought of a camp being erected in Brownsville. The people looked like the pictures in her history books of the victims of World War II and Vietnam

185

-- images of the desolate and downtrodden. While traveling through the camp, they made sure to stay together and move with haste when the clock tower rang. Because the camp was so large, they weren't quite sure where to go. They ate food, stale bread, and water when it was given. Just before the sun was about to set on another day, Alex heard a faint voice calling his name.

"Alex," called the voice.

"Karen, did you hear that?" said Alex.

"Yes I did, but from where?" said Karen.

"Maybe they're calling for someone else named Alex," said Walker.

"But the voice sounds awfully familiar," said Alex. "Let's move in the direction of the voice."

They moved through the crowds and found the source of the voice. Emerging toward them was Lieutenant Jackson. Alex and Karen ran to embrace him as soon as their eyes met.

"What on God's green Earth are you doing here?" asked Jackson.

"We were captured while driving from Brownsville. Here's the guy who drove us. Lieutenant Jackson, meet Walker."

"Sir, the pleasure is all mine," said Walker. "Now we have a lieutenant to go along with two undercover CIA agents. We'll be out of here in no time!"

Jackson chuckled loudly.

"Sir, they're as much CIA agents as we're on vacation in Hawaii," said Jackson.

Walker looked at the teens.

"You mean to tell me you're not secret CIA agents?" asked Walker.

Alex and Karen slowly shook their heads no.

"I can't believe it. You two lied to me," said Walker.

"There's no need to be angry," said Jackson. "These kids are two of the savviest and bravest people I have ever met. Don't let their ages fool you."

"We're sorry for lying to you, but we needed to get to Washington to save the President and that's the truth," said Karen.

"What do you know about the President?" asked Jackson.

"I overheard the Pope talking about getting rid of him while I was recovering in the hospital. He happened to be visiting the sick and injured in Brownsville," said Alex. "The Pope was talking to Ms. Gateway and Detective Riley. He was afraid that the President was going to tell the world the truth about the Catholic Church, aliens, and the world's governments. We tried to warn Flip, but couldn't reach him. So that's why Karen and I, along with Walker, decided to come to Washington. But we were captured and taken here. Do you know if the President is okay?"

"No, he's not," said Jackson. "He, Flip, the Major, and I were confronted by the Pope and taken at gunpoint by the rebels. Flip, the Major, and I were placed in here. The President was placed in a different location. We're not sure where."

"Where did these traitors come from?" asked Karen.

"The rebels are a product of Sétbætañ mind control, activated by reciting the sixth scroll," said Jackson. "Anyone with a BioCharge chip was affected. Unfortunately, over half the world's population has the chip. The Pope was the one who activated the command. Since the rebels have numbers on their side, they were able to seize control of the world's government and capture the President."

"Is the mind control permanent?" asked Alex.

"No," said Jackson. "It wears off in time. But the Pope has continued the brainwashing process with his propaganda."

"Well I'm not quite sure what you're talkin' about when you say that the President was going to tell the truth about the Church and aliens, but how are we gonna get out of this hellhole?" asked Walker.

"Flip, the Major, and I have a plan. And since I found you it'll be easier to execute," said Jackson.

"You know where Flip is?" asked Karen.

"Yep. Just follow me, stay close, and watch out for the rebels stationed in the watchtowers."

Jackson, Alex, Karen, and Walker quickly moved through the crowd while occasionally sneaking a peak at the clock tower. The time read five forty-five which meant they had fifteen

187

minutes before the next group was brought to the chambers. The crowds were so panicky and chaotic, Jackson worried that Flip and Major Kremley might get swept along with whoever was sentenced. It was his hope that they would return to the spot that they agreed upon five minutes before every hour.

The time read five fifty-five when Jackson and the trio arrived at the agreed-upon spot three hundred thirty yards southeast of the clock tower, at a six-foot high stone wall.

When Flip, Jackson, and Kremley arrived at Camp 349, the wall had been one of the first things they noticed. Wasn't it odd to have a brick wall in the middle of nowhere? They decided to make it their meeting point. Just before the clock struck the hour, they would move among the crowd to avoid being brought to the chambers.

The time now read five fifty-six, and Jackson began to worry about the whereabouts of Flip and Kremley.

"Where's Flip?" asked Karen.

"He's supposed to be here, along with Kremley," said Jackson. But we're gonna have to move in another two minutes or we're going to be sitting ducks."

"Why don't we just call out their names?" said Alex.

The four of them screamed for Flip and Kremley as they watched the clock approach five fifty-eight. Jackson worried that Flip and Kremley had been taken to the chambers. He felt that they could wait no longer.

"We've gotta move, now," said Jackson.

Just before the quartet was about to scramble, out of nowhere appeared Flip and Kremley.

"Flip!" screamed Alex and Karen, embracing him with bear hugs.

"Well, what took ya so long?" Flip said to Jackson. "Kids, I would love to hug ya all night but we've gotta move."

As the group began to move, the clock struck six. People scrambled in horror as the deafening chimes filled the evening air. Just in front of Alex, twenty prisoners were captured by rebels and led away to the chambers. If he'd been ten feet farther ahead, Alex would have been captured.

"Son, when we tell you to stay close, we mean for you to stay close," said Jackson.

"You see that chamber over there? That's where the rebels stored our clothes and weapons," said Flip. "We need to get in that chamber, get our stuff, and get the hell out of here."

"How do you know your stuff is in there?" asked Alex.

"Hey, we're government officials. We've been staking out this camp since we got here," said Flip.

"What's your plan for getting us in there and what's your plan once we get in?" asked Karen.

"When the clock strikes seven, we're gonna let the rebels capture us so we can get in the chamber," said Kremley. "Now let's go over what you three need to do once we're inside."

As six forty-five approached, Flip, Jackson, and Kremley gave their final instructions to the trio. Though Walker didn't quite know what was going on, he was more than willing to carry out the mission.

"Now when do I make my move?" asked Walker.

"You do it when the clock reaches six fifty-five," said Flip. "Now I'm gonna get myself ready."

At six fifty-five, Walker began to scream. This drew the attention of some of the nearby field guards.

"Hey, you, shut it up," said one of the guards.

"But my wife, I don't know where she is. Help!" said Walker, shouting and acting convincingly hysterical.

"Oh, I see we have a candidate for the chamber. Just keep it up," said another guard.

While the guards and prisoners gathered around to witness the commotion, Flip slipped behind the brick wall to defecate. In his waste was a small plastic bag of cloaking pills. He'd managed to swallow the bag just before being strip searched. He took a pill and cloaked. The timing couldn't have been more precise. The clock tower began to strike seven.

"My wife, where's my wife? I need her!" yelled Walker as the bell rang.

"You're coming with us," said a rebel guard. "Maybe you'll find your wife in the chambers."

As the guards rounded up several more prisoners, Alex, Karen, Jackson, and Kremley joined the group. They hoped that Flip was not far behind.

At the chamber, the guards knocked on the door with the butts of their weapons. The doors swung open and the prisoners were quickly pushed inside. The chamber was a dimly lit, large room. Chains, whips, ropes, cattle prods, and other torture devices adorned the blood-stained walls. Above, hanging from the ceiling, were human corpses. Some were old, some were young. As Alex looked around, he remembered the torture chamber in Vuur and how he and his father had escaped certain death.

In the far left corner of the room were piles of clothing and bags. Alex assumed that is where Flip's belongings were. Battle tested, Karen, Kremley, and Jackson were ready for action. Walker, on the other hand, talking to himself, was frightened out of his wits.

"I need a drink, boy, do I need a drink," Walker whispered. "I've got to get out of here. I'm gonna die."

"Calm yourself," ordered Kremley. "You're gonna blow the mission."

Alex guessed that there were about twenty prisoners in all. The five guards had gathered to discuss which method of execution to use.

"Okay, we want all of you to line up against the wall and take off all of your clothes," shouted one of the rebel guards. "We're gonna try to make this quick and easy. Let's move."

As the prisoners slowly made their way to the wall, they let out cries of despair. Among them were eight women and three children. Karen tried to comfort a child who'd been separated from her parents for more than a week.

"What's your name, sweetheart?" asked Karen.

"My name is Molly and I want my mommy," cried the girl. "Please, please, where's my mommy?"

Karen didn't answer but hugged the girl and softly caressed her. Eyes filling with tears, she shielded the child's face from the rebels. Alex looked at Karen, beginning to doubt that they would get out of this predicament alive.

Walker and some of the other prisoners, sensing that the end was near, began to chant prayers.

"Our Father, who art in Heaven …"

"Though I walk through the valley of the shadow of death …"

As the prisoners began to undress, the rebel guards raised their guns. Alex closed his eyes. He imagined what his body would look like as it hung from the chamber ceiling. He figured that he had tried his best and given all that he had. The reciting of the Lord's Prayer had seemed to signal for him that the end was near. He opened his eyes to peek at Karen. She was still dressed. Tears flowed from her eyes as she clutched Molly tight. He thought that she looked as beautiful as ever. He wanted to tell her that he loved her but there was no sound when he opened his mouth. He peeked around and saw Walker and the other prisoners were now chanting their prayers, tears streaming down their faces. Alex wondered what had happened to the well-thought-out plan. He opened his eyes to take a peek at Jackson but didn't see him. Then he looked over at Kremley and didn't see him, either. He took off his clothes and shut his eyes tight.

But the guard giving the orders did not say 'Fire.' What he did say sent shivers down Alex's and Karen's spines.

ⲈϨⲞⲨⲚ ⲠⲒⲢⲞ Ⲉ̀ ⲠⲒ ⲀⲦⲀϬⲚⲒ ⳘⲚ̇ⲦⲢⲢⲰⲞⲨ

It was the command of the first scroll to open the portal.

"Oh, my god!" shouted a prisoner. "What's that?"

Without opening his eyes, Alex knew that the prisoner was seeing the dimensional portal. He had figured it out. The rebel guards were going to force the prisoners to go through the portal. Alex guessed that what met them on the other side was certain death.

"Okay, I want every one of you to quickly step through the opening," ordered the guard.

But before the prisoners began to move toward the portal, an explosion of machine gun fire erupted in the chamber. Alex kept

191

his eyes closed and braced himself for impact. But he didn't feel any pain. In fact, he heard a lot of commotion, and the voices of Flip, Jackson, and Kremley. When he opened his eyes, he saw the rebels lying on the ground in pools of their own blood. The prisoners, including Alex, were stunned. Within seconds the dimensional portal had closed.

"All right, everything's fine," said Flip, as he uncloaked, appearing before them with a semi-automatic weapon in his hand.

"If you all remain calm we can get out of here," said Kremley.

"It's a miracle," the prisoners began to chant.

"God saved us," said Walker. "I saw it with my own two eyes. Those rebels went down in thin air. God is great!"

As Walker and the prisoners gave thanks, Alex, Karen, and the rest of the crew dared not say a word. Their next mission was getting out of the prison camp and they needed to make sure that prisoners were able to help others get out.

"I want everyone to listen carefully," said Flip. "I understand that everyone is happy that we were able to avoid disaster. However, think of this as just the beginning."

"Other rebels will come when they find that the rebels in charge of this chamber are missing," said Flip. "You are going to be the first to lead a revolution against the enemy. You four, come here."

Flip selected four adult male prisoners and gave them weapons and ammunition.

"I want you to protect the rest of these people and help them fight against the rebels. We have an important mission that we must attend to."

"You're leaving us? How do you expect us to fight against the rebels?" asked one of the prisoners.

Alex and Karen looked at each other in disbelief. They'd never imagined that part of Flip's plan was to leave the prisoners.

"You can't leave them here," said Karen. "We have to save them. They have no chance against the rebels."

192

Flip pulled Alex and Karen aside.

"Now listen here," said Flip, trying to remain calm. "We cannot jeopardize the mission by taking any of the prisoners, none of them. So I'm asking you two to keep your mouths shut and follow orders. Do you understand?"

"Yes, sir," they said meekly.

Flip then went back to address the concerns of the prisoners.

"You fight by believing in God. Look at what just happened here. My team and I rescued you, appearing out of thin air. Now if that isn't the hand of God I don't know what is!"

Karen, not one to easily give up, looked at Alex before offering a suggestion.

"The little girl, Molly, can we take her?" asked Karen. "She has no family."

Flip's face turned red with anger.

"I'm not sure that'll be a good idea," said Kremley.

"Don't worry, I'll watch her. I wanna stay and fight," said Walker. "These last few moments have proved that God is alive and well and that we were rescued by His angels. I'm willing to protect and watch over this little girl by raising my weapon to fight."

Kremley walked over to Walker and handed him a semi-automatic weapon and some ammunition. The team wished him good luck. Alex and Karen were especially appreciative.

"We want to thank you for all of your help," said Karen.

"Yes," said Alex. "I was a little apprehensive about you at first but you've earned my respect."

"Well I'm just tryin' to do the right thing," said Walker. "Those demons took away my wife and children. The least I can do is to try and help this little girl. I plan on fightin' them to the death."

Karen turned to the little girl to see if she would be all right with Walker. The little girl had a smile on her face.

"Molly, I want you to be a good girl, okay?" said Karen. "Walker's going to be looking after you now. Make sure you do what he says."

"I will. Thank you for looking after me," said the little girl.

193

Karen gave her a big hug.

Flip gave Alex and Karen each a cloaking pill.

"Okay, kiddies. Take your medicine so we can get out of here. We have a President to find," said Flip.

"Our sources say that he's still in the Washington, D.C., vicinity," said Jackson.

"Good," said Kremley. "Good thing he still has that homing device on him."

"We better get a move on," said Flip. "Even though we can still track the President, there's no telling if those Setties or that deranged Pope have done away with him."

Alex and Karen said goodbye to the prisoners, took their pills, and began to cloak. The prisoners looked at them as if they were angels. As Alex faded from view, he saw glimpses of hope that he hadn't seen on a civilian face in a long time.

Maybe things are finally turning for the better.

Chapter 28
The Manipulation of Molahsras

The forecast had predicted a late-winter blizzard for the majority of the east coast. Washington was slated to receive twelve to sixteen inches of snow. This new layer would fall on top of the already accumulated snow and ice that had paralyzed the city. As springtime approached, the desolate streets were patrolled by tanks driven by the Sétbætañ and their human rebel forces. Any civilian roaming the streets without proper identification was placed in a concentration camp or shot on sight. Proper identification meant having the implanted BioCharge microchip, which was now controlled by the Sétbætañ.

Those with the microchip who were not fighting alongside the Sétbætañ lived like brainwashed robots. Their days consisted of staying at home watching The Faith in God Channel, run and hosted by Pope Gregory, and the now government-censored TAPC News channel. Regular jobs were no longer necessary. Most places of business had been destroyed, and the Church and the newly structured U.S. government provided citizens a living allowance. The Faith in God Channel, which aired twenty-four hours a day, seven days a week, taught believers that God and the Catholic Church were all that mattered and that anyone who did not believe should and would be condemned to the Lake of Fire. They were promised the Return of the Savior. This was the only thing that kept up morale. When people did leave their homes, it was to gather food or to go door-to-door, spreading the Word of God. Citizens were expected to report suspected non-believers to the authorities to be stripped of their allowance and condemned.

Methods to maintain faith in the Church's teachings included a worldwide telecast via satellite on The Faith in God Channel in which non-believers and those opposed to the Church were sentenced to the fiery lake of Enervet Sine in Vuur. People taken to the concentration camp chambers were usually the ones sacrificed in order to perpetuate the Church's propaganda. First,

195

they'd be forced at gunpoint through the portal. Upon entering the portal to Vuur, they were met by the Pope or one of his many Church leaders, flanked by creatures of the Sétbætañ. Those to be condemned were judged on their supposed wrong-doings in front of millions. The creatures of the Sétbætañ would then force them into the Lake of Fire. When people saw this, they dared not question or challenge the authority of the Church for it was now confirmed that hell did exist and that those who did not abide by God's law would be punished. No longer did a person have to wait until death to be damned. The era of Armageddon, as prophesied in the Bible, included the condemning of live souls. Nearly fifteen-thousand people were being sentenced to Enervet Sine every week.

"True believers, witness the destruction of those who rebel against God," said the Pope on his daily television program. "These twelve individuals have been sentenced for crimes committed against the Church. Witness hell's angels casting them into the fire!"

Streams of lava flanked by billows of black smoke flowed into the fiery lake of Enervet Sine. Stripped naked, the accused stood on a rocky cliff with the Pope and six members of the Sétbætañ. They were of different ages, races, and ethnicities. The cliff stood one hundred and fifty feet tall, overlooking the fiery lake. The creatures, who wielded large swords and guns, made sure to block any path of escape as the Pope addressed the accused.

"Do any of you sinners have any last words before meeting your fate?" asked the Pope.

Some of them wept loudly. Some tried to escape. Others called out God's name and begged for forgiveness. Others cursed Him. A few fell to their knees and begged the Pope for forgiveness. None of their pleas would sway the Pope and his hardened soul.

"Into the fires of hell," shouted the Pope, as the accused were forced at knife and gunpoint to fall to their deaths.

Millions of television viewers witnessed the naked humans falling from the cliff into the Lake of Fire. The Sétbætañ used their swords on anyone who resisted. Each of them screamed while falling off the cliff and when their body reached the fiery surface. Explosions of fire, lava, and smoke would erupt each time a body was cast into the lake.

"True believers, you have just witnessed the destruction of those who rebelled against the Church. Do not fall victim to evil, as you will meet a similar fate," warned the Pope.

Everyone around the world was enslaved to the whims of the Church. And it was not limited to Catholics. All denominations and religions had to convert to the teachings of the Church or face death. As it had been years ago, through the use of fear and violence, the Pope had again become the most powerful man on the planet.

On Pennsylvania Avenue in the bowels of the White House, President Topher sat quietly in the corner of a small, cold, dark, empty room guarded by a young rebel. It had been two weeks since his capture. The hallways of the White House remained dark due to the Sétbætañ's attack on the city, and the darkness and cold created a dismal setting. The President, usually optimistic no matter the situation, began to have doubts about the future of the country and the world. To his surprise, he'd been treated well. Even though he shivered from the cold, he was served food and drink three times a day, given tubs of water for bathing, a fresh change of clothes, and blankets to help keep warm. There was a monitor, providing the only light in the room, showing The Faith in God and TAPC News channels. Even though he felt fortunate to be alive, the President was puzzled as to why he hadn't been put into a concentration camp or killed on the spot. He wondered what had happened to Kremley, Jackson, and Flip and what the Pope had up his sleeve. And while the President knew he was in dire straits, he tried to maintain his composure by making small talk with the rebel.

"If I were you, I would keep my mouth shut," said the young rebel. "You don't know how I take pleasure in holding you at gunpoint. I'm glad to say that I never voted for you. I've always known that you were the antichrist. And if the Pope gives me a chance, I'm going to plant a bullet right in the middle of your forehead."

The President pitied the brainwashed rebel.

"I'm not your enemy, son."

"Just keep your mouth shut," countered the rebel.

The small room in which the President was imprisoned reflected the fall of the world's governments. Former leaders of nations were jailed, killed, or made powerless. The majority of the President's staff had been killed or sent to concentration camps. Topher was alone, without allies.

He heard a shuffle outside the door. The rebel who had been guarding him peeked outside and abruptly left. Topher's blood pressure rose when he saw who'd entered.

"Good morning, Christopher. Have you been enjoying The Faith in God Channel?" asked the Pope.

"I never thought that you would stoop so low as to sacrifice innocent lives to fuel your propaganda," said the President.

"Don't you tell me about sacrificing innocent lives," scoffed the Pope. "Lives were sacrificed the moment that you and all the world's governments allowed the placement of BioCharge chips into human bodies."

"I realize that may have been a mistake," said the President. "But that chip was made to improve lives, not destroy them. Look at what you've done. Your actions alone have caused more damage than that chip and the aliens ever have."

"I see that no matter the situation, you remain arrogant as ever," said the Pope. "I am taking people back to the way things used to be. The way things ought to be. With everything revolving around the Church and God. You and your government attempted to eliminate God from the equation."

"That's not true. Unlike the Church, we wanted people to have free will. We believe that people should have the freedom of choice when it comes to choosing their own denomination. To select a religion that's not Christianity. To have a choice in whether or not to believe in God. You and the Church have reverted to the days of the Inquisition. Only this is much worse. You have proved people right. You are a heartless soul."

"I care nothing for my enemies. They'll pay for their insolence," said the Pope. "I will not deny that the Church now has unyielding power. If I wanted to I could make you disappear and not a question would be asked. But keeping you alive has a purpose of which you will soon learn. There is also someone you shall meet."

"I'm not interested in meeting or negotiating with any of your cronies," said the President.

"You have no choice," said the Pope. "Tell me Christopher, have you ever wondered why your parents left you on the doorstep of an orphanage? Or why you seemed to be different from other children? Tonight you'll find out. Just make sure to watch The Faith in God Channel."

With that warning, the Pope abruptly left the room and the rebel guard returned. The President now had a new worry: *What evil does the Pope have up his sleeve this time?*

It was after eleven o'clock and the Pope had just finished another segment on condemning people to Enervet Sine. Sickened by the images on the monitor, the President tried not to look. He began to believe that the Pope was bluffing when he'd brought up having information on Topher's past. The Pope, who still had his office in Vatican City, and traveled the world via dimensional portal, was close to signing off for the night. At this point in the program he usually welcomed his viewers to watch programmed reruns or to tune in to the TAPC News channel. Tonight, however, he stated that he had an important announcement. This caught the President's attention.

"People of the world, several weeks ago I told you that the President of the United States, Christopher Topher, went into exile because of his disbelief in the existence of God. The usual punishment for such insolence is death by the fiery lake of hell. But because Mr. Topher pleaded with the Church for

199

forgiveness, and promised to repent and accept the Church, we have decided to spare his life. He wishes to communicate with you, through the Church, that he has welcomed the opportunity to serve on the board of the newly structured World Apex Government. This new world government will no longer allow a separation of church and state. There is only one faith, and it must be followed. The new government council has unanimously agreed that all must follow the teachings of the Roman Catholic Church. Anyone who does not will face dire consequences, including death. To be broadcast later this week on both the Faith in God and TAPC News channels, Mr. Topher will confess to the world a deep sin that he has harbored all his life. I beg all of you to forgive him for his past transgressions and what he'll reveal. Now, let us pray:

"Our great Church which dwells on Earth,
How mighty is your name?
Thy kingdom come, thy will be done on Earth as it is in Heaven.
Give us this day of triumph, as we punish our enemies with death.
And lead us not from our law, but deliver us from evil.
For the kingdom, the power, and the glory of the Church are yours forever and ever.
Amen."

When the Pope's image finally left the monitor, the President could not believe what had transpired. The Pope had communicated to the world that Topher had agreed to serve as a board member of a new world government and that he would be introduced as such in front of billions of people. He was further appalled that he would report to the Pope and that the Pope had lied about him having asked for forgiveness. After the President tried to digest what he'd heard, he once again tried to talk with the rebel. At this point, he wasn't afraid of the consequences.

"Hey, did you hear that? I'm going to serve on the board of the newly formed World Apex Government. That means I'm going to report directly to the head honcho, Pope Gregory. Plus, I get to confess to some sin I don't even know about. I think I'm ready to take that bullet in the middle of my forehead."

Moments later, a loud humming sound accompanied by a flash of light filled the hallways and then disappeared. As footsteps approached the doorway, the rebel guard exited the room. When the door reopened, the Pope walked in.

"Well, Christopher, are you up for the job or what?" asked the Pope, grinning.

"What kind of game are you playing?"

"Oh, I'm not playing any kind of game. You will appear on my channel and accept your fate."

"I will not. You'll have to dump me in Enervet Sine with the rest of the innocent people you've murdered."

"Unfortunately, that's not my decision to make. You don't realize how badly I wish to take you up on that offer, but there's been a change of plans. The main reason you've been kept alive is because I have promised my business partner that you would not be harmed. We've agreed that if you are harmed, it would be at his hands only."

"Whoever it is sounds like he's the boss and you're just one of his minions. Let me guess. Is it one of your alien friends? And why is he so interested in keeping me alive?"

"Listen, I care nothing about those aliens," said the Pope. "Make no mistake. I hate them with a passion. I would cut their hearts out of their chests if I got the opportunity."

Once again, there was a loud humming sound accompanied by a brief flash of light. Only this time it was inside the room. When the President saw what emerged from the portal he fell to his knees.

"I'd like to introduce you to my partner, the mighty Ecaep," said the Pope. "Oh, and by the way, he also happens to be your father."

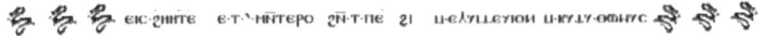

It was a little over two hundred miliyous, or six hundred earth years, ago when Ecaep had worked as a slave on one of Mataralin's farms in Urodae. He was one of hundreds of

Sétbætañ working the fields. His duties ranged from cultivating the soil to gathering the crops. Sometimes he would take the gathered crops and deliver them directly to one of Mataralin's councils. Mataralin feared Ecaep because he was strong, smart, and possessed leadership qualities. Though he wavered on whether to kill Ecaep, Mataralin felt it was best to keep a close eye on a potential enemy. And Ecaep was his best worker. Many noticed Ecaep, including Mataralin's daughter, Bwendai.

Bwendai was unlike many of the other Luçimarks. She'd never had a problem mingling with the Sétbætañ. Though she was a Luçimark princess and the daughter of one of the most notorious beings who'd ever lived, she felt that both races should live peacefully together as they had many miliyous before. This type of thinking made her father very angry. It was forbidden for Luçimarks to mingle with Sétbætañ. But Bwendai was a free spirit and also very attractive. She drew attention from Luçimark and Sétbætañ alike.

Every evening, Ecaep brought his share of crops to one of the direct councils. One day, during this delivery, he happened to run into Bwendai.

"Another bountiful crop, I see," said Bwendai. "How is it that you always outperform the other workers?"

"It's about dedication and hard work. I strive to be victorious in everything I do. Even when gathering crops."

"You know, many of my people hate you out of jealousy", said Bwendai. "Do you not fear for your life?"

"I fear not, because I am fear," said Ecaep. "Should you not fear for your life as you mingle with a Sétbætañ?"

"I have no fear for my life. I mingle with whomever I admire."

"How can you admire what is ugly and unpleasing to the eye?"

"My eyes see the beauty of your soul," said Bwendai. "And this has been seen by many others. Only the eyes of those who hate would find you unpleasing."

That night, under a shroud of secrecy, Ecaep and Bwendai fell in love. Their love would last in secret for nearly one miliyou, until Bwendai became pregnant.

"Ecaep, you must leave these parts of Urodae. My father will have you killed when he finds out."

"I'm not going anywhere. I'm willing to sacrifice my blood for the life of my child and the one I love."

"Then we must contact Suini. She will know what to do."

For the following months, Bwendai was mentored in secret by a Luçimark caretaker and midwife named Suini. The caretaker knew that if the pregnancy was discovered, the child, Ecaep, and possibly Bwendai would be executed. She assisted Bwendai in concealing her pregnancy from her father by showing her how to wear garments in a certain fashion. Meanwhile, as Ecaep gathered crops each day, he tried to formulate a plan for him, Bwendai, and their child to escape the wrath of Mataralin. Each night he would meet Bwendai at Suini's cottage.

"Soon you will give birth to the first being known to be of both Sétbætañ and Luçimark blood," stated Ecaep.

"And once the child is discovered our lives will be in danger," said Bwendai.

"You must have faith. You have many allies," said Suini.

Bwendai soon gave birth to a male child. He didn't have any of the diverse traits of a Sétbætañ, or the webbed hands and wide-set eyes of a Luçimark. He looked human. Suini, who had delivered her share of children, was flabbergasted when she saw the child.

"This child is like no other," said Suini. "The mix of the bloods has produced a being that is certain to be destroyed by Sétbætañ or Luçimark. I must take him away if he is to survive."

"No, I want my child," said Bwendai. "This child has given me reason to live. He is special. Look at how beautiful he is. His beauty surpasses that of all Luçimarks in Urodae. I choose to stay and fight for him."

Ecaep understood Suini's thinking.

"They will destroy the child," he said. "Go. Take him away so he can be safe. This child fulfills the ancient Sétbætañ prophecy foretold by our forefathers. I shall call him Molahsras, for he is the prince who shall deliver our people from the hands of Luçimark oppression."

"I understand your reasoning," a tearful Bwendai said to Ecaep and Suini. "Suini, please go and save my child."

So with Bwendai's blessing, the caretaker, with her top aide at her side, fled the village with the child. Unbeknownst to Ecaep, the princess, or Suini, Mataralin's spies had discovered their plans. Suini's cottage was ransacked and Mataralin's troops took Ecaep and Bwendai into custody. The caretaker and the child were captured just outside of the Asus Forest and taken before the Luçimark leader at Enervet Sine. Her aide was nowhere to be found.

"You fools, you thought that you could escape me? You thought that you could fool me? How dare you. All of you!" screamed Mataralin. Then he looked sadly at Bwendai. "I've been betrayed by my own daughter. You've created this abomination with this beast. Someone I knew couldn't be trusted."

He also addressed Suini.

"And you, the caretaker and midwife who raised my daughter like her own since her mother's death. Your betrayal saddens me most."

Mataralin ordered his guards to take the child from Suini. With a nod of his head, he instructed the guards to force her off the cliff into the Lake of Fire. The scream from the caretaker was so terrifying, even Ecaep was shaken.

"Take Bwendai away," Mataralin ordered his guards. The other guards held Ecaep back with swords. Mataralin was holding the child, wrapped tightly in a thick blanket.

"Now, I'll destroy this monstrosity. And I'll save you for last," said Mataralin, to Ecaep.

Without looking at the infant, Mataralin wildly flung his arms over the cliff. In an instant the child was engulfed in the fiery lake of Enervet Sine.

"Nooooo!" screamed Ecaep as he struggled to escape from Mataralin's guards.

Bwendai did escape. The loss of her child drove her to

madness. Without warning, the screaming Luçimark princess flung herself off the cliff into the Lake of Fire.

"Nooooo!" screamed Mataralin.

"Bwendai!" screamed Ecaep, his voice reverberating around Caynonã.

"I'll kill you," said Ecaep, whose anger now gave him the strength of ten Sétbætañ.

As Ecaep wrestled away from the guards, Mataralin cloaked to thwart Ecaep's attack. Mataralin's guards were not as fortunate. Ecaep grabbed one of their swords and slaughtered them one by one.

Ecaep escaped from Urodae and took up exile in Vuur, vowing to exact his revenge on Mataralin and all Luçimarks. Little did he know, other life-altering events had already been put in motion.

Prior to Suini's capture, she and her aide had arrived at a coreintel -- a Luçimark ice chamber for preserving living beings -- on the outskirts of Urodae. The Luçimarks primarily used the ice chambers to hold soldiers in suspended animation for use in future wars. They also used the chambers to preserve children. These children would repopulate the race when and if necessary. Only the wealthiest Luçimarks could afford to keep their offspring in a coreintel. There were fifty ice chambers in Urodae and each contained about thirty thousand individuals. On average, a body could survive in the chambers for up to three hundred miliyous which is nine hundred Earth years. Suini had known the owner of a coreintel for many miliyous and was now looking for a favor.

"Colox, I need your help to preserve this child," Suini said, handing the coreintel owner a bag of coins.

"Why do you wish to preserve this child and why do you bring the child here?" asked Colox.

"This is the child of Princess Bwendai. His name is Molahsras. He was fathered by the Sétbætañ Ecaep," said Suini.

Colox pulled the blanket away to get a good look at the child. He was stunned but kept his composure.

"The product of Luçimark and Sétbætañ blood appears human, though it is not. It looks as if the ancient Sétbætañ prophecy has been fulfilled. Why should I save this creature when it has been foretold that he will lead Ecaep's people from Luçimark bondage?"

"I am carrying out the wishes of the princess. When Mataralin finds out he will undoubtedly kill the child," said Suini.

"Mataralin and his spies are always watching, so the child is already dead," said Colox.

"There's nothing you can do?" asked Suini.

"If they find out I am hiding the child here, I will be executed," said Colox.

"Well here, take this. Will this change your mind?" said Suini, handing Colox another bag of coins.

"Okay, I have a plan," said the coreintel owner.

Colox took the child. He returned a few minutes later with a Luçimark child in his arms.

"Take this child in his place. I will preserve the child of Bwendai," said Colox. "But understand that you and your aide have already sacrificed your lives."

Suini looked her aide in the eyes.

"I will be the sacrifice for both of us," Suini said to the aide. "But you must promise me that you will protect the child with your life."

"I will," said the aide.

Suini took the Luçimark infant and headed toward the Asus Forest. Despite the danger, escaping to the forest gave her the best chance of survival. She had learned the ways of the forest as a child. Meanwhile, Suini's aide struck a deal with Colox to become one of his servants.

Miliyous passed, and lingering rumors that the child of Ecaep lived grew. Villagers told soldiers they'd seen two Luçimark females traveling hastily toward the outskirts of Urodae at the time the caretaker had been wanted for treason. Mataralin and his soldiers speculated that the child was being preserved in a coreintel. Each ice chamber was thoroughly searched. But Colox always kept an eye out for unwanted guests and was able to warn the aide in time.

"Hurry and grab the child. You must leave," said Colox. "Mataralin's troops are on their way. They have figured out the location of the child."

"After two hundred miliyous, they have finally caught up to us," said the aide. "Thank you for all that you've done."

"You are welcome," said Colox. "Now go."

Just as Mataralin's troops reached the entrance of the coreintel, the aide gathered the child from his chamber and chanted the command to open the dimensional portal to Earth.

ⲉⲃⲟⲩⲛ ⲡ ⲓⲣⲟ ⲉ̀ ⲡⲓ ⲁⲧⲁ6ⲛⲓ ⲙ̄ ⲧⲡⲣⲱⲟⲩ

When the aide reached Earth, she landed in an urban section of Philadelphia. Still cloaked, she spent time reviving the child from his six hundred earth years in suspended animation. Keeping her promise to Suini, she put the child on the doorstep of an orphanage. She knew that this was the best way to ensure his survival -- to be raised on Earth. Even though the baby had alien blood, he would easily pass for human. When the aide knocked on the orphanage door, a middle-aged woman answered and found the child at her feet. Alerting everyone to her discovery, she took the child inside and closed the door. The aide, still cloaked, cried as she watched the child disappear.

When the aide returned to Urodae, she was eventually captured and executed. But her mission to safeguard the child's survival had been a success. Ecaep remained unaware.

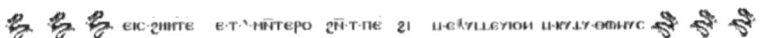 ⲉⲓⲥ-2ⲏⲡ̄ⲧⲉ ⲉⲧ·ⲙ̄ⲙⲏⲧⲉⲣⲟ ⲟⲛ̄·ⲧ·ⲡⲉ 21 ⲙ-ⲉⲁⲩⲗⲗⲉⲩⲓⲟⲙ ⲙ-ⲕⲩⲗⲩ-ⲟⲥⲟⲏⲏⲧⲥ

"Finally, after these many miliyous, I lay eyes on my son," said Ecaep. "I thought you had died at the hands of Mataralin, but you live. Now is the time to take your rightful place as leader

207

of the Sétbætañ."

"My father?" said the stunned President. "I already have a father and he's not some evil alien being."

"But facts are facts, Christopher," interjected the Pope. "The father you knew was your adoptive father. Didn't you always wonder why you were so different from others?"

"You're a filthy liar," said the President.

"I don't lie about such matters," said the Pope. "I've had my eye on you for many years. While I searched the Earth for the coveted seventh scroll, my relationship with the Sétbætañ allowed me to follow your every move, from the time you were left at the orphanage. You see, the Sétbætañ were tipped off by how brilliant you were at such a young age. When they heard of an orphan child who could recite Shakespeare; add, subtract, and multiply; and read college text, all at the age of three, we knew it was a strong possibility that you were the Sétbætañ's chosen child. Luckily for you, the foolish Luçimark leader thought you were dead, and was only concerned with finding the sacred scrolls. Never in his wildest dreams did he consider that you could be alive on Earth.

"You were number one in all of your classes, always recognized nationally. And when you began a political career that was no less than brilliant, we knew that you were the one. The alien blood that flows in you makes you superior to any human on this Earth."

"That still doesn't prove anything," said the President. "There are plenty of child prodigies who had political careers. And look at me, do I look like an alien to you?"

"On the back on your left shoulder," interjected Ecaep. "There should be a scar in the shape of a triangle enclosed by a circle with two arrows. A smaller circle is at the top of the triangle."

To the President it seemed as if time had stopped.

He sighed. "I have the scar you described. But you still fail to explain what any of this proves."

"It proves much," said Ecaep. "After you were born, I carved that mark into your skin. It is the mark of the Sétbætañ, the symbol of our salvation. The triangle represents the doorway to the dimensions of other worlds. The circle represents space and time. The two arrows that cross the triangle represent the swords of war. The small circle at the top of the triangle is the watchful eye of the Sétbætañ. Not only is this mark on your body, it's on each of the seven sacred scrolls, inscribed by our forefathers many miliyous ago. The Luçimarks tried to lay claim to the mark by erecting pyramids on this world. Notice, the pyramid is in the shape of a triangle. Human scholars have hypothesized that the apex of each pyramid points to an ancient alien world. That world is our planet, Caynonã. This was done many miliyous ago, before I existed. Yes, I am old. My age is many of your Earth years. And because of your alien blood you, too, are of an advanced age."

"How old am I?" asked the President, not sure he wanted an answer.

"You are over six hundred Earth years old," said Ecaep.

The President began to quiver, as he realized that the Pope and Ecaep were telling the truth.

"And what of my mother?" asked the President.

"Your mother was killed by grief, administered by my eternal enemy Mataralin," said Ecaep. "She herself was a Luçimark, the daughter of my enemy. She was the only Luçimark I have ever cared for."

"What happened to this Mataralin?" asked the President.

"I have taken care of him," said Ecaep.

The President stood in stunned silence. Not only had he begun to accept that he was an alien, but that he was an alien of two separate races.

"It is time for you to embrace your destiny as the heir apparent to the throne of the Sétbætañ kingdom," continued Ecaep. "Our kingdom spans from Vuur throughout Caynonã. Anyone or anything that challenges our authority shall be eradicated."

"And if I took the throne, what of the humans?" the President asked Ecaep.

"Their purpose would be to serve the Sétbætañ as we served

the Luçimarks for thousands of your Earth years."

"And if I refuse?"

"Then you and every human on Earth shall perish."

"Christopher, please consider the alternatives," injected the Pope. "If you refuse you will cause the destruction of the human race. You will confess that you are not human and will resign as President of the United States. You will be protected by the Church and your own people. If you choose to be on your own, you will be lucky if the humans don't kill you within three days."

"I'm sure you wouldn't mind that," said the President.

"You know me all too well," said the Pope.

"I guess I have no choice," said the President, with tears streaming. "Though I am not human, I feel I'm still one of them. I still feel responsible for them. Therefore, I will lead the Sétbætañ as I serve on the board of the World Apex Government. I'll also confess the truth to the world and step down as President. I think these actions should satisfy you both."

"Excellent," said the Pope. "I shall make arrangements for your announcement."

"And afterward, I shall arrange for you to meet my commanding officers. I'm sure they'll be overjoyed at your existence," said Ecaep.

The President addressed Ecaep one last time.

"Ecaep, upon accepting these responsibilities, do you give me your word as both my commander and my father that no harm will come to the humans?"

"Molahsras, you have my word," said Ecaep.

The name sent shivers down the President's spine.

Ecaep chanted to open the portal. Before entering he gave the President a long look. His look was one a proud parent would give to a child.

"After all these years, my son Molahsras lives. You shall lead our people to their long-awaited salvation."

In an instant, Ecaep and the Pope disappeared into the portal, leaving a stunned President Topher in their wake.

Chapter 29
Operation Pigskin

Alex and Karen were in a large, underground bunker in Virginia, just outside of Washington, D.C. Operation Pigskin, an oddly named directive to find the President, was to be carried out by the United Alliance Marines. Though they'd experienced much and seen plenty, the kids were in awe of the hustle and bustle around them. The vast, brightly lit bunker looked like an underground city swarming with civilians, military personnel, Luçimarks, and scientists in lab coats. These scientists spent the majority of their time researching the Sétbætañ deceased, looking for any information that would give the Alliance an advantage.

Civilians of all ages, races, colors, and beliefs walked through the huge passageways as if they didn't have a care in the world. The assurance that they were safe made it easier for them to adapt to their new environment. Though they didn't have the luxuries they were used to having above ground, they attempted to live their lives to the fullest. These were the people who were against the newly formed World Apex Government. And with the knowledge that President Topher would soon join that organization, it no longer made any sense for them to stay above ground in a society that didn't allow freedom of choice. It was estimated that a quarter of the world's remaining population lived in similar underground bunkers.

Alex, Karen, Flip, Jackson, and Kremley sat at a huge rectangular table among military officials and scientists. The group was strategizing ways to rescue the President. The presence of the teenagers did not sit well with everyone.

"You're going to have to tell me the purpose of having these two in here," said James Bronson, a steel-jawed lieutenant general who had reported to the late General Miller.

"Don't look at them as ordinary teenagers," said Kremley. "These two have been instrumental in the fight against the Sétbætañ. Alex is the young man who discovered the hidden scrolls."

"So, in other words, this is the lad who set off an interplanetary war. Am I correct in that interpretation, sir?" asked Bronson.

"Sir, I think you're being a bit harsh by saying the kid set off an interplanetary war. He found the scrolls buried in a sewer beneath a junkyard. It's not like he was looking for them," said Flip.

"I don't think I was talking to you, captain," said Bronson. "I know this kid's entire history and how his father was a traitor to the American government."

"Sir, I felt the same way for a long time," said Kremley. "But his father was trying to protect us by hiding the scrolls. He knew how dangerous they were."

"Phillip Smiley is and will always be remembered as a traitor in the eyes of the U.S. Government," said Bronson, raising his voice. "I understand that he died fighting the enemy, but it's something he probably deserved."

"How dare you talk about my father that way," said Alex. "He has more courage than anyone in this room. He was tortured, abducted, and killed, all while trying to protect this country and the world."

"You are out of line, young man," said Bronson. "You are talking to a twenty-five-year veteran of the United States military. I've paid my dues, son."

"And I've paid mine," said Alex. "Not only have I been hunted and abducted by the aliens, I have fought beside the Alliance against the Sétbætañ at the front line. I nearly lost my life in a concentration camp. I've been paralyzed. I've been chased by wolf-creatures. I spent time in an alien prison. I almost lost my best friend at the hands of an alien. And my father, after being tortured for days, died in my arms. So sir, like you, I've paid my dues. I do realize that because of my actions, I've put many people in danger, including my family and Karen. It would've been easy for me to turn my back on everything and just go home. Yet, I'm still here, ready and willing to give my life not only for the President, but for America and the free world."

212

The military officials sat in stunned silence. Even Bronson was at a loss for words. Flip, Jackson, and Kremley had slight grins on their faces. Karen, who would usually speak up for Alex at times like these, was glowing with admiration. She now knew that the shy, skinny kid with low self-esteem was long gone.

"We appreciate all that you've done for our country, young man," said a subdued Bronson. "Understand that our country and the world have never experienced anything like this before. It has placed all of us on edge."

"Alex, why don't you tell him what you heard while you were a patient in that Brownsville clinic?" said Karen.

"I overheard the Pope saying that he was going to take care of the President," said Alex.

"What did he mean by 'take care of the President?'" asked Bronson.

"I'm paraphrasing, but he said that he had a plan that would make the President step down from office," said Alex.

"And you say you heard the Pope say this?" said Bronson. "Are you sure you weren't hallucinating? I know he was scheduled to visit local hospitals and clinics, but I'm puzzled as to why he would be in Brownsville. Do you have any idea who he was talking to?"

"I was fully coherent," said Alex. "He was talking to Detective Riley and Ms. Gateway."

"Detective Riley and Ms. Gateway?" said Bronson.

"That would be agents Victor Riley and Elizabeth Gateway," said Jackson. "They are both undercover CIA."

"Do you have a history with them?" Bronson asked Alex.

"Not with the Pope, of course," said Alex. "I only knew about Riley through my father, but Ms. Gateway was one of my middle-school teachers."

"Both Riley and Gateway were assigned to Brownsville to keep an eye on your father," said Bronson. "None of our officials had any idea they'd get out of control."

"And they made Alex and his family's lives miserable," said Karen.

Bronson paused and looked at the other military officials.

213

"What? Are you surprised that we have traitors in our government?" said Flip. "These were the same people who held us at gunpoint and kidnapped the President. And do you recall that report about General Miller being killed by the aliens? Well, I'm here to inform you that it was Riley and Gateway who pulled the trigger."

"Are you sure about that, captain?" said Bronson.

"Oh, I'm sure," said Flip. "I have his spattered blood all over my military jacket to prove it."

"I can't believe they would betray their own nation and destroy so many lives. And to betray it on behalf of that religious kook?" said Bronson, referring to the Pope. "The Pope made a live broadcast telling the masses that the President would be joining the World Apex Government. And once he's part of that, there's no telling what's going to happen. So at least we know he's still alive. So to the matter at hand. How are we going to locate and rescue the President?" asked Bronson.

"A homing device was placed on his jacket just before he was taken by the Pope," said Jackson. "We have tracked his signal to the basement of the White House. I'm afraid we can't be sure he's still there. At this point, we can only hope."

"The streets are teeming with Sétbætañ and their rebel forces," said Kremley. "And they've seized many of our weapons. How are we going to reach the White House?"

"I think I may have a solution," said a voice from across the table.

It was scientist John Creighton, considered one of the world's brightest and most innovative minds. He'd worked for the government for more than thirty years. A specialist in biorobotics, Creighton was the creator of the BioCharge chip imbedded in eighty percent of the world's population. He was short and slight, wore glasses, and spoke with a British accent.

"What's your solution?" asked Bronson.

"A weapon that could trump anything created by the Sétbætañ, including the scrolls. Let's go down to the lab, shall we?"

The squad, led by Creighton, loaded into a couple of jeeps

214

and traveled to a remote part of the bunker heavily guarded by military personnel. Civilians were not allowed access except for Alex and Karen, who were granted special privilege. They rode an elevator farther down into the earth.

"The majority of our top-secret experiments are down here," said Creighton. "Some of the experiments you'll see have been around since the 1950s."

After their descent, the group found themselves in a quiet, dimly lit tunnel with four labs, two on each side. Each lab had a huge, silver, sliding, blast-proof door.

"Follow me," said Creighton, leading them down the tunnel. "The lab we are going to is the last one on the right."

"This is creeping me out," Karen whispered to Alex.

"I'm all too familiar with creepy tunnels and passageways," said Alex.

Creighton opened the door with a simple swipe of his hand. Flip took notice right away.

"Hey, you've got a BioCharge chip. Were you temporarily controlled by the Sétbætañ?"

"No, because the chip I have is not like the others," said Creighton. "Let me explain. The chips embedded in the population contained a functionality allowing the reading of emotions."

"The chip could read emotions? Why would the government allow something like that?" asked Kremley.

"It wasn't totally the government's brain child," said Creighton, leading the group through the lab. "That was the idea of the corporations."

"The corporations? What was their stake in this?" asked Flip.

"Is it really that hard to figure out, captain?" said Creighton. "Money. You see if the corporations knew what consumers wanted before producing goods, they would save a ton of money. As a matter of fact, the BioCharge chip saved corporations around the world an estimated one hundred seventy billion dollars. Why do you think we had such significant gains in the stock market in the past six years?"

"So we imbedded something in people that could read minds?

215

Sir, did you know about this?" Flip asked Bronson.

"Everyone on my level and up knew about it, including the President of the United States."

"Well, how in the hell did the Pope and the Sétbætañ find out about it?" asked Flip.

"Our government got the technology from the Nazis," said Bronson. "Years ago, the Sétbætañ engineered the technology for purposes of mind control and had plans to use it as a weapon against the Luçimarks. When the Luçimarks stole it from them, they sold it to the Nazis in exchange for weapons. When Nazi Germany was defeated, the United States and her allies gained the technology. Now that it's back in Sétbætañ hands, the Pope would know about it because they are allies."

"So our government was never concerned that a technology this dangerous could be used against us?" asked Jackson. "And why put it in the chip?"

"These BioCharge chips were originally created as a weapon to be embedded into enemy soldiers -- namely POWs," said Bronson. "When it became apparent that embedding our enemies with the chips wouldn't be worth the cost, President Topher came up with the idea of using them for commerce. He didn't realize that the chips would be mass-produced with the emotion technology included.

"We never figured there would be any issues with the emotion technology in the chips, nor did we ever imagine that the aliens would reacquire the technology. So we made the decision not to have a recall on the chips. Unfortunately, when the Sétbætañ did gain back the technology, it was easy for them to use it against us. So in hindsight, what Phillip Smiley did by hiding the scrolls was to prolong the inevitable: a total alien invasion by mind control."

"Sir, would it be a stretch to say that the government aided the aliens with this mass destruction?" said Flip. "Think about it. We knew about the scrolls. We knew about the satellites and how they were controlled by the voice-recognition technology. And lastly, we knew about the mind-control technology and put it in the chip. So tell me, sir, who's at fault here?"

Bronson didn't bother to answer. He just walked in a straight line with his jaw clenched. The story didn't surprise Alex. His mother had always warned him that the government was up to no good.

"Tell me, sir," said Alex, directing a question toward Bronson. "Since we know the satellites carry out the commands written on the scrolls, why don't we just destroy the satellites?"

"Because they're cloaked and we can't locate them. If it were that simple, don't you think we would've done it already?" said Bronson.

As the group went through the lab, many oddities caught the kids' eyes. There were embalmed alien bodies -- some whole, some in parts -- mostly Sétbætañ, but also some Luçimarks. The creatures ranged in age, size, and type.

"What were you doing with the creatures?" asked Alex.

"We wanted to see how they ticked, how we humans could benefit from them," said Creighton. "Both the Sétbætañ and the Luçimarks age very slowly. We have yet to understand why. Some scientists think it has something to do with the time difference on their planet. I think figuring this out could prove beneficial to the human race."

"Karen and I were on Caynonã for quite a while. Do you think we were affected?" asked Alex

"Quite possibly," said Creighton. "Due to the time difference between our planets, your life span would be longer on Caynonã. Whenever you returned to Earth from the other planet, you'd arrive at a point that seemed farther ahead in the future than you should have been, given how long you'd been gone. And that's why you felt you were missing time. Since you two are young, it's hard to tell what the long-term effects will be."

"I think it had the opposite effect. Y'all look old," said Flip in a joking manner.

"Hey, take that back," said Karen.

"All kidding aside, I don't think I would care to live for hundreds of years," said Flip.

The group entered a small room that held legions of close-fitting uniforms modeled on mannequins in a display case. The

217

uniforms were in a range of sizes and were green, brown, or tan.

"Behind this glass is the government's latest invention in biorobotics," said Creighton. "Artificial Robotic Intelligent Skin, the acronym is pronounced a-RISE-en. When worn, these ARISN uniforms can fire laser beams toward a target by the user just thinking it."

"Where do the beams fire from?" asked Jackson.

"From your hand or your fist," said Creighton.

"How do you acquire ammunition?" asked Alex.

"The uniform is powered by the electricity generated naturally by the human body. This creates the ammunition," said Creighton.

"Can you ever run out of ammunition?" asked Kremley.

"Well, yes and no," said Creighton. "If the body is deprived of necessary nutrients, then it's possible it will not generate enough electricity to power the uniform. As an alternative, if it's not possible for the body to quickly reenergize, the ARISN can be charged artificially and can hold a charge for up to six hours. Any additional electricity generated by the body can prolong the charge. Charging stations are located in each bunker, so it would be wise to know the bunker locations and layouts."

"How tough are these uniforms?" asked Flip.

"The uniforms are made of a durable material called interwire. This is a robotic material light enough to be comfortable on human skin yet tough enough to withstand a lot of enemy firepower, including gunfire and grenades. It won't be able to protect you from a gunshot at point-blank range, or from mines or bomb shells, so you'll have to be smart. And as you probably figured, the ARISN uniforms only protect from the neck down. You'll have to wear some type of head protection. We have yet to construct head protection to match the toughness of the ARISN."

"How powerful are the body-generated lasers?" asked Karen.

"That's the beauty of the ARISN. It can take the electricity generated from the protons and neutrons of your body, and fire a laser of more than seventeen metric tons of power," said Creighton.

"Does that laser strength hold true for everyone?" asked Alex.

"It all depends on the size of the person and how much electricity is generated. Someone like you and your friend will probably generate no more than eight metric tons of power while someone like Flip or Bronson may have the ability to as much as twenty-five metric tons of power," said Creighton.

"What's the advantage to using the ARISN technology as opposed to conventional methods?" asked Kremley.

"I, along with leaders of armed forces around the world, believe that this gives us the best chance of defeating the Sétbætañ. With ARISN not only are you given optimal protection from gunfire, but you have the ability to use firepower without the need to carry weapons. Also, it allows the wearer to fire the weapon by simply thinking it."

Deep in the bunker, on a huge field that served as a practice range for military personnel, hundreds of soldiers clad in ARISN uniforms were practicing war games for the upcoming rescue of the President and fight against the Sétbætañ. Alex and Karen were dressed for battle.

"Are you two ready?" asked Bronson.

"We're ready, sir," said Alex.

"Good, now get in there and let's see what you've got. But remember this, if you fail during the war games, there's no way I'm gonna let you fight in a real battle. Do I make myself clear?"

"Yes, sir," they said.

"Don't y'all worry," said Flip. "Y'all know you've got this."

Because of their previous experience, Alex and Karen performed superbly. They were able to hit all of their targets and avoid gunfire. Bronson was really impressed. Alex was even more impressed with the battle armor.

"This suit is amazing. It's so light it feels like I'm not wearing anything. And the weaponry is awesome. All I have to do is think about firing the lasers and they fire."

"Just make sure you keep your bodies well nourished or you'll be dependent on charging up the suit artificially," said Creighton.

"I don't know where you've been but food is scarce," said Flip. "We'll have to do the best we can with the whole nourishment thing."

Time was of the essence, so Alex and the others only had three days of training. Operation Pigskin was about to go into full effect. The Sétbætañ had their armies fully entrenched in all the world's major cities and were spreading to the smaller cities. Brownsville had experienced some of the power of the Sétbætañ, but Alex and Karen were extremely concerned that their hometown would soon bear the creatures' full wrath. Their loved ones would be in grave danger. But the first course of action was the rescue of the President. It was only a matter of time before he would come out of hiding.

Chapter 30
Backroom Deals

Never before in the history of mankind had the world been in such crisis. Since the start of the Armageddon war, over one hundred and fifty million lives had been lost. Corpses lay in fields and polluted the waters. Millions of people roamed the streets in search of shelter and food. Disease and famine were widespread. Doctors, medicine, and shelters were in short supply. Thugs controlled perishable items, weapons, medicine, and other needed supplies. It was survival of the fittest. Only those who possessed weapons or were street savvy stood a chance. Many of those were rebel forces who fought on the side of the Church and the Sétbætañ. But there were others who rejected World Apex Government law and were willing to fight back. These people were not against God, but against the laws of the Church and the way its laws were intertwined with government policy. As hard as they wanted to believe and follow Pope Gregory's counsel, their hearts and minds told them otherwise.

Many of those who did not believe in God found solace in their theories of His non-existence. They were able to conceptualize mankind fighting an Armageddon-type war without any religious explanation or reasoning. So despite the propaganda trumpeted by the World Apex Government, the war events only reinforced their atheism. Others became believers out of fear, after seeing demon-like beings and witnessing people being cast into the Lake of Fire, Enervet Sine. The unbelievers were quickly eradicated by the Church.

Most of the world's population was under the influence of the Church and their alien allies. The BioCharge microchip, originally implanted to make human lives easier, was now acting as a mind-controlling device influenced by conscious and unconscious thoughts. The Sétbætañ and the Church invoked the power of the sixth scroll any time they felt they were losing control of the populace. And now, to the delight of Ecaep and Pope Gregory, most people were willing to give their lives to the

Sétbætañ and the Church.

The relationship between Ecaep and the Pope had always been tenuous at best. After the Pope had helped Ecaep discover the whereabouts of Phillip Smiley and President Topher, it took a turn for the worse. Not only did Ecaep resent the Pope's treatment of his son, he resented the Pope's continual bashing of his people. At the Vatican with the Pope and his cardinals, Ecaep thought it best to lay some ground rules before the planned blackmail of Topher was carried out.

"So I understand that my people are monsters," Ecaep said to the Pope. "That you would cut our hearts out if you had the chance."

"Not true. I would never say such a thing."

"I understand that you plan to gain possession of the seventh scroll and destroy our race. Is this true?"

"Nothing could be further from the truth," said the Pope. "Where are you hearing these lies?"

"And what about my son?" asked Ecaep. "I understand that your hatred for him runs deep."

"I would say 'hatred' is too strong a word. I would call it more of an extreme dislike," said the Pope. "After I expose him to the world, he will relinquish his presidency. Then I can take my rightful place as the most powerful man in the world. We are still in agreement, aren't we? Or did you make an empty promise?"

Not one to suffer fools lightly, Ecaep quickly grabbed the Pope around the neck and lifted him airborne. The pressure from Ecaep's grip almost snapped the Pope's neck. The cardinals cowered in fear.

"Listen to me, you stupid human. You would be making a fatal mistake to take me for a fool. I am the lord of the Sétbætañ. My spies have roamed your world for ages. And I am privy to your plans. Do not forget that I am indirectly responsible for the God that you worship. But because I'm slow to anger, I will take the life of one of your subordinates while yours is spared."

In an instant, Ecaep dropped the Pope and grabbed one of the cardinals around the neck. He took his other hand and began to drill his boney finger into the cardinal's skull. He dropped the limp body to the floor, blood flowing out a hole in the cardinal's forehead. The shaken Pope and the other cardinals were frightened beyond belief.

"I apologize for my insolence," said the Pope. "Please do not harm anyone else."

"That will depend upon your future actions," said Ecaep. "We must be diligent in making Molahsras your planet's new ruler and making the entire human race bow to him and to me."

"I thought we'd agreed that you and I would rule the Earth," said the Pope. "You promised this as my reward for locating the one who could translate the seventh scroll and for finding your son."

"I am indebted to you for holding up your end of the bargain," said Ecaep. "You may establish your church and government as you please. I will ensure that the humans remain under control, and that they will be slaves to our commands. Because of your disrespect toward me and my people, however, I am altering the terms of the deal. Molahsras shall be crowned king and ruler of your world and you, like the others, shall bow at his feet."

The Pope's body language showed his displeasure. This once again angered Ecaep.

"Feel fortunate that I let you live," said Ecaep. "You would not be so lucky if you were in the presence of my general. Now go and prepare my son's introduction as the new ruler of Earth. Any further disrespect on your behalf will be met with a slow and painful death."

The Sétbætañ ruler quickly disappeared into the portal. The cardinals stood flabbergasted and frightened. The Pope ordered a member of the rebel forces to discard the corpse that lay limp in the middle of the floor. He needed to adjust his strategy since Ecaep no longer trusted him. And despite the ruler's cryptic promise, the arrogant Pope vented his anger at the clergy.

"How dare that creature betray me," said the Pope. "It was I who led him to the one who could translate the seventh scroll and to his idiotic son. If it weren't for me, his race would still be enslaved by the Luçimarks."

"Please, Your Holiness," said one of the cardinals. "It is probably still watching us."

"It will take more than a threat to break me," said the Pope. "I should be Earth's ruler. I am the only one who can guide the lost into the light of God. And if he thinks for one minute that I will bow down to that fool of a son of his ... I'd rather he cast me into Enervet Sine."

"But Holy Father, what about the rest of us? You saw what it did to Cardinal Morelli. It killed him," cried one of the bishops.

"For that I apologize and take full responsibility," said the Pope. "We will tell the world that Morelli was a traitor against the Church and was cast into the Lake of Fire. For the sake of our lives I will keep a low profile and follow Ecaep's commands."

Three days later, after preparing Topher's wardrobe and speech as instructed by Ecaep, the Pope, with two of his cardinals, took the portal to Vuur to meet Ecaep and his commanding officers. They shivered from the gruesomeness of the Sétbætañ beings that flanked Ecaep. The Pope and his clergy bowed in front of Ecaep's throne.

"Welcome to the cooler regions of Vuur. I know that you are already familiar with the heat of Enervet Sine. We prefer the cooler climates. But this is only temporary until we move to Urodae," said Ecaep. "Behind me are my commanding officers, and Ugnjengon, general of my army and my most trusted servant. Straboudo, Qiooing, Zriotnmtail, and Auionaral are the others."

The aliens' appearance horrified the clergy. Their grotesqueness made it hard for the Pope and his clergy to focus. Ugnjengon stared at them coldly without saying a word.

"Have you prepared Molahsras for his ascension to the throne?" asked Ecaep.

"Yes, my lord," said the Pope. "I will be meeting with him for the final touches upon my return."

"Excellent. I am sure that he will follow the script as planned. Qiooing, gather all to witness the crowning of the king. This is the day our people have been waiting for," said Ecaep.

"Is there anything else we can do for you, my lord?" asked the Pope.

"No. I am satisfied. You may go."

The Pope and his cardinals quickly entered the portal to return to Earth.

"I don't trust them, my lord, especially their leader," said Ugnjengon. "He has betrayal written on his face. I feel it in my soul."

"I understand your concerns, Ugnjengon," said Ecaep. "But revel in the crowning of The Chosen One. This is a time of joy for our people."

"Yes, my lord," said Ugnjengon.

Exiting the portal, the cardinals were confused. Even though destruction was all around them, the cardinals knew they were not on Earth.

"Where are we, Father?" asked one of the cardinals.

"We are in Urodae," said the Pope.

"Why are we here?"

"I have some friends that I wish to visit. It's about unfinished business."

Chapter 31
Back in Power

At Ecaep's request, the Sétbætañ army and thousands of other creatures gathered in Vuur. The night was even eerier than usual. One of Caynonã's four moons was under a red-moon lunar eclipse. There was a buzz of excitement among the creatures unlike any other in their history. After many years of rumors and hearsay, Ecaep was finally going to confirm what everyone believed -- that he who was chosen to redeem the Sétbætañ was alive and well, and ready to lead them to salvation. Ecaep beamed proudly as he stood high on the mountainside, looking down at four hundred thousand of his loyal subjects.

"My people, our days of glory are now upon us," said Ecaep, his voice booming through an echo chamber that carried it to the masses. "Throughout our history, the proud people of the Sétbætañ have been oppressed by the Luçimarks and their offspring races. With our resolve we have managed to crush the Luçimarks and regain what is ours -- the seven sacred scrolls. And our good fortune continues. For many miliyous, our people have looked toward the heavens anticipating the arrival of The Chosen One to lead the Sétbætañ race to salvation. Not only to crush our enemies, but to reclaim the paradise we once had in Urodae. The Chosen One shall give us a new paradise, in Urodae and also on Earth. Yes, my people. The Sétbætañ prophecy has been fulfilled. He is my offspring. He is the Son of the Most High. And he goes by the name of Molahsras, the deliverer of our people."

All in attendance went wild, from the vy-imps and wolf-creatures to the Selanon. Ugnjengon was especially excited about the arrival of the new king as he had looked forward to this news all his life. Tears fell from his eyes as he roared in jubilation.

"Yes! Yes! Our redemption has come."

"Cúbaneg has not died in vain. He shall be vindicated."

The great crowd started dancing to the rhythmic drum beats that played in the background. The Selanon celebrated with

226

synchronized dances in the sky. Wolf-creatures howled loudly in the chilly Vuur air. And the elated trolls beat the ground with their fists in celebration. Ugnjengon made his way to the front of the crowd and onto the mountainside to greet Ecaep.

"My most high lord, you have blessed us with your good news," said Ugnjengon with tears still streaming down his hideous face. "But I must ask. When shall we meet The Chosen One?"

"My child, you shall meet him tonight, after he is introduced as Earth's new king," said Ecaep.

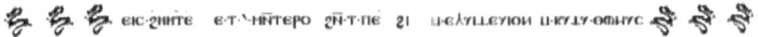

The existence of the human race was at stake. Ecaep had promised to destroy all those who did not become slaves of the creatures. The former American President was prepared to resign and serve on the board of the World Apex Government, which would deftly mix politics and religion in making political decisions. Now, the former President was slated to become the organization's minister of propaganda, misleading the public with lies and half-truths. The fact was, the organization existed only to assist the Pope and the Sétbætañ in enslaving the humans. To Topher, preservation of the human race was the only option.

Pope Gregory's aim in all of this was control. Even though Topher would become the face of the new government, in reality the Pope would be the de facto leader and Topher would do his bidding. Even though the Pope despised Ecaep and was no longer destined to be the world's ruler, the Sétbætañ leader still offered him power and control -- two things the Pope had always desired. While the humans were enslaved, the Pope could still use the President to spread the message of false hope.

"You look dashing, Christopher," the Pope said to the President, referring to his new attire and closely shaved face. "Are you ready to take your place as the world's one and only leader?"

"One and only leader?" said the President. "I thought that title

227

belonged to you."

"Things have changed," said the Pope. "Ecaep has ordered that you become the Earth's sole ruler. And I agree with his decision. We have also agreed that your alien ancestry will not be revealed."

"Wow, that was easy," said the President. "What did my father offer you in its place? The opportunity to live?"

"You should revel in your father's decision," said the Pope. "Not only will you be crowned Earth's sole leader, but you'll keep your secret."

"Well, I'm not," said the President, as makeup artists worked on his face. "I feel awful about lying to the people of the world. But I'll do anything to ensure their survival."

"Oh, don't play phony with me," said the Pope. "You have been lying to them since you agreed to mass-produce that chip. Do you deny that you knew about the mind-controlling technology and that you and the government knew it came from aliens?"

"I can't deny that I knew about it," said the President. "But I never would have done it if I'd thought it placed people in danger."

"It looks as if your naiveté has enabled eighty percent of the world's population to be controlled by the aliens at any time," said the Pope. "It brings tears to my eyes."

"Yet, you take orders from him because he allows you to spread your useless propaganda," said the President. "All you seek is power, regardless of who's sacrificed. Even if it means that people will be enslaved by an alien race. So don't you dare play phony with me."

"All I've ever wanted was for all people to live by the law. It's what God wants," said the Pope. "Your job is to convert those who resist the rules of the Church. If not, then they must suffer the consequences."

"And how do you expect me to convert them?" said Topher.

"Try using your manipulative skills. It should come easy to you," said the Pope. "While you're making your address tonight, deliver the speech with confidence. All must be converted. Their lives depend on it."

"What if I can't convince them? What if they're willing to die for their cause?" asked Topher.

"Those under the influence of the chip will be ordered to find those who rebel against the Church," said the Pope. "Then, the dissenters will be destroyed. We're talking twenty percent of the world's population. This is why it is crucial that you convert them. Make them abide by the law. Understand, the laws of the Church and the laws of Ecaep are one and the same. Think about it Christopher, we are talking about the deaths of billions. Ecaep has made it clear that he will not discriminate. Imagine men, women, and children being shot or tossed into Enervet Sine. The war has already claimed three billion lives. The human race is being exterminated. Ecaep knows that if the twenty percent are not converted, they will continue to rebel and influence the majority. This, in turn, would put bounties on our heads. It could anger Ecaep to the point where he'd authorize the destruction of all humans. Remember, the Sétbætañ have crowned you The Chosen One. They will protect you at any cost. I think you would agree that it will be in our best interest to prevent more deaths."

The Pope's last statement made Topher sick to his stomach. He had undoubtedly been framed to carry out the evil plans of his father and the Pope. But keeping the humans alive was his primary objective.

It was nine o'clock at night when the Pope and his cardinals sat at a table in front of a multitude of cameras, microphones, and other media devices on a stage at Washington's National Mall. It was time for the introduction of Topher as President of the newly formed World Apex Government. The world's eyes and ears were on the Pope. As he rose to take the podium, he felt triumphant. The Pope knew that Topher, despite having his own agenda, was the only person in the world who could rally the masses to carry out the Church's objective.

Though the Mall had suffered in the war, the new government leaders had attempted to make it presentable for the occasion. Yellow, red, and blue lighting adorned the landscaping. Large

229

purple curtains hung at every landmark and museum. Banners welcoming the new President hung from the trees. Flyers and leaflets were handed out. Spotlights illuminated the stage. More than two million people were at the event. The TAPC News and The Faith in God channels broadcast the event worldwide to four billion more. In addition, internet access was allowed for the first time in two years. Believers and skeptics tuned in. Millions watched on their mobile devices. Even those opposed to the new government, living in the underground bunkers tuned in. The pope delivered his introduction:

"First, let us pray:

> Our great Church which dwells on Earth,
> How mighty is your name?
> Thy kingdom come, thy will be done on Earth as it is in Heaven.
> Give us this day of triumph, as we punish our enemies with death
> And lead us not from our law, but deliver us from evil.
> For the kingdom, the power, and the glory of the Church are yours forever and ever.
> Amen.

"Good evening to the people of the world and to those who abide only by God's law. Several days ago I informed you that the former American President would confess a deep sin. I also said that he would serve on the board of the World Apex Government. But through the commandment of God, he has now been appointed to lead the government and all of the world's people into the future.

"A future where the word of God is valued above all else. A future in which those who oppose His law will be punished and condemned. A future in which all will live in peace and serve He who has brought retribution to our world. Yes, the man I'm about to introduce has committed many sins. Yet, he has come to us asking for forgiveness and for the opportunity to lead our world into mankind's next spiritual phase. This man has proved himself by successfully leading the United States of America and the rest of the world during the days of Armageddon. His forces

230

of God defeated Satan's armies and established His law on Earth. Now, he returns. I'd like to introduce the world to the newly appointed President of the World Apex Government, the man who has been ordained by God, Christopher Topher."

Topher passed his newly selected staff members and took to the podium as millions of people chanted his name. Staring out at the masses, cameras flashing, he found himself trying to gather his composure. Even though he had given hundreds of public speeches before, Topher was genuinely nervous for the first time in his life. He realized that his every move would be scrutinized, and that each word he uttered could mean the survival or death of those who rebelled against the World Apex Government. It was time. He adjusted his jacket and tie. As always, he appeared strong and confident. Today, however, he had a God-like aura about him.

"People of the world, fellow political leaders, and members of the Holy Church, I come to you with my head bowed, asking for forgiveness. For many years, including my years in the White House, I have lived as an unbeliever in the Church and her laws. But I have learned that in all bad things there is good. Despite the destruction and death caused by the Apocalypse, a new kingdom has been established on Earth, and I have been born again to abide by the Church's teachings.

While held as a prisoner by the Alliance, better known as the United States Government, I discovered how I was misled and lied to my entire life. While in prison, I was rescued by those who wear the armor of God, the true angels of heaven. They go by the name of the Sétbætañ. These angels have enlightened me. They have been miscast as usurpers and destroyers of mankind. They have come to this world to destroy those who deceive mankind, and battle against those who reject the Church's law. But I must give highest praise to his holiness Pope Gregory for showing me the light. People of Earth, I bear witness that the Pope, along with the Sétbætañ, rescued me from the jaws of death. They explained to me their true purpose and how we must rally against those who resist the Church. They told me anyone who was against God would be destroyed. I cried out to the

231

Pope, saying, 'How could this be? Look at them! They are hideous monsters from the depths of hell. How can they possibly be the keepers of God's law?' But through the wisdom of the Earth's Most Holy, Pope Gregory, I have learned the error of my ways. Due to my repentance, his Holiness has forgiven me and asked that I take the reins as President of the World Apex Government."

The crowd erupted in applause, chanting Topher's name. The Pope was very pleased. Topher continued.

"Now, I come to deliver the message that the war against the Church is not over. But we must show compassion and forgive our enemies as they do not understand what they do. We must pray for them so that they will not suffer the same fate as others who have challenged the Church's law. For as the Bible has taught us, we must be servants for God and submit to His glory. This is what the Church and the World Apex Government will teach all men, women, and children.

"The angels of the Church, the Sétbætañ, will protect all of God's servants. All that is asked in return is the unwavering submission of your hearts, minds, and souls. I plead with you today to submit to the authority of the World Apex Government and its church, so that with the destruction of the enemy, God's new kingdom can move forward, prosper, and establish itself here on Earth forever and ever."

The crowd erupted in a frenzy. Confetti, chants, and gunfire filled the air. Posters of Topher and the Pope were unfurled. Around the world, people huddled around government-sanctioned monitors and televisions, marveling at the spectacle. Crowds as large as five million had gathered to witness the event. Topher had captured the imagination of the entire world.

"Now I'd like to explain our new governmental structure. The individuals seated to my right will be my cabinet members. Will you please stand as I call your name? Secretary of State Wayne Hoffman, Secretary of Defense Sheldon Brown, Attorney General David Wentworth. We also have a secretary of ministry. His Holiness, Pope Gregory, has graciously accepted the position."

The crowd cheered, chanting the Pope's name.

"There is one more introduction I'd like to make," said Topher. "Please look behind me, toward the Capitol."

From the direction of the Capitol building, an extremely tall, boney, caped figure came into view. The crowd murmured and gasped. Sensing their unease, Topher quickly proceeded with the introduction.

"People of the world, I'd like to introduce you to a being who comes directly from God, as prophesied in the Bible. He's the alpha and the omega, the beginning and the end, the lord of heaven and earth, the king of kings, the mighty Ecaep."

As Ecaep took to the podium, the crowd went silent. Topher felt their awe.

"My servants, I've come before you as your leader and the destroyer of your enemy," said Ecaep. "Those who are subservient to me will live and not suffer the judgment of death. I will offer protection and comfort from those who persecute and smite you with the sword. For the majority of your existence I have witnessed your oppression by those who would deny your commitment to my law. No more shall you suffer, as you, formally the hunted, will now become the hunter. I command that you follow and serve me as the slave serves his master. All the people of the world, both ally and enemy, witness my awesome power. Turn your sight to the south."

With that, Ecaep chanted the text of the fifth scroll:

ⲡⲓⲣⲏ ⲓ̀ ⲉ̀ⲡⲉⲥⲏⲧ ⲥⲓ ⲧ̀ⲫⲉ

In the distance, over the Potomac River, fiery hail rained down from the dark skies. People around the world gazed in wonderment. There was no question that the majority of those who witnessed the event feared but also reveled in Ecaep's power. He was driven to make the humans subservient.

"Witness the splendor and the power of our king! Who would dare challenge the laws of the Church?" shouted Topher.

Once again the masses cheered. They began to chant Ecaep's

name.

"Now, my people, look around the Mall," Topher said. "Notice the hanging drapes."

As the people looked the drapes that hung on the Mall's building and monuments fell as one to the ground. Each drape had concealed the mark of the Sétbætañ. Drawn freehand in blood, the symbols were large enough for everyone in attendance to see. They'd been drawn on the buildings and monuments.

"This is the mark of the Sétbætañ," said Topher, as the new Vatican flag, also bearing the symbol, was raised. "This symbol represents peace between the Church, the Earth, and Heaven. Through his loving grace, the mighty Ecaep has shared his heavenly symbol with us. Worship this holy symbol. Spread it to those who are lost to the Church's laws. The bearer of the mark shall enter heaven and be blessed forever."

The jubilant crowd went berserk. People carved the symbol into their skin with any object they could find. Some had the symbol forcibly carved on them by others. Riots were forming around the world. At the Mall, some attempted to storm the stage. But in the blink of an eye Ecaep, the Pope, Topher, and his newly appointed team vanished through a portal. The trinity of Ecaep, Topher, and Pope Gregory had left a lasting image. God had finally returned to Earth in the form of the Father, the Son, and the Holy Ghost.

Chapter 32
Armageddon, Part Two

While the world witnessed the crowning of President Christopher Topher as leader of the World Apex Government, those in the Alliance knew they had to restore order fast. With the majority of the world's population under Sétbætañ control, and the demoralizing raising of the new Vatican flag, many were worried that this would indeed become the new way of life. Alex and Karen could not believe what they were seeing on their laptop monitors, as the former American President declared his oath to a new government.

Vice President Bernard Windows, who was now acting President of the United States, addressed the troops before they set out for war.

"Soldiers, the human race is in great peril. We have already lost more lives than in World Wars I and II combined. And we have lost many of our nation's leaders to the enemy, including American President Christopher Topher. Though we thank the heavens that he is still alive, he is now under the influence of the alien creatures.

"When you are on the battle field, remember that you are not only fighting for yourselves, you are fighting for the human race. One of our prime objectives in this mission is to rescue our former President. We are uncertain how badly his mind has been warped. So maintain extreme caution.

"I look upon you proudly as we have agreed to join together with one common goal -- to defeat the enemy and restore this once-beautiful planet we call Earth. We have banded together and will smash the enemy by any means necessary.

"As you know, the aliens are controlling roughly eighty percent of the population via the BioCharge chip. This makes this mission even more daunting, as you may find yourself facing off to the death against a fellow human -- even a former loved one. Do all that you can to save our brothers and sisters. You have orders from Lieutenant General Bronson to cut the chip from their hands. But protect yourselves at all costs if the

235

task proves too daunting.

"Now, let us rise up and march into war, whether by land, sea, or air. The existence of the human race is at stake. We will leave all that we have on the fields of battle. And may God bless you for your perseverance and bravery."

The Alliance was inspired by the Vice President's speech. Nearly all troops were set to converge on the White House at oh three hundred. For the first time since their adventure had begun, Alex and Karen were in different units within the Alliance. Alex was in a unit led by Bronson, and Karen was in a unit led by Flip. The day before Operation Pigskin, around six o'clock in the evening, Alex and Karen spoke while eating what they knew could be their final meal.

"Are you ready for tomorrow?" asked Alex.

"As ready as I'm going to be," said Karen. "You'd better make sure you eat well or your suit won't work."

"Don't worry. I've eaten my share," said Alex. "Plus, you never know when we'll get to pig out like this again."

Karen smiled. "Do you realize that this will be the first time we've been apart since you ran off to Vuur to rescue your father?"

"Yes, I do," said Alex. "And that seems so long ago. I asked Lieutenant General Bronson if we could be together and he literally growled at me."

Karen laughed. "Yeah, he's pretty hardcore. I didn't even bother to ask Flip. He's done enough favors for us, anyway."

"Have you heard from our parents?" asked Alex. "I haven't spoken to my mother in about a week. She was frightened to death when I told her I was going to fight for the Alliance."

"I spoke to mine yesterday. My mom said that your mom is doing fine. She told me to tell you that Mrs. Smiley says she's really proud of you," said Karen. "You know, you should keep in touch with your mom. You're the only one she has left and there are no guarantees that you'll be here past tomorrow."

Alex smiled, but a tear trickled down his cheek.

"Yeah, I guess you're right," he said. "I'll make sure I call her before lights out."

236

"Good," said Karen. "Well I'm gonna head in early and get some rest."

As they got up from the table, Karen reached across and met Alex with a short but meaningful kiss before rushing off to her bunker. Alex dropped back down in his seat, stunned.

He had always liked Karen, and suspected that she liked him, but he didn't know how much. He'd never had the courage to tell her how he felt because he was afraid of being rejected. It was now clear that she had the same feelings toward him. As he looked out at the red-tinted but peaceful sky, he smiled and daydreamed of them someday getting married and living a long life together.

If we make it out of this alive I'm going to ask her to be my girlfriend, Alex thought to himself, realizing that they were still too young to get married.

The forecast predicted a mixture of snow and freezing rain, which was unusual for this time of year. People were warned by the new government to find shelter. As the locals obeyed orders and looked to protect themselves from the weather, they were unaware of the storms of war set to descend on them in the morning.

In order to execute a successful rescue of the President, and attack the creatures, the Alliance planned to use a combination of cloaking and dimensional intraportalization. Thanks to the homing device, the Alliance intelligence had confirmed that the creatures, the President, and the Pope were stationed in two places: the White House and its surrounding area, and Vatican City.

After rescuing the President, the Alliance planned to administer deep psychological counseling. Whether his former mental state could be restored was undetermined.

The situation surrounding the Pope was less complicated. Many of the remaining clergy followed him only through fear. In fact, many clergy never liked Pope Gregory and had wanted him

237

ousted prior to the alien takeover. They'd always found him to be mean-spirited, power-hungry, and simply the wrong person to represent the Roman Catholic Church. When and if captured, the Alliance would arrest the Pope and charge him with crimes against humanity, accessory to mass murder, and high treason.

The Alliance didn't have much information on Ecaep. They simply considered him the leader of a hostile alien race working in concert with the Pope and a brainwashed Topher. He was wanted, dead or alive.

"Let's make sure we come up on 'em nice and slow," whispered Flip, as his unit converged on a multitude of trolls guarding the White House. Nervous sweat impaired Karen's vision as the unit got closer to the targets.

As the sixty Alliance soldiers moved toward one of the secret White House doors, the vile smell of the trolls caused one of the soldiers to gag audibly, putting the trolls on alert. Flip thought it would be in their best interest to get the party started.

"Attack!" he yelled, as the troops emerged from their cloaked positions. The unit riddled the trolls with ARISN firepower. Karen put down a troll with a shot to the head. The rest of the trolls surrounding the White House rallied to join the battle.

"Fire!" yelled Flip, as more creatures converged on the unit. Wolf-creatures, vy-imps, and other creatures joined the battle. Despite having the element of surprise, the Alliance was outnumbered and the creatures, armed with automatic weapons and hand grenades, pushed them back. Selanon attacked from the air, grabbing soldiers and dropping them from the sky. Vy-imps maimed many of the Alliance soldiers by strategically detonating mines. They used interportalization to counter the Alliance's sneak attack. Despite these disadvantages, the Alliance pressed on. They managed to take out several Selanon by firing rocket launchers into the sky.

"Yeah, got 'em good. Let's pick these ugly birds right out the sky," shouted a jubilant Flip as he watched Selanon crash to the earth. "Soldiers, keep firing those launchers. Killin' those flying things will help us with our ground attack."

Flip and his unit were making headway toward the White

238

House when the Sétbætañ used a trick of their own. A twenty-foot-tall, tree-like creature rose out of the ground to attack the Alliance. This species of Sétbætañ, known as the Arbogog, dwell in the northern parts of the Asus Forest. Their ability to camouflage among the trees kept them safe from the Luçimarks. They can stretch their strong limbs in different directions in order to reach and crush their opponents. Now, the creature used its branch-like limbs to quickly destroy the rocket launchers and pierce or crush the soldiers' bodies, allowing the Selanon to continue its aerial assault uninterrupted.

"Karen, look out!" Flip screamed, as he saw one of the tree-monster's limbs descend toward her. Thanks to her athletic ability as a junior-high soccer player, she was able to avoid the blow and deliver one of her own.

"Take that!" shouted Karen, letting loose on the creature with some laser missiles from her suit.

Karen's heroics made the creature angry and it focused directly on her.

"Karen, to your left! Right! Roll back!" yelled Flip and other soldiers as she rolled on the ground avoiding blow after fatal blow.

"Flip, you watch out!" Karen screamed as a vy-imp stabbed the unfocused Flip in the foot with a knife dripping with poison. He screamed in pain before eliminating the little creature with one of his lasers.

While Karen continued to roll around and avoid getting struck by the Arbogog, several soldiers set the tree-creature ablaze. It swayed its branches, screeching in pain. Karen quickly stood and took off running. When she was at a safe enough distance, she delivered a final blow to the creature's trunk, causing it to topple to the ground. It was a small victory. The Sétbætañ army was besting the Alliance in every other battle.

"Retreat! Retreat!" shouted Flip, realizing his unit was no match for the aliens. The Sétbætañ had a counter for every Alliance attack. He recited the command to open the portal:

†ⲬⲞⲘ ⲠⲒⲚⲓⲱ† ⲚⲞⲨⲢⲞ ⲪⲎⲈⲦⲌⲈⲘⲤⲒ ⲌⲒⲬⲈⲚ ⲠⲒⲐⲢⲞⲚⲞⲤ ⲟⲧⲱⲛ †ⲫⲉ

The power of the king who sits on the throne opens the heavens.

The Alliance soldiers escaped through the intradimensional portal.

As the troops gathered at their secret bunker, Flip was at a loss for words. He had never imagined that the creatures would rally to defend their position so quickly and decisively. He wondered how the Alliance, so outnumbered, could possibly rescue the President, let alone defeat the enemy. Looking around the bunker he saw a demoralized group of soldiers. Many were injured. Some had missing limbs. All were trying to deal with the mental anguish of the failed battle. Many soldiers had been killed.

Flip had begun to feel weak as the poison entered his bloodstream. The medics came to his aid as he collapsed to the floor. Karen, despite her encounter with the Arbogog, had escaped unscathed. As she sat down and leaned her back against the wall, she looked around at the miserable unit. Just like Flip, she was beginning to wonder if the creatures could be defeated. Then her mind wandered to Alex. She wondered how he and his unit were faring against the creatures.

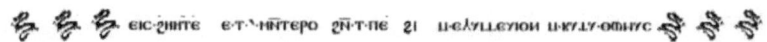

It was unseasonably warm in the Italian capital of Rome. A mixture of heat, darkness, and steady rain created a stifling, tropical atmosphere that was nearly unbearable for Bronson's unit. Reports from Washington relayed the grim news that Flip's unit had been unable to penetrate the aliens' defense and gain access to the White House. Now that night had fallen in Rome, it was time for Bronson's unit to descend on Vatican City.

Hours before the unit was scheduled to execute its attack, Alex rested in his bunk reading verses in Psalms. His mother had recommended reading the Bible and praying during times of peril. Alex wasn't deeply religious, but he had few other sources

240

of comfort. He remembered going to church regularly with his family as a young child. The sweet songs of praise and the inspirational sermons by the pastor brought joy to the Smileys' hearts. Mr. Smiley's blackmailing by the government had dampened the family's faith. Alex and his father rarely referred to religion. Mr. Smiley's faith had already been shaken when he'd discovered the secret behind the scrolls. By then, only Mrs. Smiley held fast to her faith. Now, years later, and despite all he had learned, Alex was experiencing a spiritual rebirth. He'd begun to think that God was something bigger than the government and the aliens. Perhaps, just perhaps, God Himself had set all of this in motion, for reasons beyond human comprehension.

The only other comfort for Alex was thinking of Karen. He'd been doing so since her family had moved into the neighborhood, when they were in elementary school. He would tell his mother that an angel had moved into the house next door and that he was going to try and be her friend. When Alex was being bullied, he was able to cope by thinking about Karen. And now, years later, Alex felt even more strongly about her. Instead of worrying about bullies and their assaults on nerds, he was worrying about aliens and the destruction of mankind. Nevertheless, despite the seriousness of the situation, regularly looking at his cell-phone photo of Karen helped sooth his nerves and ease his mind.

As the troops prepared for their assault, deep inside the Vatican City walls the Pope, Topher, and Ecaep were strategizing.

"It has not yet been five days and the humans have already disobeyed my commands," said Ecaep. "Move forth in destroying them!"

"My lord, please be more merciful," said Topher. "We were attacked by the humans' army. Civilians had nothing to do with that. I beg that you show restraint."

"The humans do not show restraint. Why should my army? My spies tell me that they are here and plan to attack. This despite the fact that our armies eradicated them in your former home," Ecaep said to Topher.

"Perhaps we can use Christopher to negotiate with them," injected the Pope. "We can threaten to kill him if they advance their armies. I believe we can use fear to our advantage."

Topher glared at the Pope.

"Threaten him? And how would this be done?" asked Ugnjengon.

"We can show him to the Alliance with a gun pointed at his head. Ugnjengon, I believe they would clearly get the message if you did the honors," said the Pope.

"You continue to show disrespect to the child of Ecaep. And if you show disrespect to Molahsras, you show disrespect to the Father. Off with his head!" shouted Ugnjengon.

"No," said Ecaep. "The human has a good plan. There is no intent to bring harm to my son."

The Pope smiled slyly. Ugnjengon gave him a look of death.

"Now that that's settled, why don't we put Topher in front of the Alliance before they attack," said the Pope.

"No. I have another plan," said Ecaep.

Bronson's unit was three hundred deep, east of Vatican City. They were ordered to advance over the Viminal and Quirinal hills, through the Field of Mars and across the Tiber River to the Vatican. Although they no longer controlled the weapons stockpile, the Alliance had managed to arm themselves with twenty tanks. Though Alex wished he'd been assigned to one of the tanks, Bronson assigned him to a grounds special forces unit to rescue the President.

In the steady downpour, the Alliance quickly advanced through the buildings and monuments on the Viminal and Quirinal hills. When they reached their downslope, they were met on the Field of Mars by more than five hundred armed Sétbætañ soldiers. The enemy troops were a mix of aliens and men. The men stood silent and still as if they were in a trance. They were the brainwashed slaves of the Sétbætañ.

Ecaep had released the power of the sixth scroll. Several of the men carried or waved the new Vatican flag displaying the mark of the Sétbætañ. Each had had the mark engraved on his body. They were equipped with tanks and myriad weapons which had once been owned by the Italian military. A creature named Ichielkak stood among them. He was a general of the Sétbætañ army and Ugnjengon's protégé. The Sétbætañ military looked upon Ichielkak with great favor. Ugnjengon treated him like a son. Their army was ready for any attack by the Alliance. At the edge of the Field of Mars, just before the Tiber River, Ugnjengon stood on a platform holding Topher tightly and pointing a gun at his head.

"Earthlings, if you value the life of this human, I would advise that you return whence you came. If you do not abide by the commands of our lord, I will kill the human, and then we will turn the waters of this planet red with human blood," shouted Ugnjengon.

Bronson, who was skilled at interrogation techniques, decided to call his bluff.

"I command you to release the prisoner," shouted Bronson through a megaphone. "If you do not release the prisoner to us, we will be forced to scatter the brains of the Sétbætañ throughout our lands, providing food to our Earthly animals for years to come."

Ugnjengon's anger knew no bounds.

"Soldiers, attack," he ordered.

Within seconds, the rebel-led Sétbætañ fired a missile from one of their tanks, killing several Alliance soldiers.

"Go! Go! Go!" shouted Bronson, as his unit met the enemy head on.

Despite being outnumbered, the Alliance soldiers used their suits' built-in weapons to deliver swift and effective blows. The lasers burned through the enemy's flesh with precision. At first, the Alliance was selective in their attacks. For aliens, their lasers were set to kill; for rebel soldiers, to stun. They wanted to capture rather than kill their fellow human beings. As the battle wore on, however, the rebels forced Bronson's unit to keep the lasers in kill mode regardless of the target.

Alex's lasers were fixed at stun. He wasn't sure why, considering he had experience killing aliens, but his suit was not

243

equipped with kill mode. In time, Alex felt glad about this limitation, because he could fire his lasers at will without worrying about killing another human being. And even though he wasn't on the front line, Alex delivered some good stun shots against the enemy, including one laser shot directly into Ichielkak's knee. The creature was caught up in battle with another Alliance soldier when Alex delivered the shot. Bronson, who took pleasure in killing the aliens, decided it would be advantageous to capture the creature instead of killing him. So Bronson finished Alex's work by stunning the creature into submission. The defeat of Ichielkak proved a devastating blow to the Sétbætañ army. Their front line had been broken. Retaliating missiles and perfectly placed grenades had killed scores of rebels. The Alliance had the Sétbætañ army reeling. As they chased the alien troops toward the Tiber River, Alex managed to get himself cornered by a rebel. Bronson recognized him as a private by the name of Hewlett Bronson. He had served under Flip in the U.S. Army and was Bronson's one and only son.

"It's time for you to die. You are against God. For the Chosen One has told me!" said Hewlett.

Before Alex attempted to use his lasers, Bronson intervened. Hewlett was wielding a knife at Alex.

"General, I'm ready to take him down," said a flustered Alex.

"No! If anyone does anything to him it'll be me. Let me handle this," said Bronson.

"We don't want to hurt you, son," Bronson calmly said to Hewlett. "Put down your weapon."

When Hewlett refused to obey, Bronson stunned the private with his built-in lasers. He then took the rebel and carried him to shelter. The rest of the rebels were in full retreat. Though Ecaep was angry, he was not surprised by the loss and decided to fight for another day. His idea of using the rebels for war had backfired. He now saw that they lacked the military skills necessary for interplanetary war. Except for the most basic assignments, the rebels were worthless.

As the Alliance advanced across the Tiber River and stormed the Vatican, Ecaep and the rest of the Sétbætañ used the portal to transport to Vuur. The Alliance had killed three hundred aliens and about fifty rebels. Seventy-five rebels had been detained as prisoners of war. The rest had escaped, but the capture of Ichielkak was a feather in the Alliance's cap.

Bronson was overjoyed to discover that his son was still alive. He hadn't heard from him for nearly fourteen months and had figured he was dead. It was just by chance that he found Hewitt on the battlefield and was able to capture him unscathed. His next challenge was to figure out a way to free his son's mind. He tried speaking with the young man at the prison camp.

"You stay away from me! You serve not the lord. You serve evil," screamed Hewlett.

Statements such as these were common among the captured, brainwashed rebels.

"Hewlett, do you know who I am?" asked Bronson.

"You are an agent of Satan," Hewlett responded.

"Okay, I've already heard enough. I'm gonna have to find that chip and get it out of him," Bronson said to Lieutenant Jackson. "I'll need you and a couple of the men to hold him."

While the men held Hewlett down, Bronson searched his hand for the chip. Hewlett continued to scream platitudes.

"My Lord shall give me salvation against all evil. I am loved by his angels that dwell in the heavens."

"Ah ha, here it is," said Bronson, locating the chip in the palm of Hewlett's right hand. Holding his son's hand tight, Bronson took a sharp army knife and cut the chip out. Hewlett's scream echoed throughout the prison camp before he lost consciousness.

"Now, hopefully, he'll be back to himself when he wakes up. Let's bandage him up and get the rest of these prisoners chip-free," ordered Bronson.

"Sir, I have to say that you led an impressive victory," said Jackson.

"I hope this is the beginning of many more victories and that we will reclaim our planet. But don't give me all the credit. Our soldiers fought really well and thanks to Alex, we got an alien creature behind bars," Bronson said proudly.

Ichielkak was a unique creature. He was six feet tall, with wings similar to the Selanon's. He had a devil-like head and tail but human-like hands and feet. His face was almost handsome. Light brown hair covered his body. His knee was severely swollen from Alex's laser shot. He stood behind the steel bars quietly, not making a sound and avoiding eye contact with the humans.

"Get the devices out for him," said Bronson. "We're gonna see what we can get out of him and see if we can't change the direction of this war."

Finding his son and capturing an alien had Bronson giddy. He was giving everyone he could find laughs and high-fives.

"How did you like my response when he made the comment about 'making our waters red with human blood?'"

"A stroke of genius, sir," said Jackson. "That creature was so mad that I thought his head would explode."

"Weren't you afraid he was going to kill the President?" asked Alex.

"Not at all," said Bronson. "If they wanted to they would have killed him already. He's really important to them somehow. We just need to find out why."

For hours, Bronson stayed by his son's side. Uncertain about the outcome, Bronson found himself praying for Hewlett's recovery. On occasion, Alex would sneak a peek to see how Bronson was coping.

After a while, Hewlett regained consciousness.

"Dad?"

"Son!"

With the chip removed, Hewlett made a full recovery and was back to his old self. He didn't remember anything from the time when his mind was controlled by the Sétbætañ. Bronson didn't care. He was just happy that his son was back. As the father and son embraced, Alex thought back to when his father had been alive. He wished that he had embraced his father more. The ordeal that they'd gone through together taught him to place a higher value on time spent with loved ones.

The other prisoners of war had begun to come out of their

stupors. As with Hewitt, they were returned to themselves once their chips were removed.

Back in Vuur the mood was darker than usual among the Sétbætañ. Not only had they lost the battle against an undermanned army, they had also lost Ichielkak. It was the first battle they had lost in a while and their use of human rebels was being questioned.

"My lord, understand that I respect your leadership and all that you command," said Ugnjengon. "But I feel we used the wrong strategy against the Alliance. Please forgive me, my lord."

"You are forgiven," said Ecaep. "You are the lead general of all of my armies. So your opinion is valued. I'd wanted to test the human rebels to see how they fought as soldiers. And as I predicted, they failed miserably. You should be rest assured that I will never put the human rebels on the front lines of our battles again. I will trust your leadership as general to make the decisions regarding our military."

"Thank you, my lord, for your understanding," said Ugnjengon.

Later that night, Ugnjengon was meditating in one of the castle's rooms. He was abruptly disturbed by the Pope.

"I don't think you should have questioned Ecaep. His wisdom is superior to anything in this universe."

"How dare you interrupt my meditation," said Ugnjengon. "And why are you in this section of the castle? It is off-limits to humans."

"I wanted to understand what you had planned for a counteroffensive against the Alliance," said the Pope. "We must ensure that there are no more mistakes in strategy."

An angered Ugnjengon slowly rose to his feet and walked toward the Pope. He bent his massive body down so that he could meet the Pope eye to eye.

"Understand that you have no power, nor authority, to make commands here," said Ugnjengon. "I would strip your skin from your bones and eat you as a delicacy if you were not favored by Ecaep. I would recommend that you stay out of my way and keep your opinions to yourself. Furthermore, I do not wish to see you in this part of the castle ever again. If you disobey my orders, I will be forced, of my own accord, to act contrary to Ecaep's wishes."

"Forgive my disobedience," said the Pope, turning to leave the room. "I just would feel more certain of victory if our armies were led by the late, great Cúbaneg."

"Out!" shouted Ugnjengon. "Leave me."

The next day, while Ecaep was in meditation, Topher, Ugnjengon, the Pope, and several military officials sat at a round table discussing their next move.

"Our spies tell me that Ichielkak lives," said Ugnjengon. "He is a prisoner of war."

"Maybe we can get him back if I'm allowed to negotiate with the Alliance, ask for peace," said Topher. "Perhaps they will accept both of our races coexisting on Earth."

"The humans will never agree to that solution and you know it," said the Pope. "Plus, you tried that when you were introduced as President of the World Apex Government. The Alliance has shown their disobedience and must be punished."

"Wait a minute. What are we trying to do here?" asked Topher. "I was willing to join the Sétbætañ to preserve human lives. Now, you want to just blow everything up? What is it? Are you so power hungry that you would risk more war, which would likely result in the elimination of humans from the face of the Earth? What are you looking to gain?"

"As I have explained before, I do not wish for Ecaep to eliminate all human lives, only those who are disobedient. That would mean those who do not abide by the laws of the Church and those who fight for the Alliance," said the Pope. "Completely destroying the Alliance is the only way to achieve peace. We must eliminate all resistance to Ecaep's plans."

"But if the Alliance does not go quietly, then the citizens of the world will feel Ecaep's wrath," said Topher. "I beg all of you to let me negotiate with them. I assure you that we will get

Ichielkak back and that Ecaep will get what he wants -- human slaves that will abide by his every command."

"Okay then, go. I'm sure Ugnjengon would agree that it would be best if he accompanied you," said the Pope. "If the humans do not obey, it will force Ecaep's hand."

Making decisions independently from Ecaep was rare for the Sétbætañ. Topher, however, being The Chosen One among the aliens, had the unquestioned right to make his own decisions on behalf of his people.

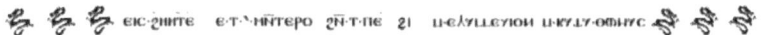

Back in Virginia, the Alliance was feeling better than ever. Not only had they posted victories in Vatican City, but the reports out of Paris, London, Moscow, San Francisco, Chicago, and New York were also favorable. Not only did the ARISN uniforms prove to be a rousing success, the Alliance also altered their tactics and used intradimensionality to attack the aliens. Alex and Karen embraced when they saw each other. A bedridden Flip, still recovering from the alien poison, was happy to see Alex. Bronson bragged about how Alex had handled himself during the battle. He even talked about Alex getting some kind of award.

All the captured rebels had had the BioCharge chips removed. Most of them had no memory of their actions with the aliens and were able to return to duty as Alliance soldiers. Some suffered from depression and were cared for by the military medics.

Ichielkak was put in solitary confinement. He was scheduled for questioning by Bronson later that day. Even though the creature knew what was coming, he maintained a calm demeanor.

As the day settled into afternoon, several military officers armed with machine guns and rifles came to take the creature for questioning. For the first time in months, the earth's sky was blue and a warm spring sun shined through the windows. Worldwide, hope had begun to return. Thanks to the technologically advanced ARISN uniforms, the humans had the aliens set back on their heels for the first time in years.

The creature stood before Vice President Windows, Bronson, and several world military officials for questioning. Alex and Karen looked on.

"Creature, you stand before world leaders and the United Alliance Marines for crimes against humanity," said Vice President Windows. "How do you plead?"

Still surrounded by military officers, the creature did not respond.

"Your crimes are punishable by death. We will consider lessening your sentence if you cooperate with the Alliance," said Vice President Windows. "Do you understand what I am telling you?"

The creature remained quiet, acknowledging no one.

"Either you do not understand, or you refuse to acknowledge us," said Bronson. "Your people have murdered millions of human beings. I am of the opinion that you refuse to answer. You give us no choice but to use more aggressive measures."

The creature still did not respond. Windows and Bronson looked at each other. Bronson gave a nod to a military officer. The officer held an electric-shock baton. He was ordered to use it on the alien. As soon as the officer raised the weapon, the creature spread its wings and let out a high, piercing shrill, enough to deafen anyone within thirty feet. Everyone in the room reached for his ears and cowered in pain. The creature began to speak:

"I am Ichielkak, a high-ranking general of lord Ecaep's army. I am a Selanon, a people of the Sétbætañ race. You have done yourselves a great disservice in waging war against our people. Now you shall pay for your stupidity with death."

"Oh, I think you're the ones who are going to pay," said Bronson, struggling to recover from the noise. "You have murdered millions of innocent people and the tide of war is turning. The skies are no longer red. Your armies around the world are retreating. It would be best for you and your race to go back from where you came."

250

"You delude yourselves if you think the tide of war is turning. You have won a few battles and your Earthly skies are no longer cursed. But it is because of the forgiving hand of lord Ecaep that you have had some good fortune. Our lord can easily command that your skies return red. Nothing in the universe happens without Ecaep's willing it."

"I've seen this Ecaep, or whatever you call him. He's public enemy number one," said Bronson. "We are willing to make you a deal. You hand over this Ecaep character and we'll make sure that you and the rest of your kind return to your planet unharmed. Do we have a deal?"

"Foolish human, you have no idea who you're dealing with," said Ichielkak.

"Okay, this is going nowhere," said Windows. "Let's take him down."

As the officers raised their weapons to strike, a bright light and humming sound appeared. Alex, like everyone else, knew what was happening. A dimensional portal was opening. Emerging from the portal were Ugnjengon and former U.S. President Christopher Topher. Alex, Karen, and the rest of the crowd were stunned.

"Mr. President, are you okay?" asked Windows, keeping his distance because of Ugnjengon.

"I am, thank you, Bernard," said Topher.

"Okay, now get back," Bronson said to Ugnjengon, aiming an M1 Carbine rifle.

"No, you get back," said Ugnjengon, aiming a Mauser 98.

"Everyone, please calm down," shouted Topher. "We've come in peace."

"What exactly do you mean when you say 'we've?'" asked Bronson.

"I come to you as President of the World Apex Government which abides by the laws of the Church," said Topher. "And our law states that all beings should live in harmony and worship lord Ecaep."

"I'm sorry, Chris, but we do not recognize your government," said Windows.

"Plus, I understand that your law states that humans should be subservient to the aliens," said Bronson. "Is this what's wanted from your 'lord?'"

"Our lord is angry but forgiving," said Topher. "You must understand that he created us to serve him and his people. He is responsible for civilization on Earth."

"That's not true," chimed in Jackson. "The Luçimarks gave us our first languages and structures."

"Jackson, you have been misled. The Luçimarks stole all the Sétbætañ had created and claimed it for themselves. The Luçimarks can only rightfully claim to be our biological forefathers," said Topher. "This is why the alien races have been fighting each other for millennia."

"It sounds like a problem between the alien races. We should be left out of it," said Windows.

"No. Lord Ecaep is giving us the chance to earn his forgiveness through subservience to him and his people. I would suggest that we acquiesce," said Topher.

"And if we don't?" asked Windows.

"Then you would force lord Ecaep to destroy all humans," said Topher.

Everyone was waiting for Windows' or Bronson's response when Alex emerged from the back of the room to confront Topher.

"How could you do this, Mr. President? How could you betray your own people like this? My friend and I were kidnapped by that monster standing behind you and those aliens killed my father. I will never be a slave to them. Never!"

"Ah, so you've met Ugnjengon," said Topher. "Look, son, I'm sorry about what happened to your father. But it was the result of man's past sins against lord Ecaep. Do you remember when we first met? When you and your friend told me about your adventure? I knew then that I had to do all that I could to save human lives, even if it meant befriending the aliens. Understand that we are an inferior race and that no matter how we try we will not be able to defeat them. The Alliance continuing on its current path will mean the certain destruction

252

of the human race. So I've come here asking for peace."

"You know, I used to respect you," said Flip, who'd worked himself to the front of the room. "I never imagined in a million years that you would betray your own."

In the blink of an eye, Topher grabbed Alex from behind and held him tightly around his neck. Karen let out a scream.

"Why are you doing this?" asked Windows.

"The spirit of lord Ecaep has sent me here to retrieve Ichielkak. I would advise that you turn him over to me unharmed," said Topher.

"You're bluffing," said Bronson. "You know darn well that you will not harm that boy."

"For the survival of the human race?" asked Topher. "No, I'm not bluffing. Now hand over the creature so that no harm comes to the boy."

Windows ordered the officers to release the creature. Ugnjengon nodded at Ichielkak as he joined him at his side.

"We kept our end of the bargain. Now let go of the boy," said Windows.

"Yes, Vice President," said Topher. "But remember verse four, chapter thirteen, in the book of Romans. 'For he is God's servant for your good. But if you do wrong, be afraid, for he does not bear the sword in vain. For he is the servant of God, an avenger who carries out God's wrath on the wrongdoer.'"

Still holding Alex, Topher chanted the command to open the portal. Before entering, he took a handheld device from behind his back and quickly branded a mark on the side of Alex's neck. He pushed away a screaming Alex and disappeared into the portal with Ugnjengon and Ichielkak. Alex fell to the floor, writhing in pain. Karen and the medics ran to him.

"Alex, are you okay?" Karen asked.

"Get a doctor, now," ordered Bronson.

As Alex lay on the medical bed smelling the burning flesh from his neck, anger he hadn't felt since his father's death burned within him. To be betrayed and assaulted by the former President of the United States, a leader, a person he had believed in no matter what his critics had said, made him lose hope. He

253

tried to convince himself that the President was under the influence of the aliens. But while he was in the President's grasp, the look in his eye let Alex know he had his wits about him and was acting of his own accord. As Alex faded in and out of consciousness, his thoughts moved at a mile a minute. But the one thought that remained consistent was the image of his mother telling him what she had believed for years about the President -- that he was evil. With this act, Christopher Topher had proved to Alex that his mother had indeed been correct.

🐿 🐿 🐿 🐿 🐿 🐿

With the return of Ichielkak, the Sétbætañ army wasted no time rallying their troops and preparing them for battle. This time, to Topher's dismay, they had a different strategy. Now back in Vuur, Ugnjengon presented his plans to the army with newfound vigor.

"Now, as our great warrior Ichielkak returns to us, I have come, by the spirit of Ecaep, to change our destiny. We have lost numerous battles around the Earth due to the humans' newly created technology. They appeared to have rallied in the Earth's most populated areas. And our losses have had another negative effect. Many of the humans are no longer under our control and have joined the battle against us.

"The new strategy will work in our favor. We will abandon Earth's most populated areas and conquer those that are less-populated. As we leave their metropolises, the humans will believe they are on the verge of winning the war. We will pillage and destroy their less-populated lands and everyone within them. Their armies will scatter throughout the Earth and buy time until lord Ecaep introduces the command from the seventh scroll."

After addressing the army, Ugnjengon, Ichielkak, and Topher met in the bowels of the castle.

"Your plan is brilliant," said Ichielkak. "Which lands will we first conquer?"

"One of the areas we shall first conquer has already witnessed a small dose of the mighty Sétbætañ," said Ugnjengon. "This is

254

the land of the human who had originally possessed the scrolls."

"We must think of another way of making the humans succumb to us," said Topher. "The war is causing destruction to both races."

"No," said a voice from the hallway.

It was Ecaep. He emerged from the darkness and stood before them.

"My lord," said Ugnjengon. "We are blessed to once again bask in the glory of your presence."

"You return to us, my lord," said Ichielkak.

"Son, I have heard your plea for the humans," said Ecaep. "But I am in agreement with Ugnjengon. It is time for the destruction of the human race."

"No," said Topher. "The plan was to make them your slaves."

"And the condition was that they obey my laws," said Ecaep. "But they chose to disobey and to destroy our people."

"My lord, destroying the smaller cities and towns will not turn the tide of war," said Topher. "We must agree to a peaceful solution."

"Your time on Earth has made your Sétbætañ blood weak," said Ecaep. "There will be no peaceful solution. Peace will only come after the destruction of the humans. I will release the command of the seventh scroll. This act shall complete our people's revenge against our most hated enemies, the Luçimarks."

"Does that include me? Have you forgotten that Luçimark blood also flows through my veins?" said Topher.

"You will be included if you choose to disobey. The choice is now yours, Molahsras," said Ecaep before he walked away.

Alex woke to the joyful whistling of an old friend. In the bunk beside him was Flip, still recovering from the poison knife wound he'd suffered in the battle on the White House lawn. He was getting stronger and was nearly back to his old self.

"Don't worry, she's been here five times already," said Flip.

"How long have I been out?" Alex asked.

"Eh, a couple of days. They gave you a high dose of pain killers to keep you sedated," said Flip.

That reminded Alex of the burn on his neck, wrapped tightly with bandages. The mere thought of having the mark of the Sétbætañ made him depressed.

"How's the Alliance doing? Do we have them on the ropes?"

"Well, yes and no," said Flip. "The good news is that we're running them out of the higher populated areas."

"And the bad?"

"The bad is that the aliens are now attacking the smaller cities and towns. And we believe that may include Brownsville, though we're not quite sure. We've sent our troops to police the area," Flip said.

The thought of the Sétbætañ in Brownsville gave Alex an anxiety attack. Nervous sweat began to drip from his body. He worried that his mother would fall victim to the aliens. This would be the third time the creatures had invaded the town. Alex guessed that if they went in again it would be to finish the job.

"Flip, I need your phone," said Alex.

Flip gave Alex the phone. He dialed his aunt's number to find it was out of order. He dialed his own number, which was also out of order. He tried Karen's parents. Every number he dialed with the Brownsville area code was out of order.

"Flip, I have to go back to Brownsville," said Alex, staggering out of his bunk.

"Son, you're still weak. You need to let the troops handle it. I'm sure they'll find your mom."

"I've lost my father to those monsters and I'm not about to lose my mother. I have to go back to see if she's all right."

"Alex, what about Karen? If you go back there you'll worry her crazy," said Flip.

"She won't know I went back," said Alex.

"Fair enough. Look, I won't try to stop you. I realize what you're going through. Just understand that you're treading in very dangerous waters out there. And in the shape you're in, if you run into a situation where you need to defend yourself, you

256

may have trouble because you have very low energy. Your suit may not release any ammunition."

"Then I can get it artificially charged. How long would it take?" asked Alex.

"It can take up to six hours for a full charge, and you'll need at least a two-hour charge for the uniform to be effective at all," said Flip.

"I don't have two hours and I sure enough don't have six. It's just a chance I've got to take," said Alex as he put on his ARISN uniform.

"Good luck, son," said Flip.

 eic-2нн̄те e·т·'·нн̄теро 2н̄·т·пе 21 ʟ·ɛʎʏʟʟɛʎɪoн ɪɪ·ĸʏ·ʟʏ·oꝏн̄ʏc

Alex reached the end of the portal and stepped onto Brownsville soil. The entire town looked to be destroyed. Wonder Circle, the street where his aunt and uncle lived, was completely silent. Every other house had been reduced to shards of wood. Fortunately, his aunt's house was still intact. As Alex looked through the windows, he could see nothing but emptiness. He rang the doorbell several times but got no response. He went around back and saw that the hatchway to the cellar was open. It was obvious that the house had been looted. Alex entered, calling out to his family.

"Mom, are you here? Aunt Vickie? Uncle Shawn? It's Alex."

He checked all over the house. Besides a few clothes that remained in the closet, there were no signs of life. Panic began to creep up on Alex.

Maybe she's been rescued by the Alliance. Or maybe she went home, Alex thought as beads of sweat dropped from his forehead.

Heather Avenue, which had been one of the noisiest and busiest streets in town, was desolate and quiet. Houses and businesses had been razed. Animals roamed the streets. Brownsville Middle School had been destroyed. He took a moment to pause at the former site of his educational experience and reflect on his good and mostly bad times in its classrooms and hallways.

Alex approached the town junkyard. It was where his adventure -- Armageddon and the attempted destruction of the human race -- had begun. Compared with its surroundings, the junkyard still looked the same as it always had. It had a peaceful aura. Seagulls still made the journey from the Great Lakes to flock on the mountains of trash that scraped the now-blue skies. As he cut through the junkyard he didn't hear any dogs barking, only the buzzing of flies that swarmed over animal carcasses. Alex soon arrived at the open manhole cover that led to the sewer. Once again, anxiety seized him and his heart began to pound like a jackhammer in his chest.

On his block, most of the houses were still intact. Most important, despite unkempt landscaping, both Karen's house and his house stood strong. The front door of Alex's house was ever-so-slightly ajar. He slowly pushed it open and entered. Every room had been ransacked. Furniture was overturned and copies of his father's research papers were scattered about. Only the posters and paraphernalia that hung in the living room looked to be untouched.

"Mom," Alex shouted as he searched for her throughout the house. "Mom, are you here? It's Alex."

In the bathroom Alex took off his helmet. He didn't like what he saw in the mirror. It reflected someone worn down and dejected. It reflected someone beginning to lose hope in the trustworthiness of humans. The government had trashed his house looking for documents related to the scrolls. And with the latest situation involving Christopher Topher, Alex wondered just whose interests the government was protecting.

As he looked in the mirror to adjust his glasses, Alex felt his neck getting itchy. It was probably because his wound was healing. Before he could remove the bandages, he heard the sounds of pots dropping to the floor in the kitchen. When he reached the kitchen it didn't take long recognize that he was in trouble. He was confronted by a mallie dragon.

This creature was huge, much larger than any of the dragons he'd encountered in Vuur. Alex had two options: run or fight the creature head on.

"Have some of this!" he shouted, as the laser from his uniform split the creature in half. He began coming to the realization that if there were mallie dragons in the house, there was a good chance that his mother had not survived. He walked out of the house, sat on the front stoop, and began to cry.

Mom, I'm sorry. I'm so, so sorry.

As Alex walked back through the neighborhood, he heard muffled sounds from under some debris.

That sounds like someone is trapped. I've gotta check it out.

Pulling aside the debris, Alex reached for something the size of a baby. What he found was a vy-imp willing and eager to take a bite out of him. As the alien shook off the debris, a confronted Alex decided to shoot first and ask questions later. Unfortunately, his sapped body did not have enough energy to power the suit's lasers. Fortunately, he still had his legs.

Like a jackrabbit, Alex took off down the street with the vy-imp in pursuit. He quickly grew winded, but if the creature caught him it would mean his end. When he realized he'd be unable to outrun the vy-imp, Alex mustered enough energy to think his way out of his predicament.

†ⲭⲟⲙ ⲡⲓⲛⲓⲱ† ⲛ̀ⲟⲩⲣⲟ ⲫⲏⲉⲧ2ⲉⲙⲥⲓ 2ⲓⲭⲉⲛ ⲡⲓⲑⲣⲟⲛⲟⲥ ⲟⲩⲱⲛ †ⲫⲉ

The power of the king who sits on the throne opens the heavens.

Alex ran through the portal with the vy-imp literally nipping at his heels. The alien tried to stab Alex with its knife. Going through the portal was taking a lifetime. When he reached the end and stepped into the Alliance bunker, the creature had come through with him. Flip quickly shot it down.

"Now you're bringing the aliens to us? We're tryin' to get away from those things," joked Flip, who was looking the best he had since being injured in battle.

Alex was not in a joking mood. He may have lost his mother.

He sprawled on the floor and wept for her, and for Karen's parents. Instead of giving him more words of encouragement, Flip felt the best he could do was to get Karen. She sat on the floor next to Alex and embraced him. Flip watched them embrace. He glanced over at the dead creature and fired more shots into it before leaving the room. Frustrated that the tide of war seemed to be turning again to favor the aliens, Flip knew the breaking point was near.

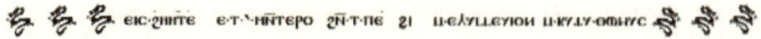

The Pope's bony hands fidgeted with the lock on a vault in one of the castle's rooms. He was surprised by a low, growling voice and a bright flashlight, as Ugnjengon and Ichielkak uncloaked into the darkness, ready to confront him.

"What are you doing here?" shouted Ugnjengon. "You were told that humans are not allowed in this section of the castle. Yet, you disobey. And now I find you in the hallowed areas of the castle that harbor the many secrets of my people. According to lord Ecaep, such crimes are punishable by death. You were already warned. Now, you shall die."

The Pope looked unconcerned.

"You speak as if you have control of things. Yet, you do not," said the Pope. "Not only do you lack leadership, but the same can be said about your lord Ecaep."

"This is blasphemy," screamed Ugnjengon. "Off with his head!"

As Ichielkak reached for his sword, six Luçimarks uncloaked. One of the Luçimarks fired an arrow straight into Ichielkak's chest, bringing him to his knees. The remaining Luçimarks surrounded Ugnjengon and secured him with strong steel rope. They kept him in a standing position and bound him at his neck, arms, and legs. The Pope gloated at the creature in bondage.

"As I said, you control nothing," said the Pope. "As your winged warrior gasps his last breath, I become the lord of this universe. While you and your so-called lord Ecaep spent your waking hours plotting to destroy the humans, I and my new friends have gained possession of the seventh scroll."

"You will pay for this betrayal," said Ugnjengon, struggling to speak.

"No, it is you who shall pay," the Pope said. "Now that I have the scroll, the Luçimarks and I will restore Earth to the way it was. The only exception being that I will be the head of the New World Order. And it means that your lord and his son will be eliminated from the equation."

Ichielkak began to cough up blood.

"Oh what's the matter, my winged friend? Having trouble breathing?" said the Pope. "Where's your loud, piercing cry? Oh, that's right. Your sound comes from your chest muscles. What a pity."

"Don't worry. We're about to put you out of your misery," said one of the Luçimarks.

Six arrows pierced Ichielkak's body. He fell limp to the ground with a thud.

"I want his wings for my trophy case," said one of the Luçimarks.

The Luçimark cut the wings off the creature. Tears flowed down Ugnjengon's face. He could not bear to watch.

"What's the matter, Ugnjengon? You don't like the way they're mutilating your friend? Are you feeling left out? Well, don't worry. I'm sure they have plans for you. Perhaps they'll use you as a bear rug," said the Pope.

"You may kill me, but you will meet certain destruction at the hands of our lord," said Ugnjengon.

"For such a repulsive creature you have much faith," said the Pope. "But before you die I'm going to let you in on a secret. There are over ten thousand Luçimarks marching toward this castle right now. While your troops struggle against the humans, Ecaep and the rest of your people will be easy pickings."

Ugnjengon struggled with all his might to break free from the rope, letting out a roar that echoed through all of Vuur. The arrows pierced his body and he fell silent, believing that his lord Ecaep would conquer the Luçimarks and avenge his death.

261

Chapter 33
The Seventh Scroll

The night was chaotic. Alliance troops were being deployed to smaller cities and towns all over the world to help defend against the Sétbætañ. After comforting Alex for most of the day, Karen was deployed to a town right outside Chicago, not too far from Brownsville. Alex, who eventually fell asleep after his return from trying to find his mother, woke up with anger in his heart, ready to go into action. Unfortunately, most of his cohorts had already been deployed. Alex wondered why he hadn't been called to duty.

"Sir, why wasn't I called to duty?" Alex asked an officer.

"We needed soldiers that were ready to go," said the officer. "You were not."

"We'll I'm ready now, sir. I heard rumors that Topher is at the Vatican. I'm willing to be deployed there," said Alex.

"I'm afraid not," said the chuckling officer. "You don't get to choose where you are deployed to. Plus, we already have more-experienced soldiers doing the job of capturing Topher. We would need you to help civilians. But on a more serious note, you don't seem to obey orders. Your disobedience brought a hostile creature back to our bunker, putting troops in danger. I've been told that you should remain in the bunker until further notice."

"But, sir, --"

The officer left the room, ignoring Alex's pleas. For the first time in a long time, Alex felt helpless. If only he could fight once more with the Alliance to bring down the enemy.

Alex walked to the bathroom to wash his face. As he dried himself and put his glasses back on, he noticed that he no longer felt pain on his neck.

I don't need this anymore, Alex thought, removing the bandages. Looking long and hard in the mirror, he saw something much worse than the mark of the Sétbætañ. It looked to be an ancient alien message. Alex was boiling mad. He felt he was being mocked by the creatures.

"No!" Alex shouted.

Incredibly angry, Alex ran back to his quarters and opened the portal. By the time anyone had noticed him missing, Alex was long gone.

The majority of his troops were scattered on Earth when Ecaep heard reports of the Luçimarks advancing toward his castle. With little more than two thousand troops at his disposal, and despite the loss of Ugnjengon and Ichielkak, Ecaep still felt confident that he would be victorious. When he'd been told that the bodies of Ugnjengon and Ichielkak were discovered in the castle, pierced by Luçimark arrows, Ecaep vowed to avenge their deaths. The stage was set for another faceoff between the Sétbætañ and the Luçimarks, and Ecaep's back was against the wall.

The Luçimarks got off to a great start. They killed many of the Sétbætañ with arrows and gun weaponry they'd received from the humans. The Sétbætañ tried to counter with the Selanon but were still driven back.

As the Luçimarks approached the castle, they were met by the Arbogog. At first the creatures were able to fend off the Luçimarks using their long, branch-like limbs. But the Luçimarks proved too much for the Sétbætañ. The difference in their numbers was too great.

King Camalabridge, son of the late King Mataralin, led the Luçimark army. Camalabridge was even more arrogant and condescending than his father. As his troops surrounded Ecaep and his remaining troops, he rode up to Ecaep on his horse-like creature and looked him square in the eye. Ecaep rode his xyheilamander.

"I finally meet the scum that killed my father -- the mighty Ecaep," said Camalabridge. "Now I get to avenge my father's death."

"You will avenge nothing," countered Ecaep. "I will dispose of you as I did your father."

263

"You fool, I have already disposed of your generals and your army is weak. They are fighting for their lives against the humans. To surrender now would spare your race from certain destruction. It may now be best that you listen to your son," said Camalabridge.

"I surrender to no one, especially Luçimark scum. And what business of my son's do you know?" asked Ecaep.

"I know that your son prefers not to fight. He wants to save lives," Camalabridge said sarcastically.

Topher, meanwhile, was watching events unfold from the castle. He saw a figure among the soldiers that made him head down to the battlefield.

"Anyway, enough chatter," said Camalabridge. "Since you are unwilling to surrender, are you and your people ready to die?"

Ecaep didn't respond.

"Before I dispose of your troops, destroy your castle, and sever your head, I thought it would be appropriate for you to meet the one who helped us murder your generals and gave us possession of the sacred seventh scroll."

Emerging from the pack of soldiers, riding a white horse-like creature, was the Pope. Ecaep stared at the Pope with anger.

"Does this surprise you, my lord?" said the Pope. "Does it surprise you that your death will be at the hands of a human? If not, then what a pity. You broke your promise of giving me world domination. So I break my promise of being obedient to you and to your people."

"You shall pay dearly for your murderous betrayal," said Ecaep.

"No. You shall pay for your betrayal," said the Pope. "Do I have to remind you that it was I who led you to the one who could translate the seventh scroll? That it was I who found your fool of a son? Yet, I had to follow his orders. That, my friend, was a mistake. If you had left me in charge, all humans would be subservient to you. By the way, I took great pleasure in watching those two beastly generals of yours die. The pain from those arrows must have been excruciating. I pity anyone who suffers a

264

slow death. Only the slow, painful deaths of you and Christopher will give me greater pleasure."

Ecaep's eyes filled with rage.

"So this is what this is all about? Power? World domination?" asked Topher, who'd made his way to stand beside Ecaep.

"You can call it what you want, Christopher," said the Pope. "But after your deaths, order on Earth will be restored, with Camalabridge acting as God, and I as king."

"Well, this couldn't have worked out any better," said Camalabridge. "I get to kill Ecaep, his son, and all these soldiers at the same time. Avenging my father and my people will be completed. Any of your people who survive will become slaves to the Luçimarks. Now it's time for you and your soldiers to die."

Camalabridge opened a saddlebag on his horse-like creature and removed a scroll. He then proceeded to read aloud its Coptic text:

ПЄ ТА ХО·ОС N̄·NЄЄІ·ШАХЄ

·NА ҀІNЄ МОY`

Camalabridge repeated the command, but louder:

ПЄ ТА ХО·ОС N̄·NЄЄІ·ШАХЄ

·NА ҀІNЄ МОY`

Then for a third time:

ПЄ ТА ХО·ОС N̄·NЄЄІ·ШАХЄ

·NА ҀІNЄ МОY`

"What is wrong? The command is not working," said Camalabridge, directing his anger at the Pope.

265

"Give me the scroll," said the Pope.

ⲡⲉ ⲧⲁ ⲭⲟ·ⲟⲥ ⲛ̄·ⲛⲉⲉⲓ·ϣⲁⲭⲉ

·ⲛⲁ ϭⲓⲛⲉ ⲙⲟⲩ`

ⲡⲉ ⲧⲁ ⲭⲟ·ⲟⲥ ⲛ̄·ⲛⲉⲉⲓ·ϣⲁⲭⲉ

·ⲛⲁ ϭⲓⲛⲉ ⲙⲟⲩ`

ⲡⲉ ⲧⲁ ⲭⲟ·ⲟⲥ ⲛ̄·ⲛⲉⲉⲓ·ϣⲁⲭⲉ

·ⲛⲁ ϭⲓⲛⲉ ⲙⲟⲩ`

"I don't know what's wrong," said the Pope, flustered.
"Perhaps I can help," said Ecaep. "What you read is not the seventh scroll, although what it says is true."

ⲡⲉ ⲧⲁ ⲭⲟ·ⲟⲥ ⲛ̄·ⲛⲉⲉⲓ·ϣⲁⲭⲉ

·ⲛⲁ ϭⲓⲛⲉ ⲙⲟⲩ`

"The translation of what you've both just recited is: *'Whoever speaks these words will find Death.'*"
"I knew you would betray me," Ecaep continued. "Ugnjengon told me so. I believe you wanted this command:"

ⲁⲉⲓ·ⲛⲟⲩⲭⲉ ⲛ̄·ⲟⲩ·ⲕⲱ̄ϩⲧ` ⲉ.ⲭⲛ̄· ⲡ·ⲕⲟⲥⲙⲟⲥ

ⲥⲁⲭⲓ ⲛ̄ϭⲟⲓⲥ

"The translation is: *'I have cast a fire upon the world, says the Lord.'*"
When Ecaep shouted the last command, laser beams fired down from the sky upon Camalabridge's army. The laser beams, made out of amplified concentrated plutonium, measured three

hundred and fifty feet in diameter. Powered by the alien satellites, these nuclear beams of electromagnetic radiation destroyed anyone and anything in its path. Ecaep had pulled the ultimate trick.

ⲗⲉⲓ·ⲚⲞⲨⲭⲉ Ⲛ·ⲞⲨ·ⲔⲰⲣⲦ` ⲉⲭⲚ· ·Ⲡ·ⲔⲞⲤⲘⲞⲤ
ⲥⲁⲭⲓ Ⲛⲥⲟⲓⲥ

Ecaep chanted again, and the beams continued to rain down. Ecaep's troops slew any Luçimark that didn't fall victim to the lights of radiation. Camalabridge's army tried to escape, to no avail. Ecaep recited the chant over and over:

ⲗⲉⲓ·ⲚⲞⲨⲭⲉ Ⲛ·ⲞⲨ·ⲔⲰⲣⲦ` ⲉⲭⲚ· ·Ⲡ·ⲔⲞⲤⲘⲞⲤ
ⲥⲁⲭⲓ Ⲛⲥⲟⲓⲥ

ⲗⲉⲓ·ⲚⲞⲨⲭⲉ Ⲛ·ⲞⲨ·ⲔⲰⲣⲦ` ⲉⲭⲚ· ·Ⲡ·ⲔⲞⲤⲘⲞⲤ
ⲥⲁⲭⲓ Ⲛⲥⲟⲓⲥ

Before long, the battle had ended. The onslaught resulted in the deaths of more than ten thousand Luçimarks. Camalabridge was the only surviving Luçimark. The Pope, cowering on the ground, had also managed to survive. Topher had taken shelter during the battle. He emerged unharmed and joined his father. Ecaep sat on his xyheilamander, surveying his victims.

"As I've said before, you will avenge nothing," he said to Camalabridge.

"Please, spare my life," said a whimpering Camalabridge.

"You beg like your father did before I cut off his head," said Ecaep. "Come before me and kneel."

"Spare me, please. I will be your slave."

"Very well," said Ecaep. "I am merciful. I will not kill you."

"Thank you. Oh, thank you, my lord."

"But my pet does not show mercy. Feed on his flesh."

267

In an instant, the xyheilamander pounced on Camalabridge and sunk its razor like teeth into his neck. The creature proceeded to eat the Luçimark. The sound of crunching bone made Topher and the Pope turn away in disgust.

"Now it's time for you to meet your fate," Ecaep said to the Pope.

"Please spare me, oh lord. Forgive my sins. I wish not to be eaten," said the Pope, sobbing between each word.

"It will not be I who decides your fate, but Molahsras."

"Oh, Christopher, or Molahsras -- however you wish to be addressed -- please spare me, for I have sinned."

Topher did not respond. He looked down at the Pope with pity.

"Please, Christopher. Please let me live," said the Pope, tears flowing.

"I've decided that I will not be the one to determine your fate, either," said Topher.

"Then I shall determine his fate," said an angry Ecaep.

Ecaep grabbed the Pope by his mozetta and pulled him onto the xyheilamander. They rode off toward the Vuur Mountains, leaving Topher in their wake. At the other side of the mountains, they arrived at the fiery lake of Enervet Sine. Ecaep pulled the Pope off the xyheilamander and slowly dragged him towards the rocky ledge. The unforgiving serrated Vuur landscape tore through the Pope's old and weathered skin.

"No! Please God, no! Don't do this to me!"

"I think this would be a just punishment," said Ecaep, grinning. "Besides, didn't you once say that 'you'd rather be cast into Enervet Sine?' Just think of this as paying for your sins."

As Ecaep continued his ascent towards the ledge, dragging the pope over the jagged mountainous terrain, the pope began reciting the Lord's Prayer.

> "Our father, who art in heaven
> Hallowed be thy name.
> Thy kingdom come, thy will be done
> On earth as it is in heaven
> Give us this day our daily bread

And forgive us our trespasses

As we forgive those who trespass against us. And lead us not into temptation –"

Before the Pope could finish, Ecaep slung him off the cliff. As the Pope fell, he could be heard finishing the prayer.

"But deliver us from evil.

Amen."

This was followed by screams of agony.

"Now, all of my people of the Sé-bætañ race, gather with me and my army for the final battle. The destruction of the human race is at hand," screamed Ecaep as he opened the portal to Earth.

I wonder if Topher is here, thought Alex. He sat cloaked, just outside of the Vatican gates, which were surrounded by guard trolls.

In his anger, Alex had failed to think through the possible scenarios. Would Topher be in Washington or in Vatican City? Unsure of where to go, Alex went with his gut, and his gut told him Vatican City.

The problem was that he had been in the city for nearly three hours and everything was quiet. It was very possible that Topher was somewhere inside the Vatican walls. But the Vatican was guarded like a fortress and penetrating its walls would be nearly impossible. Alex was looking for any sign that told him of Topher's whereabouts.

I'm gonna wait another fifteen minutes then I'm headed to Washington.

Alex got the sign he was looking for. From behind the gates a bright light and a silent lightning strike filled the dark night. It was a dimensional portal from which Ecaep and his army had just emerged.

Great, Topher should be appearing any minute now. And when he does, he'll be greeted with a hole in the side of his neck.

Unfortunately, Alex didn't get the chance to wait.

Immediately after emerging from the portal, the Sétbætañ leader began to chant the command of the seventh scroll:

ⲗⲉⲓ·ⲛⲟⲩϫⲉ Ⲛ·ⲟⲩ·ⲕⲱ͞ⲣⲧ` ⲉϫⲛ̄· ·ⲡ·ⲕⲟⲥⲙⲟⲥ

ⲥⲁϫⲓ ⲙ̄ϭⲟⲓⲥ

Almost instantly, a laser beam shot from the sky and fired on the citizens of Vatican City. It destroyed everything in its path.

ⲗⲉⲓ·ⲛⲟⲩϫⲉ Ⲛ·ⲟⲩ·ⲕⲱ͞ⲣⲧ` ⲉϫⲛ̄· ·ⲡ·ⲕⲟⲥⲙⲟⲥ

ⲥⲁϫⲓ ⲙ̄ϭⲟⲓⲥ

Ecaep's chanting caused laser beams to shoot down from the sky at the speed of sound. Alex moved to find shelter in St. Peter's Basilica, joining thousands of others who prayed for protection.

"Lord, please protect us from this evil. Please spare us. Forgive us for our sins. The Lord is angry. The almighty hand of God has sent hellfire from the heavens," shouted the faithful.

Among the noises of chaos and destruction, Alex heard another sound -- the humming of a portal. He was sure that Topher had arrived. Alex left the safety of St. Peter's to take a closer look.

Outside, Alex saw Ecaep's army wreaking havoc on the city. Any human who survived the nuclear beams fell victim to the Sétbætañ creatures. But just as Alex turned back to St. Peter's, he saw a figure headed toward the Apostolic Palace. It was Christopher Topher.

"Hey you, Topher," Alex screamed over the chaos. He wasn't sure if Topher had heard him. Once Alex began his pursuit, Topher made a dash toward the Palace.

"Stop. I have unfinished business with you," Alex yelled.

Topher didn't respond. Nor did he look back. He continued straight through the doors of the Palace. Alex cloaked to avoid the two large trolls guarding the doors. As he quietly

270

approached, Alex almost gave himself away by gagging from the smell of the creatures. The trolls also took notice. They smelled human scent. After communicating with grunts, however, they determined that the smell must have been from Topher. Alex snuck past the creatures and into the Palace.

It was the first time Alex had ever been in the Palace.

Which way should I go?

The building was vast and very quiet. There were no signs of Topher or anyone else. Not a priest, not a creature, no one. But the death-like quiet didn't frighten Alex, nor was he intimidated. Led by a burning desire for revenge, he decided to uncloak.

"Topher, I know you're here," shouted Alex. His voice echoed off the walls.

"Topher, come out and show yourself. I just want to talk. I need to understand why you did what you did. Why did you betray your country? Why did you betray the world?"

As Alex traveled deeper into the Palace he heard a sound like a small marble being dropped on the floor. He put his lasers in stun mode.

"Mr. Topher, is that you? Mr. President, it's okay. I just wanna talk."

Alex heard a thud and stopped in his tracks. It sounded like a person falling to the floor. From under a staircase, he looked up. Dozens of vy-imps were standing at the top of the stairs, ready to pounce. He attempted to use his lasers, but his energy reserves were too low. So Alex took flight.

The creatures chased Alex down the hall. He slipped and slid on the waxed floors, making it difficult to go full speed. He ducked into a small room.

Think Alex, think. How do I dodge these creatures? I can't stay in here forever.

He heard a sound from inside the room. It was vy-imps, uncloaking right in front of him. Alex felt a hard, sharp pain rip across his head. He blacked out.

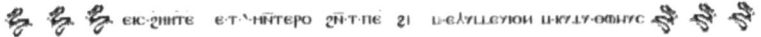

The majority of Alliance troops that had been stationed worldwide came to Vatican City to meet the enemy head on. This was the most dangerous challenge they'd yet faced. Russian intelligence confirmed that the fiery lasers raining from the sky were coming from the invisible alien satellites. Intelligence agencies all over the world were frantically trying to find and destroy the satellites. Vice President Windows, Flip, Bronson, and many other military officials got together to strategize. Karen, who'd returned from the town outside Chicago, was allowed to listen in.

"What we face is the alien leader of the Sétbætañ causing mass destruction by uttering the command of the seventh scroll," said Windows. "Over the last twelve hours, hundreds of thousands of people in Rome and Vatican City have been murdered. At this rate, within twenty-four hours, nearly a million people will be dead, and up to five million will be dead by week's end. If the aliens are not stopped within the next forty-eight hours, we have no doubt that the devastation will be worldwide. People, I want you to understand. We very well may be witnessing the extermination of mankind. We need ideas, now."

"Where exactly are these alien satellites located?" asked Flip.

"They're scattered somewhere behind our satellites," said Bronson.

"Can we somehow strategically shoot down the alien satellites by firing missiles behind ours? I know the odds are against us, but we may get lucky enough to hit some," said Flip.

"Yeah, and who cares if we occasionally hit our own satellites? Half of them aren't working anyway," said Kremley.

"Okay, we'll put that idea on the table. Anyone else?" asked Windows.

"Why don't we do the obvious and get rid of the source of the problem -- Ecaep?" chirped in Karen.

"Well, why didn't we think of that?" Bronson said sarcastically.

"Look, Ecaep is the only one who knows the command. If we eliminate him then we stop the lasers," said Karen.

272

"Hon, don't let him discourage you. That's a great idea," said Flip. "Except that Ecaep has over a thousand aliens surrounding him like a fortress. Their defensive front is darn near impossible to penetrate."

"Even if that idea seems obvious, I say put it on the table," said Windows. "Finding a way to kill Ecaep may be easier than shooting invisible satellites from space."

"By the way, did you check on Alex before coming out here?" asked Flip.

"No, he wasn't in his bunker. I thought he came with you guys," said Karen.

Flip leaned back against the wall and sighed.

"No, he didn't come with us. But I have a feeling where he might be," said Flip.

Alex arose from the hard marble floor with a splitting headache. He was locked inside a small but elegant room with no windows. On the walls hung many photos of the Pope meeting with world leaders. Alex found it odd that he didn't see a single photo of the Pope with President Christopher Topher.

On the floor was a television tray that held a plate of baked chicken and rice. Famished, Alex quickly devoured the food, scraping the plate clean. He longed for a tall glass of water.

"Are you thirsty?" said a voice from inside the room.

It was Topher's image projected on a flatscreen. Alex's blood pressure shot up when he saw Topher's face. He instinctively aimed to fire a laser at the flatscreen. It was only then that he noticed that the gloves from his uniform had been removed.

"You can't shoot at me without your gloves," said Topher. "I ask again. Are you thirsty?"

Alex's thirst was stronger than his pride.

"Yes," he said.

The flatscreen went black and the door slowly opened.

Now I'm going to get him.

But when the door opened it wasn't Topher. It was a wolf-

273

creature delivering water. Alex stumbled back in fear. The creature set down a glass and a pitcher of water on a nearby table.

"You thought I was going to deliver the water?" said Topher, reappearing on the flatscreen. "You're still angry."

"Because you're a traitor," yelled Alex. "You helped mastermind the aliens' dominance over us. You contributed to the deaths of nearly a billion people. And it was you who indirectly contributed to the deaths of my parents. How can you sit there and question that I'm angry? Why? Why did you do it? I believed in you. I looked up to you. The world believed in you, and you betrayed us. You're nothing but a coward."

Topher appeared unmoved by Alex's rant.

"Alex, I want to show you something."

Topher removed his shirt and showed Alex the scar on the back of his shoulder blade.

"I'm sure you're familiar with this mark. It's the mark of the beast. The mark of the Sétbætañ. And I'm gonna let you in on a little secret. This mark was given to me by my father, Ecaep. I know this is a lot for you to take in but you must know the truth. I'm not human. I am of Sétbætañ and Luçimark blood."

Alex looked at Topher in stunned silence.

"I am well over six hundred years old. My real name is Molahsras. I was introduced to your world when I was placed on the doorstep of an orphanage. My alien blood gave me superior intelligence and as I matured I was able to use it to my advantage.

"You're already aware that the Luçimarks are the forefathers of the human race and the eternal enemy of the Sétbætañ. Lord Ecaep wants the Luçimarks and their offspring destroyed. I have tried to compromise with the humans so that they could avoid destruction. All I wanted to do was save lives," said Topher.

"And what was your compromise? For us to be slaves of your people?" asked Alex. "We'd rather die if we can't be free!"

Topher didn't respond. He put back on his shirt.

"I have one other question for you," said Alex. "Why did you give me this scar?"

274

"Just think of it as my present to you," said Topher.

The flatscreen went black.

Within minutes, Sétbætañ creatures stormed the room and seized Alex. He had no idea where they were taking him. He figured that he had seen his best days and that his life was coming to a close. The creatures took him outside to the Courtyard of Sixtus V and bound him upright, in a sacrificial manner. As Alex was being tied up he looked toward the star-lit sky and saw an array of lasers coming down from the heavens. *Is this truly the end of mankind?* Alex knew that his time was short. Unless a miracle occurred, he would never know the answer to his question.

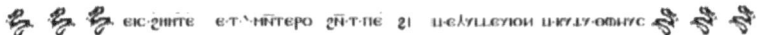

Flip and Karen arrived at the Apostolic Palace with guns blazing. They took down nearly every Sétbætañ creature that crossed their paths. Flip had guessed that Alex went looking for Topher in Vatican City. Karen, who was growing more attached to Alex each day, insisted on being by Flip's side. Bronson and some of the other military officials were angry at Flip for going against protocol. But after all that Flip and Alex had gone through together, Flip felt it was his duty to come to the boy's rescue. Flip had developed a deep fondness for both Alex and Karen, and there was no way he was going to let either of them down.

"Where could he be?" asked Karen.

"I dunno. This place is too darn big. Let's head down this hallway. Just make sure that your lasers are set to kill mode," said Flip.

Alex was still in the center of the courtyard when a large group of Sétbætañ began to gather around him. All sorts of things were running through his mind as the volume of the creatures' chatter increased. Alex noticed that the sky was no longer filled with lasers but with Selanon. They looked to be joining the group of creatures that surrounded him. Topher made his way to face Alex. With him was the supreme evil incarnate,

Ecaep.

"He is ready for you, my lord. He's ready for the sacrifice," said Topher.

"Excellent," said Ecaep.

Ecaep addressed his army.

"For many miliyous our people have been the servant, the hunted, and the sacrificed. But this night marks a new era for the Sétbætañ. An era in which we are the masters. An era in which we are the hunters. An era in which others are sacrificed to us. My son, Molahsras, has brought us together for a celebration of victory and to claim our new palace, our new kingdom, and our new world. Molahsras has taught me how humans worship their gods and that part of this worship is done through sacrifice. Now my son has brought me this sacrificial lamb to be slaughtered and its blood drunk in the names of Ecaep, Molahsras, and Cúbaneg. Prepare me."

The creatures prepared Ecaep for the ritual. They marked his face with mallie-dragon blood and handed him a long, piercing sword. Alex had given up hope. After all he'd been through, he was going to be killed and his blood would be drained from him and drunk like wine. Even as his life began to flash before his eyes, his mind kept returning to his conversation with Topher about the scar on his neck. "*Just think of it as my present to you.*"

Out of nowhere, Flip and Karen fired on the crowd of aliens. They were able to kill ten before Flip was taken down by an alien's automatic rifle. Karen screamed as she went to help him. Blood gushed from Flip's chest as he gasped wildly.

"It looks as if two more have joined the party," crowed Ecaep. "There will be plenty for all of us to feast on."

Ecaep looked down at Flip and Karen in disgust and then looked at Alex. Then he smirked.

"Finally, I get my revenge on the one who possessed the scrolls," said Ecaep. "I see that you are still weak. Your female companion has more warrior blood than you. I'm going to enjoy draining your blood until you are dry. Afterward, your companions will be sacrificed to my Sétbætañ followers."

Alex, still tied, stared at the ground.

276

"Do you have any last words?" asked Ecaep, drawing his sword.

Closing his eyes, Alex thought about his mom and dad. He thought about how he discovered the scrolls and his wild adventure. He thought about Karen and how he had fallen for her. He thought about Topher. He thought about the image of the scar on his neck. Then he smiled. Though he was weak, he slowly began to whisper something.

"What?" asked Ecaep.

ⲀⲈⲒ·ⲚⲞⲨⲬⲈ Ⲛ·ⲞⲨ·ⲔⲰ̅Ⲣ̅Ⲧ̀ ⲈⲬⲚ̄· ·Ⲡ·ⲔⲞⲤⲘⲞⲤ

ⲤⲀⲬⲒ Ⲛ̄ⲤⲟⲒⲤ

ⲀⲈⲒ·ⲚⲞⲨⲬⲈ Ⲛ·ⲞⲨ·ⲔⲰ̅Ⲣ̅Ⲧ̀ ⲈⲬⲚ̄· ·Ⲡ·ⲔⲞⲤⲘⲞⲤ

ⲤⲀⲬⲒ Ⲛ̄ⲤⲟⲒⲤ

This time Alex shouted for all to hear.

ⲀⲈⲒ·ⲚⲞⲨⲬⲈ Ⲛ·ⲞⲨ·ⲔⲰ̅Ⲣ̅Ⲧ̀ ⲈⲬⲚ̄· ·Ⲡ·ⲔⲞⲤⲘⲞⲤ

ⲤⲀⲬⲒ Ⲛ̄ⲤⲟⲒⲤ

"No!" screamed Ecaep.

In an instant, beams of light discharged from the heavens and knifed their way through the crowd. The laser beams showed no mercy to those they struck. Unable to avoid the lights of radiation, a part of a laser beam struck Ecaep and he was sliced in half at the waist. Face up on the ground he stared at Alex with his fiery eyes. They became distant and emotionless, then not too long after, lifeless. He uttered no words and died instantly. As he lay mutilated on the ground, the creatures went into full panic mode. Some turned on one another while others killed themselves.

For the first time in centuries, the Sétbætañ were without their leader. Devoid of hope, the surviving creatures opened a portal

277

back to Vuur. Around the world, the Sétbætañ were returning to their home planet, never to return.

Rising from beneath the bodies of dead aliens, Karen took an alien's sword and cut the ropes binding Alex. The dead bodies had shielded her and Flip from the onslaught of radiation. She then quickly returned to Flip.

"How did you do it, boy?" Flip said, coughing up blood. "You saved mankind. How did you know the command?"

"From President Topher," said Alex. "It was the command of the seventh scroll that he'd burned onto my neck."

"Well you got 'em good," said Flip.

Holding Alex's and Karen's hands, Flip took his final breath. Captain Franklin 'Flip' Powers had uttered his last words, leaving them standing above him, crying. Flip was another friend, another loved one, Alex and Karen had lost to the war.

Though it appeared that mankind was now safe, Alex wanted answers. Where had Topher been in all the chaos?

"Where do you think he went?" asked Karen.

"I have an idea," said Alex, still crying over the loss of Flip. "Come on, let's go."

Alex took Karen by the hand and entered a dimensional portal to Vuur. Alex's hunch had been correct. Standing on the rocky ledge above Enervet Sine was Christopher Topher.

"Mr. President, why didn't you tell me?" shouted Alex over the noise of the fire and brimstone.

"Because you were our only hope, Alex," said Topher. "The only hope for mankind. I knew you could read it. You were the only one besides Ecaep who could."

"You had me confused," said Alex. "I thought that you were against us."

"Never," said Topher. "It was my plan to assist in the survival of the humans."

"Why are we standing on this ledge?" asked Karen.

Yeah. Let's go back, Mr. President," said Alex.

"No. You were right, Alex. I assisted in killing millions. And yes, I am a coward. Now's the time for me to pay for my sins."

"No! You don't have to do this," screamed Alex.

278

"I know. But this is what I choose to do," said Topher.

Then, with a slight grin on his face, he tossed himself over the ledge. Alex and Karen watched in horror as Topher fell to his death into the fiery lake of Enervet Sine.

"We've gotta get out of here," screamed Karen. It was the start of an earthquake.

ⲈϧⲞⲨⲚ ⲠⲒⲢⲞ Ⲉ̀ ⲠⲒ ⲀⲦⲀϬⲚⲒ ⲘⲚⲦⲢⲢⲰⲞⲨ

Alex shouted the command as he grabbed Karen's hand and they ran into the portal.

Reaching Earth, they felt the tension leave their bodies. They kissed with great passion. It was Alex's first. The Alliance arrived to see to Flip's and the rest of the humans' bodies. The dead aliens were piled up and set afire.

Chapter 34
Aftermath

Through advanced technology, the worldwide Alliance was eventually able to locate and destroy the hidden satellites orbiting the Earth. Any scroll command uttered would be useless. The scrolls were confiscated by the U.S Government. The remaining people implanted with the BioCharge chip had them removed. With the death of Christopher Topher, the World Apex Government was disbanded and Bernard Windows was sworn in as the new American President.

One year after the final battle, the world governments ratified the Windows–Bronson Pact, prohibiting the embedment of mind-altering technology into human bodies. All government officials who sided with the aliens and who were not under the chip's influence were court-martialed and imprisoned. This included Victor Riley and Elizabeth Gateway. With plans to rebuild the Earth's cities and towns underway, the first task at hand was recognizing those who'd played a part in the defeat of the aliens. More than two million people gathered at the National Mall in Washington, D.C., for the celebration and to hear President Windows' speech:

"I welcome the people of this great nation and the world to celebrate a new era in mankind's existence. We have proved that with the defeat of the aliens we are not Americans, or Russians, or Chinese, or any other nationality. We have proved that we are human beings first and the joint protectors of our great world. And if any hostile civilization attempts to threaten us, we shall meet it with much resistance -- sending them back whence they came.

"Throughout our three-and-a-half-year struggle, there have been many heroes. The United Alliance Marines were formed to protect our citizens from the alien invasion. And there were many other military factions that joined in the war against our enemies.

But there are two people I would like to present with the newly minted Franklin Powers Medal -- now recognized as our nation's highest award for honor and bravery. There's no telling where the nation or world would be if it wasn't for these two youngters. They are Alexander Smiley and Karen Stubblefield."

Alex and Karen took the stage and the crowd cheered. Bronson, Kremley, and Jackson smiled at them like proud parents. Never before had Alex and Karen stood in front of so many people. Karen's parents joined her on the stage. She let her emotions show as they embraced.

"There is one more medal I would like to present," said President Windows. "This medal will be awarded posthumously to Phillip Smiley. Accepting the award is his lovely widow, Marion Smiley."

Once again the crowd went wild. Alex embraced his mother with all of his emotions on display.

"I thought I'd lost you, mom," said Alex.

"You should have known that I would be too tough for those creatures," said Mrs. Smiley. "When rumors surfaced that the creatures were not hell-spawned but actually aliens, I knew God would triumph!"

"But where were you? I searched everywhere."

"Your uncle, aunt, and I stayed in one of the underground bunkers, thank God!" said Mrs. Smiley. "For months I had no means of communication so I was unable to contact you. After martial law was lifted, we put out flyers wherever we could, hoping that someone could help us find you. When we didn't get a response, I thought that you had perished and I fell into a deep depression. I needed to leave Brownsville. We ended up moving to Aunt Vickie's mother's house in Northern Wisconsin. It was one of the few places the aliens didn't invade so all the towns were intact. But by the grace of God I was located by the Alliance and they told me you were alive. And now I'm here to witness my son's finest moment."

Alex looked out at the cheering crowd. He'd never felt more proud. He was with his best friend, united with his mother, and his father had been publicly vindicated.

After the corruption of the Roman Catholic Church had surfaced, the Church worked hard to restore its image and regain members. Part of the Church's restructuring was the ouster of all those who'd assisted the late Pope Gregory. This convinced the populace that the Church was serious about the morality of those who led the institution. Another part of their revamping was introducing the idea that the aliens were also God's creatures. People returned to the pews in droves, and new worshipers joined them. The Church was now seen as a more open and progressive institution. It was apparent that no matter what truths had come out during the alien invasion, people still wanted to believe in God.

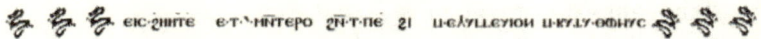

The Sétbætañ had divided themselves into multiple factions upon returning to Vuur. Lacking leadership and direction, the creatures struggled to survive. Several had risen to lead, but were quickly assassinated. Internal wars had become the norm. The Luçimarks quickly reestablished themselves in Urodae and appointed a new king by the name of Philimoncenty.

Philimoncenty made half-hearted attempts to live peacefully alongside the Sétbætañ, but made it clear that the races must remain segregated. The destruction of the satellites orbiting Earth meant that interplanetary travel by dimensional portal was no longer possible. No one on Earth knew if the remaining scroll technology was still in use on Caynonã, or what the future held for the planet's races.

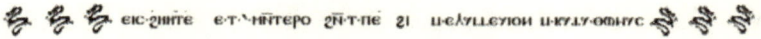

When Alex returned to his home in Brownsville, there was much work to be done. Several exterminators were called to rid the house of mallie dragons. Most of the creatures were destroyed and some were kept for scientific research. Alex and

Mrs. Smiley collected all of the scattered paperwork on Mr. Smiley's scroll discovery and placed it, along with the medals for honor and bravery, in a safe-deposit box. They also helped the Stubblefields' get their house in order when they found the time, which was often.

A year and a half after the final battle, Alex still had nightmares. He made sure to attend counseling each week. The scar on his neck would be a lifetime reminder of his past trials and tribulations.

Under the Windows-Jackson Act, Earth's reconstruction was well under way. The town of Brownsville wasn't left out. Office buildings, houses, and schools were rebuilt. The majority of kids who'd been unable to attend school during the Armageddon Wars were now home-schooled. Alex, who had no desire to return to middle school, fell into this category. The mall destroyed by the Krieatine was rebuilt. Families slowly returned to the neighborhood. Everything was looking up.

Late one evening, Mrs. Smiley sent Alex to the store to get some cleaning supplies. Karen tagged along. As they walked, they passed the new middle school, built on the former location of the junkyard.

"That's where everything started," said Karen.

"At least we don't have to look at that junkyard anymore," said Alex. "I don't think I'll ever look at a junkyard the same way again."

After they shared a laugh, they kissed and resumed their walk, holding hands.

When Alex and Karen left the store, Alex was struck on the back of the head with a rock. A crowd of kids that had seemed to come out of nowhere erupted in laughter. Leading the pack was none other than Lenopolous Gary.

"Hey, punk, what are you doing with my girlfriend?"

Alex desperately wanted to avoid confrontation. He just wanted to take his purchases and go home.

"It's been years and you're still acting like a creep," said Karen.

"Aw, did I hurt your feelings? What about yours, Alex?"

Alex tried to ignore him.

"Karen, let's go. It makes no sense feeding into it," said Alex.

"Hey, punk, are you talking about me? You think you're special because you got some lame medal?" asked Lenopolous.

"That lame medal was for bravery and honor. Something that you don't know anything about," said Karen.

"Oh, you have to stick up for your boyfriend? Or is he your girlfriend?"

Somehow, even after spending more than three years of his life fighting aliens on the front lines with the Alliance, Alex still feared Lenopolous. But if he had learned one thing, it was how to face his fears. And Alex was nearing his breaking point.

"Why don't you go back to school and learn something for a change? Or better yet, the detention center. Everyone knows that you need to work your way up to qualify for special ed," said Karen.

That set Lenopolous off.

"So you think I'm trouble, huh? You think I'm stupid? Well I'm gonna show you who's stupid."

"You're not going to show anyone anything," said Alex.

"Oh, look who's grown a pair," said Lenopolous. "This is none of your business. This is between me and the lady."

"Her business is my business. Now leave her alone."

"Alex, you don't need to do this," said Karen.

"You best listen to the lady," said Lenopolous.

"Karen, I need to face my fears. I could have saved millions if I'd done so before," said Alex.

Karen nodded, leaving Alex to square off against Lenopolous.

"You know what? I'm gonna pound your face in, for old time's sake," said Lenopolous.

With that, Lenopolous rushed Alex. He swung and missed wildly with a right cross.

"Come on," said Lenopolous.

Lenopolous missed again with a left hook and Alex countered with a kick to the shin.

"Ouch! I'm gonna kill you."

With the growing crowd chanting "fight, fight, fight," Lenopolous connected a punch to Alex's midsection, sending him to the ground. He got on top of Alex and pinned him down.

"Now, I'm gonna pummel your face so hard, no one will recognize you."

Lenopolous began to punch Alex. But to the surprise of the crowd, Alex delivered a hard blow with his knee right to Lenopolous' groin, temporarily paralyzing him with pain. Alex pushed him off. Standing, Alex took Karen by the hand and ran as fast as he could.

"I'm gonna get you," said Lenopolous, rolling on the ground in pain.

"Where did you learn that?" Karen asked, laughing.

"From Flip," said Alex.

"Do you think Lenopolous will come after you?"

"Who cares?" said Alex. "If he does I'll just give him another knee."

Karen laughed.

"See you tomorrow?" Alex asked Karen, as he walked her back to her house.

"Sure," said Karen.

After Alex left Karen with a kiss, he looked up at the star-filled sky and wondered if there were other alien races that planned to visit the Earth. After taking time to ponder, he headed home.

Beaming with unbridled confidence, Alex was no longer the fear-filled twelve-year-old kid with low self-esteem. He was a sixteen-year-old young man who had bravely battled aliens and bullies, and fought side-by-side with the United Alliance Marines. He had helped save the world.

The End

Appendix A
Characters and Places of Interest

Akaie – (A-kye) Luçimark general

Alexander Smiley –twelve-year-old boy with low self-esteem

Arowana – (air-o-WANN-ah) submarine used to navigate Lake Jymhamasbad

Asus Forest – (A-zeus) an ancient forest in Caynonã that separates Urodae and Vuur

Bernard Windows – U.S. Vice President

Brent – a soldier in Flip's brigade

Brownsville – Alex's hometown

Bwendai – (BWIN-day) princess of the Luçimarks, daughter of Mataralin

Camalabridge - (cam-AHLA-bridge) son of Mataralin and subsequent king of the Luçimarks

Cambridge Tower – a secret post of the Luçimarks located in Urodae

Camp 349 – Sétbætañ concentration camp located outside Washington, D.C.

Cardinal Morelli – a cardinal of the Catholic Church under Pope Gregory

Caynonã (kay-NO-na) – the home planet of the Luçimarks and the Sétbætañ

Caynonã mill worms – worms native to Caynonã

Christopher Marcellus Topher (TOE-fer) – U.S. President

Colox – owner of a coreintel

Coreintel (core-in-TELL) – Luçimark ice chamber

Cúbaneg (COO-ba-neg) – lead general of the Sétbætañ army

Darius Miller – a general of the Alliance

David Wentworth – W.A.G. attorney general

Duayne – one of Lenopolous' minions

Ecaep (EE-sep) – leader of the Sétbætañ

Eloysina (eh-low-SEE-na) – one of the Luçimark native

Enervet Sine (eh-ner-VET sign) – a fiery lake in Vuur

Flying Dragons – winged creatures that fight alongside the Sétbætañ

Franklin "Flip" Powers – U.S. Army captain
Granger Jackson – U.S. military lieutenant and scientist
Hewlett Bronson – a soldier and the son of James Bronson
Ichielkak (eye-chill-KAK) – general of the Sétbætañ army and leader of the Selanon
Inspyron (in-SPY-ron) – Luçimark Prime Minister
James Bronson – a lieutenant general of the Alliance
John Creighton – British scientist, inventor of the BioCharge chip and the ARISN uniform
John Kremley – U.S. military major
Jymhamasbad (gym-HAHM-is-bahd) – an island thirty miles southwest of Vuur
Karen Stubblefield – Alex's best friend and confidant
Krieatine (KREE-a-tin) – ancient warrior of the Sétbætañ
Lake Arnold – located in Brownsville
Lenopolous Gary – the town bully
Luçimarks (LUKE-ee-marks) – an alien race from Caynonã, creators of humans and their ally during the Armageddon wars
Maczell Galaxy (mack-ZELL) – Caynonã's galaxy, seven hundred fifty thousand light years from Earth
Mallie dragon – snakelike creature native to Caynonã
Mataralin – leader of the Luçimarks
Molahsras (mo-LAH-ras) – birth name of Christopher Topher
Molly – a little girl at Camp 349
Phillip Smiley – Alex's father
Marion Smiley – Alex's mother
Elizabeth Gateway – Alex's insensitive schoolteacher and undercover CIA agent
NONWES treaty (No Nuclear Weapons treaty) – between the Earth's nations to eliminate all nuclear weaponry
Paul James III – Roman Catholic Pope preceding Gregory
Philimoncenty (fil-eh-mon-SEN-ty) - Luçimark king
Pope Gregory – Roman Catholic Pope
Rane Mackie – master sergeant and commander of the Arowana
Selanon (SELL-a-non) – winged, gargoyle-like Sétbætañ creatures
Sétbætañ (SET-bee-tan) – an alien race from Caynonã, enemy of

the Luçimarks and humans

Sheldon Brown – W.A.G. secretary of defense

Straboudo (stra-BOO-doh), Qiooing (KO-ing), Zriotnmtail (RITE-en-till), Auionaral (arr-ee-ON-all) – Ecaep's commanding officers

Suini (SUE-nee) – a Luçimark caretaker and midwife

TAPC News Channel (The American Political and Congressional News Channel) – a highly partisan news outlet

Trolls – large, malodorous Sétbætañ creatures

Ugnjengon (oo-ja-GON) – general of the Sétbætañ army

United Alliance Marines (U.A.M.) – military unit created by President Topher to battle the aliens

United People's Act – allowing the creation and implantation of the BioCharge chip

Urodae (YOUR-o-day) – land of the Luçimarks

Victor Riley – CIA agent

Vuur (vurr) – land of the Sétbætañ

Vy-imps –Sétbætañ creatures about the size of a chimpanzee

Walker – man from Brownsville who drives Alex and Karen to Washington, D.C.

Wayne Hoffman – W.A.G. secretary of state

World Apex Government (W.A.G.) – new world government put in place by Ecaep and Pope Gregory after the first Armageddon war

Xyheilamander (zy-HEEL-a-MAN-der) – bearlike creature native to Caynonã

Zixselec (ZICK-sil-ick) – Luçimark military of defense leader

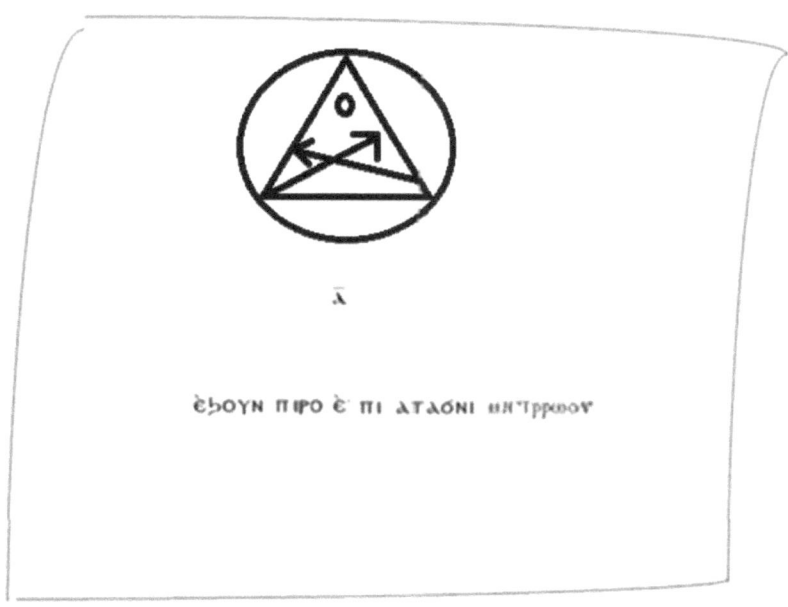

Ā

ⲉϧⲟⲩⲛ ⲡⲓⲣⲟ ⲉ̀ ⲡⲓ ⲁⲧⲁⲟ́ⲛⲓ ⲙ̀ⲛ̀ⲧ̄ⲣⲣⲱⲟⲩ

This is a drawing of the Scroll Number 1, which opens a dimensional portal --a wormhole in time and space -- between Earth and Caynonã. The Coptic translates as:

Enter the door into the new kingdom.

B̄

ⲥ̀ⲙⲟⲩ ⲉ̀ⲣⲟϥ ⲕⲁⲧⲁ ⲡ̀ⲁϣⲁⲓ ⲛ̀ⲧⲉ ⲧⲉϥⲙⲉⲧⲛⲓϣ̀ⲧ ⲑⲱⲗⲉⲃ ⲧ̀ⲫⲉ

This is a drawing of Scroll Number 2, which turns the sky red. The alien satellites emit rays toward the sun, and the sun releases red gamma rays into Earth's atmosphere. The Coptic translates as:

Bless Him according to the abundance of His greatness as He spoils the heavens.

290

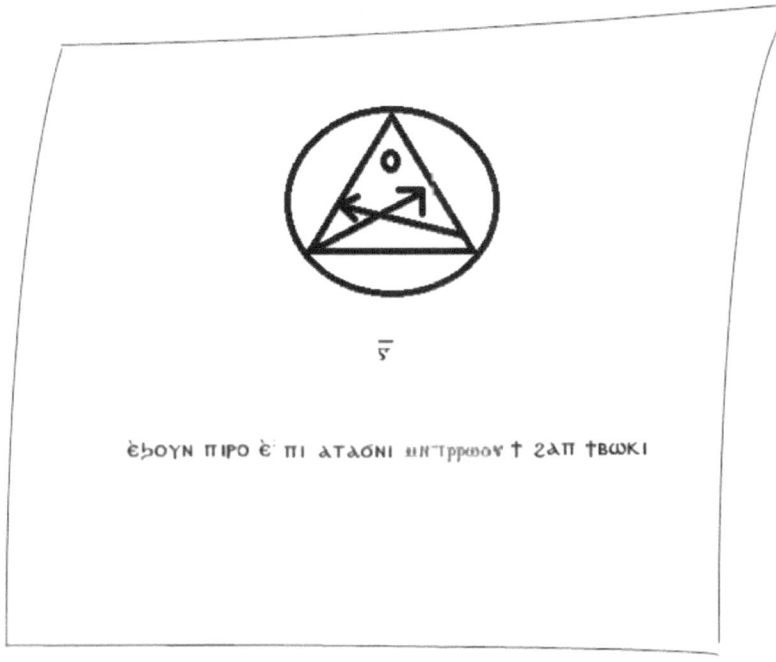

ⲉ̀ϩⲟⲩⲛ ⲡⲓⲣⲟ ⲉ̀ ⲡⲓ ⲁⲧⲁϬⲛⲓ ⲙⲛ̄ⲧⲣⲣⲱⲟⲩ † ⲍⲁⲡ †ⲃⲱⲕⲓ

This is a drawing of Scroll Number 5, which allows the transport of multiple objects through a dimensional portal. The Coptic translates as:

Enter the door into the new kingdom to condemn the slave.

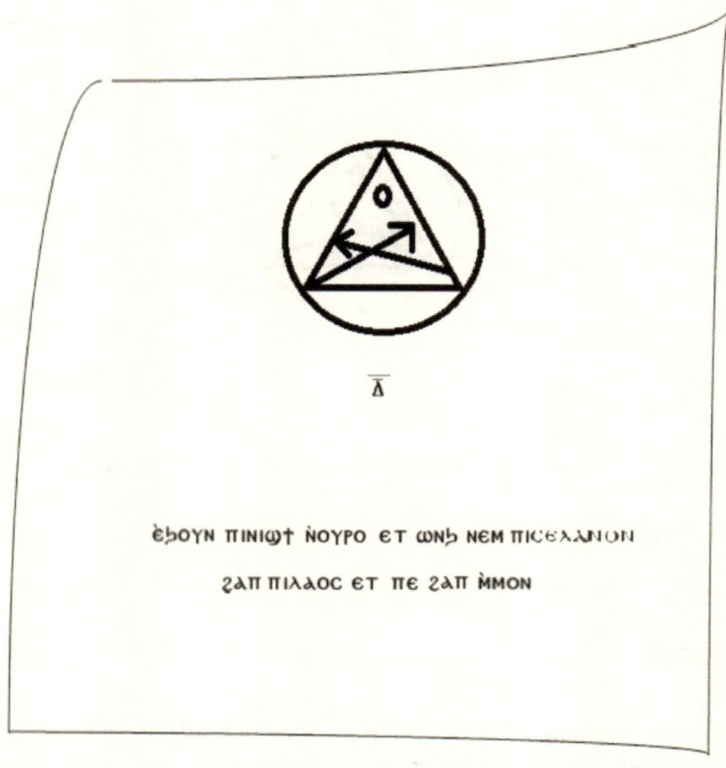

èϩⲟⲩⲛ ⲡⲓⲛⲓⲱϯ ⲛ̇ⲟⲩⲣⲟ ⲉⲧ ⲱⲛϩ ⲛⲉⲙ ⲡⲓⲥⲉⲗⲁⲛⲟⲛ

ϩⲁⲡ ⲡⲓⲗⲁⲟⲥ ⲉⲧ ⲡⲉ ϩⲁⲡ ⲙ̇ⲙⲟⲛ

This is a drawing of Scroll Number 4, which brings forth the Selanon and awakens the monstrous Krieatine. The Coptic translates as:

Enter the great king who lives with the Selanon. Condemn those who condemn us.

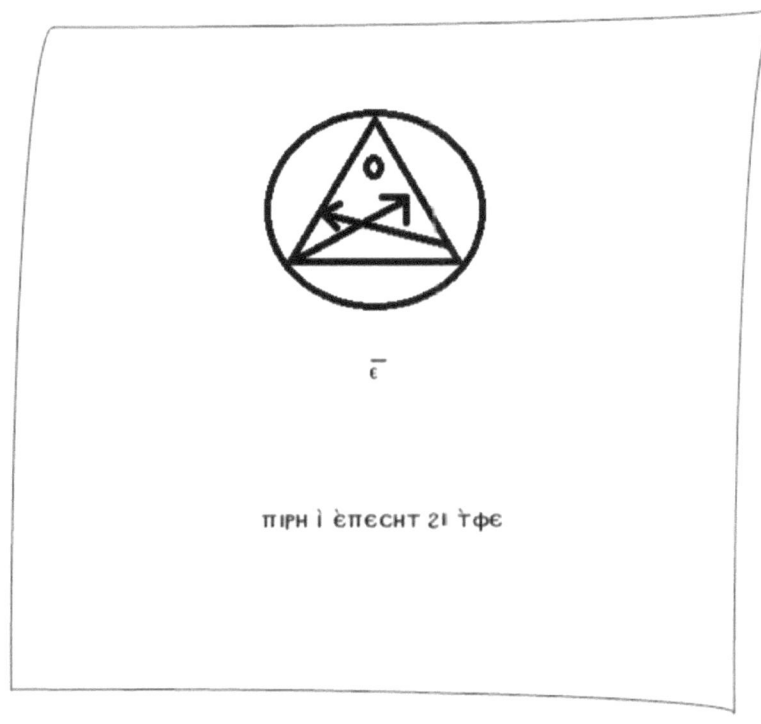

This is a drawing of Scroll Number 5, which causes fire and brimstone to rain from the sky. The Coptic translates as:

The sun will come down from the heavens.

‾ᴦ

†ϫⲟⲙ ⲡⲓⲛⲓⲱ† ⲛ̀ⲟⲩⲣⲟ ⲫⲏⲉⲧϩⲉⲙⲥⲓ ϩⲓϫⲉⲛ ⲡⲓⲑⲣⲟⲛⲟⲥ ⲟⲩⲱⲛ †ⲫⲉ

ⲛⲉⲃⲥⲉ ϩⲓⲧⲉⲛ ⲛⲓ̇ⲡⲣⲉⲥⲃⲓ̇ⲁ ⲛ̀ⲧⲉ ⲡⲓⲱ̇ⲁϣ̇ϥ ⲛ̀ⲁⲣⲭⲏⲁⲅⲅⲉⲗⲟⲥ ⲛⲉⲙ ⲛⲓⲧⲁⲅⲙⲁ ⲛ̀ⲉ̇ⲡⲟⲩⲣⲁⲛⲓⲟⲛ ϫⲱⲣ ⲡⲓⲗⲁⲟⲥ ⲉⲧ ⲡⲉ ϩⲁⲡ ⲙ̀ⲙⲟⲛ

This is a drawing of Scroll Number 6. It is unique in that it has two commands: one allows intradimensional travel, the other enables mind control. The Coptic translates as:

The power of the king who sits on the throne opens the heavens.

Awaken through the pleadings of the seven archangels and the heavenly hosts. Destroy those who condemn us.

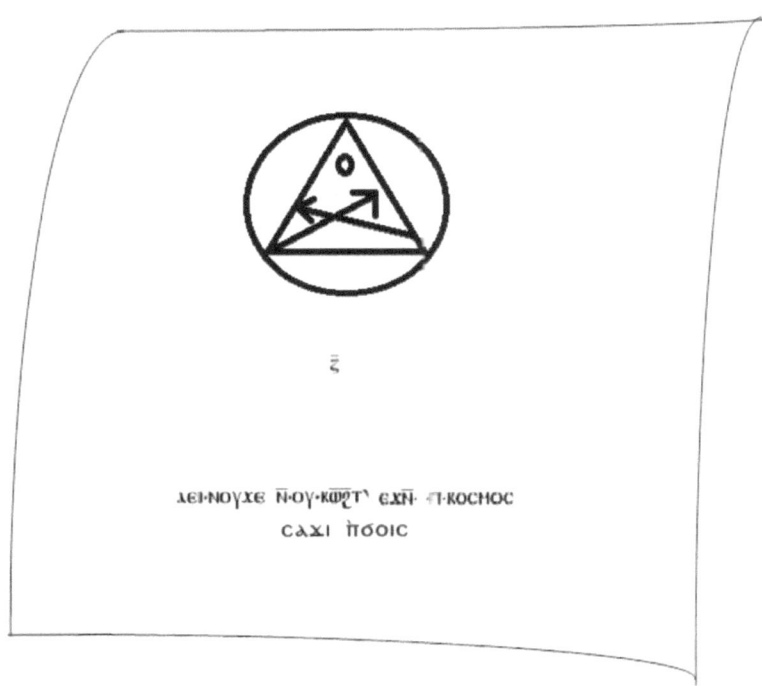

This is a drawing of Scroll Number 7, which causes lasers to fire from the alien satellites that orbit the Earth. The Coptic translates as:

I have cast a fire upon the world, says the Lord.

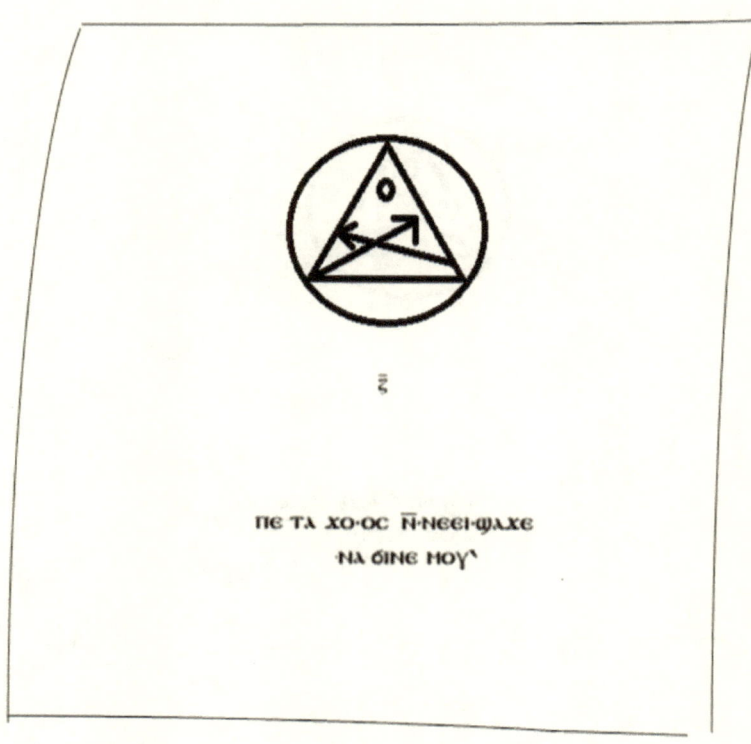

This is a drawing of the false seventh scroll, created by Ecaep. The Coptic translates as:

Whoever speaks these words will find Death.

Appendix C

This is the flag of the World Apex Government. It is simply the Vatican flag defiled with the bloody mark of the Sétbætañ.

CHГb ṄTE ΠI CЄTBΛЄTΛII

Mark or sign of the Sétbætañ

Appendix E

A sample of weapons, tanks, and planes exchanged between the humans and the aliens:

- bazooka
- Beretta Model 38 submachine gun
- Boeing P-12 pursuit aircraft
- Browning M2HB machine gun
- Fiat 3000 tank
- Glock 26 subcompact semi-automatic pistol
- grenades
- Heinkel bomber aircraft
- Luger P.08 pistol
- M16 rifle
- M-80 fireworks
- M2 carbine automatic rifle
- Gewehr 98 rifle
- Mauser C96 semi-automatic pistol
- Sturmgewehr 44 rifle
- T30 tank
- Uzi submachine gun
- various swords and knives
- M1 Carbine rifle

For more information on 'The Secret of Christopher Topher' or other novels written by Gee Williams or published by 'The Omen Experience', please visit: www.theomenexperience.com